Praise for *New York Times* bestselling author Lindsay McKenna

"McKenna provides heartbreakingly tender romantic development that will move readers to tears. Her military background lends authenticity to this outstanding tale, and readers will fall in love with the upstanding hero and his fierce determination to save the woman he loves."
—*Publishers Weekly* on *Never Surrender*

"Talented Lindsay McKenna delivers excitement and romance in equal measure."
—*RT Book Reviews* on *Protecting His Own*

"Lindsay McKenna will have you flying with the daring and deadly women pilots who risk their lives... Buckle in for the ride of your life."
—*Writers Unlimited* on *Heart of Stone*

NEW YORK TIMES BESTSELLING AUTHOR

LINDSAY McKENNA

&

MELISSA SENATE

A COWBOY TO TRUST

2 Heartfelt Stories
The Cougar & The Most Eligible Cowboy

HARLEQUIN

Special thanks and acknowledgment are given to
Melissa Senate for her contribution to the Montana Mavericks:
The Real Cowboys of Bronco Heights miniseries.

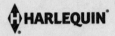

ISBN-13: 978-1-335-50836-2

A Cowboy to Trust

Copyright © 2023 by Harlequin Enterprises ULC

The Cougar
First published in 1998. This edition published in 2023.
Copyright © 1998 by Lindsay McKenna

The Most Eligible Cowboy
First published in 2021. This edition published in 2023.
Copyright © 2021 by Harlequin Enterprises ULC

Recycling programs
for this product may
not exist in your area.

For questions and comments about the quality of this book,
please contact us at CustomerService@Harlequin.com.

Harlequin Enterprises ULC
22 Adelaide St. West, 41st Floor
Toronto, Ontario M5H 4E3, Canada
www.Harlequin.com

Printed in U.S.A.

CONTENTS

Lindsay McKenna is proud to have served her country in the US Navy as an aerographer's mate third class—also known as a weather forecaster. She was a pioneer in the military romance subgenre and loves to combine heart-pounding action with soulful and poignant romance. True to her military roots, she is the originator of the long-running and reader-favorite Morgan's Mercenaries series. She does extensive hands-on research, including flying in aircraft such as a P3-B Orion sub-hunter and a B-52 bomber. She was the first romance writer to sign her books in the Pentagon bookstore. Visit her online at lindsaymckenna.com.

Books by Lindsay McKenna

Shadow Warriors

Running Fire
Taking Fire
Never Surrender
Breaking Point
Degree of Risk
Risk Taker
Down Range

The Wyoming Series

Out Rider
Night Hawk
Wolf Haven
High Country Rebel
The Loner
The Defender
The Wrangler
The Last Cowboy
Deadly Silence

Visit the Author Profile page
at Harlequin.com for more titles.

THE COUGAR

Lindsay McKenna

To my cyberfriends: Melissa Weaver, Carla Rowan,
Maria Theresa Bohle and Carol B. Willis

Chapter 1

"This wasn't a very good idea, Rachel Donovan." The words rang out briefly in the interior of the brand-new car that Rachel was driving. Huge, fat snowflakes were falling faster and faster. It was early December. Why shouldn't it be snowing in Oak Creek Canyon, which lay just south of Flagstaff, near Sedona? Her fingers tightened around the steering wheel. Tiredness pulled at her. A nine-hour flight from London, and then another six hours to get to Denver, Colorado, was taking its toll on her. As a homeopathic practitioner, she was no stranger to the effects of sleep deprivation.

Rubbing her watering eyes, she decided that the Rachel of her youth, some thirty years ago, was at play this morning. Normally, she wasn't this spontaneous, but in her haste to see her sisters as soon as possible, she'd changed her travel plans. Instead of flying into Phoenix, renting a car and driving up to Sedona, she'd flown into Denver and taken a commuter flight to Flagstaff, which was only an hour away from her home, the Donovan Ranch.

Home... The word made her heart expand with warm feelings. Yes, she was coming home—for good. Her older sister, Kate, had asked Rachel and their younger sister, Jessica, to come home and help save the ranch, which was teetering on the edge of bankruptcy. A fierce kind of sweetness welled up through Rachel. She couldn't wait to be living on the ranch with her sisters once again.

Glancing at her watch, she saw it was 7:00 a.m. She knew at this time of year the highways were often icy in the world-famous canyon. There was a foot of snow on the ground already—and it was coming down at an even faster rate as she drove carefully down the twisting, two-lane asphalt highway. On one side the canyon walls towered thousands of feet above her. On the other lay a five-hundred-foot-plus drop-off into Oak Creek, which flowed at the bottom of the canyon.

How many times had she driven 89A from Sedona to Flag? Rachel had lost count. Her eyes watered again from fatigue and she took a swipe at them with the back of her hand. Kate and Jessica were expecting her home at noon. If she got down the canyon in one piece, she would be home at 9:00 a.m. and would surprise them. A smile tugged at the corners of her full mouth. Oh, how she longed to see her sisters! She'd missed them so very much after leaving to work in England as a homeopath.

The best news was that Kate was going to marry her

high school sweetheart, Sam McGuire. And Jessica had found the love of her life, Dan Black, a horse wrangler who worked at the ranch. Both were going to be married seven days from now, and Rachel was going to be their maid of honor. Yes, things were finally looking up for those two. The good Lord knew, Kate and Jessica deserved to be happy. Their childhood with their alcoholic father, Kelly Donovan, had been a disaster. As each daughter turned eighteen, she had fled from the ranch. Kate had become a rebel, working for environmental causes. Jessica had moved to Canada to pursue her love of flower essences. And Rachel—well, she'd fled the farthest away—to England.

Rachel felt the car slide. Instantly, she lifted her foot off the accelerator. She was only going thirty miles an hour, but black ice was a well-known problem here in this part of Arizona. It killed a lot of people and she didn't want to be the next victim. As she drove down the narrow, steep, road, dark green Douglas firs surrounded her. Ordinarily, Rachel would be enthralled with the beauty and majesty of the landscape—this remarkable canyon reminded her of a miniature Grand Canyon in many respects. But she scarcely noticed now. In half an hour, she would be home.

Her hands tightened on the wheel as she spotted a yellow, diamond-shaped sign that read 15 mph. A sharp hairpin curve was coming up. She knew this curve well. She glanced once again at the jagged, unforgiving face of a yellow-and-white limestone cliff soaring thousands of feet above her and disappearing into the heavily falling snow. Gently she tested her brakes on the invisible, dangerous black ice. The only thing between her and the cliff that plunged into the canyon was a guardrail.

Suddenly, Rachel gasped. Was she seeing things? Without thinking, she slammed on the brakes. Directly in front of her, looming out of nowhere, was a huge black-and-gold cat. Her eyes widened enormously and a cry tore from her lips as the car swung drunkenly. The tires screeched as she tried to correct the skid. Impossible! Everything started to whirl around her. Out of the corner of her eye, she saw the black-and-gold cat, as large as a cougar, jump out of the way. Slamming violently against the cliff face, Rachel screamed. The steering wheel slipped out of her hands. A split second later, she watched in horror as the guardrail roared up at her.

The next moment there was a grinding impact. Throwing up her hands to protect her face, she felt the car become airborne. Everything seemed to suddenly move into slow motion. The car was twisting around in midair. She heard the glass crack as her head smashed against the side window. The snow, the dark shapes of the fir trees, all rushed at her. The nose of the car spiraled down—down into the jagged limestone wall well below the guardrail. Oh, no! She was going to die!

A thousand thoughts jammed through her mind in those milliseconds. What had been up on that highway? It wasn't a cougar. What *was* it? Had she hallucinated? Rachel knew better than to slam on brakes on black ice! How stupid could she be! But if she hadn't hit the brakes, she'd have struck that jaguar. Had there been a jaguar at all? Was it possible? She had to be seeing things! Now she was going to die!

Everything went black in front of Rachel. The last

thing she recalled was the motion of her car as it arched down like a shot fired from a cannon, before hitting the side of the cliff. The last sound she heard was her own scream of absolute terror ringing through the air.

Warm liquid was flowing across Rachel's parted lips. She heard voices that seemed very far away. As she slowly became conscious, the voices grew stronger—and closer. Forcing open her eyes, she at first saw only white. Groggily, she looked closer and realized it was snow on part of the windshield. The other half of the windshield was torn away, the white flakes lazily drifting into the passenger's side of the car.

The accident came back to her as the pain in her head and left foot throbbed in unison. Suddenly she realized she was sitting at an angle, the car twisted around the trunk of a huge Douglas fir.

Again she heard a voice. A man's voice. It was closer this time. Blinking slowly, Rachel lifted her right arm. At least *it* worked. The seat belt bit deeply into her shoulder and neck. The airbag, deflated now, had stopped her from being thrown through the windshield. A branch must have gouged out the right half of the windshield. If anyone had been sitting there, they'd be dead.

It was cold with the wind and snow blowing into the car. Shivering, Rachel closed her eyes. The image of the jaguar standing in the middle of that icy, snow-covered highway came back to her. How stupid could she have been? She knew not to slam on brakes like that. Where had the jaguar come from? Jaguars didn't exist in Arizona! Her head pounded as she tried to make sense of everything. She was in trouble. Serious trouble.

Again, a man's voice, deep and commanding, drifted into her semiconscious state. Help. She needed medical help. If only she could get to her homeopathic kit in the back seat. Arnica was what she needed for tissue trauma. Her head throbbed. She was sure she'd have a goose egg. Arnica would reduce the swelling and the pain.

The snowflakes were falling more thickly and at a faster rate now. How long had she been unconscious? Looking at her watch, Rachel groaned. It was 8:00 a.m. She'd been down here an hour? She had to get out! Rachel tried to move, but her seat belt was tightly constricting. She hung at a slight angle toward the passenger side of the car. Struggling weakly, she tried to find the seat belt latch, but her fingers were cold and numb.

"Hey! Are you all right?"

Rachel slowly lifted her head. Her vision was blurred for a moment, and when it cleared she noticed her side window was gone, smashed out, she guessed, in the crash. A man—a very tall, lean man with dark, short hair and intense blue eyes, wearing a navy blue jacket and pants—anchored himself against the car. He was looking at her, assessing her sharply. Rachel saw the patch on his jacket: EMT. And then she saw another patch: Sedona Fire Department.

"No…no… I'm not all right," she whispered, giving up on trying to find the seat belt latch.

"Okay…just hold on. Help's here. My name is Jim. We're from the Sedona Fire Department. We got a 911 call that an auto had flipped off the highway. Hold on while I get my buddies down here."

Rachel sank back, feeling relief. This man… Jim… radiated confidence. Somehow she knew she'd be okay with him. She watched through half-closed eyes as he lifted the radio to his strong-looking mouth and talked to someone far above them. The snow was thickening. The gray morning light accentuated his oval face, his strong nose and that mouth. He looked Indian. Rachel briefly wondered what kind. With his high cheekbones and dark hair, he could be Navajo, Hopi or from one of many other tribal nations.

Something about him made her feel safe. That was good. Rachel knew that he could get her out of this mess. She watched as he snapped the radio onto his belt and returned his full attention to her, trying to hide his worry.

"Helluva way to see Arizona," he joked. "The car is wrapped around this big Douglas fir here, so it and you aren't going anywhere. My buddies are bringing down a stretcher and some auto-extrication equipment. My job is to take care of you." He smiled a little as he reached in the window. "What's your name?"

"Rachel…" she whispered.

"Rachel, I'm going to do a quick exam of you. Do you hurt anywhere?"

She closed her eyes as he touched her shoulder. "Yes…my head and my foot. I—I think I've got a bump on my head."

His touch was immediately soothing to her, though he wore latex gloves. But then, so did she when she had to examine a patient. With AIDS, HIV and hepatitis

B all being transmissible via blood and fluids, medical people had to protect themselves accordingly. As he moved his hands gently across her head, she could feel him searching for injury. Something in her relaxed completely beneath his ministrations. She felt his warm, moist breath, his face inches from hers as he carefully examined her scalp.

"Beautiful hair," he murmured, "but you're right— you've got a nice goose egg on the left side of your head."

One corner of her mouth turned up as she lay against the car seat. "If that's all, I'm lucky. I hate going to hospitals."

Chuckling, Jim eased a white gauze dressing against her hair and then quickly placed a bandage around her head. "Yeah, well, you'll be going to Cottonwood Hospital, anyway. If nothing more than to make sure you're okay."

Groaning, Rachel barely opened her eyes. She saw that he'd unzipped his jacket and it hung open, revealing a gold bar over the left top pocket of his dark blue shirt that read J. Cunningham. *Cunningham.* Frowning, she looked up at him as he moved his hands in a gentle motion down her neck, searching for more trauma.

"Cunningham's your last name?" she asked, her voice sounding faint even to her.

"Yeah, Jim Cunningham." He glanced down at her. She was pasty, her forest green eyes dull looking. Jim knew she was in shock. He quickly pressed his fingertips against her collarbone, noticing her pale pink angora sweater and dark gray wool slacks. Under any other circumstance, she would turn a man's head. "Why?" he teased, "has my reputation preceded me?" He quickly felt her arms for broken bones or signs of bleeding. There were some minor cuts due to flying glass from the windshield, but otherwise, so far, so good. He tried not to show his worry.

"Of the Bar C?" she asked softly, shutting her eyes as he leaned over her and pressed firmly on her rib cage to see if she had any broken ribs. How close he was! Yet his presence was utterly comforting to Rachel.

"Yes…how did you know?" Jim eased his hands down over her hips, applying gentle pressure. If she had any hip or pelvic injuries, they would show up now. He watched her expression closely. Her eyes were closed, her thick, dark lashes standing out against her pale skin. She'd had a nosebleed, but it had ceased. Her lips parted, but she didn't answer his question. Looking down and pushing aside the deflated airbag, he saw that her left foot was caught in the wreckage. *Damn.* That wasn't a good sign. His mind whirled with possibilities. He needed to get a cuff around her upper arm and check her blood pressure. What if her foot was mangled? What if an artery was severed? She could be losing a lot of blood. She could die on them.

He had to keep her talking. Easing out of the car window, he reached into his bright orange EMT bag. Looking up, he saw his partner, Larry, coming down, along with four other firefighters bringing the stretcher and ropes as well as auto-extrication equipment.

"Well," Jim prodded, as he pushed up her sleeve and slipped the blood-pressure cuff around her upper left arm, "am I a wanted desperado?"

Rachel needed his stabilizing touch and absorbed it

hungrily. Consciousness kept escaping her. For some reason she would slip away, only to be brought back by his deep, teasing voice. "Uh, no…."

"You sound like you know me. Do you?" He quickly put the stethoscope to her arm and pumped up the cuff. His gaze was focused on the needle, watching it closely as he bled off the air.

Rachel rallied. Opened her eyes slightly, she saw the worry in Jim's face. The intensity in his expression shook her. "You don't remember me, do you?" she said, trying to tease back. Her voice sounded very far away. What was going on? Why wasn't she able to remain coherent?

Damn! Jim kept his expression neutral. Her blood pressure wasn't good. Either she had a serious head injury or she was bleeding somewhere. He left the cuff on her arm and removed the stethoscope from his ears. She lay against the seat, her eyes closed, her body limp. Her breathing was slowly becoming weaker and weaker. His medical training told him she was losing a lot of blood. Where? It *had* to be that foot that was jammed in the wreckage.

He *had* to keep her talking. "I'm sorry," he apologized, "I don't remember you. I wish I did, though." And that was the truth. She was a beautiful woman. *Stunning* was a word Jim would use with her. Her dark brown hair was thick and long, like a dark cape across her proud shoulders.

"Listen, I'm going to try and get this door open." Jim made a signal to Larry to hurry even faster down the slippery incline. Studying the jagged cliff, Jim realized that if the car hadn't wrapped itself around this fir tree, it would have plunged another three hundred feet. More than likely, Rachel would be dead.

Larry hurried forward. He was a big man, over six feet tall, and built like a proverbial bull.

"Yeah, Cougar, what are the stats?" He dropped his bag and moved gingerly up to Jim.

Scowling, Jim lowered his voice so no one but his partner would hear. "She's dumping on us. I think she's hemorrhaging from her left foot, which is trapped beneath the dash of the car. Help me get this door open. I need to get a cuff on her upper leg. It'll have to act like a tourniquet. Then those extrication guys can get in here and cut that metal away so we can get her foot free to examine it."

"Right, pard."

Rachel heard another male voice, but it was Jim's voice she clung to. Her vision was growing dim. What was wrong with her? She heard the door protest and creak loudly as it was pulled opened in a series of hard, jerking motions. In moments, she heard Jim's voice very close to her ear. Forcing open her eyes, she saw that he was kneeling on the side of the car where the door was now open. She felt his hand moving down her left leg, below her knee.

"Can you feel that?" he demanded.

"Feel what?" Rachel asked.

"Or this?"

"No…nothing. I feel nothing, Jim."

Jim threw Larry a sharp look. "Hand me your blood-pressure cuff. We're going to apply a tourniquet." In the gray light of the canyon, with snowflakes twirling lazily around them, Jim saw that her left foot and ankle had been twisted and trapped in the metal upon impact. With Larry's help, he affixed the cuff around her slim calf and then inflated it enough to halt the blood flow in that extremity.

Four other firefighters arrived on scene. Larry put a warm, protective blanket across Rachel. He then got into the back seat and held her head straight while Jim carefully placed a stabilizing cervical collar around her neck, in case she had an undetected spinal injury. He was worried. She kept slipping in and out of consciousness.

As he settled into the passenger seat beside her, and the firefighters worked to remove the metal that trapped her leg, Jim tried to draw her out of her semiconscious state.

"Rachel," he called, "it's Jim. Can you hear me?"

She barely moved her lips. "Yes…"

He told her what the firefighters were going to do, and that there would be a lot of noise and not to get upset by it. All the while, he kept his hand on hers. She responded valiantly to his touch, to his voice, but Jim saw Larry shake his head doubtfully as he continued to gently hold her head and neck.

"You said you heard of me," Jim teased. He watched her lashes move upward to reveal her incredible eyes. Her pupils were wide and dilated, black with a crescent of green around them. "Well? Am I on a wanted poster somewhere?" he asked with a smile.

Jim's smile went straight to Rachel's heart. It was boyish, teasing, and yet he was so male that it made her heart beat a little harder in her chest. She tried to smile back and realized it was a poor attempt. "No…

not a wanted poster. I remember you from high school. I'm Rachel Donovan. You know the Donovan Ranch?"

Stunned, Jim stared. "Rachel Donovan?" His head whirled with shock. That was right! He recalled Jessica Donovan telling him over a month ago that Rachel, the middle daughter, was moving home from England to live at the ranch.

"That's me," Rachel joked softly. She forced her eyes open a little more and held his gaze. "You used to pull my braids in junior high, but I don't think you remember that, do you?"

Jim forced a grin he didn't feel at all. "I do now." And he did. Little Rachel Donovan had been such a thin stick of a girl in junior high. She had worn her long, dark brown flowing mane of hair in braids back then, like her mother, Odula, an Eastern Cherokee medicine woman. Rachel was the spitting image of her. Jim recalled the crush he'd had on little Rachel Donovan. She'd always run from him. The only way he'd get her attention was to sneak up, tweak one of her braids and then run away himself. It was his way of saying he liked her, for at that age, Jim had been too shy to tell her. Besides, there were other problems that prevented him from openly showing his affection for her.

"You were always teasing me, Jim Cunningham," Rachel said weakly. Her mouth was dry and she was thirsty. The noise of machinery filled the car. If it hadn't been for Jim's steadying hand on her shoulder, the sound would have scared her witless.

"Hey, Cougar, we're gonna have to take the rest of this windshield out. Gotta pull the steering wheel up and away from her."

Jim nodded to Captain Cord Ramsey of the extrication team. "Okay." He rose up on his knees and took a second blanket into his hands.

"Rachel," he said as he leaned directly over her, "I'm going to place a blanket over us. The firefighters have to pull the rest of the window out. There's going to be glass everywhere, but the blanket will protect you."

Everything went dark before Rachel's eyes. Jim Cunningham had literally placed his body like a wall between her and the firefighters who were working feverishly to free her. She felt the heat of his body as he pulled the blanket over their heads. How close he was! She was overwhelmed by the care he showed toward her. It was wonderful.

When he spoke, his voice was barely an inch from her ear.

"Okay, they're going to pull that windshield any moment now. You'll hear some noise and feel the car move a bit. It's nothing to be concerned about."

"You're wonderful at what you do," Rachel whispered weakly. "You really make a person feel safe... that everything's going to be okay even if it isn't...."

Worried, Jim said, "Rachel, do you know what blood type you are?"

"AB positive."

His heart sank. He struggled to keep the disappointment out of his voice. "That's a rare blood type."

She smiled a little. "Like me, I guess."

He chuckled. "I have AB positive blood, too. How about that? Two rare birds, eh?"

Rachel heard the windshield crack. There was one brief, sharp movement. As Jim eased back and removed the blanket, she looked up at him. His face was hard and expressionless until he looked down to make sure she was all right. Then his features became very readable. She saw concern banked in his eyes.

"Listen, Jim, in the back seat there's a kit. A homeopathic kit. It's important you get to it. There's a remedy in there. It's called Arnica Montana. I know I'm bleeding. It will help stop it. Can you get it for me? Pour some pellets into my mouth?"

He frowned and looked in the back seat. There was a black physician's bag there on the seat next to Larry. "You a doctor?"

"No, a homeopath."

"I've vaguely heard about it. An alternative medicine, right?" He reached over the back seat and brought the leather case up front, resting it against his thigh as he opened it. He found a small plastic box inside along with a lot of other medical equipment. "This box?" he asked, holding it up for her to look at.

"Yes...that's the one. I'll need two pills."

Opening it, Jim located the bottle marked Arnica. He unscrewed the cap and put a couple of white pellets into her mouth.

"Thanks...." Rachel said. The sweetness of the small pellets tasted good to her. "It will help stop the shock and the bleeding."

Jim put the bag aside. Worriedly, he took another blood-pressure reading. She was no longer dumping as before. He suspected the tourniquet on her lower leg had halted most of the bleeding, and that was good news.

"Did I hear someone call you Cougar?"

Distracted because the extrication team was finally

prying the metal away from her foot, Jim nodded. "Yeah, that's my nickname."

"H-how did you get it?" Rachel felt the power of the homeopathic remedy begin to work on her immediately. "Listen, this remedy I took will probably make me look like I'm unconscious, but I'm not. It's just working to stabilize me, so don't panic, okay?"

Jim nodded and placed himself in front of Rachel to protect her again as the extrication equipment began to remove the metal from around her foot. "Okay, sweetheart, I won't panic." He watched her lashes drift down as he shielded her with his body. Her color was no longer as pasty, and that was promising. Still, her blood pressure was low. Too low.

Looking up at Larry, Jim said, "As soon as we get her out of here, have Ramsey call the hospital and see if they've got AB positive blood standing by. We're going to need it."

"Right."

Rachel savored Jim's nearness. She heard the screech of metal as it was being torn away to release her foot. She hoped her injury wasn't bad. She had a wedding to attend in a week. Her foot couldn't be broken!

"What's the frown for?" Jim asked. Her face was inches from his. He saw the soft upturn of the corners of her mouth. What a lovely mouth Rachel had. The spindly shadow of a girl he'd known was now a mature swan of indescribable beauty.

"Oh…the weddings—Katie and Jessica. I'm supposed to be their maid of honor. My foot… I'm worried about my foot. What if I broke it?"

"We'll know in just a little while," he soothed. Instinctively, he placed his hand on her left shoulder. The last of the metal was torn away.

"Cougar?"

"Yeah?" Jim twisted his head toward Captain Ramsey.

"She's all yours. Better come and take a look."

Rachel felt Jim leave her side. Larry's hands remained firm against her head and neck, however.

Cunningham climbed carefully around the car. The temperature was dropping, and the wind was picking up. Blizzard conditions were developing fast. Jim noted the captain's wrinkled brow as he made his way to the driver's side. Getting down on his hands and knees, squinting in the poor light, he got his first look at Rachel's foot.

He'd been right about loss of blood. He saw where an artery on the top of her foot had been sliced open. Quickly examining it, he placed a dressing there. Turning, he looked up at the captain.

"Get the hospital on the horn right away. We're definitely going to need a blood transfusion for her. AB positive." Rachel had lost a lot of blood, there was no doubt. If he hadn't put that blood-pressure cuff on her lower leg when he did, she would have bled to death right in front of him. Shaken, Jim eased to his feet.

"Okay, let's get her out of the car and onto a spine board." When he looked up to check on Rachel, he saw that she had lost consciousness again. So many memories flooded back through Jim in those moments. Good ones. Painful ones. Ones of yearning. Of unrequited love that was never fulfilled. Little Rachel Donovan. He'd had a crush on her all through school.

As Jim quickly positioned the spine board beneath Rachel with the help of the firefighters, he suddenly felt hope for the first time in a long time. Maybe, just maybe, life was giving him a second chance with Rachel. And then he laughed at himself. The hundred-year-old feud between the Cunninghams and Donovans was famous in this part of the country. Still he wondered if Rachel had ever had any feelings for him?

Right now, Jim couldn't even think about the past. His concern was for Rachel's loss of blood and her shock. The clock on the car had stopped at 7:00 a.m. That was when the accident had probably occurred. And it had taken them an hour to get here. Whether he wanted to admit it or not, her life hung in a precarious balance right now.

"Hey," Ramsey said, getting off the radio, "bad news, Cougar."

"What?" Jim eased Rachel onto the spine board and made her as comfortable as possible.

"No AB positive blood at Cottonwood."

Damn! "Try Flagstaff."

Ramsey shook his head. "None anywhere."

Placing another blanket across Rachel, Jim glanced up at his partner. "You tell Cottonwood to stand by for a blood transfusion, then," he told the captain. "I've got AB positive blood. She needs at *least* a pint or we aren't going to be able to save her."

"Roger," Ramsey grunted, and got on the radio again to the hospital.

Chapter 2

The first thing Rachel was aware of was a hand gently caressing her hair. It was a nurturing touch, almost tender as it brushed across her crown. Unfamiliar noises leaked into her groggy consciousness, along with the smell of antiseptic. Where was she? Her head ached. Whoever was caressing her hair soothed the pain with each touch. Voices. There were so many unfamiliar voices all around her. Struggling to open her eyes, she heard a man's voice, very low and nearby.

"It's okay, Rachel. You're safe and you're going to be okay. Don't try so hard. Just lay back and take it easy. You've been through a lot."

Who was that? The voice was oddly familiar, and yet it wasn't. The touch of his hand on her head was magical. Rachel tried to focus on the gentle caress. Each time he followed the curve of her skull, the pain went away, only to return when he lifted his hand. Who was this man who had such a powerful touch? Rachel was no stranger to hands-on healing. Her mother, Odula, used to lay her hands on each of them when they were sick with fever or chills. And amazingly, each time, their aches and pains had disappeared.

The antiseptic smell awakened her even more—the smell of a hospital. She knew the scent well, having tended many patients at the homeopathic hospital in London. Her mind was fuzzy, so she continued to focus on the man's hand and his nearness. She felt his other hand resting on her upper arm, as if to give her an anchor in the whirling world of gold-and-white light beneath her lids.

Gathering all her strength, Rachel forced her lashes to lift. At first all she saw was a dark green curtain in front of her. And then she heard a low chuckle to her right, where the man was standing—the one who caressed her as if she were a very beloved, cherished woman. His warm touch was undeniable. Her heart opened of its own accord and Rachel felt a rush of feelings she thought had died a long time ago. Confused by the sights and sounds, she looked up, up at the man who stood protectively at her side.

Jim's mouth pulled slightly. "Welcome back to the real world, Rachel." He saw her cloudy, forest green eyes rest on him. There was confusion in their depths. Nudging a few strands of long, dark brown hair away from her cheek, he said in a low, soothing tone, "You're at the Flagstaff Hospital. We brought you here about an hour ago. You had a wreck up on 89A coming out of Flag earlier this morning. Do you remember?"

Rachel was mesmerized by him, by his low tone, which seemed to penetrate every cell of her being like a lover's caress. He had stilled his hand, resting it against her hair. His smile was kind. She liked the tenderness burning in his eyes as he regarded her. Who was he? His face looked familiar, and yet no name would come. Her mouth felt gummy. Her foot ached. She looked to the left, at her surroundings.

"You're in ER, the emergency room, in a cubical," Jim told her. "The doc just got done looking at you. He just stitched up your foot where you severed a small artery. You took a pint of whole blood, and he said the bump on your head is going to hurt like hell, but it's not a concussion."

Bits and pieces of memory kept striking her. The jaguar. The jaguar standing in the middle of that ice-covered highway. Rachel frowned and closed her eyes.

"The cat…it was in the middle of the road," she began, her voice scratchy. "I slammed on the brakes. I didn't want to hit it…. The last thing I remember is spinning out of control."

Jim tightened his hand slightly on her upper arm. He could see she was struggling to remember. "A cat? You mean a cougar?"

Everything was jumbled up. Rachel closed her eyes. She felt terribly weak—far weaker than she wanted to feel. "My kit…where is it?"

Jim saw a dull flush of color starting to come back to her very pale cheeks. The blood transfusion had halted her shock. He'd made sure she was covered with extra blankets and he'd remained with her in ER throughout the time, not wanting her to wake up alone and confused.

"Kit?"

"Yes…" She moved her lips, the words sticking in her dry mouth. "My homeopathic kit…in my car. I need it…."

He raised his brows. "Oh…your black bag. Yeah, I brought it in with me. Hold on, I'll be right back."

Rachel almost cried when he left her side. The strong, caring warmth of his hand on her arm was very stabilizing. The noise in ER was like a drum inside her head. She heard the plaintive cry of a baby, someone else was groaning in pain—familiar sounds to her as a homeopath. She wished she could get up, go dispense a remedy to each of them to ease their pain and discomfort. She wasn't in England any longer, though; she was in the U.S. Suddenly she felt disoriented.

Her ears picked up the sound of a curtain being drawn aside. She opened her eyes. He was back, with her black leather physician's bag.

"Got it," he said with a smile, placing the bag close to her blanketed leg.

As he opened it, Rachel tried to think clearly. "Who are you? I feel like I know you…but I'm not remembering names too well right now."

His mouth curved in a grin as he opened the bag. "Jim Cunningham. I'm the EMT who worked with you out at the accident scene." He pulled out the white, plastic box and held it where she could see it.

"Oh…"

Chuckling, he said, "Man, have I made a good impression on you. Here you are, the prettiest woman I've seen in a long time, and you forget my name."

His teasing warmth fell across her. Rachel tried to smile, but the pain in her head wouldn't let her. There was no denying that Jim Cunningham was a very good-looking man. He was tall, around six foot two, and lean, like a lithe cougar with a kind of boneless grace that told her he was in superb physical condition. The dark blue, long-sleeved shirt and matching pants he wore couldn't hide his athletic build. The silver badge on his left pocket, the gold nameplate above it and all the patches on the shoulders of his shirt gave him a decided air of authority.

Wrinkling her nose a little, she croaked, "Don't take it personally. I'm feeling like I have cotton stuffed between my ears." She lifted her hand and found it shaky.

"Just tell me which one you want," he said gently. "You're pretty weak yet. In another couple of hours you'll feel a lot better than you do right now."

Alarmed at her weakness, Rachel whispered, "Get me the Arnica."

"Ah, the same one you used out at the accident site. Okay." He hunted around. There were fifty black-capped, amber bottles arranged by alphabetical order in the small case. Finding Arnica, he uncapped it.

"Now what?"

"My mouth. Drop a couple of pellets in it."

Jim carefully put two pellets on her tongue. "Okay, you're set." He capped the amber bottle. "What is this stuff, anyway? The ER doc wanted to know if it had side effects or if it would cause any problems with prescription drugs."

The pellets were sugary sweet. Rachel closed her eyes. She knew the magic of homeopathy. In a few minutes, her headache would be gone. And in a few more after that, she'd start feeling more human again.

"That's okay," Jim murmured as he replaced the vial into the case, "you don't have to answer the questions right now." He glanced up. "I called your family. I talked to Kate." He put the box back into Rachel's bag and set it on a chair nearby. "They're all waiting out in the visitors' lounge. Hold on, I'll get them for you."

Rachel watched through half-closed eyes as Jim opened the green curtain and disappeared. She liked him. A lot. What wasn't there to like? she asked herself. He was warm, nurturing, charming—not to mention terribly handsome. He had matured since she'd known him in school. He'd been a tall, gangly, shy kid with acne on his face. She remembered he was half-Apache and half-Anglo and that they'd always had that common bond—being half-Indian.

So many memories of her past—of growing up here in Sedona, of the pain of her father's alcoholism and her mother's endless suffering with the situation—flooded back through her. They weren't pleasant memories. And many of them she wanted to forget.

Jim Cunningham… In school she'd avoided him like the plague because Old Man Cunningham and her father had huge adjoining ranches. The two men had fought endlessly over the land, the often-broken fence line and the problems that occurred when each other's cattle wandered onto the other's property. They'd hated one another. Rachel had learned to avoid the three Cunningham boys as a result.

Funny how a hit on the head pried loose some very old memories. A crooked smile pulled at Rachel's mouth. And who had saved her? None other than one of the Cunninghams. What kind of karma did she have? She almost laughed, and realized the pain in her head was lessening quickly; her thoughts were rapidly clearing. Thanks to homeopathy. And Jim Cunningham.

"Rachel!"

She opened her eyes in time to see Jessica come flying through the curtains. Her younger sister's eyes were huge, her face stricken with anxiety. Reaching out with her right hand, Rachel gave her a weak smile.

"Hi, Jess. I'm okay…really, I am…."

Then Rachel saw Kate, much taller and dressed in Levi's and a plaid wool coat, come through the curtains. Her serious features were set with worry, too.

Jessica gripped Rachel's hand. "Oh, Rachel! Jim called us, bless him! He didn't have to do that. He told us everything. You could have died out there!" She gave a sob, then quickly wiped the tears from her eyes. Leaning down, she kissed Rachel's cheek in welcome.

Kate smiled brokenly. "Helluva welcome to Sedona, isn't it?"

Grinning weakly, Rachel felt Kate's work-worn hand fall over hers. "Yes, I guess it is."

Kate frowned. "I thought you were flying into Phoenix, renting a car and driving up from there?"

Making a frustrated sound, Rachel said, "I was going to surprise you two. I got an earlier flight out of Denver directly into Flag. I was going to be at the ranch hours earlier that way." She gave Kate a long, warm look. "I really wanted to get home."

"Yeah," Kate whispered, suddenly choked up as she gripped her sister's fingers, "I guess you did."

Sniffing, Jessica wiped her eyes. "Are you okay, Rachel? What did the doctor say?"

Rachel saw the curtains part. It was Jim Cunningham. Her heart skipped a beat. She saw how drawn his face was and his eyes seemed darker than she recalled. He came and stood at the foot of the gurney where she was lying.

"Dr. Forbush said she had eight stitches in her foot for a torn artery, and a bump on the head," he told them. He held Rachel's gaze. She seemed far more alert now, and that was good. When he'd stepped into the cubicle, he'd noticed that her cheeks were flushed. Pointing to her left foot, he said, "She lost a pint of blood out there at the wreck. She got that replaced and the doc is releasing her to your care." And then he smiled teasingly down at Rachel. "That is, unless you want to spend a night here in the hospital for observation?"

Rachel grimaced. "Not on your life," she muttered defiantly. "I work in them, I don't stay in them."

Chuckling, Jim nodded. He looked at the three Donovan sisters. "I gotta get going, but the head nurse, Sue Young, will take care of getting you out of this place." He studied Rachel's face and felt a stirring in his heart. "Stay out of trouble, you hear?"

"Wait!" Rachel said, her voice cracking. She saw surprise written on his features when he turned to her again. "Wait," she pleaded. "I want to thank you...." Then she smiled when she saw deviltry in his eyes as he stood there, considering her plea.

"You serious about that?"

"Sure."

"Good. Then when you get well, have lunch with me?"

Stunned, Rachel leaned back onto the bed. She saw Jessica's face blossom in a huge smile. And Kate frowned. Rachel knew what her older sister was thinking. He was a Cunningham, their enemy for as long as any of them could recall.

"Well…"

Jim raised his hand, realizing he'd overstepped his bounds. "Hey, I was just teasing. I'll see you around. Take care of yourself…."

"I'll be right back," Kate murmured to her sisters, and she quickly followed after him.

Jim was headed toward the small office in the back of ER where EMTs filled out their accident report forms when he heard Kate Donovan's husky voice.

"Jim?"

Turning, he saw her moving in his direction. Stepping out of the ER traffic, he waited for her. The serious look on her face put him on guard. She was the oldest of the three Donovan daughters and the owner of a ranch, which was teetering precariously on the edge of bankruptcy. He knew she had worked hard since assuming the responsibilities of the ranch after Kelly died in an auto accident earlier in the year. Because of that, Jim also knew she had more reason to hate a Cunningham than any of the sisters. Inwardly, he tried to steel himself against anything she had to say. His father, unfortunately, had launched a lawsuit against Kate's ranch right now. There was nothing Jim could do about it, even though he'd tried to talk his father into dropping the stupid suit. Driven by the vendetta against Kelly Donovan, he'd refused to. It made no difference to him that the daughters were coming home to try and save their family ranch. The old man couldn't have cared less.

With such bad blood running between the two families, Jim was trying to mend fences where he could. His two older brothers weren't helping things, however. They derived just as much joy and pleasure out of hurting people, especially the Donovans, as their old man. Jim was considered the black sheep of the family, probably because he was the only Cunningham who wasn't into bad blood or revenge. No, he'd come home to try and fix things. And in the months since he'd been home, Jim had found himself living in hell. He found his escape when he was on duty for the fire department. But the rest of the time he was a cowboy on the family ranch, helping to hold it together and run it. Ordinarily, he'd loved the life of a rancher, but not anymore. These days his father was even more embittered toward the Donovans, and now he had Bo and Chet on his side to wage a continued war against them.

As Kate Donovan approached him, Jim understood how she felt toward him. It wasn't anything personal; it was just ancient history that was still alive and injuring all parties concerned. Even him. The darkness in her eyes, the serious set of her mouth, put him on guard. He studied her as she halted a few feet away from him, jamming her hands into the deep pockets of the plaid wool jacket she wore.

"I want to thank you," Kate rasped, the words coming out strained.

Reeling, Jim couldn't believe his ears. He'd expected

to catch hell from Kate for suggesting lunch with Rachel. He knew she had a lot of her father in her and could be mule headed, holding grudges for a long time, too.

"You didn't have to call us," Kate continued. "You could have left that to a nurse here in ER, I know." Then she looked up at him. "I found out from the nurse before I went in to see Rachel that you saved her life—literally."

Shrugging shyly, Jim said, "I did what I could, Kate. I'd do it for anyone." He didn't want her to think that he'd done something special for Rachel that he wouldn't do for others. In his business as an EMT, his job was to try and save lives.

"Damn, this is hard," Kate muttered, scowling and looking down at her booted feet. Lifting her head, she pinned him with a dark look. "I understand you just gave her a pint of your blood. Is that true?"

He nodded. "Rachel's blood type is a rare one." Looking around the busy hospital area, he continued, "This is a backwoods hospital, Kate. They can't always have every rare blood type on hand. Especially in the middle of Arizona, out in the wilds." He tried to ease her hard expression with his teasing reply.

Kate wasn't deterred in the least. "And your partner, Larry, who I just talked to out at the ambulance, said you'd stopped Rachel from losing even more blood by putting a tourniquet on her leg?"

"I put a blood-pressure cuff around Rachel's lower leg to try and stop most of the bleeding, yes." Inwardly, Jim remained on guard. He never knew if Kate Donovan was going to pat him on the head or rip out his jugular. Usually it was the latter. He saw her expression go from anger to confusion and then frustration, and he almost expected her to curse him out for volunteering his own blood to help save Rachel's life. After all, it was Cunningham blood—the blood of her arch enemy. The enemy that her father had fought against all his life.

Kate pulled her hand out of her pocket and suddenly thrust it toward him. "Then," she quavered, suddenly emotional, "I owe you a debt I can't begin to pay back."

Staring at her proffered hand, Jim realized what it took for Kate to do that. He gripped her hand warmly. The tears in her eyes touched him deeply. "I'm glad it was me. I'm glad I was there, Kate. No regrets, okay?"

She shook his hand firmly and then released it. "Okay," she rasped nervously, clearing her throat. "I just wanted you to know that I know what really happened."

He gave her a slight smile. "And there's nothing to pay back here. You understand?" He wanted both families to release the revenge, the aggressive acts against one another. Kelly Donovan was dead, though Jim's father was still alive and still stirring up trouble against their closest neighbors. Kate was struggling to keep the ranch afloat, and Jim admired her more than he could ever say. But if he told her that she wouldn't believe him, because he was a Cunningham—bad blood.

Nodding, she wiped her eyes free of tears. "You sure know how to balance ledgers, don't you?"

Scrutinizing her closely, Jim said quietly, "I assume you're talking about the ledger between our two families?"

"Yes." She stared up at him. "I can't figure you out—yet."

"There's nothing to figure out, Kate."

"Yes," she growled, "there is."

His mouth curved ruefully. "I came home like you did—to try and fix things."

"Then why does your old man have that damned lawsuit against us?"

Kate's frustration paralleled his own. Opening his hands, Jim rasped, "I'm trying to get him to drop the suit, Kate. It has no merit. It's just that same old revenge crap from long ago, that's all."

She glared at him. "We are hitting rock bottom financially and you and everyone else knows it. Rachel came home to try and make money to help us pay the bills to keep our ranch afloat. If I have to hire a lawyer and pay all the court costs, that's just one more monetary hemorrhage. Can't *you* do anything to make him stop it?"

"I'm doing what I can."

She looked away, her mouth set. "It's not enough."

Wearily, Jim nodded. "Kate, I want peace between our families. Not bloodshed or lawsuits. My father has diabetes and often refuses to take his meds, so he exhibits some bizarre behavior."

"Like this stupid lawsuit?"

"Exactly." Glancing around, Jim pulled Kate into the office, which was vacant at the moment. Shutting the door, he leaned against it as he held her stormy gaze. "Let's bury the hatchet between us, okay? I did not come home to start another round of battles with you or anyone else at the Donovan Ranch."

"You left home right after high school," Kate said in a low voice. "So why did you come back now?"

"I never approved of my father's tactics against you or your family. Yes, I left when I was eighteen. I became a hotshot firefighter with the forest service. I didn't want to be a part of how my father was acting or behaving. I didn't approve of it then and I don't now. I'm doing what I can, Kate. But I've got a father who rants and raves, who's out of his head half the time. Then he stirs up my two brothers, who believe he's a tin god and would do anything he told them to do. They don't stop to think about the consequences of their actions."

Kate wrapped her arms against her body and stared at him, the silence thickening. "Since you've come back, things have gotten worse, not better."

Releasing a sigh, Jim rested against the edge of the desk. "Do you know what happens when a diabetic doesn't watch his diet or doesn't take his meds?" he asked in a calm tone.

"No," she muttered defensively. "Are you going to blame your old man's lawsuit and everything else on the fact that he's sick and won't take the drugs he's supposed to take?"

"In part, yes," Jim said. "I'm trying to get my brothers to work with me, not against me, on my father taking his medication daily. I'm trying to get our cook to make meals that balance my father's blood sugar and not spike it up so he has to be peeled off the ceiling every night when I get home."

Kate nodded. "If you think I feel sorry for you, I don't."

"I'm not telling you this to get your sympathy, Kate,"

he said slowly. "I'm trying to communicate with you and tell you what's going on. The more you understand, the less, I hope, you'll get angry about it."

"Your father is sick, all right," Kate rattled. "He hasn't changed one iota from when I was a kid growing up."

"I'm trying to change that, but it takes time." Jim held her defiant gaze. "If I can keep channels of communication open between us, maybe I can put out some brushfires before they explode into a wildfire. I'd like to be able to talk with you at times if I can."

Snorting, Kate let her arms fall to her sides. "You just saved Rachel's life. Your blood is in her body. I might be pigheaded, Cunningham, but I'm not stupid. I owe you for her life. If all you want in return is a little chat every once in a while, then I can deal with that."

Frustration curdled Jim's innards. He'd actually given one and a half pints of blood and he was feeling light-headed, on top of being stressed out from the rescue. But he held on to his deteriorating emotions. "I told you, Kate—no one owes me for helping to save Rachel's life."

"I just wonder what your father is going to say. This ought to make his day. Not only did you save a Donovan's neck, you gave her your blood, too. Frankly," Kate muttered, moving to the door and opening it, "I don't envy you at all when you go home tonight. You're going to have to scrape that bitter old man of yours off the ceiling but good this time."

Jim nodded. "Yeah, he'll probably think I've thrown in with the enemy." He said it in jest, but he could tell as Kate's knuckles whitened around the doorknob, she had taken the comment the wrong way.

"Bad blood," she rasped. "And it always will be."

Suddenly he felt exhausted. "I hope Rachel doesn't take it that way even if you do." There was nothing he could do to change Kate's mind about his last name, Cunningham. As her deceased father had, she chose to associate all the wrongdoings of the past with each individual Cunningham, whether involved in it or not. And in Jim's case, he was as much the victim here as were the Donovan sisters. He'd never condoned or supported what his father had done to Kelly Donovan over the years, or how he'd tried to destroy the Donovan Ranch and then buy it up himself. But Kate didn't see it—or him—as separate from those acts of his father. She never would, Jim thought tiredly.

"Rachel's a big girl," Kate muttered defiantly. "I'm not going to brainwash her one way or another about you Cunninghams."

"Right now, Rachel needs peace and quiet," Jim answered. "She was in pretty deep shock out there. If you could give her two or three days of rest without all this agitation, it would help her a lot."

Kate nodded. "I'll make sure she gets the rest."

The office turned silent after Kate Donovan left. Sighing, Jim rubbed his brow. What a helluva morning! His thoughts moved back to Rachel. Old feelings he'd believed had died a long time ago stirred in his chest. She was so beautiful. He wondered if she had Kate's bitterness toward the Cunninghams. Jim cared more about that than he wanted to admit.

First things first. Because he'd given more than a pint

of blood, he'd been taken off duty by the fire chief, and another EMT had been called in to replace him on the duty roster. Well, he'd fill out the accident report on Rachel and then go home. As he sat down at the desk and pulled out the pertinent form, Jim wondered if news of this event would precede him home. He hoped not— right now, he was too exhausted to deal with his father's ire. What he felt was a soul tiredness, though, more than just physical tiredness. He'd been home almost a year now, and as Kate had said, not much had changed.

Pen in hand, the report staring up at him, Jim tried to order his thoughts, but all he could see was Rachel's pale face and those glorious, dark green eyes of hers. What kind of woman had she grown into after she'd left Sedona? He'd heard she'd moved to England and spent most of her adult life there. Jim understood her desire to escape from Kelly Donovan's drunken, abusive behavior, just as he'd taken flight from his own father and his erratic, emotional moods. Jim's fingers tightened around the pen. Dammit, he was drawn to Rachel—right or wrong. And in Kate Donovan's eyes, he was dead wrong in desiring Rachel.

With a shake of his head, he began to fill out the form. Why the hell had he asked Rachel out to lunch? The invitation had been as much a surprise to him as it had been to the Donovan women. Kate was the one who'd reacted the most to it. Jessica was too embroiled in worry for Rachel to even hear his teasing rejoinder. And Rachel? Well, he'd seen surprise in her green eyes, and then something else…. His heart stirred again— this time with good, warm feelings. He wondered at the fleeting look in Rachel's eyes when he'd made his sudden invitation.

Would she consider going to lunch with him? Was he crazy enough to hold on to that thought? With a snort, Jim forced his attention back to his paperwork. Right now, what he had to look forward to was going back to the Bar C and hoping his father hadn't heard what had happened. If he had, Jim knew there would be a blisteringly high price to pay on his hide tonight.

Chapter 3

"I heard you gave blood to one of those Donovan bitches."

Jim's hand tightened on the door as he stepped into the Cunningham ranch house. Frank Cunningham's gravelly voice landed like a hot branding iron on him, causing anger to surge through Jim. Slowly shutting the door, he saw his father in his wheelchair sitting next to the flagstone fireplace. The old man was glaring at him from beneath those bushy white eyebrows, his gray eyes flat and hard. Demanding.

Jim told himself that he was a grown man, that his gut shouldn't be clenching as it was now. He was over thirty years old, yet he was having a little boy's reaction to a raging father. Girding himself internally, Jim forced himself to switch to his EMT mode. Shrugging out of his heavy jacket, he placed it on a hook beside the door.

"Looks like news travels fast," he said as lightly as possible. Judging from the wild look in his father's eyes, he guessed he hadn't taken his diabetes medication.

"Bad news always does, dammit!" Frank punched a finger at Jim as he sauntered between the leather couch and chair. "What are you doing, boy? Ruining our good name? How could you?"

Halting in front of him, Jim placed his hands on his hips. He was tired and drained. Ordinarily, giving blood didn't knock him down like this. It was different knowing who the accident victim was, though. He was still reeling from the fact that it was little Rachel Donovan, the girl he'd had a mad crush on so long ago.

"Have you taken your pill for your sugar problem?" Jim asked quietly.

Cursing richly, Frank Cunningham snarled, "You answer my questions, boy! Who the *hell* do you think you are, giving blood to—"

"You call her a bitch one more time and it will be the last time," Jim rasped, locking gazes with his angry father. "Rachel doesn't deserve that from you or anyone. She could have died out there early this morning."

Gripping the arms of his wheelchair with swollen, arthritic fingers, Frank glared at him. "You don't threaten me, boy."

The word *boy* grated on Jim's sensitized nerves. He reminded himself one more time that he'd come home to try and pull his family together. To try and stop all the hatred, the anger and fighting that the Cunninghams were known for across two counties. Maybe he'd been a little too idealistic. After all, no one had even invited him back. It was one thing to be called home. It was quite another to wonder every day whether he'd have a home to come back to. Frank Cunningham had thrown him out when he was eighteen and Jim had never returned, except for Christmas. Even then, the holidays became a battleground of sniping and snarling, of dealing with the manipulations of his two brothers.

"Look, Father," Jim began in a strained tone, "I'm a little out of sorts right now. I need to lie down for a while and rest. Did you take your medicine this morning at breakfast? Did Louisa give it to you?"

Snorting, Frank glared at the open fireplace, where a fire crackled and snapped. "Yes, she gave it to me," he muttered irritably.

A tired smile tugged at the corners of Jim's mouth. "Did you take it?"

"No!"

In some ways, at seventy-five, Frank was a pale ghost of his former self. Jim recalled growing up with a strapping, six-foot-five cowboy who was tougher than the drought they were presently enduring. Frank had made this ranch what it was: the largest and most prosperous in the state of Arizona. Jim was proud of his heritage, and like his father, he loved being a cowboy, sitting on a good horse, working ceaselessly during calving season and struggling through all the other demanding jobs of ranching life.

Pulling himself out of his reverie, Jim walked out to the kitchen. There on the table were two tiny blue tablets, one for diabetes and one for high blood pressure. He picked them up and got a glass of water. He knew his father's mood was based directly on his blood sugar level. If it was too high, he was an irritable son of a bitch. If it was too low, he would go into insulin shock, keel over unconscious and fall out of his wheelchair. Jim had lost track of how many times he'd had to pull his father out of insulin shock. He could never get it through Frank's head that he might die from it. His father didn't seem to care. Frank's desire to live, Jim realized, had left when their mother died.

Jim walked back out into the living room. It was a huge, expansive room with a cathedral ceiling and the stuffed heads of elk, deer, peccary and cougar on the cedar walls. The aged hardwood floor gleamed a burnished gold color. A large Navajo rug of red, black and gray lay in the center of the room, which was filled with several dark leather couches and chairs set around a rectangular coffee table.

"Here, Dad, take it now," Jim urged gently.

"Damn stuff."

"I know."

"I *hate* taking pills! Don't like leaning on anything or anyone! That's all these are—crutches," he said, glaring down at the blue pill in his large, callused palm.

Jim patiently handed him the glass of water. Neither of his brothers would ensure that Frank took his medicine. If they even saw the pills on the kitchen table, they ignored them. Jim had once heard Bo say that it would be just that much sooner that the ranch would be given to him.

As he stood there watching his father take the second pill, Jim felt his heart wrench. Frank was so thin now. His flesh, once darkly tanned and hard as saddle leather, was washed out and almost translucent look-ing. Jim could see the large, prominent veins in his fa-ther's crippled hands, which shook as he handed the glass back to him.

"Thanks. Now hit the hay. You look like hell, son."

Jim smiled a little. Such gruff warmth from his father was a rare gift and he absorbed it greedily. There were moments when Frank was human and compassionate. Not many, but Jim lived for them. "Okay, Dad. If you need anything, just come and get me."

Rubbing his hand through his thick silver hair, Frank grunted. "I got work to do in the office. I'll be fine."

"Okay...."

Jim was sitting on his bed and had pushed off his black boots when he heard someone coming down the hardwood hall. By the sound of the heavy footsteps, he knew it was Bo. Looking up, he saw his tall, lean brother standing in the doorway. By the state of his muddied Levi's and snow-dampened sheepskin coat, Bo had been out working. Taking off his black Stetson hat, he scowled at Jim.

"What's this I hear about you giving blood to one of those Donovan girls? Is that true? I was over at the hay and feed store and that was all they were talkin' about."

With a shake of his head, Jim stretched out on top of his double bed, which was covered with a brightly colored, Pendleton wool blanket. Placing his hands be-hind his head, he looked up at the ceiling.

"Gossip travels faster than anything else on earth," he commented.

Bo stepped inside the room. His dark brows drew down. "It's true, then?"

"Yeah, so what if it is?"

Settling the hat back on his head, Bo glared down at him. "Don'tcha think your goody two-shoes routine is a little out of control?"

Smarting at Bo's drawled criticisms, Jim sat up. "I know you wish I'd crawl back under a rock and disappear from this ranch, Bo, but it isn't going to happen."

Bo's full lips curved into a cutting smile. "Comin' home to save all sinners is a little presumptuous, don't you think?"

Tiredness washed across Jim, but he held on to his deteriorating patience. "Someone needs to save this place."

"So you gave blood to Rachel Donovan. Isn't that a neat trick. You think by doing that, you'll stop the war between us?"

Anger lapped at him. "Bo, get the hell out of here. I'm beat. If you want to talk about this later, we'll do it then."

Chuckling indulgently, Bo reached for the doorknob. "Okay, little bro. I'll see you later."

Once the door shut, Jim sighed and lay back down. Closing his eyes, he let his arm fall across his face. The image of Rachel Donovan hovered beneath his eyelids. Instantly, he felt warmth flow through his tense body, washing away his irritation with his father, his anger toward his older brother. She had the most incredible dark green eyes he'd ever seen. Jim recalled being mesmerized by them as a young, painfully shy boy in junior high. He'd wanted to stare into them and see how many gold flecks he could find among the deep, forest green depths.

Rachel had been awkward and skinny then. Now she was tall, elegant looking and incredibly beautiful. The prettiest, he felt, of the three sisters. She had Odula's face—high cheekbones, golden skin, dark brown hair that hung thick and heavy around her shoulders. Finely arched brows and large, compassionate eyes. Her nose was fine and thin; her mouth—the most delectable part of her—was full and expressive. Jim found himself wondering what it would be like to kiss that mouth.

At that thought, he removed his arm and opened his eyes. What the hell was he doing? His father would have a stroke if he suspected Jim liked Rachel Donovan. Frank Cunningham would blow his top, as usual, and spout vehemently, "That's like marrying the plague!" or something like that. Donovan blood, as far as Frank was concerned, was contaminated filth of the worst kind. Jim knew that to admit his interest in Rachel would do nothing but create the worst kind of stress in this household. His older brothers would ride roughshod over him, too. He was sure Frank would disown him—again—as he had when Jim was eighteen.

Jim closed his eyes once more and felt the tension in his body. Why the hell had he come home? Was Bo right? Was he out to "save" everyone? Right now, he was trying to juggle his part-time job as an EMT and work full time at the ranch as a cowboy. Jim didn't want his father's money, though Bo had accused him of coming home because their father was slowly dying from diabetes. Bo thought Jim was hoping to be written back

into the will. When Jim had left home, Frank had told
him that the entire ranch would be given to Bo and Chet.

Hell, Jim couldn't care less about who was in the will
or who got what. That didn't matter to him. What did
matter was family. His family. Ever since his mother
had died, the males in the family had become lost and
the cohesiveness destroyed. His mother, a full-blooded
Apache, had been the strong, guiding central core of
their family. The backbiting, the manipulation and
power games that Bo and Chet played with their father
wouldn't exist, Jim felt, if she were still alive. No, ever
since his mother's death when he was six years old,
the family unit had begun to rot—from the inside out.

Jim felt the tension bleeding out of him as he dwelled
on his family's history. He felt the grief over losing his
mother at such a young, vulnerable age. She had been a
big woman, built like a squash, her black, flashing eyes,
her copper skin and her playful smile so much a part of
her. She'd brought joy and laughter to the ranch. When
she died, so had the happiness. No one had laughed
much after that. His father had changed drastically. In
the year following his mother's death, Jim saw what loving and losing a person did to a man. Frank had turned
to alcohol and his rages became known county wide.
He'd gotten into bar fights. Lawsuits. He'd fought with
Kelly Donovan on almost a daily basis. Frank Cunningham had gone berserk over his wife's passing. Maybe
that's why Jim was gun-shy of committing to a relationship. Or maybe Rachel Donovan had stolen his heart
at such a young age that he wanted no one but her—
whether he could ever have her or not.

All Jim could do back then, was try to hold the rest

of his suffering, grieving family together. He hadn't had time for his own grief and loss as he'd tried to help Bo and Chet. Even though he was the youngest, he was always the responsible one. The family burden had shifted to Jim whenever their father would disappear for days at a time. Frank would eventually return, unshaven and dirty, with the reek of alcohol on his breath. The weight of the world had been thrust upon Jim at a young age. Then, at eighteen, right after high school graduation, Jim had decided he had to escape. And he did—but the price had been high.

Slowly, ever so slowly, Rachel's face formed before his closed eyes again. Jim felt all his stress dissolve before the vision. She had such a peaceful look about her. Even out there at the accident site, she hadn't panicked. He admired her courage under the circumstances.

Suddenly, anger rose within him. Dammit, he *wanted* to see her again. How could he? If Frank knew, he'd hit the ceiling in a rage. Yet Jim refused to live his life knowing what his father's knee-jerk reaction would be. Still, it was hell having to come back to the ranch and take a gutful of Frank's verbal attacks. But if Jim moved to his own place in Sedona, which was what he wanted to do, who would make sure his father took his meds?

Feeling trapped, he turned on his side. He felt the fingers of sleep encroaching on his worry and his desires. The last thing he saw as he drifted off was Rachel trying to smile gamely up at him in the ER when she regained consciousness. He recalled how thick and silky her hair had felt when he'd touched it. And he'd seen how his touch had affected her. In those moments, he'd felt so clean and hopeful again—two things he hadn't felt in a long, long time. Somehow, some way, he was going to find a way to see her again. He *had* to.

Rachel absorbed the warmth of the goose-down quilt lying over her. She was in her old bed, in the room she'd had as a child. She was back at the Donovan Ranch. Gloomy midafternoon light filtered through the flowery curtains at the window. Outside, snowflakes were falling slowly, like butterflies. The winter storm of this morning had passed on through.

Her foot ached a little, so she struggled to sit up. On the bed stand was her homeopathic kit. Opening it, she found the Arnica and took another dose.

"You awake?"

Rachel heard Jessica's hopeful voice at her door before her younger sister smiled tentatively and entered the room. Jessica's gold hair was in two braids and the oversize, plaid flannel shirt she wore highlighted her flushed cheeks.

"Come on in," Rachel whispered.

Pushing a few strands of hair off her face, Jessica sat down at the bottom of the bed and faced Rachel. "I thought you might be awake."

"I slept long and hard," Rachel assured her as she placed the kit back on the bed table. She put a couple of pillows behind her and then pushed the quilt down to her waist. The flannel nightgown she wore was covering enough in the cool room. There was no central heating in the huge, main ranch house. Only the fireplace in the living room provided heat throughout the winter. Rachel didn't mind the coolness, though.

Jessica nodded and surveyed her. "How's your foot?"

"Okay. I just took another round of Arnica."

"What does that do for it?"

Rachel smiled, enjoying her sister's company. Jessica was so open, idealistic and trusting. Nothing like Kate, who distrusted everyone, always questioning their motives. "It reduces the swelling of the soft tissue. The pain will go away in about five minutes."

"Good." Jessica rubbed her hands down her Levi's. "I was just out checking on my girls—my orchids. The temperature is staying just fine out there in the greenhouse. This is the first big snow we've had and I was a little worried about them."

Rachel nodded. "Where's Kate?"

"Oh, she and Sam and Dan are out driving the fence line. Earlier today, she got a call from Bo Cunningham who said that some of our cattle were on their property—again."

Groaning, Rachel said, "Life doesn't change at all, does it, Jess?"

Giggling, Jessica shook her head. "No, it doesn't seem to, does it? Don't you feel like you're a teenager again? We had the same problems with the Cunninghams then as we do now." She sighed and opened her hands. "I wish they wouldn't be so nasty toward us. Frank Cunningham hates us."

"He hates everything," Rachel murmured.

"So how did Jim turn out to be so nice?"

"I don't know." Rachel picked absently at the bedcover. "He *is* nice, Jess. You should have seen him out there with me, at the accident. I was in bad shape. He was so gentle and soothing. I had such faith in him. I knew I'd be okay."

"He's been home almost a year now, and he's trying to mend a lot of fences."

"Are you saying he was nice to me because of the feud between our families?"

Jessica shook her head. "No, Jim is a nice guy. Somehow, he didn't get Frank's nasty genes like the other two boys did." She laughed. "I think he has his mother's, instead."

Rachel smiled. "I know one thing. I owe Jim my life."

"You owe him more than that," Jessica said primly as she tucked her hands in her lap. "Did he tell you he gave a pint of *his* blood to you?"

"What?" Rachel's eyes grew wide.

"Yeah, the blood transfusion. You lost a lot from the cut across your foot," she said, pointing to Rachel's foot beneath the cover. "I found out about it from the head nurse in ER when we came in to see how you were. Jim had called us from hospital and told us what had happened. Well," she murmured, "he was selective in what he told us. He really downplayed his part in saving you. He's so humble that way, you know? Anyway, I was asking the nurse what all had been done for you, because we don't have medical insurance and I knew Kate would be worrying about the bill. I figured I'd do some investigating for her and get the info so she wouldn't have to do it later." Clasping her hands together, she continued, "You have a rare type of blood. They didn't have any on hand at the hospital, nor did they have any in Cottonwood. So I guess Jim volunteered his on the spot. He has the same blood type as you do." She smiled gently. "Wasn't that sweet of him? I mean, talk about a symbolic thing happening between our two families."

Rachel sat there, digesting her sister's explanation. Jim's blood was circulating in her body. It felt right. And good. "I—see...." Moistening her lips, she searched Jessica's small, open face. She loved her fiercely for her compassion and understanding. "How do you feel about that?"

"Oh, I think it's wonderful!"

"And Kate?" Tension nagged at Rachel's stomach over the thought of her older sister's reaction. Kate held grudges like their father did.

Jessica gazed up at the ceiling and then at her. "Well, you know Kate. She wasn't exactly happy about it, but like she said, you're alive and that's what counts."

"I'm glad she took the high road on this," Rachel murmured, chuckling.

Jessica nodded. "We owe Jim so much. Kate knows that and so do I. I think he's wonderful. He's trying so hard to patch things up between the two families."

"That's a tall order," Rachel said. She reached for the water pitcher on the bed stand. Pouring herself a glassful, she sipped it.

"I have faith in him," Jessica said simply. "His integrity, his morals and values are like sunshine compared to the darkness of the Cunningham ranch in general. I believe he can change his father and two brothers."

"You're being overidealistic," Rachel cautioned.

"Maybe," she said. Reaching out, she ran her hand along Rachel's blanketed shin. "We're all wondering *what* made you skid off 89A. You know that road like the back of your hand. And you're used to driving in snow and ice."

Setting the glass on the bed table, Rachel frowned. "You're probably going to think I'm crazy."

Laughing, Jessica sat up. "Me? The metaphysical brat of the three of us? Nooo, I don't think so, Rachel." Leaning forward, her eyes animated, she whispered, "So tell me what happened!"

Groaning, Rachel muttered, "I saw a jaguar standing in the middle of 89A as I rounded that last hairpin curve."

Jessica's eyes widened enormously. "A jaguar? You saw a jaguar?"

Rachel grimaced. "I told you you'd think I was crazy."

Leaping up from the bed, her sister whispered, "Oh, gosh! This is *really* important, Rachel." Typical of Jessica, when she got excited she had to move around. She quickly rounded the bed, her hands flying in the air. "It was a jaguar? You're positive?"

"I know what I saw," Rachel said a bit defensively. "I know I was tired and I had jet lag, but I've never hallucinated in my life. No, it *was* a jaguar. Not a cougar, because I've seen the cougars that live all around us up here. It was a jaguar, with a black-and-gold coat and had huge yellow eyes. It was looking right at me. I was never so startled, Jess. I slammed on the brakes. I know I shouldn't have—but I did. If I hadn't, I'd have hit that cat."

"Oh, gosh, this is *wonderful!*" Jessica cried. She clapped her hands together, coming to a sudden halt at the end of Rachel's bed.

"Really? What's so wonderful about it? If this story ever gets out, I'll be the laughingstock of Sedona. There're no jaguars in Arizona."

Excitedly, Jessica whispered, "My friend Moyra, who is from Peru, lived near me for two years up in Canada. She helped me get my flower essence business going, and tended my orchid girls with me. What a mysterious woman she was! She was very metaphysical, very spiritual. Over the two years I knew her, she told me that she was a member of a very ancient order called the Jaguar Clan. She told me that she took her training in the jungles of Peru with some very, very old teachers who possessed jaguar medicine."

Rachel opened her mouth to reply, but Jessica gripped her hand, her words tumbling out in a torrent. "No, no, just listen to me, okay? Don't interrupt. Moyra told me that members of the Jaguar Clan came from around the world. They didn't have to be born in South America to belong. I guess it has something to do with one's genes. Anyway, I saw some very strange things with Moyra over the two years she was with me."

"Strange?"

"Well," she said, "Moyra could read minds. She could also use mental telepathy. There were so many times I'd start to ask her a question and she'd answer before I got it out of my mouth! Or…" Jessica paused, her expression less animated "…when Carl, my ex-husband, was stalking me and trying to find out where I was hiding, Moyra told me that she'd guard me and make sure he never got to me. I remember four different times when she warned me he was close and protected me from being found by him."

"You mean," Rachel murmured, "she *sensed* his presence?"

"Something like that, but it was more, much more. She had these heightened senses. And—" Jessica held her gaze "—I saw her do it one day."

"Do what?"

Jessica sighed and held up her right hand. "I *swear* I'm telling you the truth on this, Rachel. I was taking a walk in the woods, like I always did in the afternoon when I was done watering my girls in the greenhouse. It was a warm summer day and I wanted to go stick my feet in the creek about half a mile from where we lived. As I approached the creek, I froze. You won't believe this, but one minute I saw Moyra standing in the middle of the creek and in the next I saw a jaguar! Well, I just stood there in shock, my mouth dropping open. Then suddenly the jaguar turned back into Moyra. She turned around and looked right at me. I blinked. Gosh, I thought I was going crazy or something. I thought I was seeing things."

Jessica patted her sister's hand and released it. "There were two other times that I saw Moyra change into a jaguar. I don't think she meant for me to see it—it just happened."

"A woman who turns into a jaguar?" Rachel demanded.

"I know, I know," Jessica said. "It sounds crazy, but listen to this!" She sat down on the edge of the bed and faced Rachel. "I got up enough courage to ask Moyra about what I'd seen. She didn't say much, but she said that because she was a member of this clan, her spirit guide was a male jaguar. Every clan member has one. And that this spirit guide is her teacher, her protector, and she could send it out to help others or protect others if necessary." Excitedly, Jessica whispered, "Rachel, the last thing Moyra told me before I drove down here to live was that if I ever needed help, she would be there!"

Stymied, Rachel said, "That jaguar I saw was Moyra—or Moyra's spirit guardian?" Rachel had no trouble believing in spirit guardians, because Odula, their mother, had taught them from a very early age that all people had such guides from the invisible realms. They were protectors, teachers and helpers if the person allowed them to be.

"It must have been one or the other!" Jessica exclaimed in awe.

"Because," Kate Donovan said, walking through the door and taking off her damp wool coat, "about half a mile down 89A from where you crashed, there was a fuel-oil tanker that collided with a pickup truck." She halted and smiled down at Jessica, placing her coat on a chair. "What you don't know, Rachel, is that five minutes after you spun out on that corner, that pickup truck slid into that tanker carrying fuel oil. There was an explosion, and everyone died."

Stunned, Rachel looked at Jessica. "And if I hadn't spun out on that corner..."

Kate brought the chair over and sat down near her bed. "Yep, *you* would have been killed in that explosion, too."

"My God," Rachel whispered. She frowned.

Jessica gave them both a wide-eyed look. "Then that jaguar showing up saved your life. It really did!"

Kate combed her fingers through her long, dark hair, which was mussed from wearing a cowboy hat all day.

"I heard you two talking as I came down the hall. So you think it was your friend's jaguar that showed up?"

Jessica nodded. "I have no question about it. Even now, about once a month, I have this dream that's not a dream, about Moyra. She comes and visits me. We talk over what's happening in our lives. Stuff like that. She's down at a place called the Village of the Clouds, and she said she's in training. She didn't say for what. She's very mysterious about that."

"So, your friend comes in the dream state and visits with you?" Rachel asked. Odula had placed great weight and importance on dreaming, especially lucid dreaming, which was a technique embraced wholeheartedly by the Eastern Cherokee people.

"Yes," Jessica said in awe. "Wow...isn't that something?" She looked up at Kate. "How did you find this out?"

"At the ER desk as I was signing Rachel out. Once they had you extricated from your rental car," Kate told Rachel, "Jim's ambulance had to drive up to Flagstaff to get you ER care because of that mess down on 89A. There was no way they could get through to the Cottonwood Hospital. There were fire trucks all over the place putting out the fire from that wreck."

Rachel studied her two sisters. Kate looked drawn and tired in her pink flannel shirt, Levi's and cowboy boots. She worked herself to the bone for this ranch. "Once upon a time, jaguars lived in the Southwest," Rachel told them.

"Yeah," Kate muttered, "until the good ol' white man killed them all off. I hear, though, they're coming back. There're jaguars living just over the border in Mexico. It wouldn't surprise me if they've already reached here." She rubbed her face. "And this Rim country where we live is ideal habitat for them." She smiled a little. "Maybe what you saw wasn't from the spirit world, after all. Maybe it was a live one. The first jaguar back in the States?"

"Oh," Jessica said with a sigh, "that would be neat, too!"

They all laughed. Rachel reached out and gripped Kate's work-worn hand. "It's so good to be home. It feels like old times, doesn't it? The three of us in one or the other's bedroom, chatting and laughing?"

"Yeah," Kate whispered, suddenly emotional as she gripped Rachel's hand. "It's nice to have you both here. Welcome home, sis."

Home. The word sent a tide of undeniable warmth through Rachel. She saw tears in Jessica's eyes and felt them in her own.

"If it wasn't for Jim Cunningham," Rachel quavered, "I wouldn't be here at all. We owe him a lot."

Kate nodded grimly. "Yes, we do."

"Tomorrow I want to see him and thank him personally," Rachel told them. "Jessica, can you find out if he's going to be at the fire department in Sedona?"

"Sure, no problem." She eased off the bed and wiped the tears from her eyes. "He's the sweetest guy."

Kate snorted. "He's a Cunningham. What's the old saying? A tiger can't change his stripes?"

Rachel grinned at her older sister's sour reaction. "Who knows, Kate? Jim may not be a tiger at all. He may be a jaguar in disguise."

"You know his nickname and his Apache name are both Cougar," Jessica said excitedly.

"Close enough for me," Rachel said with a smile.

Chapter 4

"Hey, Cunningham, you got a visitor!"

Jim lifted his head as his name was shouted through the cavernous area where the fire trucks and ambulance sat waiting for another call. The bay doors were open and bright winter sunlight poured inside the ambulance where Jim sat, repacking some of the shelves with necessary items.

Who could it be? Probably one of his brothers wanting to borrow some money from him as usual. With a grunt he eased out of the ambulance and swung around the corner.

His eyes widened and he came to an abrupt halt. Rachel Donovan! Swallowing his surprise, he stood watching as she slowly walked toward him. Noontime sunlight cascaded down, burnishing her long dark hair with hints of red and gold. She wore conservative, light gray woolen slacks and a camel-colored overcoat.

Struck by her beauty, her quiet presence as she met and held his gaze, he watched her lips lift into a smile. Heat sheeted through him as he stood there. Like a greedy beggar, he absorbed her warm gaze. Her green eyes sparkled with such life that he felt his breath momentarily hitch. This wasn't the woman he'd met at the car accident. Not in the least. Amazed that she seemed perfectly fine three days after nearly losing her life, Jim managed a shy grin of welcome.

"Hey, you look pretty good," he exclaimed, meeting her halfway across the bay.

Rachel felt heat sting her cheeks. She was blushing again! Her old childhood response always seemed to show up at the most embarrassing times. She studied the man before her; he was dressed in his usual dark blue pants and shirt, the patches for the fire department adorning the sleeves. When he offered his hand to her, she was struck by the symbolic gesture. A Donovan and a Cunningham meeting not in anger, but in friendship. As far as she knew it was a first, and Rachel welcomed it.

As she slid her hand into his big square one she felt the calluses and strength of it. Yet she could feel by his grip that he was carefully monitoring that strength. But what Rachel noticed most of all was the incredible warmth and joy in his eyes. It stunned her. He was a Cunningham, she, a Donovan. Nearly a century-old feud stood between them, and a lot of bad blood.

"I should hope I look better," Rachel replied with a low, husky laugh. "I'm not a homeopath for nothing."

Jim forced himself to release Rachel's long, thin fingers. She had the hands of a doctor, a surgeon, maybe. There was such a fluid grace about her as she moved. Suddenly he remembered that she could have bled to death the other day if they hadn't arrived on scene to help her when they had, and he was shaken deeply once again.

"I'm just finishing up my shift." He glanced at his watch. "I have to do some repacking in the ambulance. Come on back and keep me company?"

She touched her cheek, knowing the heat in it was obvious. "I didn't want to bother you—"

"You're not a bother, believe me," he confided sincerely as he slid his hand beneath her elbow and guided her between the gargantuan fire trucks to the boxy ambulance that sat at the rear.

As Rachel allowed him to guide her, she saw a number of men and women firefighters, most of them watching television in the room off the main hangar. Yet she hardly noticed them. So many emotions were flowing through her as Jim cupped her elbow. What she recalled of him from junior high was a painfully shy teenager who couldn't look anyone directly in the eye. Of course, she understood that; she hadn't exactly been the homecoming queen type herself. Two shadows thrown together by life circumstance, Rachel thought, musing about their recent meeting.

Once they reached the back of the ambulance, Jim urged her to climb in. "You can sit in the hot seat," he joked, and pointed to the right of the gurney, where the next patient would lie.

Rachel carefully climbed in. She sat down and looked around. "Is this the one I was in?"

Jim smiled a little and opened up a box of rolled bandages. He counted out six and then stepped up into the ambulance. "Yes, it was," he said, sliding the plastic door on one of the shelves to one side to arrange the bandages. "We call her Ginger."

"I like that. You named your truck."

"Actually, my partner, Larry, named her." Jim made a motion toward the front of the ambulance. "All the fire trucks are ladies and they all have names, too." He studied Rachel as he crouched by one of the panels. "You look like your accident never happened. How are you feeling?"

With a slight laugh, she said, "Well, let's put it this way—my two sisters, Kate and Jessica, are getting married this Saturday out at the ranch. I'm their maid of honor. I could *not* stay sick." She pointed to her foot, which sported a white dressing across the top. "I had to get well fast or they'd have disowned me for not showing up for their weddings."

"You look terrific," Jim murmured. "Like nothing ever happened."

She waved her hands and laughed. "*That* was thanks to you and homeopathy. When I got back to the ranch, I had Jessica bathe the wound with tincture of Calendula three times a day." She patted her injured foot. "It really speeded up the healing."

"And that stuff you took? What did you call it? Arnica? What did it do for you?"

She was pleased he remembered the remedy. "Arnica reduces the swelling and trauma to injured soft tissue."

He slid the last door shut, his inventory completed. "That's a remedy we could sure use a lot of around here. We scrape so many people up off the highway that it would really help."

Rachel watched as he climbed out of the ambulance. There was no wasted motion about Jim Cunningham. He was lithe, like the cougar he was named after. And she liked the sense of steadiness and calmness that emanated from him like a beacon. His Apache blood was obvious in the color of his skin, his dark, cut hair and high cheekbones. What she liked most were his wide, intelligent eyes and his mouth, which was usually crooked in a partial smile. Jim was such an opposite to the warring Cunningham clan he'd been born into. He was like his mother, who had been known for her calm, quiet demeanor. Rachel knew little more about her, except that she'd been always full of laughter, with a twinkle in her eye.

"We're done here," Jim said genially, holding out his hand to her. He told himself he was enjoying Rachel too much. He wondered if she was married, but he didn't see a wedding ring on her left hand as he took it into his own. She stepped carefully out of the ambulance to the concrete floor beside him. "And I'm done with my shift." He glanced at his watch. "Noon, exactly." And then he took a huge risk. "If I recall, up at the Flag hospital I offered you lunch. I know a great little establishment called the Muse Restaurant. Best mocha lattes in town. How about it?" His heart pumped hard once, underscoring just how badly he wanted Rachel to say yes.

Jim saw her forest green eyes sparkle with gold as he asked her the question. Did that mean yes or no?

He hoped it meant yes and found himself holding his breath, waiting for her answer. As he studied her up-turned face, he felt her undeniable warmth and compassion. There was a gentleness around her, a Zenlike quality that reminded him of a quiet pool of water—serene yet very deep and mysterious.

"Actually," Rachel said with a laugh, "I came here to invite *you* to lunch. It was to be a surprise. A way of thanking you for saving my neck."

A powerful sensation moved through Jim, catching him off guard. It was a delicious feeling.

"That's a great idea," he murmured, meaning it. "But I asked first, so you're my guest for lunch. Come on, we'll take my truck. It's parked just outside. I'll bring you back here afterward."

Rachel couldn't resist smiling. He looked boyish as the seriousness in his face, the wrinkle in his brow disappeared in that magical moment. Happiness filled her, making her feel as if she were walking on air. Once again Jim cupped his hand on her elbow to guide her out of the station. She liked the fact that he matched his stride to hers. Normally she was a fast walker, but the injury to her foot had slowed her down.

Jim's truck was a white Dodge Ram with a shiny chrome bumper. It was a big, powerful truck, and there was plenty of Arizona—red mud which stuck to everything—on the lower half of it, probably from driving down the three-mile dirt road to the Cunningham ranch. He opened the door for her and she carefully climbed in.

Rachel was impressed with how clean and neat the interior was, unlike many men's pickups. As she hooked the seat belt, she imagined the orderliness came from him working in the medical field and understanding the necessity of cleanliness. She watched as Jim climbed in, his face wonderfully free of tension. He ran his fingers through his short, dark hair and then strapped himself in.

"Have you thought about the repercussions of being seen out in public with me?" he drawled as he slipped the key into the ignition. The pickup purred to life, the engine making a deep growling sound.

Wrinkling her nose, Rachel said, "You mean the gossip that will spread because a Cunningham and a Donovan broke bread together?"

Grinning, he nodded and eased the truck out of the parking spot next to the redbrick building. "Exactly."

"I was over at Fay Seward's, the saddle maker's, yesterday, and she was telling me all kinds of gossip she'd heard about us."

Moving out into the traffic, slow moving because of the recent snow, Jim chuckled. "I'll bet."

Rachel looked out the window. The temperature was in the low thirties, the sky bright blue and filled with nonstop sunlight. She put her dark glasses on and simply enjoyed being near Jim as he drove from the tourist area of Sedona into what was known as West Sedona. "I really missed this place," she whispered.

The crimson rocks of Sedona created some of the most spectacular scenery he'd ever seen. Red sandstone and white limestone alike were capped with a foot of new, sparkling snow from the storm several days before. With the dark green mantle of forest across the top of the Rim, which rose abruptly to tower several thousand feet above Sedona, this was a place for an artist and photographer, he mused.

Glancing over at her, he asked, "Why did you stay away so long?"

Shrugging, Rachel met his inquiring gaze. "Isn't it obvious? Or is it only to me?"

Gripping the steering wheel a little more tightly, he became serious. "We both left when we were kids. Probably for similar reasons. I went into the forest service and became a firefighter. Where did you go? I heard you moved overseas?"

Pain moved through Rachel. She saw an equal amount in Jim's eyes. It surprised her in one way, because the men she had known never allowed much emotion to show. "I moved to England," she said.

"And Jessica went to Canada and Kate became a tumbleweed here in the States."

"Yes."

Jim could feel her vulnerability over the issue. "Sorry, I didn't mean to get so personal." He had no right, but Rachel just seemed to allow him to be himself, and it was much too easy to become intimate with her. Maybe it was because she was in the medical field; she had a doctor's compassion, but more so.

With a wave of her hand, she murmured, "No harm done. I knew when I moved home to try and help save our ranch that there were a lot of buried wounds that needed to be aired and cleaned out and dressed."

"I like your analogy. Yeah, we all have old wounds, don't we?" He pulled into a shopping center with a huge fountain that had been shut off for the winter. Pointing up the walk, he said, "The Muse—a literary café. All the writers and would-be writers come here and hang out. Since you're so intelligent, I thought you might enjoy being with your own kind."

Smiling, Rachel released the seat belt. "How did you know I'm writing a book?"

Jim opened his door. "Are you?"

With a laugh, she said, "Yes, I am." Before she could open her own door, Jim was there to do it. He offered his hand and she willingly took it because the distance to the ground was great and she had no desire to put extra stress on the stitches still in her foot.

"Thank you," she said huskily. How close he was! How very male he was. Rachel found herself wanting to sway those few inches and lean against his tall, strong frame. Jim's shoulders were broad, proudly thrown back. His bearing was dignified and filled with incredible self-confidence.

Unwilling to release her, Jim guided Rachel up the wet concrete steps. "So what are you writing on?" The slight breeze lifted strands of her dark hair from her shoulders, reminding him how thick and silky it was. His fingers itched to thread through those strands once again.

"A book on homeopathy and first aid. I'm almost finished. I already have a publisher for it, here in the States. It will be simultaneously published by an English firm, too."

He opened the door to the restaurant for her. "How about that? I know a famous person."

With a shake of her head, Rachel entered the warm restaurant, which smelled of baking bread. Inhaling the delicious scent, she waited for Jim to catch up with her. "Mmm, homemade bread. Doesn't it smell wonderful?"

He nodded. "Jamie and his partner, Adrian, make everything fresh here on the premises. No canned anything." He guided her around the corner to a table near the window. Each table, covered in white linen, was decorated with fresh, colorful flowers in a vase. The music was soft and New Age. In each corner stood towering green plants. Jim liked the place because it was alive with plants and flowers.

Rachel relinquished her coat to Jim. He placed it on one of several hooks in the corner. The place was packed with noontime clientele. In winter and spring, Sedona was busy with tourists from around the world who wanted to escape harsh winters at home. The snowfall earlier in the week was rare. Sedona got snow perhaps two to four times each winter. And usually, within a day or two, it had melted and been replaced with forty-degree weather in the daytime, thirty-degree temperatures at night.

Sitting down, Jim recognized some of the locals. He saw them watching with undisguised interest. The looks on their face said it all: a Cunningham and Donovan sitting together—peacefully—what a miracle! Frowning, Jim picked up the menu and then looked over at Rachel, who was studying hers.

"They've got great food here. Anything you pick will be good."

Rachel tried to pay attention to the menu. She liked the fact that Jim sat at her elbow and not across from her. It was so easy to like him, to want to get to know him better. She had a million questions to ask him, but knew she had to remain circumspect.

After ordering their lunch, and having steaming bowls of fragrant mocha latte placed in front of them, Rachel began to relax. The atmosphere of the Muse was low-key. Even though there wasn't an empty table, the noise level was low, and she appreciated that. Setting the huge bowl of latte down after taking a sip, she pressed the pink linen napkin briefly to her lips. Settling the napkin back in her lap, she met and held Jim's warm, interested gaze. He wasn't model handsome. His face had lines in it, marks of character from the thirty-some years of his life. His thick, dark brows moved up a bit in inquiry as she studied him.

"I know what you're thinking," he teased. "I'll bet you're remembering this acne-covered teenager from junior high school, aren't you?"

She folded her hands in front of her. "No, not really. I do remember you being terribly shy, though."

"So were you," he said, sipping his own latte. Jim liked the flush that suddenly covered her cheeks. There was such painfully obvious vulnerability to Rachel. How had she been able to keep it? Life usually had a way of knocking the stuffing out of most people, and everyone he knew hid behind a protective mask or wall as a result. Rachel didn't, he sensed. Maybe that was a testament to her obvious confidence.

"I was a wallflower," Rachel conceded with a nervous laugh. "Although I did attend several clubs after school."

"Drama and photography, if my memory serves me."

Her brows rose. "That's right! Boy, what a memory

you have." She was flabbergasted that Jim would remember such a thing. If he remembered that, what else
did he recall? And why would he retain such insignifi-
cant details of her life, anyway? Her heart beat a little
harder for a moment.

With a shy shrug, Jim sipped more of his latte. "If
the truth be told, I had a terrible crush on you back
then. But you didn't know it. I was too shy to say anything, much less look you in the eyes." He chuckled
over the memory.

Gawking, Rachel tried to recover. "A crush? On me?"

"Ridiculous, huh?"

She saw the pain in his eyes and realized he was
waiting for her to make fun of him for such an admit-
tance. Rachel would never do that to anyone. Especially Jim.

"No!" she whispered, touched. "I didn't know...."

"Are you sorry you didn't know?" Damn, why had
he asked that? His stomach clenched. Why was it so important that Rachel like him as much as he had always
liked her? His hands tightened momentarily around
his bowl of latte.

"Never mind," he said, trying to tease her, "you don't
have to answer that on the grounds it may incriminate
you—or embarrass me."

Rachel felt his tension and saw the worry in his eyes.
A scene flashed inside her head; of a little boy cow-
ering, as if waiting to get struck. Sliding her fingers
around her warm bowl of latte, she said, "I wish I had
known, Jim. That's a beautiful compliment. Thank
you."

Unable to look at her, he nervously took a couple of

sips of his own. Wiping his mouth with the napkin, he muttered, "The past is the past."

Rachel smiled gently. "Our past follows us like a good friend. I'm sure you know that by now." Looking around, she saw several people staring openly at them with undisguised interest. "Like right now," she mused, "I see several locals watching us like bugs under a microscope." She met and held his gaze. Her lips curved in a grin. "Tell me our pasts aren't present!"

Glancing around, Jim realized Rachel was right. "Well, by tonight your name will be tarnished but good."

"What? Because I'm having lunch with the man who saved my life? I'd say that I'm in the best company in the world, with no apology. Wouldn't you?"

He felt heat in his neck and then in his face. Jim couldn't recall the last time he'd blushed. Rachel's gently spoken words echoed through him like a bell being rung on a very clear day. It was as if she'd reached out and touched him. Her ability to share her feelings openly was affecting him deeply. Taking in a deep breath, he held her warm green gaze, which suddenly glimmered with tears. Tears! The soft parting of her lips was his undoing. Embarrassed, he reached into his back pocket and produced a clean handkerchief.

"Here," he said gruffly, and placed it in her hand.

Dabbing her eyes, Rachel sniffed. "Don't belittle what you did for me, Jim. I sure won't." She handed it back to him. He could barely meet her eyes, obviously embarrassed by her show of tears and gratitude. "You and I are in the same business in one way," she continued. "We work with sick and injured people. The only difference is your EMT work is immediate, mine is more long-term and certainly not as dramatic."

He refolded the handkerchief and stuffed it back into his rear pocket. "I'm not trying to make little of what we did out there for you, Rachel. It wasn't just me that saved your life. My partner, Larry, and four other firefighters were all working as a team to save you."

"Yes, but it was your experience that made you put that blood-pressure cuff on my leg, inflate it and stop the hemorrhaging from my foot."

He couldn't deny that. "Anyone would have figured that out."

"Maybe," Rachel hedged as she saw him begin to withdraw from her. Why wouldn't Jim take due credit for saving her life? The man had great humility. He never said "I," but rather "we" or "the team," and she found that a remarkable trait rarely seen in males.

Lowering her voice, she added, "And I understand from talking to Kate and Jessica, that you gave me a pint of your blood to stabilize me. Is that so?"

Trying to steel himself against whatever she felt about having his blood in her body, Jim lifted his head. When he met and held her tender gaze, something old and hurting broke loose in his heart. He recalled that look before. Rachel probably had forgotten the incident, but he never had. He had just been coming out of the main doors to go home for the day when he saw that a dog had been hit by a car out in front of the high school. Rachel had flown down the steps of the building, crying out in alarm as the dog was hurled several feet onto the lawn.

Falling to her knees, she had held the injured animal.

Jim had joined her, along with a few other concerned students. Even then, Rachel had been a healer. She had torn off a piece of her skirt and pressed it against the dog's wounded shoulder to stop the bleeding. Jim had dropped his books and gone to help her. The dog had had a broken leg as well.

Jim remembered sinking to his knees directly opposite her and asking what he could do to help. The look Rachel was giving him now was the same one he'd seen on her face then. There was such clear compassion, pain and love in her eyes that he recalled freezing momentarily because the energy of it had knocked the breath out of him. Rachel had worn her heart on her sleeve back then, just as she did now. She made no excuses for how she felt and was bravely willing to share her vulnerability.

Shaken, he rasped, "Yeah, I was the only one around with your blood type." He opened his hands and looked at them. "I don't know how you feel about that, but I caught hell from my old man and my brothers about it." He glanced up at her. "But I'm not sorry I did it, Rachel."

Without thinking, Rachel slid her hand into his. Hers was slightly damp, while his was dry and strong and nurturing. She saw surprise come to his eyes and felt him tense for a moment, then relax.

As his fingers closed over Rachel's, Jim knew tongues would wag for sure now about them holding hands. But hell, nothing had ever felt so right to him. Ever.

"I'm grateful for what you did, Jim," Rachel quavered. "I wouldn't be sitting here now if you hadn't been there to help. I don't know how to repay you. I really don't. If there's a way—"

His fingers tightened around hers. "I'm going hiking in a couple of weeks, near Boynton Canyon. Come with me?" The words flew out of his mouth. What the hell was he doing? Jim couldn't help himself, nor did he want to. He saw Rachel's eyes grow tender and her fingers tightened around his.

"Yes, I'd love to do that."

"Even though," he muttered, "we'll be the gossip of Sedona?"

She laughed a little breathlessly. "If I cared, really cared about that, I wouldn't be sitting here with you right now, would I?"

A load shifted off his shoulders. Rachel was free in a way that Kate Donovan was not, and the discovery was powerful and galvanizing. Jim very reluctantly released her hand. "Okay, two weeks. I'm free on Saturday. I'll pack us a winter picnic lunch to boot."

"Fair enough," Rachel murmured, thrilled over the prospect of the hike. "But I have one more favor to ask of you first, Jim."

"Name it and it's yours," he promised thickly.

Rachel placed her elbows on the table and lowered her voice. "It's a big favor, Jim, and you don't have to do it if it's asking too much of you."

Scowling, he saw the sudden worry and seriousness on her face. "What is it?"

Moistening her lips, Rachel picked up her purse from the floor and opened it. Taking out a thick, white envelope, she handed it to him. "Read it, please."

Mystified, Jim eased the envelope open. It was a

wedding invitation—to Kate and Jessica's double wedding, which would be held on Saturday. He could feel the tension in Rachel. His head spun with questions and few answers. Putting the envelope aside, he held her steady gaze.

"You're serious about this…invitation?"

"Very."

"Look," he began uneasily, holding up his hands, "Kate isn't real comfortable with me being around. I understand why and—"

"Kate was the one who suggested it."

Jim stared at her. "What?"

Rachel looked down at the tablecloth for a moment. "Jim," she began unsteadily, her voice strained, "I've heard why you came back here, back to Sedona. You want to try and straighten out a lot of family troubles between yourself, your father and two brothers. Kate didn't trust you at first because of the past, the feud between our families…actually, between our fathers, not us for the most part." She looked up and held his dark, shadowed gaze. "Kate doesn't trust a whole lot of people. Her life experiences make her a little more paranoid than me or Jessica, but that's okay, too. Yesterday she brought this invitation to me and told me to give it to you. She said that because you'd saved my life, she and Jessica wanted you there. That this was a celebration of life—and love—and that you deserved to be with us."

He saw the earnestness in Rachel's eyes. "How do you feel about it? Having the enemy in your midst?"

"You were never my enemy, Jim. None of you were. Kelly had his battles with your father. Not with me, not with my sisters. Your brothers are another thing. They aren't invited." Her voice grew husky. "I *want* you to be there. I like Kate's changing attitude toward you. It's a start in healing this wound that festers among us. I know you'll probably feel uncomfortable, but by showing up, it's a start, even if only symbolically, don't you think? A positive one?"

In that moment, Jim wished they were anywhere but out in a public place. The tears in Rachel's eyes made them shine and sparkle like dark emeralds. He wanted to whisper her name, slide his hands through that thick mass of hair, angle her head just a little and kiss her until she melted into his being, into his heart. Despite her background, Rachel was so fresh, so alive, so brave about being herself and sharing her feelings, that it allowed him the same privilege within himself.

He wanted to take her hand and hold it, but he couldn't. He saw the locals watching them like proverbial hawks now. Jim didn't wish gossip upon Rachel or any of the Donovan sisters. God knew, they had suffered enough of it through the years.

One corner of his mouth tugged upward. "I'll be there," he promised her huskily.

Chapter 5

"**W**here you goin' all duded up?" Bo Cunningham drawled as he leaned languidly against the open door to Jim's bedroom.

Jim glanced over at his brother. Bo was tall and lean, much like their father. His dark good looks had always brought him a lot of attention from women. In high school, Bo had been keenly competitive with Jim. Whatever Jim undertook, Bo did too. The rivalry hadn't stopped and there was always tension, like a razor, between them.

"Going to a wedding," he said.

He knotted his tie and snugged it into place against his throat. In all his years of traveling around the U.S. as a Hotshot, he'd never had much call for wearing a suit. But after having lunch with Rachel, he'd gone to

Flagstaff and bought one. Jim had known that when his two brothers saw him in a suit, they'd be sure to make fun of him. Uniform of the day around the Bar C was jeans, a long-sleeved shirt and a cowboy hat. He would wear his dark brown Stetson to the wedding, however. The color of his hat would nearly match the raw umber tone of his suit. A new white shirt and dark green tie completed his ensemble.

Bo's full lips curled a little. "I usually know of most weddin's takin' place around here. Only one I know of today is the Donovan sisters."

Inwardly, Jim tried to steel himself against the inevitable. "That's the one," he murmured, picking up his brush and moving it one last time across his short, dark hair. It was nearly 1:00 p.m. and the wedding was scheduled for 2:00. He had to hurry.

"You workin' at bein' a traitor to this family?"

Bo's chilling question made him freeze. Slowly turning, he saw that his brother was no longer leaning against his bedroom door, but standing tensely. The stormy look on his face was what Jim expected.

Picking up his hat, Jim stepped toward him. "Save your garbage for somebody who believes it, Bo." Then he moved past him and down the hall. Since Jim had come home, Bo had acted like a little bantam rooster, crowing and strutting because their father was planning on leaving Bo and Chet the ranch—and not Jim. Frank Cunningham had disowned his youngest son the day he'd left home years before. As Jim walked into the main living area, he realized he'd never regretted that decision. What he did regret was Bo trying at every turn to get their father to throw him off the property now.

As Jim settled his hat on his head, he saw his father positioned near the heavy cedar door that he had to walk through to get to his pickup. The look on his father's face wasn't pleasant, and Jim realized that Bo, an inveterate gossip, had already told him everything.

"Where you goin', son?"

Jim halted in front of his father's wheelchair. As he studied his father's eyes, he realized the old man was angry and upset, but not out of control. He must have remembered his meds today. For that, Jim breathed an inner sigh of relief.

"I'm going to a wedding," he said quietly. "Kate and Jessica Donovan are getting married. It's a double wedding."

His father's brows dipped ominously. "Who invited you?"

"Kate did." Jim felt his gut twist. He could see his father's rage begin to mount, from the flash of light in his bloodshot eyes to the way he set his mouth into that thin, hard line.

"You could've turned down the invitation."

"I didn't want to." Jim felt his adrenaline start to pump. He couldn't help feeling threatened and scared— sort of like the little boy who used to cower in front of his larger-than-life father. When Frank Cunningham went around shouting and yelling, his booming voice sounded like thunder itself. Jim knew that by coming back to the ranch he would go through a lot of the conditioned patterns he had when he was a child and that he had to work through and dissolve them. He was a man now, not a little boy. He struggled to remain mature in his reactions with his father and not melt into a quivering mass of fear like he had when he was young.

"You had a choice," Frank growled.

"Yes." Jim sighed. "I did."

"You're doin' this on purpose. Bo said you were."

Jim looked to his right. He saw Bo amble slowly out of the hallway, a gleeful look in his eyes. His brother *wanted* this confrontation. Bo took every opportunity to make things tense between Jim and his father in hopes that Jim would be banned forever from the ranch and their lives. Jim knew Bo was worried that Frank would change his will and give Jim his share of the ranch. The joke was Jim would never take it. Not on the terms that Frank would extract from him. No, he wouldn't play those dark family games anymore. Girding himself against his father's well-known temper, Jim looked down into his angry eyes.

"What I do, Father, is my business. I'm not going to this wedding to hurt you in any way. But if that's what they want you to believe, and you want to believe it, then I can't change your mind."

"They're *Donovans!*" Frank roared as he gripped the arms of his wheelchair, his knuckles turning white. His breathing became harsh and swift. "Damn you, Jim! You just don't get it, do you, boy? They're our enemies!"

Jim's eyes narrowed. "No, they're not our enemies! You and I have had this argument before. I'm not going to have it again. They're decent people. I'm not treating them any differently than I'd treat you or a stranger on the street."

"Damn you to hell," Frank snarled, suddenly leaning back and glaring up at him. "If I wasn't imprisoned in this damned chair, I'd take a strap to you! I'd stop you from going over there!"

"Come on, Pa," Bo coaxed, sauntering over and patting him sympathetically on the shoulder. "Jim's a turncoat. He's showin' his true colors, that's all. Come on, lemme take you to town. We'll go over to the bar and have a drink of whiskey and drown our troubles together over this."

Glaring at Bo, Jim snapped, "He's diabetic! You know he can't drink liquor."

Bo grinned smugly. "You're forcing him to drink. It's not my fault."

Breathing hard, Jim looked down at his father, a pleading expression in his eyes. Before Frank became diabetic, he'd been a hard drinker. Jim was sure he was an alcoholic, but he never said so. Now Jim centered his anger on Bo. His brother knew a drink would make his father's blood sugar leap off the scale, that it could damage him in many ways and potentially shorten his life. Jim knew that Bo hated his father, but he never showed it, never confronted him on anything. Instead, Bo used passive-aggressive ways of getting what he wanted. This wasn't the first time his brother had poured Frank a drink or two. And Bo didn't really care what it did to his father's health. His only interest was getting control of the ranch once Frank died.

Even his father knew alcohol wasn't good for his condition. But Jim wasn't about to launch into the reasons why he shouldn't drink. Placing his hand on the doorknob, he rasped, "You're grown men. You're responsible for whatever you decide to do."

* * *

The wedding was taking place at the main ranch house. The day was sunny and the sky a deep, almost startling blue. As Jim drove up and parked his pickup on the graveled driveway, he counted more than thirty other vehicles. Glancing at his watch, he saw that it was 2:10 p.m. He was late, dammit. With his stomach still in knots from his confrontation with his father, he gathered up the wedding gifts and hurried to the porch of the ranch house. There were garlands of evergreen with pine cones, scattered with silver, red and gold glitter, framing the door, showing Jim that the place had been decorated with a woman's touch.

Gently opening the door, he saw Jessica and Kate standing with their respective mates near the huge red-pink-and-white flagstone fireplace. Rachel was there, too. Reverend Thomas O'Malley was presiding and sonorously reading from his text. Walking as quietly as he could, Jim felt the stares of a number of people in the gathered group as he placed the wrapped gifts on a table at the back of the huge room.

Taking off his hat, he remained at the rear of the crowd that had formed a U around the two beautiful brides and their obviously nervous grooms. Looking up, he saw similar pine boughs and cones hung across each of the thick timbers that supported the ceiling of the main room. The place was light and pretty compared to the darkness of his father's home. Light and dark. Jim shut his eyes for a moment and tried to get a hold on his tangled, jumbled emotions.

When he opened his eyes, he moved a few feet to the left to get a better look at the wedding party. His heart opened up fiercely as he felt the draw of Rachel's natural beauty.

Both brides wore white. Kate had on a long, traditional wedding gown of what looked to Jim like satin, and a gossamer veil on her hair. Tiny pearl buttons decorated each of her wrists and the scoop neck of her dress. Kate had never looked prettier, with her face flushed, her eyes sparkling, her entire attention focused on Sam McGuire, who stood tall and dark at her side. In their expressions, Jim could see their love for one another, and it eased some of his own internal pain.

Jessica wore a tailored white wool suit, decorated with a corsage of several orchids. In her hair was a ringlet of orchids woven with greenery, making her look like a fairy. Jim smiled a little. Jessica had always reminded him of some ethereal being, someone not quite of this earth, but made more from the stuff of heaven. He eyed Dan Black, dressed in a dark blue suit and tie, standing close beside his wife-to-be. Jim noticed the fierce love in Black's eyes for Jessica. And he saw tears running down Jessica's cheeks as she began to repeat her vows to Dan.

The incredible love between the two couples soothed whatever demons were left in him. Jim listened to Kate's voice quaver as she spoke the words to Sam. McGuire, whose face usually was rock hard and expressionless, was surprisingly readable. The look of tenderness, of open, adoring love for Kate, was there to be seen by everyone at the gathering. Jim's heart ached. He wished he would someday feel that way about a woman. And then his gaze settled on Rachel.

The ache in his heart softened, then went away as

he hungrily gazed at her. He felt like a thief, stealing glances at a woman he had no right to even look at twice. How she looked today was a far cry from how she'd looked out at the accident site. She was radiant in a pale pink, long-sleeved dress that brushed her thin ankles. A circlet of orchids similar to Jessica's rested in her dark, thick hair, which had been arranged in a pretty French braid, and she carried a small bouquet of orchids and greenery in her hands. She wore no make-up, which Jim applauded. Rachel didn't need any, he thought, struck once again by her exquisite beauty.

Her lips were softly parted. Tears shone in two paths across her high cheekbones as the men now began to speak their vows to Kate and Jessica. Everything about Rachel was soft and vulnerable, Jim realized. She didn't try to hide behind a wall like Kate did. She was open, like Jessica. But even more so, in a way Jim couldn't yet define. And then something electric and magical happened. Rachel, as if sensing his presence, his gaze burning upon her, lifted her head a little and turned to look toward him. Their eyes met.

In that split second, Jim felt as if a lightning bolt had slammed through him. Rachel's forest green eyes were velvet, and glistening with tears. He saw the sweet curve of her full lips move upward in silent welcome. Suddenly awkward, Jim felt heat crawling up his neck and into his face. Barely nodding in her direction, he tried to return her smile. He saw relief in her face, too. Relief that he'd come? Was it personal or symbolic of the fragile union being forged between their families? he wondered. Jim wished that it was personal. He felt shaken inside as Rachel returned her attention to her sisters, but he felt good, too.

The dark mass of knots in his belly miraculously dissolved beneath Rachel's one, welcoming look. There was such a cleanness to her and he found himself wanting her in every possible way. Yet as soon as that desire was born, a sharp stab of fear followed. She was a Donovan. He was a Cunningham. Did he dare follow his heart? If he did, Jim knew that the hell in his life would quadruple accordingly. His father would be outraged. Bo would use it as another lever to get him to look unworthy to Frank. Jim had come home to try and change the poisonous condition of their heritage. What was more important—trying to change his family or wanting to know Rachel much, much better?

There was a whoop and holler when both grooms kissed their brides, and the party was in full swing shortly after. Jim recognized everyone at the festive gathering. He joined in the camaraderie, the joy around him palpable. The next order of business was tossing the bridal bouquets. Jim saw Rachel stand at the rear of the excited group, of about thirty women, and noticed she wasn't really trying to jockey for a position to possibly catch one of those beautiful orchid bouquets. Why not?

Both Kate and Jessica threw their bouquets at the same time. There were shrieks, shouts and a sudden rush forward as all the women except Rachel tried to catch them. Ruby Forester, a waitress in her early forties who worked at the Muse Restaurant, caught Jessica's. Kate's bouquet was caught by Lannie Young, who worked at the hardware store in Cottonwood. Both women beamed in triumph and held up their bouquets.

Remaining at the rear of the crowd, Jim saw two wedding cakes being rolled out of the kitchen and into the center of the huge living room. From time to time he saw Rachel look up, as if searching for him in the crowd of nearly sixty people. She was kept busy up front as the cakes were cut, and then sparkling, nonalcoholic grape juice was passed around in champagne glasses.

After the toast, someone went over to the grand piano in the corner, and began to play a happy tune. The crowd parted so that a dance floor was spontaneously created. A number of people urged Kate and Sam out on the floor, and Jim saw Jessica drag Dan out there, too. Jim felt sorry for the new husbands, who obviously weren't first-rate dancers. But that didn't matter. The infectious joy of the moment filled all of them and soon both brides and grooms were dancing and whirling on the hardwood oak floor, which gleamed beneath them.

Finishing off the last of his grape juice, Jim saw a number of people with camcorders filming the event. Kate and Jessica would have a wonderful memento of one of the happiest days of their lives. He felt good about that. It was time the Donovans had a little luck, a little happiness.

After the song was finished, everyone broke into applause. The room rang with laughter, clapping and shouts of joy. The woman at the piano began another song and soon the dance floor was crowded with other well-wishers. Yes, this was turning into quite a party. Jim grinned and shook a number of people's hands, saying hello to them as he slowly made his way toward the kitchen. He wanted to find Rachel now that her duties as the maid of honor were pretty much over.

The kitchen was a beehive of activity, he discovered as he placed his used glass near the sink. At least seven women were bustling around placing hors d'oeuvres on platters, preparing them to be taken out to serve to the happy crowd in the living room. He spotted Rachel in the thick of things. Through the babble he heard her low, husky voice giving out directions. Her cheeks were flushed a bright pink and she had rolled up the sleeves on her dress to her elbows. The circlet of orchids looked fetching in her hair. The small pearl earrings in her ears, and the single-strand pearl necklace around her throat made her even prettier in his eyes, if that were possible.

Finally, the women paraded out, carrying huge silver platters piled high with all types of food—from meat to fruit to vegetables with dip. Jim stepped to one side and allowed the group to troop by. Suddenly it was quiet in the kitchen. He looked up to see Rachel leaning against the counter, giving him an amused look.

He grinned a little and moved toward her. The pink dress had a mandarin collar and showed off her long, graceful neck to advantage. The dress itself had an empire waistline and made her look deliciously desirable.

"I got here a little late," he said. "I'm sorry."

Pushing a strand of dark hair off her brow, Rachel felt her heart pick up in beat. How handsome and dangerous Jim looked in his new suit. "I'm just glad you came," she whispered, noting the genuine apology in his eyes.

"I am, too." He forced himself not to reach out and touch her—or kiss her. Right now, Rachel looked so damned inviting that he had to fight himself. "Doesn't look like your foot is bothering you at all."

"No, complete recovery, thanks to you and a little homeopathic magic." She felt giddy. Like a teenager. Rachel tried to warn herself that she shouldn't feel like this toward any man again. The last time she'd felt even close to this kind of feeling for a man, things hadn't ended well between them. Trying to put those memories aside, Rachel lifted her hands and said, "You clean up pretty good, too, I see."

Shyly, Jim touched the lapel of his suit. "Yeah, first suit I've had since… I don't remember when."

"Well," Rachel said huskily, "you look very handsome in it."

Her compliment warmed him as if she had kissed him. Jim found himself wanting to kiss her, to capture that perfect mouth of hers that looked like orchid petals, and feel her melt hotly beneath his exploration. He looked deep into her forest green eyes and saw gold flecks of happiness in them. "I hope by coming in late I didn't upset anything or anyone?"

She eased away from the counter and wiped her hands on a dish towel, suddenly nervous because he was so close to her. Did Jim realize the power he had over her? She didn't think so. He seemed shy and awkward around her, nothing like the take-charge medic she'd seen at her accident. No, that man had been confident and gentle with her, knowing exactly what to do and when. Here, he seemed tentative and unsure. Rachel laughed at herself as she fluttered nervously around the kitchen, realizing she felt the same way.

"I have to get back out there," she said a little breathlessly. "I need to separate the gifts. They'll be opening them next."

"Need some help?"

Hesitating in the doorway, Rachel laughed a little. "Well, sure.... Come on."

Jim and Rachel took up positions behind the linen-draped tables as the music and dancing continued unabated. He felt better doing something. Occasionally, their hands would touch as they closed over the same brightly wrapped gift, and she would jerk hers away as if burned. Jim didn't know how to interpret her reaction. He was, after all, a dreaded Cunningham. And more than once he'd seen a small knot of people talking, quizzically studying him and then talking some more. Gossip was the lifeblood of any small town, and Sedona was no exception. He sighed. Word of a Cunningham attending the Donovan weddings was sure to be the chief topic at the local barbershop come Monday morning.

Worse, he would have to face his father and brothers tonight at the dinner table. His stomach clenched. Trying to push all that aside, he concentrated on the good feelings Rachel brought up in him. Being the maid of honor, she had to make sure everything ran smoothly. It was her responsibility to see that Kate and Jessica's wedding went off without a hitch. And it looked like everything was going wonderfully. The hors d'oeuvres were placed on another group of tables near the fireplace, where flames were snapping and crackling. Paper plates, pink napkins and plenty of coffee, soda and sparkling grape juice would keep the guests well fed in the hours to come.

It was nearly 5:00 p.m. by the time the crowd began to dissipate little by little. Jim didn't want to go home. He had taken off his coat, rolled up his shirtsleeves and was helping wash dishes out in the kitchen, along with several women. Someone had to do the cleanup. Kate and Sam had gone to Flagstaff an hour earlier, planning to stay at a friend's cabin up in the pine country. Jessica and Dan had retired to their house on the Donovan spread, not wanting to leave the ranch.

Jim had his hands in soapy water when Rachel reappeared. He grinned at her as she came through the doorway. She'd changed from her pink dress into a pair of dark tan wool slacks, a long-sleeved white blouse and a bright, colorful vest of purple, pink and red. Her hair was still up in the French braid, but the circlet of orchids had disappeared. The pearl choker and earrings were gone, too.

She smiled at him as she came up and took over drying dishes from one of the older women. "I can see the look on your face, Mr. Cunningham."

"Oh?" he teased, placing another platter beneath the warm, running water to rinse it off.

"The look on your face says, 'Gosh, you changed out of that pretty dress for these togs.'"

"You're a pretty good mind reader." And she was. Jim wondered if his expression was really that revealing. Or was it Rachel's finely honed observation skills that helped her see through him? Either way, it was disconcerting.

"Thank you," she said lightly, taking the platter from him. Their fingers touched. A soft warmth flowed up her hand, making her heart beat a little harder.

"I'm sorry I didn't get to dance with you," Rachel said in a low voice. There were several other women in the kitchen and she didn't want them to overhear.

Jim had asked her to dance earlier, but she had reluctantly chosen kitchen duties over his invitation. He'd tried not to take her refusal personally—but he had. The Cunningham-Donovan feud still stood between them. He understood that Rachel didn't want to be seen in the arms of her vaunted enemy at such a public function.

"That's okay. You were busy." Jim scrubbed a particularly dirty skillet intently. Just the fact that Rachel was next to him and they were working together like a team made his heart sing.

"I wished I hadn't been," Rachel said, meaning it. She saw surprise flare in his eyes and then, just as quickly, he suppressed his reaction.

"You know how town gossip is," Jim began, rinsing off the iron skillet. "You just got home and you don't need gossip about being caught in the arms of a Cunningham haunting your every step." He handed her the skillet and met her grave gaze.

Pursing her lips, Rachel closed her fingers over his as she took the skillet. She felt a fierce longing build in her. She saw the bleakness in Jim's eyes, and heard the past overwhelming the present feelings between them. She wanted to touch him, and found herself inventing small ways of doing just that. The light in his eyes changed as her fingertips brushed his. For an instant, she saw raw, hungry desire in his eyes. Or had she? It had happened so fast, Rachel wondered if she was making it up.

"That had nothing to do with it, Jim," she said,

briskly drying the skillet. "Kate told me you'd come home to try and mend some family problems. She told me how much you've done to try and make that happen. I find it admirable." Grimacing, she set the skillet aside and watched him begin to scrub a huge platter. "I really admire you." And she did.

Jim lifted his chin and glanced across his shoulder at her. There was pleasure in his eyes. Shrugging her shoulders, Rachel said, "I don't know if you'll be successful or not. You have three men who want to keep the vendetta alive between us. And I'm *sure*," she continued huskily, holding his gaze, "that you caught hell today for coming over here."

Chuckling a little, Jim nodded and began to rinse the platter beneath the faucet. "Just a little. But I don't regret it, Rachel. Not one bit."

She stood there assessing the amount of discomfort she heard in his voice. She was a trained homeopath, taught to pay attention to voice tone, facial expressions and body language, and sense on many levels what was really being felt over what was being verbally said. Jim was obviously trying to make light of a situation that, in her gut, she knew was a huge roadblock for him.

"Did your father get upset?"

Obviously uncomfortable, Jim handed her the rinsed platter. "A little," he hedged.

"Probably a lot. Has Bo changed since I saw him in school? He used to be real good at manipulating people and situations to his own advantage."

Jim pulled the plug and let the soapy water run out of the sink. "He hasn't changed much," he admitted, sadness in his voice.

"And Chet? Is he still a six-year-old boy in a man's body? And still behaving like one?"

Grinning, Jim nodded. "You're pretty good at pegging people."

Drying the platter, Rachel said, "It comes from being a homeopath for so many years. We're trained to observe, watch and listen on many levels simultaneously."

Jim rinsed off his soapy hands and took the towel she handed him. "Thanks. Well, I'm impressed." He saw her brows lower in thought. "So, what's your prescription for my family, Doctor?"

She smiled a little and put the platter on the table behind them. The other women had left, their duties done, and she and Jim were alone—at last. Rachel leaned against the counter, with no more than a few feet separating them. "When you have three people who want a poisonous situation to continue, who don't want to change, mature or break certain habit patterns, I'd say you're in over your head."

Unable to argue, he hung the cloth up on a nail on the side of the cabinet next to the sink. Slowly rolling his sleeves down, Jim studied her. "I won't disagree with your assessment."

Her heart ached for him. In that moment, Rachel saw a vulnerable little boy with too much responsibility heaped upon his shoulders at too young an age. His mother had died when he was six, as she recalled, leaving three little boys robbed of her nurturing love. Frank Cunningham had lost it after his wife died. Rachel remembered that story. He'd gone on a drinking binge that lasted a week, until he finally got into a fight at a local bar and they threw him in the county jail to cool down. In the meantime, Bo, Chet and Jim had had to run the ranch without their grief-stricken father. Three very young boys had been saddled with traumatic responsibilities well beyond their years or understanding. Rachel felt her heart breaking for all of them.

"Hey," she whispered, "everyone's leaving. I'd love to have some help moving the furniture back into place in the living room. It's going to quiet down now. Do you have time to help me or do you have to go somewhere?"

Jim felt his heart pound hard at the warmth in her voice, the need in her eyes—for his company. Her invitation was genuine. A hunger flowed through him. He ached to kiss Rachel. To steal the goodness of her for himself. Right now he felt impoverished, overwhelmed by the situation with his family, and he knew that by staying, he was only going to make things worse for himself when he did go home. His father expected him for dinner at 6:00 p.m. It was 5:30 now.

As Jim stood there, he felt Rachel's soft hand, so tentative, on his arm. Lifting his head, he held her compassionate gaze. "Yeah, I can stick around to help you. Let me make a phone call first."

Smiling softly, Rachel said, "Good."

Chapter 6

Jim enjoyed the quiet of the evening with Rachel. The fire was warm and cast dancing yellow light out into the living room, where they sat on the sofa together, coffee in hand. It had taken them several hours to get everything back in order and in place. Rachel had fixed them some sandwiches a little while ago—a reward for all their hard work. Now she sat on one end of the sofa, her long legs tucked beneath her, her shoes on the floor, a soft, relaxed look on her face.

Jim sat at the other end, the cup between his square hands. Everything seemed perfect to him—the quiet, the snowflakes gently falling outside, the beauty of a woman he was drawn to more and more by the hour, the snap and crackle of the fire, the intimacy of the dimly lit room. Yes, he was happy, he realized—in a way he'd never been before.

Rachel studied Jim's pensive features, profiled against the dark. He had a strong face, yet his sense of humor was wonderful. The kind of face that shouted of his responsible nature. Her stomach still hurt, they had laughed so much while working together. Really, Rachel admitted to herself, he was terribly desirable to her in every way. Rarely had she seen such a gentle nature in a man. Maybe it was because he was an EMT and dealt with people in crisis all the time. He was a far cry from her father, who had always been full of rage. Maybe her new relationship with Jim was a good sign of her health—she was reaching out to a man of peace, not violence.

Pulling herself from her reverie, she said, "Did I ever tell you what made me slam on my brakes up there in the canyon?"

Jim turned and placed his arm across the back of the couch. "No. I think you said it was a cat."

Rachel rolled her eyes. "It wasn't a cougar. When I got home from ER, I asked Jessica to bring me an encyclopedia. I lay there in bed with books surrounding me. I looked under *L* for leopard, and that wasn't what I saw. When I looked under *J* for jaguar..." She gave him a bemused look. "That was what I saw out there, Jim, in the middle of an ice-covered highway that morning—a jaguar." She saw the surprise flare in his eyes. "I thought I was hallucinating, of course, but then something very unusual—strange—happened."

"Oh?" Jim replied with a smile. He liked the way her mouth curved into a self-deprecating line. Rachel had no problem poking fun at herself—she was confident enough to do so. As she moved her hand to punctuate her story, he marveled at her effortless grace. She was like a ballet dancer. He wanted to say that she had the grace of a jungle cat—a boneless, rhythmic way of moving that simply entranced him.

"Jessica and Kate came in about an hour later to check on me, and when I showed them the picture in the encyclopedia, well, Jessica went bonkers!" Rachel chuckled. "She began babbling a mile a minute—you know how Jess can get when she's excited—and she told me the following story, which I've been meaning to share with you."

Interested, Jim placed his empty coffee cup on the table. The peacefulness that surrounded Rachel was something he'd craved. Any excuse to remain in her company just a few minutes longer he'd take without apology. "Let's hear it. I like stories. I recall Mom always had a story for me at bedtime," he said wistfully, remembering those special times.

Sipping her coffee thoughtfully, Rachel decided to give Jim all the details Jessica had filled her in on since the day she'd come home from the hospital. "Awhile back, Morgan Trayhern and his wife, Laura, visited with us. They were trying to put the pieces of their lives back together after being kidnapped by drug lords from South America. An Army Special Forces officer by the name of Mike Houston was asked to come and stay with them and be their 'guard dog' while they were here with us. Dr. Ann Parsons, an MD and psychiatrist who worked for Morgan's company, Perseus, also stayed here." Rachel gestured to the north. "They each stayed in one of the houses here at the ranch.

"Jessica made good friends with Mike and Ann while

we were here for the week following Kelly's funeral. At the time, I was too busy helping Kate to really get to know them, although we shared a couple of meals with them and I helped Morgan and Laura move into the cabin up in the canyon, where they stayed." She frowned slightly. "One of the things Jessica said was that she confided in Mike. She asked how he, one man, could possibly protect anyone from sneaking up on Morgan and Laura if they wanted to, the ranch was so large. I guess Mike laughed and said that he had a little help. Jessica pressed him on that point, and he said that his mother's people, the Quechua Indians, had certain people within their nation who had a special kind of medicine. 'Medicine,' as you know, means a skill or talent. He said he was born with jaguar medicine."

Laughing, Rachel placed her cup on the coffee table. The intent look in Jim's eyes told her he was fascinated with her story. He wasn't making fun of her or sitting there with disbelief written across his face, so she continued. "Well, this little piece of information really spurred Jessica on to ask more questions. You know how she is." Rachel smiled fondly. "As 'fate' would have it, Jessica's good friend, Moyra, who lived up in Vancouver, was also a member of a Jaguar Clan down in Peru. And, of course, Mike was stationed in Peru as a trainer for Peruvian soldiers who went after the drug lords and stopped cocaine shipments from coming north to the U.S. Jessica couldn't let this little development go, so she really nagged Mike to give her more information.

"Mike told her that he was a member of the Jaguar Clan. He teasingly said that down there, in Peru, they called him the Jaguar god. Of course, this really excited

Jessica, who is into paranormal things big-time." Again, Rachel laughed softly. "She told Mike that Moyra had *hinted* that members of the Jaguar Clan possessed certain special 'powers.' Did he? Mike tried to tease her and deflect her, but she just kept coming back and pushing him for answers. Finally, one night, just before she left to go home to Canada, Mike told her that people born with Jaguar Clan blood could do certain things most other people could not. They could heal, for one thing. And when they touched someone they cared about or loved, that person could be saved—regardless of how sick or wounded he or she was. Mike admitted that he'd gotten his nickname out in the jungles fighting cocaine soldiers and drug lords. He told her that one time, one of his men got hit by a bullet and was bleeding to death. Mike placed his hand over the wound and, miraculously, it stopped bleeding. The man lived. Mike's legend grew. They said he could bring the dying back to life."

Fascinated, Jim rested his elbows on his knees and watched her shadowed features. "Interesting," he murmured.

"I thought so. But here's the really interesting part, Jim." She moved to where he was sitting, keeping barely a foot between them. Opening her hands, she whispered. "Jessica also told me more than once that Moyra had a jaguar spirit guardian. Jessica is very clairvoyant and she can 'see' things most of us can't. She told me that when Carl, her ex-husband, was stalking her, Moyra would know he was nearby. One afternoon, Jessica was taking a walk in the woods when she came to a creek and saw Moyra." Rachel shook her head. "This is going to sound really off-the-wall, Jim."

He grinned a little. "Hey, remember my mother was Apache. I was raised with a pretty spiritually based system of beliefs."

Rachel nodded. "Well, Jessica swears she saw Moyra standing in the middle of the creek, and then the next moment she saw a jaguar there instead!"

"Moyra turned into a jaguar?"

Rachel shrugged. "Jessica swears she wasn't seeing things. She watched this jaguar trot off across the meadow and into the woods. Jessica was so stunned and shocked that she ran back to the cabin, scared to death! When Moyra came in a couple hours later, Jessica confronted her on it. Moyra laughed, shrugged it off and said that shape shifting was as natural as breathing to her clan. And wasn't it more important that she and her jaguar guardian be out, protecting Jessica from Carl?"

With a shake of his head, Jim studied Rachel in the firelight. How beautiful she looked! He wanted to kiss her, feel her ripe, soft lips beneath his mouth. Never had he wanted anything more than that, but he placed steely control over that desire. He liked the intimacy that was being established between them. If he was to kiss her, it might destroy that. Instead, he asked, "How does this story dovetail into your seeing that jaguar?"

Rachel laughed a little, embarrassed. "Well, what you didn't tell me was that there was a terrible accident a mile below where I'd crashed!"

He nodded. "That's right, there was. I didn't want to upset you."

Rachel reached out and laid her hand on his arm.

She felt his muscle tense beneath her touch. Tingles flowed up her fingers and she absorbed the warmth of his flesh. Reluctantly, she withdrew her hand. The shadows played against his strong face, and she felt the heat of his gaze upon her, making her feel desired. Heat pooled within her, warm and evocative.

Clearing her throat, she went on. "Jessica was the one who put it all together. She thinks that the jaguar was protecting me from becoming a part of that awful wreck down the road. We calculated later that if I hadn't spun out where I did, I could easily have been involved in that fiery wreck where everyone was burned to death." Rachel placed her arms around herself. "I know it sounds crazy, but Jessica thinks the jaguar showed up to stop me from dying."

"You almost did, anyway," Jim said, scowling.

She relaxed her arms and opened her hands. "I never told you this, Jim. I guess I was afraid to—afraid you'd laugh at me. But I did share it with my sisters. Until you arrived, I kept seeing this jaguar. I saw it circle my car. I thought I was seeing things, of course." She frowned. "Did *you* see any tracks around the car?"

"I wasn't really paying attention," he said apologetically. "All my focus was on you, the stability of the car, and if there were any gas leaks."

Nodding, Rachel said, "Of course…"

"Well…" Jim sighed. "I don't disbelieve you, Rachel."

She studied him in the growing silence. "I thought you might think I was hallucinating. I *had* lost a lot of blood."

"My mother's people have a deep belief in shape-shifters—people who can turn from human into animal, reptile or insect form, and then change back into a human one again. I remember her sitting me on her knee and telling me stories about those special medicine people."

"Jessica thinks it was Moyra who came in the form of a jaguar to protect me until you could arrive on scene." She laughed a little, embarrassed over her explanation.

Jim smiled thoughtfully. "I think because we're part Indian and raised to know that there is an unseen, invisible world of spirits around us, that it's not really that crazy an explanation. Do you?"

Somberly, Rachel shook her head. "Thanks for not laughing at me about this, Jim. There's no question you helped save my life." She held his dark stare. "If it wasn't for you, I wouldn't be sitting here right now." She eased her hand over his. "I wish there was some way I could truly pay you back for what you did."

His fingers curled around her slender ones, as his heart pounded fiercely in his chest. "You're doing it right now," he rasped, holding her soft, glistening gaze. The fact that Rachel could be so damned open and vulnerable shook Jim. He'd met so few people capable of such honest emotions. Most people, including himself, hid behind protective walls. Like Kate Donovan did, although she was changing, most likely softened because of her love for Sam McGuire.

Rachel liked the tender smile on his mouth. "Now that the weddings are over, I have a big job ahead of me," she admitted in a low voice. "My sisters are counting on me to bring in some desperately needed money to keep the ranch afloat." Looking up, she stared out the window. A few snowflakes twirled by. "If we don't get good snowfall this winter, and spring rains, we're doomed, Jim. There's just no money to keep buying the hay we need to feed the cattle because of the continued drought."

"It's bad for every rancher," he agreed. "How are you going to make money?"

She leaned back on the couch and closed her eyes, feeling content despite her worry. The natural intimacy she felt with Jim was soothing. "I'm going to go into Sedona on Monday to find an office to rent. I'm going to set up my practice as a homeopath."

"If you need patients, I'll be the first to make an appointment."

She opened her eyes and looked at him. He was serious. "I don't see anything wrong with you."

Grinning a little, he said, "Actually, it will be for my father, who has diabetes. Since meeting you, I did a little research on what homeopathy is and how it works. My father refuses to take his meds most of the time, unless I hand them to him morning and night."

"Can't your two brothers help out?" She saw his scowl, the banked anger in his eyes. Automatically, Rachel closed her fingers over his. She enjoyed his closeness, craved it, telling herself that it was all right. Part of her, however, was scared to death.

"Bo and Chet aren't responsible in that way," he muttered, sitting up suddenly. He knew he had to get home. He could almost feel his father's upset that he was still at the Donovan Ranch. Moving his shoulders as if to get rid of the invisible loads he carried, he turned toward Rachel. Their knees met and touched. He released her hand and slid his arm to the back of the couch behind her. The concern in her eyes for his father was genuine. It was refreshing to see that she could still feel compassion for his father, in spite of the feud.

"Your father's diabetes can worsen to a dangerous level if he doesn't consistently take his meds."

"I know that," Jim said wearily.

"You're carrying a lot of loads for your family, aren't you?"

Rachel's quietly spoken words eased some of the pain he felt at the entire situation. "Yes…"

"It's very hard to change three people's minds about life, Jim," she said gently.

One corner of his mouth lifted in a grimace. "I know it sounds impossible, but I have to try."

Feeling his pain and keeping herself from reacting to it the way she wanted to was one of the hardest things Rachel had ever done. In that moment, she saw the exhaustion mirrored in Jim's face, the grief in his darkened eyes.

"You go through hell over there, don't you?"

He shrugged. "Sometimes."

Rachel sat up. "You'll catch a lot of hell being over here for the wedding."

"Yes," he muttered, slowly standing up, unwinding his long, lean frame. It was time to go, because if he didn't, he was going to do the unpardonable: he was going to kiss Rachel senseless. The powerful intimacy that had sprung up between them was throbbing and alive. Jim could feel his control disintegrating moment by moment. If he didn't leave—

Rachel stood up and slipped her shoes back on her

feet. "I'll walk you to the door," she said gently. Just the way Jim moved, she could tell he wasn't looking forward to going home. Her heart bled for him. She knew how angry and spiteful Old Man Cunningham could be. As Jim picked up his suit coat and shrugged it across his broad shoulder, Rachel opened the door for him, noticing how boyish he looked despite the suit he wore. He'd taken off the tie a long time ago, his open collar revealing dark hair on his chest.

They stood in the foyer together, a few inches apart. Rachel felt the power of desire flow through her as she looked up into his burning, searching gaze. Automatically, she placed her hand against his chest and leaned upward. In all her life she had never been so bold or honest about her feelings. Maybe it was because she was home, and that gave her a dose of security and confidence she wouldn't have elsewhere. Whatever it was, Rachel followed her heart and pressed her lips to the hard line of his mouth.

She had expected nothing in return from Jim. The kiss was one to assuage the pain she saw banked in his eyes—the worry for his father and the war that was ongoing in his family. Somehow, she wanted to soothe and heal Jim. He had, after all, unselfishly saved her life, giving his blood so that she might live. She told her frightened heart that this was her reason for kissing him.

As Rachel's soft lips touched his mouth, something wild and primal exploded within Jim. He reached out and captured her against him. For an instant, as if in shock, she stiffened. And then, just as quickly, she melted against him like a stream flowing gently against hard rock. Her kiss was unexpected. Beautiful. Necessary. He opened his mouth and melded her lips more fully against his. Framing her face with his hands, he breathed her sweet breath deep into his lungs. The knots in his gut, the worry over what was waiting for him when he got home tonight, miraculously dissolved. She tasted of sweet, honeyed coffee, of the spicy perfume she'd put on earlier for the wedding. Her mouth was pliant, giving and taking. He ran his tongue across her lower lip and felt her tremble like a leaf in a storm beneath his tentative exploration.

How long had it been since he'd had a woman he wanted to love? Too long, his lonely heart cried out. Too long. His craving for her warmth, compassion and care overrode his normal control mechanisms. Hungrily, Jim captured Rachel more fully against him. Her arms slid around his shoulders and he felt good and strong and needed once again. Just caressing the soft firmness of her cheek, his fingers trailing across her temple into the softness of her hairline, made him hot and burning all over. He felt her quiver as he grazed the outside curve of her breast, felt her melting even more into his arms, into his searching mouth as it slid wetly across her giving lips. He was a starving thief and he needed her. Every part and cell of her. His pulse pounded through him, the pain in his lower body building to an excruciating level.

Rachel spun mindlessly, enjoying the texture of his searching mouth as it skimmed and cajoled, his hands framing her face, his hard body pressing her against the door. She felt him trembling, felt his arousal against her lower body, and a sweet, hot ache filled her. It would be so easy to surrender to Jim in all ways. So easy! Her heart, however, was reminding her of the last time she'd given herself away. Fear began to encroach upon her joy. Fear ate away at the hot yearning of her body, her burning need for Jim.

"No…"

Jim heard Rachel whisper the word. Easing away from her lips, which were now wet and soft from his onslaught, he opened his eyes and looked down at her. Though her eyes were barely opened, he saw the need in them. And the fear. Why? Had he hurt her? Instantly, he pulled back. The tears in her eyes stunned him. He *had* hurt her! *Damn!* He felt her hands pressing against his chest, pushing him away. She swayed unsteadily and he cupped her shoulders. Breathing erratically, he held her gently. She lifted her hand to touch her glistening lips. A deep flush covered her cheeks and she refused to look up at him.

Angry with himself for placing his own selfish needs before hers, he rasped, "I'm sorry, Rachel.…"

Still spinning from the power of his kiss, Rachel couldn't find the right words to reply. Her heart had opened and she'd felt the power of her feelings toward Jim. Stunned in the aftermath of his unexpected response, she whispered, "No.…" and then she couldn't say anything else. Rocking between the past and the present, she closed her eyes and leaned against the door.

"I shouldn't have done it," Jim said thickly. "I took advantage.… I'm sorry, Rachel.…" Then he opened the door and disappeared into the dark, cold night.

Rachel was unable to protest Jim's sudden departure. She could only press her hand against her wildly beating heart and try to catch her breath. One kiss! Just one kiss had made her knees feel like jelly! Her heart had opened up like a flower, greedy for love, and she was left speechless in the wake of his branding kiss. When had *any* man ever made her feel like that? At the sound of the engine of a pickup in the distance, her eyes flew open. She forced herself to go out to the front porch. Wanting to shout at Jim, Rachel realized it was too late. He was already on the road leading away from the ranch, away from her.

She stood on the porch, the light surrounding her, the chill making her wrap her arms around herself. A few snowflakes twirled lazily down out of an ebony sky as she watched Jim drive up and out of the valley, the headlights stabbing the darkness. What had she done? Was she crazy? Sighing raggedly, she turned on her heel and went back into the ranch house.

As she quietly shut the huge oak door, she felt trembly inside. Her mouth throbbed with the stamp of Jim's kiss and she could still taste him on her lips. Moving slowly to the couch, she sat down before she fell down, her knees still weak in the aftermath of that explosive, unexpected joining. Hiding her face in her hands, Rachel wondered what was wrong with her. She couldn't risk getting involved again. She couldn't stand the possible loss; she remembered how badly things had ended the last time—all the fears that had kept her from happiness before threatened to ruin her relationship again. But Jim was so compelling she ached to have him, explore him and know him on every level. He was so unlike the rest of his family. He was a decent human being, a man struggling to do the right thing not only for himself, but for his misguided, dysfunctional family. With a sigh, she raised her head and stared into the bright

flames of the fire. Remembering the hurt in his eyes
when she'd stopped the kiss, she knew he didn't know
why she'd called things to a halt. He probably thought
it had to do with him, but it hadn't. Somehow, Rachel
knew she had to see him, to tell him the truth, so that
Jim didn't take the guilt that wasn't his.

Worriedly, Rachel sat there, knowing that he would
be driving home to a nasty situation. Earlier, she'd seen
the anguish in his eyes over his family. Taking a pillow, she pressed it against her torso, her arms wrapped
around it. How she ached to have Jim against her once
again! Yet a niggling voice reminded her that he had
a dangerous job as an EMT. He went out on calls with
the firefighters. Anything could happen to him, and
he could die, just like… Rachel shut off the flow of
her thoughts. Oh, why did she have such an overac-
tive imagination? She sighed, wishing she had handled
things better between her and Jim. He probably felt bad
enough about her pushing him away in the middle of
their wonderful, melting kiss. Now he was going to be
facing a very angry father because he had been here, on
Donovan property. Closing her eyes, Rachel released
another ragged sigh, wanting somehow to protect Jim.
But there was nothing she could do for him right now.
Absolutely nothing.

"Just where the hell have you been?" Frank Cunningham snarled, wheeling his chair into the living room as
Jim entered the ranch house at 9:00 p.m.

Trying to quell his ragged emotions, Jim quietly shut
the door. He turned and faced his father. The hatred
in Frank's eyes slapped at him. Jim stood in silence,

his hands at his sides, waiting for the tirade he knew was coming. Glancing over at the kitchen entrance, he saw Bo and Chet standing on alert. Bo had a smirk on his face and Chet looked drunker than hell. Inhaling deeply, Jim could smell the odor of whiskey in the air. What had they been doing? Plying their father with liquor all night? Feeding his fury? Playing on his self-righteous belief that Jim had transgressed and committed an unpardonable sin by spending time at the Donovans? Placing a hold on his building anger toward his two manipulative brothers, Jim calmly met his father's furious look.

"You knew where I was. I called you at five-thirty and told you I wouldn't be home for dinner."

Frank glared up at him. His long, weather-beaten fingers opened and closed like claws around the arms of the chair he was imprisoned in. "Damn you, Jim. You know better! I've begged you not to consort with those Donovan girls."

Jim shrugged tensely out of his coat. "They aren't girls, Father. They're grown women. Adults." He saw Bo grin a little as he leaned against the door, a glass of liquor in his long fingers. "And you know drinking whiskey isn't good for your diabetes."

"You don't care!" Frank retorted explosively. "I drank because you went over there!"

"That's crap," Jim snarled back. "I'm not responsible for what you do. I'm responsible for myself. You're not going to push that kind of blame on me. Guilt might have worked when we were kids growing up, Father, but it doesn't cut it now." His nostrils quivered as he tried to withhold his anger. He saw his father's face grow stormy and tried to shield himself against what would come next. A part of him was so tired of trying to make things better around here. He'd been home nearly a year, and nothing had changed except that he was the scapegoat for the three of them now—just as he had been as a kid growing up after their mother's death.

"Word games!" Frank declared. He wiped the back of his mouth with a trembling hand. "You aren't one of us. You are deliberately going over to the Donovan place and consorting with them to get at me!"

Jim raised his gaze to Bo. "Who told you that, Father? Did Bo?"

Bo's grin disappeared. He stood up straight, tense.

Frank waved his hand in a cutting motion. "Bo and Chet are my eyes and ears, since I can't get around like I used to. You're sweet on Rachel Donovan, aren't you?"

Bo and Chet were both smiling now. Anger shredded Jim's composure as he held his father's accusing gaze.

"My private life is none of your—or their—business." He turned and walked down the hall toward his bedroom.

"You go out with her," Frank thundered down the hall, "and I'll disown you! Only this time for good, damn you!"

Jim shut the door to his bedroom, his only refuge. In disgust, he hung up his suit coat and looped the tie over the hangar. Breathing hard, he realized his hands were shaking—with fury. It was obvious that Bo and Chet had plied their father with whiskey, nursing all his anger and making him even more furious. Sitting down on the edge of his old brass bed, which creaked with his sudden weight, Jim slipped off his cowboy boots.

Beginning at noon tomorrow, he was on duty for the next forty-eight hours. At least he'd be out of here and away from his father's simmering, scalding anger, his constant sniping and glares over his youngest son's latest transgression.

Undressing, Jim went to the bathroom across the hall and took a long, hot shower. He could hear the three men talking in the living room. Without even bothering to try and listen, Jim was sure it was about him. He wanted to say to hell with them, but it wasn't that easy. As he soaped down beneath the hot, massaging streams of water, his heart, his mind, revolved back to Rachel, to the kiss she'd initiated with him. He hadn't expected it. So why had she suddenly pushed him away? He didn't want to think it was because his last name was Cunningham. That would hurt more than anything else. Yet if he tried to see her when he got off duty, his family would damn him because she was a Donovan.

Scrubbing his hair, he wondered how serious Frank was about disowning him. The first time his father had spoken those words to him, when he was eighteen, Jim had felt as if a huge, black hole had opened up and swallowed him. He'd taken his father's words seriously and he'd left for over a decade, attempting to remake his life. Frank had asked him to come home for Christmas—and that was all.

Snorting softly, Jim shut off the shower. He opened the door, grabbed a soft yellow towel and stepped out. He knew Frank would follow through on his threat to kick him out of his life—again. This time Jim was really worried, because neither Bo nor Chet would make sure Frank took his meds for his diabetic condition. If

Jim wasn't around on a daily basis to see to that, his father's health would seriously decline in a very short time. He didn't want his father to die. But he didn't want to lose Rachel, either.

Rubbing his face, he drew in a ragged breath. Yes, he liked her—one helluva lot. Too much. How did a man stop his heart from feeling? From wanting? Rachel fit every part of him and he knew it. He sensed it. Could he give her up so that his father could live? What the hell was he going to do?

Chapter 7

"Dammit all to hell," Chet shouted as he entered the ranch house. He jerked off his Stetson and slammed the door behind him. Dressed in a sheepskin coat, red muffler and thick, protective leather gloves, he headed toward his father, who had just wheeled into the living room.

Jim was rubbing his hands in the warmth of the huge, open fireplace at one end of the living room when Chet stormed in. His older brother had a glazed look in his eyes, a two-day beard on his cheeks and an agitated expression on his face.

"Pa, that dammed cougar has killed another of our cows up in the north pasture!" Chet growled, throwing his coat and gloves on the leather couch. "Half of her is missing. She was pregnant, too."

Frank frowned, stopped his wheelchair near the fireplace where Jim was standing. "We've lost a cow every two weeks for the last four months this way," he said, running his long, large-knuckled hands through his thick white hair.

As Jim turned to warm his back, Chet joined them at the fireplace, opening his own cold hands toward the flames. Chet's eyes were red and Jim could smell liquor on his breath. His brother was drinking like Frank used to drink before contracting diabetes, he realized with concern. Jim sighed. The last three days, since he'd come back from the Donovan wedding party, things had been tense around the house. He was glad his forty-eight hours of duty had begun shortly thereafter, keeping him on call for two days with the ambulance and allowing him to eat and sleep at the fire station down at Sedona. Luckily, things had been quiet, and he'd been able to settle down from the last major confrontation with his father.

"Have you seen the spoor, Chet?" Jim asked.

"Well, shore I have!" he said, wiping his running nose with the back of his flannel sleeve. "Got spoor all over the place. There's about a foot of snow up there. The tracks are good this time."

"We need to get a hunting party together," Frank growled at them. "I'm tired of losing a beef every other week to this cat."

"Humph, we're losin' two of 'em, Pa. That cat's smart—picks on two for one."

"You were always good at hunting cougar," Frank said, looking up at Jim. "Why don't you drive up there and see what you can find out? Arrange a hunting party?"

Jim was relieved to have something to do outside the house. Usually he rode fence line, did repairs and helped out wherever he could with ranching duties. His father had ten wranglers who did most of the hard work, but Jim always looked for ways to stay out of the house when he was home between his bouts of duty at the fire station.

"Okay. How's the road back into that north pasture, Chet?"

"Pretty solid," he answered, rubbing his hands briskly. "The temps was around twenty degrees out there midday. Colder than hell. No snow, but cold. We need the snow for the water or we're going to have drought again," he muttered, his brows moving downward.

"I'll get out of my uniform and go check on it," Jim told his father.

With a brisk nod, Frank added, "You find that son of a bitch, you shoot it on sight, you hear me? I don't want any of that hearts and flower stuff you try to pull."

Jim ignored the cutting jab as he walked down the darkened hall to his bedroom. Moving his shoulders, he felt the tension in them ease a little. In his bedroom, he quickly shed his firefighter's uniform and climbed into a pair of thermal underwear, a well-worn set of Levi's, a dark blue flannel shirt and thick socks. As he sat on the bed, pulling on his cowboy boots, his mind—and if he were honest, his heart—drifted back to Rachel and that sweet, sweet kiss he'd shared with her. It had been three days since then.

He'd wanted to call her, but he hadn't. He was a coward. The way she'd pulled away from him, the fear in her eyes, had told him she didn't like what they'd shared. He felt rebuffed and hurt. Anyone would. She was a beautiful, desirable woman, and Jim was sure that now that she was home for good, every available male in Sedona would soon be tripping over themselves to ask her out. Shrugging into his sheepskin coat, he picked up the black Stetson that hung on one of the bedposts, and settled it on his head.

As he walked out into the living room, he saw Chet and his father talking. In another corner of the room was a huge, fifteen-foot-tall Christmas tree. It would be another lonely Christmas for the four of them. As he headed out the door, gloves in hand, he thought about Christmas over at the Donovan Ranch. In years past, they'd invited in the homeless and fed them a turkey dinner with all the trimmings. Odula, their mother, had coordinated such plans with the agencies around the county, and her bigheartedness was still remembered. Now her daughters were carrying on in her footsteps. Rachel had mentioned that her sisters would be coming back on Christmas Eve to help in the kitchen and to make that celebration happen once again.

Settling into the Dodge pickup, Jim looked around. The sky was a heavy, gunmetal gray, hanging low over the Rim country. It looked like it might snow. He hoped it would. Arizona high country desperately needed a huge snow this winter to fill the reservoirs so that the city of Phoenix would have enough water for the coming year. Hell, they needed groundwater to fill the aquifer below Sedona or they would lose thousands of head of cattle this spring. His father would have to sell some of his herd off cheap—probably at a loss—so that the cattle wouldn't die of starvation out on the desert range.

Driving over a cattle guard, Jim noticed the white snow lying like a clean blanket across the red, sandy desert and clay soil. He enjoyed his time out here alone. Off to his left, he saw a couple of wranglers on horseback in another pasture, moving a number of cows. His thoughts wandered as he drove and soon Rachel's soft face danced before his mind's eye. His hands tightened momentarily on the wheel. More than anything, Jim wanted to see Rachel again. He could use Christmas as an excuse to drop over and see her, apologize in person for kissing her unexpectedly. Though he knew he'd been out of line, his mouth tingled in memory of her lips skimming his. She'd been warm, soft and hungry. So why had she suddenly pushed away? Was it him? Was it the fact that he was a Cunningham? Jim thought so.

Ten miles down the winding, snow-smattered road, Jim saw the carcass in the distance. Braking, he eased up next to the partially eaten cow. The wind was blowing in fierce gusts down off the Rim and he pulled his hat down a little more tightly as he stepped out and walked around the front of the truck.

As he leaned down, he saw that the cow's throat was mangled, and he scowled, realizing the cat had killed the cow by grabbing her throat and suffocating her. There was evidence of a struggle, but little blood in the snow around her. Putting his hand on her, he found that she was frozen solid. The kill had to have occurred last night.

Easing up to his full height, he moved carefully

around the carcass and found the spoor. Leaning down, his eyes narrowing, he studied them intently. The tracks moved north, back up the two-thousand-foot-high limestone and sandstone cliff above him. Somewhere up there the cat made his home.

Studying the carcass once again, Jim realized that though the cat had gutted her and eaten his fill, almost ninety percent of the animal was left intact and unmolested. That gave him an idea. Getting to his feet, he went back to the pickup, opened the door and picked up the mike on his radio to call the foreman, Randy Parker.

"Get a couple of the boys out here," Jim ordered when Randy answered, "to pick up this cow carcass. Put it in the back of a pickup and bring it to the homestead. When it gets there, let me know."

"Sure thing," Randy answered promptly.

Satisfied, Jim replaced the mike on the console. He smiled a little to himself. Yes, his plan would work— he hoped. Soon enough, he'd know if it was going to.

Rachel was in the kitchen, up to her wrists in mashed potatoes, when she heard a heavy knock at the front door. Expecting no one, she frowned. "I'm coming!" she called out, quickly rinsing her hands, grabbing a towel and running through the living room. It was December 23, and she had been working for three days solid preparing all the dishes for the homeless people's Christmas feast. Her sisters would be home tomorrow, to help with warming and serving the meal for thirty people the following day.

When she opened the door, her eyes widened enormously. "Jim!"

He stood there, hat in hand, a sheepish look on his face. "Hi, Rachel."

Stunned, she felt color race up her throat and into her face. How handsome he looked. His face was flushed, too, but more than likely it was from being outdoors in this freezing cold weather. "Hi…." she whispered. The memory of his meltingly hot kiss, which was never far from her heart or mind, burned through her. She saw his eyes narrow on her and she felt like he was looking through her.

"Come in, it's cold out there," she said apologetically, moving to one side.

"Uh…in a minute." He pointed to his truck, parked near the porch. "Listen, we had a cow killed last night by a cat. Ninety percent of it is still good meat. It's frozen and clean. I had some of our hands bring it down in a pickup. I brought it here, thinking that you might be able to use the meat for your meal for the homeless on Christmas Day."

His thoughtfulness touched her. "That's wonderful! I mean, I'm sorry a cougar killed your cow…but what a great idea."

Grinning a little, and relieved that she wasn't going to slam the door in his face, he nervously moved his felt hat between his gloved fingers. "Good. Look, I know you have a slaughter-freezing-and-packing area in that building over there. I'm not the world's best at carving and cutting, but with a couple of sharp knives, I can get the steaks, the roasts and things like that, in a couple of hours for you."

Rachel smiled a little. "Since we don't have any other hands around, I'd have to ask you to do it." She looked at him intently. "Are you *sure* you want to do that? It's an awful lot of work."

Shrugging, Jim said, "Want the truth?"

She saw the wry lift of one corner of his mouth. Joy surged through her. She was happy to see Jim again, thrilled that her display the other night hadn't chased him away permanently. "Always the truth," she answered softly.

Looking down at his muddy boots for a moment, Jim rasped, "I was looking for a way to get out of the house. My old man is on the warpath again and I didn't want to be under the same roof." He took a deep breath and then met and held her compassionate gaze. "More important, I wanted to come over here and apologize to you in person, and I had to find an excuse to do it."

Fierce heat flowed through Rachel. She saw the uncertainty in Jim's eyes and heard the sorrow in his voice. Pressing her hand against her heart, which pounded with happiness at his appearance, she stepped out onto the porch. The wind was cold and sharp.

"No," she whispered unsteadily, "you don't need to apologize for anything, Jim. It's me. I mean…when we kissed. It wasn't your fault." She looked away, her voice becoming low. "It was me…my past…."

Stymied, Jim knew this wasn't the time or place to question her response. Still, relief flooded through him. "I thought I'd overstepped my bounds with you," he said. "I wanted to come over and apologize."

Reaching out, Rachel gripped his lower arm, finding the thick sheepskin of his coat soft and warm. "I've got some ghosts from my past that still haunt me, Jim."

The desire to step forward and simply gather her

slender form against him was nearly his undoing. His arm tingled where she'd briefly touched him. But when he saw her nervousness, he held himself in check, understood it. Managing a lopsided, boyish smile, he said, "Fair enough. Ghosts I can handle."

"I wish I could," Rachel said, rolling her eyes. "I'm not doing so well at it."

Settling his hat back on his head, he turned and pointed toward a building near the barn. "How about I get started on this carcass? I'll wrap the meat in butcher paper and put it in your freezer."

She nodded. "Fine. I'm up to my elbows in about thirty gallons of mashed potatoes right now, or I'd come over to help you."

He held up his hand. "Tell you what." Looking at the watch on his dark-haired wrist, he said, "How about if I get done in time for dinner, I take you out to a restaurant? You're probably tired of cooking at this point and you deserve a break."

Thrilled, Rachel smiled. "I'd love that, Jim. What a wonderful idea! And I can fill you in on my new office, which I rented today!"

He saw the flush of happiness on her face. It made him feel good, and he smiled shyly. "Okay," he rasped, "it's a date. It's going to take me about four hours to carve up that beef." By then, it would be 7:00 p.m.

"That's about how much time I'll need to finish up in the kitchen." Rachel turned. "I've got sweet potatoes baking right now. Fifty of them! And then I've got to mash them up, mix in the brown sugar, top them with marshmallows and let them bake a little more."

"You're making me hungry!" he teased with a grin.

How young Rachel looked at that moment. Not like a thirty-year-old homeopath, but like the girl with thick, long braids he remembered from junior high. Her eyes danced with gold flecks and he absorbed her happiness into his heart. The fact that Rachel would go to dinner with him made him feel like he was walking on air. "I'll come over here when I'm done?"

Rachel nodded. "Yes, and I'm sure you'll want to shower before we go."

"I'm going to have to." Now he was sorry he hadn't brought a change of clothes.

"Sam McGuire didn't take all his shirts with him on his honeymoon. I'll bet he'd let you borrow a clean one," she hinted with a broadening smile.

"I'm not going to fight a good idea," Jim said. He turned and made his way off the porch. He didn't even feel the cold wind and snow as he headed back to his truck. Rachel was going to have dinner with him. Never had he expected that. The words, the invitation, had just slipped spontaneously out of his mouth. Suddenly, all the weight he carried on his shoulders disappeared. By 7:00 p.m. he was going to be with Rachel in an intimate, quiet place. Never had he looked forward to anything more than that. And Jim didn't give a damn what the locals might think.

Jim took Rachel to the Sun and Moon Restaurant. He liked this place because it was quiet, the service was unobtrusive and the huge, black-and-white leather booths surrounded them like a mother's embrace. They sat in a corner booth; no one could see them and the sense of privacy made him relax.

Rachel sat next to him, less than twelve inches away, in a simple burgundy velvet dress that hung to her ankles. It sported a scoop neck and formfitting long sleeves, and she wore a simple amethyst pendant and matching earrings. Her hair, thick and slightly curly, hung well below her shoulders, framing her face and accenting her full lips and glorious, forest green eyes.

Jim had taken a hot shower and borrowed one of Sam's white, long-sleeved work shirts. Jim had wanted to shave but couldn't, so knew he had a dark shadow on his face. Rachel didn't seem to care about that, however.

After the waitress gave them glasses of water and cups of mocha latte, she left so they could look over the menu.

"That burgundy dress looks good on you," Jim said, complimenting Rachel.

She touched the sleeve of her nubby velvet dress. "Thanks. It's warm and I feel very feminine in this. I bought it over in England many years ago. It's like a good friend. I can't bear to part with it." She liked the burning look in his eyes—it made her feel desirable. But she was scared, too, though. Jim was being every bit the gentleman. She hungered for his quiet, steady male energy. His quick wit always engaged her more serious side and he never failed to make her laugh.

"I'm glad we have this time with each other," he told her as he laid the menu aside. "I'd like to hear about your years over in England. What you did. What it was like to live in a foreign country."

She smiled a little and sipped the frothy mocha latte, which was topped with whipped cream and cinnamon sprinkles. "First I want to hear how we came by this gift of beef you brought us." She set her cup aside.

Jim opened his hands. "It's the strangest thing, Rachel. For the last four months, about once every two weeks, a cat's been coming down off the Rim and killing one of the cows. My father's upset about it and he wants me to put together a hunting party and kill it."

"This isn't the first time we've had a cougar kill stock," Rachel said.

"That's true." He frowned and glanced at her. Even in the shadows, nothing could mar Rachel's beauty. He saw Odula's face in hers, those wide-set eyes, the broadness of her cheekbones. "But I'm not sure it's a cougar."

"What?"

Shaking his head, Jim muttered, "I saw the spoor for myself earlier today. We finally got enough snow up there so we had some good imprints of the cat's paws." He held up his hand. "I know cougar." Smiling slighty, he said, "My friends call me Cougar. I got that name when I was a teenager because I tracked down one of the largest cougars in the state. He had been killing off our stock for nearly a year before my father let me track him for days on end up in the Rim country." Scowling, he continued, "I didn't like killing him. In fact, after I did it, I swore I'd never kill another one. He was a magnificent animal."

"I saw the other night that you wear a leather thong around your neck," Rachel noted, gesturing toward the open collar of his shirt, which revealed not only the thong, but strands of the dark hair of his upper chest.

Jim pulled up the thong, revealing a huge cougar claw set in a sterling silver cap and a small medicine bag. "Yeah, my father had me take one of the claws to a Navajo silversmith. He said I should wear it. My mother's uncle, who used to come and visit us as kids, was a full-blood Apache medicine man. He told me that the spirit of that cougar now lived in me."

"Makes sense."

"Maybe to those of us who are part Indian," he agreed.

Rachel smiled and gazed at the fearsome claw. It was a good inch in length. She shivered as she thought of the power of such a cougar. "How old were you when you hunted that cougar?"

"Fifteen. And I was scared." Jim chuckled as he closed his hands around the latte. "Scared spitless, actually. My father sent me out alone with a 30.06 rifle, my horse and five days' worth of food. He told me to find the cougar and kill it."

"Your father had a lot of faith in you."

"Back then," Jim said wistfully. "Maybe too much." He gave her a wry look. "If I had a fifteen-year-old kid, I wouldn't be sending him out into the Rim country by himself. I'd want to be there with him, to protect him."

"Maybe your father knew you could handle the situation?"

Shrugging painfully, Jim sipped the latte. "Maybe." He wanted to get off the topic of his sordid past. "That spoor I saw today?"

"Yes?"

"I'm sure it wasn't a cougar's."

Rachel stared at him, her cup halfway to her lips. "What then?"

"I don't know *what* it is, but I know it's not what my

father thinks. I took some photos of the spoor, measured it and faxed copies of everything to a friend of mine who works for the fish and game department. He'll make some inquiries and maybe I can find out what it really is."

Setting the cup down, Rachel stared at him. "This is going to sound silly, but I had a dream the other night after we…kissed…."

"At least it wasn't a nightmare."

She smiled a little nervously. "No…it wasn't, Jim. It never would be." She saw the strain in his features diminish a little.

"What about this dream you had?"

"Being part Indian, you know how we put great stock in our dreams?"

"Sure," he murmured. "My uncle Bradford taught all of us boys the power of dreams and dreaming." Jim held her gaze. Reaching out, he slipped his hand over hers, to soothe her nervousness. "So, tell me about this dream you had."

Rachel sighed. His hand was warm and strong. "My mother, Odula, was a great dreamer. Like your uncle, she taught us that dreaming was very important. That our dreams were symbols trying to talk to us. Of course," she whispered, amused, "the big trick was figuring out what the dream symbology meant."

"No kidding," Jim chortled. He liked the fact that Rachel was allowing him to hold her hand. He didn't care who saw them. And he didn't care what gossip got back to his father. For the first time, Jim felt hopeful that his father wouldn't disown him again. Frank Cunningham was too old, too frail and in poor health. Jim was hoping that time had healed some of the old wounds between them and that his father would accept that Rachel was a very necessary part of his life.

"Well," Rachel said tentatively, "I was riding up in the Rim country on horseback. I was alone. I was looking for something—someone... I'm not sure. It was a winter day, and it was cold and I was freezing. I was in this red sandstone canyon. As we rode to the end of it, it turned out to be a box canyon. I was really disappointed and I felt fear. A lot of fear. I was looking around for something. My horse was nervous, too. Then I heard this noise. My horse jumped sideways, dumping me in the snow. When I got to my feet, the horse was galloping off into the distance. I felt this incredible power surround me, like invisible arms embracing me. I looked up..." she held his intense gaze "...and you won't believe what I saw."

"Try me. I'm open to anything."

"That same jaguar that caused me to wreck the car, Jim." Leaning back, Rachel felt his fingers tighten slightly around her hand. "The jaguar was there, no more than twenty feet away from me. Only this time, I realized a lot more. I knew the jaguar was a she, not a he. And I saw that she was in front of a cave, which she had made into a lair. She was just standing there and looking at me. I was scared, but I didn't feel like she was going to attack me or anything."

"Interesting," Jim murmured. "Then what happened?" Noting the awe in Rachel's eyes as she spoke, he knew her story was more than just a dream; he sensed it.

"I felt as if I were in some sort of silent communication with her. I *felt* it here, in my heart. I know how strange that sounds, but I sensed no danger while I was with her. I could feel her thoughts, her emotions. It was weird."

"Sort of like…" he searched for the right words "…mental telepathy?"

"Why, yes!" Rachel stared at him. "Have you been dreaming about this jaguar, too?"

He grinned a little and shook his head. "No, but when I finally met and confronted that big male cougar, we stared at one another for a long moment before I fired the gun and killed him. I *felt* him. I felt his thoughts and emotions. It was strange. Unsettling. After I shot him, I sank to my knees and I cried. I felt terrible about killing him. I knew I'd done something very wrong. Looking back on it, if I had it to do all over again, I wouldn't have killed him. I'd have let him escape."

"But then your father, who's famous for his hunting parties, would have gotten a bunch of men together and hunted him down and treed him with dogs." Rachel shook her head. "No, Jim, you gave him an honorable death compared to what your father would have done. He'd have wounded the cat, and then, when the cougar dropped from the tree, he'd have let his hounds tear him apart." Grimly, she saw the pain in Jim's eyes and she tightened her fingers around his hand. "Mom always said that if we prayed for the spirit of the animal, and asked for it to be released over the rainbow bridge, that made things right."

He snorted softly. "I did that. I went over to the cougar, held him in my skinny arms and cried my heart out. He was a magnificent animal, Rachel. He knew I was going to kill him and he just stood there looking at me with those big yellow eyes. I swear to this day that I felt embraced by this powerful sense of love from him. I *felt* it."

"Interesting," she murmured, "because in my dream about this jaguar, I felt embraced by her love, too."

"Was that the end of your dream?"

"No," she said. "I saw the jaguar begin to change."

"Change?"

Rachel pulled her hand from his. She didn't want to, but she saw the waitress was taking an order at the next table and knew she'd soon come to take theirs. "Change as in shape shifting. You told me last time we spoke that you knew something about that."

"A little. My uncle, the Apache medicine man, said that he was a shape-shifter. He said that he could change from a man into a hawk and fly anywhere he wanted, that he could see things all over the world."

"The Navajo have their skin-walkers," Rachel said in agreement, "sorcerers who change into coyotes and stalk the poor Navajo who are caught out after dark."

"That's the nasty side of shape shifting," Jim said. "My uncle was a good man, and he said he used this power and ability to help heal people."

"My mother told us many stories of shape-shifters among her people, too. But this jaguar, Jim, changed into a woman!" Her voice lowered with awe. "She was an incredibly beautiful woman. Her skin was a golden color. She had long black hair and these incredible green eyes. You know how when leaves come out on a tree in early spring they're that pale green color?"

He nodded. "Sure."

"Her eyes were like that. And what's even more strange, she wore Army camouflage pants, black military boots, an olive green, sleeveless T-shirt. Across her shoulders were bandoliers of ammunition. I kid you not! Isn't that a wild dream?"

He agreed. "Did she say anything to you?"

"Not verbally, no. She stood there and I could see her black boots shifting and changing back into the feet of the jaguar. She was almost like an apparition. I was so stunned by her powerful presence that I just stood there, too, my mouth hanging open." Rachel laughed. "I felt her looking *through* me. I felt as if she were looking for someone. But it wasn't me. I could feel her probing me mentally. This woman was very powerful, Jim. I'm sure she was a medicine woman. Maybe from South America. Then I saw her change back into the jaguar. And she was gone!" She snapped her fingers. "Just like that. Into thin air."

"What happened next?"

"I woke up." Rachel sighed. "I got up, made myself some hot tea and sat out in the living room next to the fireplace, trying to feel my way through the dream. You had kissed me hours before. I was wondering if my dream was somehow linked to that, to you."

Shrugging, Jim murmured, "I don't know. Maybe my friend at the fish and game department will shed some light on that spoor print. Maybe it's from a jaguar." He gauged her steadily. "Maybe what you saw on the highway that day was real, and not a hallucination."

Rachel gave a little laugh. "It looked pretty physical and real to me. *If* it is a jaguar, what are you going to do?"

Grimly, Jim said, "Number one, I'm not going to kill it. Number two, I'll enlist the help of the fish and game department to track the cat, locate its lair and then lay a trap to harmlessly capture it. Then they can take the cat out of the area, like they do the black bears that get too close to civilization."

Rachel felt happiness over his decision. "That's wonderful. If it is a jaguar, it would be a crying shame to shoot her."

He couldn't agree more. The waitress came to their table then, and once they gave her their orders, Jim folded his hands in front of him and caught Rachel's sparkling gaze. Gathering up his courage, he asked, "Could you use another hand on Christmas Day to help feed the homeless? Things are pretty tense around home. I'll spend Christmas morning with my father and brothers, but around noon, I want to be elsewhere."

"You don't have to work at the fire department?" Rachel's heart picked up in beat. More than anything, she'd love to have Jim's company. Kate would have Sam at her side, and Jessica would be working with Dan. It would be wonderful to have Jim with her. She knew Kate was settling her differences with Jim, so it wouldn't cause a lot of tension among them. Never had Rachel wanted anything more than to spend Christmas with Jim.

"I have the next three days off," he said. He saw hope burning brightly in Rachel's eyes. The genuine happiness in her expression made him feel strong and very sure of himself. "So, you can stand for me to be underfoot for part of Christmas Day?"

Clapping her hands enthusiastically, Rachel whispered, "Oh, yes. I'd love to have you with us!"

Moving the cup of latte in his hands, Jim nodded. "Good," he rasped. He didn't add that he'd catch hell for this decision. His father would explode in a rage. Bo and Chet would both ride him mercilessly about it. Well, Jim didn't care. All his life, he'd try to follow his heart and not his head. His heart had led him into wildfire fighting for nearly ten years. And then it had led him home, into a cauldron of boiling strife with his family. Now it whispered that with Rachel was where he longed to be.

As he saw the gold flecks in her eyes, he wanted to kiss her again—only this time he wanted to kiss her senseless and lose himself completely in her. She was a woman of the earth, no question. He was glad they shared a Native American background. They spoke the same language about the invisible realms, the world of spirit and the unseen. Jim never believed in accidents; he felt that everything, no matter what it was, had a purpose, a reason for happening. And the best thing in his life was occurring right now.

A powerful emotion moved through him, rocking him to the core. Could it be love? Studying Rachel as she delicately sipped her latte, her slender fingers wrapped around the cup, he smiled to himself. There was no doubt he loved her. The real question was did she love him? Could she? Or would she never be able to because she was a Donovan and he a Cunningham? Would Rachel always push him away, because of all the old baggage and scars between their two families?

Jim had no answers. Only questions that ate at him, gnawed away at the burgeoning love he felt toward Rachel. He knew he had to take it a day at a time with her.

He had to let her adjust to her new life here in Sedona. He had to use that Apache patience of his and slow down. Let her set the pace so she would be comfortable with him. Only then, Jim hoped, over time, she would grow to love him, and want him in her life as much as he wanted her.

Chapter 8

Rachel tried to appear unaffected by the fact that Jim Cunningham was in the kitchen of their home on Christmas Day. Both Kate and Jessica kept grinning hugely with those Cheshirelike smiles they always gave her when they knew something she didn't. Jim had arrived promptly at noon and set to work in the kitchen with the two men while the Donovan sisters served the sumptuous meal to thirty homeless people in their huge living room.

Christmas music played softly in the background and there was a roaring blaze in the fireplace. The tall timbers were wreathed in fresh pine boughs, and the noise of people laughing, talking and sharing filled the air. Rachel had never felt so happy as she passed from one table to another with coffeepot in hand, refilling cups. Among the people who had come were several families with children. Kate and Sam had gone to stores in Flagstaff and asked for donations of presents for the children. They'd spent part of their honeymoon collecting the gifts and then wrapping them.

Each child had a gift beside his or her plate. Each family would receive a sizable portion of Jim's beef to take back to the shelter where they were living. Jessica and Dan had worked with the various county agencies to see that those who had nowhere to go would have a roof over their head for the winter. Yes, this was what Christmas was *really* all about. And it was a tradition their generous, loving mother had started. It brought tears to Rachel's eyes to know that Odula's spirit still flowed strongly through them. Like their mother, the three daughters felt this was the way to gift humanity during this very special season.

The delight on the children's faces always touched Rachel deeply. For some odd reason, whenever she looked at a tiny baby in the arms of its mother, she thought of Jim. She felt a warm feeling in her lower body, and the errant, surprising thought of what it might be like to have Jim's baby flowed deliciously through her. With that thought, Rachel almost stumbled and fell on a rug that had been rolled to one side. She felt her face suffuse with heat. When she went back to the kitchen to refill her coffee urn, she avoided the look that Jim gave her as he busily carved up one of the many turkeys. Dan was spooning up mash potatoes, gravy and stuffing onto each plate that was passed down the line. Sam added cranberries, Waldorf salad and candied yams topped with browned marshmallows.

Rachel wished for some quiet time alone with Jim. When he'd arrived, they were already in full swing with the start of the dinner. The kiss they'd shared, the intimacy of their last meal together, all came back to her. She found herself wanting to kiss him again. And again. Oh, how she wished her past would disappear! If she could somehow move it aside.... There was no question she desired Jim. And she knew she wanted to pursue some kind of relationship with him. But fear was stopping her. And it was giving him mixed signals. Sighing, Rachel looked forward to the evening, when things would quiet down and they would at last be alone. She had her own house at the ranch, and she could invite Jim over for coffee later and they could talk.

"Heck of a day," Jim said, sipping coffee at Rachel's kitchen table. Her house, which had been built many years ago by Kelly Donovan, was smaller than the other two he'd built for his daughters, but it was intimate and Jim liked that. Although Rachel had only recently moved into it, he could see her feminine touches to the pale pink kitchen. There were some pots on the windowsill above the sink where she had planted some parsley, chives and basil. The table was covered with a creamy lace cloth—from England, she'd told him.

"Wasn't it though?" Rachel moved from the stove, bringing her coffee with her. She felt nervous and ruffled as she looked at Jim. How handsome he was in his dark brown slacks, white cowboy shirt and bolo tie made of a cougar's head with a turquoise inset for the eye. His sleeves were rolled up from all the kitchen duty, the dark hair on his arms bringing out the deep gold color of his weathered skin.

"When you came in at noon, you looked pretty stressed out," Rachel said, sitting down. Their elbows nearly touched at the oval table. She liked sitting close to him.

With a shrug, Jim nodded. "Family squabble just before I left," he muttered.

"Your father didn't want you to come over here, right?" She saw the shadowy pain in his eyes as he avoided her direct look.

"Yeah, you could say that." Jim sipped his coffee grimly.

"And you have dark shadows under your eyes."

He grinned a little and looked at her. "You don't miss much, do you?"

"I'm trained to observe," Rachel teased. Placing her hands around the fine, bone china cup, she lost her smile. "Why do you stay at your father's house if it's so hard on you?"

Pain serrated Jim. His brows dipped. "I don't know anymore," he rasped. "I thought I could help make a difference, turn the family around, but no one wants to change. They want me to change into one of them and I'm not going to do it."

"In homeopathy, it's known as an obstacle to cure," Rachel said. "They don't want to change their dysfunctional way of living because it suits their purposes to stay that way." She gave Jim a tender look. "You wanted to be healthy, not dysfunctional, so you left as soon as you could and you stayed away until just recently. I've treated thousands of people over the years and I know from experience that if they don't want to leave the job, the spouse or the family that is causing them to remain sick or unhealthy, there's little I, a homeopathic remedy or anything else can do about it."

"Sort of like the old saying you can lead a horse to water but you can't make her drink?"

"Yes," Rachel replied with a sigh, trying to give him a smile. Jim looked exhausted. She had seen that look before when a person was tired to the bones with a struggle they were losing, not winning. She opened her hands tentatively. "So, what are your options? Could you move out and maybe see your father, whom you're worried about, from time to time?"

Rearing back on two legs of the chair, Jim gazed over at her. The lamp above the table softly lit Rachel's features. He was hungry for her compassion, her understanding of the circumstances that had him caught like a vise. He valued her insights, which were wise and deep. "I've been thinking about that," he admitted reluctantly. "Only, who will make sure my father takes his meds twice daily?"

"How long has your father had diabetes?"

"Ten years."

"And how did he survive that long without you being there to make sure he took his meds?"

Wryly, he studied her in the ensuing silence. "Touché."

"Could you find a house to rent in Sedona?"

"Maybe," he said. "I'll just have to see how it goes."

"What was the fight about before you left to come to our ranch?"

His mouth quirked. "Chet's all up in arms about this

cat that killed the beef. He's whipping up Bo and my father into forming a hunting party tomorrow to go track the cat, tree it and kill it. I argued not to do that, to call the fish and game department and work with them to trap the cat and take it somewhere else, into a less-populated area."

Rachel felt sudden fear grip her heart. "And what did they decide?"

Easing the chair down on all four legs, Jim muttered, "They're going out tomorrow morning to hunt the cat down and kill it."

She gasped. "No!"

"I'm with you on this." Again, he studied her. "After hearing your dream, and talking more to Jessica today, I'm convinced it's a jaguar up there on the Rim, not a cougar, Rachel. Jessica's sure that it's a shape-shifter. She's worried that it's Moyra, her friend, coming to check on her, on the family." Shrugging, he eased out of the chair and stood up, coffee cup in hand. "I don't know if I believe her or not, but it really doesn't matter. I don't care if it's a cougar or a jaguar—I don't want to see it treed and killed." Leaning his hip against the counter, he asked, "Want to come with me tomorrow to track the cat? I've got the day off. I called Bob Granby, my friend from the fish and game department, and told him I was going to ride out early tomorrow, get a jump on my brothers' plan, and try to find the cat first. I'll be carrying a walkie-talkie with me. Bob promised that if I could locate the cat, he'd meet us, establish jurisdiction and make my family stop the hunt. Then we could lay out bait to lure the cat into a humane device."

Her heartbeat soared. "Yes, I'd love to go with you."

Then she laughed a little. "I haven't thrown a leg over a horse in a long time, but that's okay. You know, Sam and Dan are good trackers, too. They could help."

Jim shook his head. "No. If my brothers saw them, they'd probably open fire on them. Besides, this is on Cunningham land and they don't want them trespassing. I can't risk a confrontation, Rachel."

"What about me? What if they see me with you?"

"That's a little different. They don't get riled with a woman. They will with a man, though. Some of the Old West ethics are still alive and well in them." He smiled briefly.

"Just tell me your plans," she said, "and I'll come with you."

"If you can pack us a lunch and dinner, I hope to be able to track the cat and locate it by no later than tomorrow afternoon. We'll have a two-hour head start on their hunting party. If we could use Donovan horses, that would keep what I'm doing a secret."

Rachel felt her stomach knot a little. "What will your brothers do if they find out you've beat them to the punch on this?"

"Scream bloody blue murder, but that's all." Jim chuckled. "They've had enough tangles with the law of late. Neither of them wants to see the inside of a county jail again for a long time. Once they know I'm working for the fish and game department, they'll slink off."

Sighing, Rachel nodded. "Okay, I'll let Kate know. I'm sure Sam will make sure we've got two excellent trail and hunting horses. I'll pack our food."

Jim nodded, then looked at his watch. It was nearly midnight. "I need to get going," he said reluctantly, not wanting to leave. Setting the coffee cup on the table, he reached into his back pocket and brought out a small, wrapped gift. "It's not much, but I wanted to give you something for Christmas."

Touched, Rachel took the gift, thrilling as their fingers met. "Why, thank you! I didn't expect anything...." She removed the bright red ribbon and the gold foil wrapping.

Jim felt nervous. Settling his hands on his hips, he watched the joy cross Rachel's face. Her eyes, her beautiful forest green eyes, sparkled. It made him feel good. Better than he'd felt all day. Would Rachel like his gift? He hadn't had much time to find something in Sedona that he thought she might want. He hoped she'd like it at least.

Rachel gasped as the paper fell away. Inside were two combs for her hair. They were made of tortoise shell, and each one had twelve tiny, rounded beads of turquoise across the top. Sliding her fingers over them, she saw they were obviously well crafted.

"These are beautiful," she whispered, as she gazed up at his shadowed, worried features. "I've never seen anything like them...."

Shyly, Jim murmured, "I have a Navajo silversmith friend, and I went over to his house yesterday. You have such beautiful hair," he continued, gesturing toward her head. "And I knew he was working on a new design with hair combs." He smiled a little as he saw that she truly did treasure his gift. "When I saw these, I knew they belonged to you."

Without a word, Rachel got up and threw her arms around his neck, pressing herself to him. "Thank you," she quavered near his ear. She felt Jim tense for a moment, as if surprised, and then his arms flowed around her, holding her tightly, his hand sliding up her spine. Heat flared in her and she lifted her face from his shoulder to look up at him. His eyes were hooded and burning—with desire. Breathless and scared, Rachel felt the old fear coming up. She didn't care. She was in the arms of a man who was strong and good and caring. Although his gift was small, it was thoughtful and it touched her like little else could.

Closing her eyes, Rachel knew he was going to kiss her. Nothing had ever seemed so right! As her lips parted, she felt the powerful stamp of his mouth settle firmly upon hers and she surrendered completely to him, to his strong, caring arms and to the heat that exploded violently within her. His lips were cajoling and skimmed hers teasingly at first. She felt his moist breath against her cheek. The taste of coffee was present on his lips. His beard scraped her softer skin, sending wild tingles through her. His fingers moved upward, following the line of her torso, barely brushing the curvature of her firm breasts.

More heat built within her and she felt an ache between her thighs. How long had it been since she'd made love? Far too long. Her body screamed out for Jim's continued touch, for his hands to cup her breasts more fully, to touch and tease them. Instead, he slid his hand across her shoulders, up the slender expanse of her neck to frame her face. He angled her jaw slightly so that he could have more contact with her mouth. His tongue trailed a languid pattern of fire across her lower lip. She quivered violently. He groaned. Their breaths mingled, hot, wild and swift. Her heart pounded in her breast as his mouth settled firmly over hers. She lost herself in the power of him as a man, in the cajoling tenderness he bestowed upon her, the give and take of his mouth upon hers and the sweet, hot wetness that was created between them.

Slowly, ever so slowly, Jim eased away from her mouth. Rachel wanted to cry out that she wanted more of him, of his touch. The dark gleam in his eyes showed the primal side of him, and she shivered out of need, wondering what it would be like to go all the way with Jim. She felt his barely leashed control, felt it in the tremble of his hands along the sides of her face as he continued to hungrily press her into himself in those fragile moments strung between them.

"If I don't go now," he told her thickly, "I won't leave...." The pain in his lower body attested to his need of Rachel. She was soft, supple and warm in his arms. He saw the drowsy look in her eyes, how much his capturing kiss had affected her. Gently, he ran his hands across her crown and down the long, thick strands of her hair. She swayed unsteadily, and he held her carefully in his arms. It was too soon, his mind shrilled at him. Rachel had to have time to get to know him. And vice versa. He'd learned patience a long time ago when it came to relationships. And more than anything, Jim wanted his relationship with Rachel to develop naturally, and not become a pressure to her. When he saw the question in her gaze, he knew he'd made the right decision. Despite the desire burning in her eyes, he also saw fear banked in their depths. She was afraid of something. Him? Her past? Maybe a man she had known in

England. That thought shattered him more than any other. Yes, he had to back off and find out more about her and what she wanted out of life—and if he figured in her dream at all.

Easing away, he smiled a little. "We're going to be getting up at the crack of dawn to leave. We need to get some sleep." What Jim really wanted was to sleep with Rachel in his arms. But he didn't say that.

"Yes…" Rachel whispered, her voice faint and husky. She wanted Jim to stay, and the words were almost torn from her. But it wouldn't be fair to him—or her. If she was lucky, maybe tomorrow, as they tracked the cat, she could share her fears, her hopes and dreams with him.

The snort of the horses, the jets of white steam coming from their nostrils, were quickly absorbed by the thick pine forest that surrounded them as Rachel rode beside Jim. They had been in the saddle for nearly three hours and the temperature hovered in the low thirties up on the Rim. Bundled up, Rachel had never felt happier. And she knew why. It was because she was with Jim. They had spoken little since he'd started tracking. The spoor was still visible, thanks to the snow that hadn't yet melted off the Rim. Down below on the desert floor, the drifts had already disappeared.

Jim rode slightly ahead on a big black Arabian gelding. There was a rifle in the leather case along the right side of his saddle, beneath his leg. Rachel knew he didn't want to use it, but if the cat attacked, they had to defend themselves. It was a last resort. His black Stetson was drawn low across his brow as he leaned over the horse, looking for spoor. There weren't many, and

Rachel was amazed at how well he could track on seemingly nothing. Occasionally he'd point out a tiny broken twig on a bush, a place where the snow had melted, a part of an imprint left in the pine needles—rocks that she wouldn't have seen without Jim's expertise.

Unable to get their heated kiss out of her head, Rachel waited for the right time to talk to him. Right now, he needed silence in order to concentrate. They were two hours ahead of his family's hunting party. Bo and Chet weren't great at tracking, and Jim hoped his brothers would lose the trail, anyway.

He held up his hand. "Let's stop here for a bite to eat." He twisted around in the saddle, resting his hand on the rump of his gelding. Rachel was beautiful in her dark brown Stetson. She had a red wool muffler wrapped around her neck, and she wore a sheepskin jacket, Levi's, boots and thick, protective gloves. He was glad she'd dressed warmly, even though the temperature was rising and he was sure it would get over thirty-two degrees in the bright sunshine. Dismounting, he dropped the reins on the gelding, knowing that a ground-tied horse, once the reins were dropped, would not move.

Coming around, he held out his hands to Rachel, placing them around her waist and lifting her off the little gray Arabian mare she rode. He saw surprise and then pleasure in her eyes as she settled her own hands trustingly on his upper arms while he gently placed her feet on the ground. It would have been so easy to lean down and take her ripe, parted lips, so easy… Tearing himself out of that mode, Jim released her.

"What have you brought for us to eat?" He took the

horses and tied them to a nearby tree. The trail had led them into a huge, jagged canyon of red-and-white rock. Noticing a limestone cave halfway up on one wall, he realized it was a perfect place for a cat to have a lair.

Rachel felt giddy. Jim's unexpected touch was exhilarating to her. Taking off her gloves, she opened up one of the bulging saddlebags. "I know this isn't going to be a surprise to you. Turkey sandwiches?"

Chuckling, Jim grinned and came and stood next to her. "We'll sit over there," he said. There were some black lava rocks free of snow that had dried in the sunlight. "I like turkey."

"I hope so." Rachel laughed softly. She purposely kept her voice low. When tracking, making noise wasn't a good idea.

"Come on," he urged, taking the sandwich wrapped in tinfoil. "Let's rest a bit. Your legs have to be killing you."

Rachel was happy to sit with her back against his on the smooth, rounded surface of the lava boulder. It was a perfect spot, the sunlight lancing down through the fir, spotlighting them with warmth. She removed her hat and muffler and opened up her coat because it was getting warmer. Picking up her sandwich, she found herself starved. Between bites, she said, "My legs feel pretty good. I'm surprised."

"By tonight," he warned wryly, "your legs will be seriously bowed."

She chortled. "That's when I take Arnica for sore muscles."

He grinned and ate with a contentment he'd rarely felt. The turkey tasted good. Rachel had used a seven-grain, homemade brown bread. Slathered with a lot of mayonnaise and a little salt on the turkey, the sandwich tasted wonderful. Savoring in the silence of the forest, the warmth of the sun, the feel of her resting against his back and left shoulder, he smiled.

"This is the good life."

Rachel nodded. "I love the peace of the forest. As a kid, I loved coming up on the Rim with my horse and just hanging out. When I was in junior high and high school, I was in the photography club, so I used to shoot a lot of what I thought were 'artistic' shots up here." She laughed and shook her head. "The club advisor, a teacher, was more than kind about my fledgling efforts."

Smiling, Jim said, "I almost joined the photography club because you were in it."

Her brows arched and she twisted around and caught his amused gaze. "You're kidding me!"

"No," he said, holding up his hand. "Honest, I had a crush on you for six years. Did you know that?"

Even though he'd already confessed his boyhood crush, his words still stunned her. Maneuvering around so that she sat next to him, their elbows touching, she finished off her sandwich and leaned down to wipe her fingers in the snow and pine needles to clean them off. "I still can't believe you had a crush on me."

"Why is that so hard to believe? I thought you were the prettiest girl I'd ever seen." And then his smile softened. "You still are, Rachel."

Her heart thumped at the sincerity she heard in Jim's voice, and the serious look she saw on his face. "Oh," she said in a whisper, "I never knew back then, Jim...."

Chuckling, he took a second sandwich and unwrapped it. "Well, who was going to look at a pimply faced teenager? I wasn't the star running back of the football team like Sam was. I was shy. Not exactly good-looking. More the nerd than the sports-hero type." He chuckled again. "You always had suitors who wanted your attention."

"Well," she began helplessly, "I didn't know..."

He caught and held her gaze. "Let's face it," he said heavily, "back then, as kids, we wouldn't have stood a chance, anyway. You were a hated Donovan. If my father had seen me get interested in you, all hell would've broken loose."

Glumly, Rachel agreed. "He'd have probably beaten you within an inch of your life. Come to think of it, so would my dad."

"Yeah, two rogue stallions against one scrawny teen-age kid with acne isn't exactly good odds, is it?"

Laughing a little, Rachel offered him some of the corn chips she'd bagged up for them. Munching on the salty treat, she murmured, "No, that's not good odds. Maybe it's just as well I didn't know, then...."

The silence enveloped them for a full five minutes before either spoke again. Rachel wiped the last of the salt and grease from the chips off on her Levi's. There was something lulling and healing about being in a forest. It made what she wanted to share with Jim a little easier to undertake. Folding her hands against her knees, she drew them up against her.

"When I moved to England, a long time ago, Jim, I went over there to get the very best training possible to become a homeopath. I had no desire to live at the ranch. I knew my mother wanted all of us girls to come home, but none of us could stomach Kelly's drinking habits." She shook her head and glanced at Jim. His eyes were dark and understanding. "I loved my mother so much, but I just couldn't bring myself to come back home after I graduated from four years' training at Sheffield College. I went on to become a member of the Royal Society of Homeopaths and worked with several MDs at a clinic in London. I really loved my work, and how homeopathy, which was a natural medicine, could cure terrible illnesses and chronic diseases.

"I was very good at what I did, and eventually, the administrator at Sheffield College asked me to come back and teach. They offered me not only a teaching position, but said I could write a book on the topic and keep practicing through clinic work at their facility."

"It sounds like a dream come true for you," Jim said.

"Well, it was even more than that," she said ruefully, leaning down and picking up a damp, brown pine needle. Stroking it slowly with her fingertip, she continued, "I met Dr. Anthony Armstrong at the clinic. He was an MD. Over time, we fell in love." She frowned. "Because of my past, my father, I was really leery of marriage. I didn't want to get trapped like my mother had been. Tony was a wonderful homeopath and healer. We had so much in common. But I kept balking at setting a wedding date. This went on for five years." Rachel shook her head. "I guess you could say I was gun-shy."

Jim's heart sank. "You had good reason to be," he answered honestly. "Living with Kelly was enough to make all three of you women gun-shy of marriage and of men in general." And it was. Jim had feared Kelly himself. Nearly anyone with any sense had. The man had been unstable. He'd blow up and rage at the slightest indiscretion, over things that didn't warrant such a violent reaction. As much as Jim tried to imagine what it had been like for Rachel and her sisters, he could not. What he did see, however, was the damage that it had done to each of them, and he realized for the first time how deeply wounded Rachel had been by it as well.

"I was scared, Jim," she said finally, the words forced out from between her set lips. "Tony was a wonderful friend. We loved homeopathy. We loved helping people get well at the clinic. We had so much in common," she said again.

"But did you love him?"

Rachel closed her eyes. Her lips compressed. "Do you always ask the right question?" She opened her eyes and studied Jim's grave face. His ability to see straight through her, to her core, was unsettling but wonderful. Rachel had never met a man who could see that deep inside her. And she knew her secret vulnerabilities were safe with Jim.

"Not always," Jim murmured, one corner of his mouth lifting slightly, "but I try, and that's what counts." Seeing the fear and grief in Rachel's eyes, he asked gently, "So what happened? Did you eventually marry him?"

Allowing the pine needle to drop, she whispered, "No... I was too scared, Jim. Tony and I—well, we were good friends. I gradually realized I really didn't love him—not like he loved me. Maybe, in my late twenties, I was still gun-shy and wasn't sure about love, or what it was really supposed to be. I had a lot of phone conversations with my mother about that. I just wasn't sure what love was."

Seeing the devastation on Rachel's face, hearing the apology in her husky voice, he bit back the question that whirled in his head: *And now? Do you know what love is? Do you know that what we have is love?* "Time heals old wounds," he soothed. "I've seen it for myself with my father. When I left at age eighteen, I hated him. It took me ten years to realize a lot of things, and growing up, maturing, really helped."

"Doesn't it?" Rachel laughed softly as she lifted her head and looked up at the bright blue sky. The sunlight filtered delicately down among the fir boughs, dancing over the snow patches and pine needles.

"That's why I came home. Blood is thicker than water. I thought I could help, but I haven't been able to do a damned thing." Ruefully, he held her tender gaze. "The only good thing that's happened out of it is meeting you again."

Her throat tightened with sudden emotion and she felt tears sting the backs of her eyes. Her voice was off-key when she spoke. "When I became conscious in that wreck and saw you, your face, I knew I was going to be okay. I didn't know how, but I knew that. You had such confidence and I could feel your care. You made me feel safe, Jim, in a way I've never felt safe in my life." She tried to smile, but failed. Opening her hands, Rachel pushed on, because if she didn't get the words out, the fear would stop her from ever trying again.

"I know we haven't known each other long, but I feel so good around you. I like your touch, your kindness, the way you treat others. There's nothing not to like about you." She laughed shyly. Unable to meet his gaze because she was afraid of what she might see, she went on. "I'm so afraid to reach out…to—to like you… because of my past. I hurt Tony terribly. I kept the poor guy hanging on for five years thinking that I could re-make myself, or let go of my paranoia about marriage, my fear of being trapped by it. I thought it would go away with time, but that didn't happen. I felt horrible about it. That poor man waited in hope for five years for me to get my act together—and I never did." Sorrowfully, Rachel turned and met Jim's gaze. It took the last of her courage to do that because he deserved no less than honesty from her.

"Now I've met you. And what I feel here—" she touched her heart with her hand "—is so strong and good and clean that I wake up every morning happy, so happy that I'm afraid it's all a dream and will end. That's stupid, I know. I know better than that. It's not a dream…."

Gently, Jim turned and captured her hands in his. "Maybe it's a dream that's been there all along, but due to life and circumstances, you couldn't dream it—until now?"

Just the tenderness of his low voice made her vision blur with tears. Rachel hung her head. She felt Jim's hands tighten a little around hers. "I'm so scared, Jim… of myself, of how I feel about you…of the fact that your family would come unglued if—if I let myself go and allow the feelings I have for you to grow. I'm scared of myself. I wonder if I'll freeze again like I did with Tony. I don't want to hurt anyone. I don't want to make you suffer like I did him."

"Listen to me," Jim commanded gruffly as he placed his finger beneath Rachel's chin, making her look up at him. Tears beaded her thick, dark lashes and there was such misery in her forest green eyes. "Tony was a big boy. He knew the score. You weren't teenagers. You were adults. And so are we, Rachel." Jim slid his hand across the smooth slope of her cheek. "I know you're scared. Now I know why. That's information that can help us make decisions with each other." He brushed several strands of dark hair away from her delicate ear. "I couldn't give a damn that my last name is Cunningham and yours is Donovan. The feud our fathers and grandfathers waged with one another stops here, with us. We aren't going to fight anymore. It's this generation that has to begin the healing. I know you know that. So does Kate and Jessica. My family doesn't—not yet. And maybe they never will. But I can't live my life for them. I have to live my life the way I think it should go."

Rachel closed her eyes as he stroked her cheek. His hand was roughened from hard work, from the outdoors, and she relished his closeness, his warmth.

"I guess," Jim rasped in a low voice, "I never got over my crush on you, Rachel." He saw her eyes open. "What I felt as an awkward, gawky teenager, I feel right now. When I saw it was you trapped in that car, I almost lost it. I almost panicked. I was so afraid that you were going to die. I didn't want you to leave me." He shook his head and placed his hand over hers again. "When you needed that rare blood type, and I had the same type, I knew something special was going down. I knew it here, in my heart. I was glad to give my blood to you. For me, with my Apache upbringing, I saw it symbolically, as if the blood from our two families was now one, in you." He gazed into her green eyes and hoped she understood the depth of what he was trying to share with her.

"In a way, we're already joined. And I want to pursue what we have, Rachel—if you want to. I'm not here to push you or shove you. You need to tell me if I have a chance with you."

Chapter 9

Before Rachel could answer, both horses suddenly snorted and started violently. Jim and Rachel jumped to their feet and turned toward the fir tree, where the horses were firmly tied and standing frozen, their attention drawn deeper into the canyon.

Rachel's eyes widened enormously and her heart thudded hard in her chest. There, no more than a hundred feet away on the wall of the canyon next to the cave, stood a huge, stocky jaguar. The cat switched its tail, watching them.

Jim moved in front of her, as if to protect her. She could feel the fine tension in his body, and she gasped. The jaguar was real! Though the cat was a hundred feet above them and unable to leap toward them, her emotions were screaming in fear.

"Don't move," Jim rasped. His eyes narrowed as he slowly turned and fully faced the jaguar. For some reason, he sensed it was a female, just as in Rachel's dream. The cat was positively huge! He'd seen photos and films of jaguars, but never one in the wild. They were a lot stockier than the lithe cougar and weighed a helluva lot more. The cat's gold-and-black fur looked magnificent against the white limestone cliff. Between her jaws was a limp jackrabbit she'd obviously brought back to her lair to enjoy.

The snort of the horses echoed warningly down the canyon walls and Jim automatically put his arm out, as if to stop Rachel from any forward movement. He felt her hand on the back of his shoulder.

Rachel was mesmerized by the stark beauty of the jaguar as the cat lowered her broad, massive head and gently placed the dead rabbit at her feet. Looking down at them as if she were queen of all she surveyed and they mere subjects within her domain.

"She's beautiful!" Rachel whispered excitedly. "Look at her!"

Jim barely nodded. He was concerned she would attack. Fortunately, both horses were trained for hunting and were able to stand their ground rather than tear at their reins to get away—which any horse in its right mind would have done under the present circumstances. He estimated how long it would take to reach his gelding, unsnap the leather scabbard, pull out the rifle, load it and aim it. The odds weren't in his favor.

"She's not going to harm us," Rachel whispered. Moving closer to Jim, their bodies nearly touching as she dug her fingers into his broad shoulder. "This is so odd, Jim. I feel like she's trying to communicate with us. Look at her!"

He couldn't deny what Rachel had voiced. The cat lazily switched her tail, but showed no sign of alarm at being so near to them. Instead, she eased to the ground, the rabbit between her massive front paws. Sniffing the morsel, she raised her head and viewed them again.

"Listen to me, Rachel," Jim said in a very low voice, keeping his eyes on the jaguar. "I want you to slowly back away from me. Mount your horse and, as quietly as you can, *walk* it out of the canyon. Once you get down the hill, take the walkie-talkie you have in the saddlebag and make a call to Bob. Tell him we've located the cat and it's a jaguar. The walkie-talkie won't work up here in the fir trees. You need an open area. It might take you fifteen minutes to ride down this slope to the meadow below. Call him and then wait for him down there. I know he's on 89A waiting for us. He can drive through the Cunningham ranch. Tell him to go to the northernmost pasture. We'll meet him there."

"What are you going to do?"

"Stay here."

Alarmed, Rachel asked, "Why? Why not come with me?"

"Because if she wants to charge someone, I'd rather it be me, not you." He reached behind him and his hand found her jean-clad thigh. Patting her gently, he said, "Go on. I'll come down the hill fifteen minutes from now. I just want to give you a head start. The cat isn't going to follow you if she has me here. Besides, she's eating her lunch right now. If she's starving, that rabbit will put a dent in her appetite and she'll be far less likely to think of us as a meal."

Rachel understood his logic. "Okay, I'll do it." Her heart still pounded, but it wasn't fear she felt in the jaguar's presence, just a thrilling excitement.

He nodded slowly. "I'll see you in about twenty minutes down below in that meadow?"

Compressing her lips, Rachel reached out and squeezed his hand. "Yes," she said. "*You* be careful."

He smiled tensely. "I don't get any sense she's going to attack us."

"Me neither." Rachel released his hand. "She's so beautiful, Jim! And she's the one I saw standing in the middle of 89A. I'd swear it because I remember that black crescent on her forehead. I thought it looked odd, out of place there. It's impossible that two jaguars would have that same identical marking, isn't it?"

"Yeah, they're all marked slightly different," he agreed. "Sort of like fingerprints, you know?" He felt safe enough to turn his head slightly. Rachel's eyes were huge and full of awe as she gazed up on the cliff wall at the cat. Her cheeks were deeply flushed with excitement. Hell, he was excited, too.

"I think this is wonderful!" she gushed in a low voice. "The jaguars are back in Arizona!"

Chuckling a little, Jim said, "Well, *some* people will be thrilled with this discovery and others won't be. Like my family. Now we know who's been eating a beef every two weeks."

Frowning, Rachel sighed. "Thank goodness the fish and game department will capture her and take her someplace where she won't get killed by man."

"I talked to Bob this morning. He said jaguars were not only protected in South and Central America, but that they would be federally protected here if they ever migrated far enough north to cross the border."

"Well," Rachel said, "she certainly has. It's nice to know she can't be shot by your brothers, though they'd probably do it anyway if they had the chance, I'm sorry to say."

Glumly, Jim agreed. "No argument there. Better get going."

She patted his shoulder. "This whole day has been an incredible gift. I'll see you in about twenty minutes." Then she slowly backed away from him.

Jim tensed when the jaguar snapped up her head as Rachel began to move. Would the cat attack? Run away? He watched, awed by the beauty and throbbing power that seemed to emanate from the animal. She was a magnificent beast—so proud and queenly in the way she lifted her head to observe them. As Rachel mounted her horse and walked it out of the canyon, the cat flicked its tail once and then resumed eating her kill.

Recalling the time he'd hunted and trapped the mountain lion up here on the Rim, Jim realized this was a far cry from that traumatic event. Glancing down at his watch, he decided to give Rachel twenty minutes before he mounted up to go back down the slope and join her in the meadow. If the truth be known, he savored this time with the jaguar. He felt privileged and excited. This time he didn't have to kill, as he had with the mountain lion. The memory caused shame to creep through him as he stood there observing the jaguar. After he'd killed the cougar, his father had slapped him on the back, congratulating him heartily. Jim had felt like crying. He'd killed something wild and beautiful and had seen no sense to it.

His Apache mother had given each of her sons an Apache name when they were born. Even though it wasn't on his birth certificate, she'd called him Cougar. He remembered how she had extolled his cougar medicine, and how she made him realize how important it was. Even though he'd only been six years old when she died, her passionate remarks had made a lasting impression on him.

The past unfolded gently before him as he stood there. His mother had always called him Cougar because Jim was a white man's name, she'd told him teasingly. In her eyes and heart, he was like the cougar, and he knew he would learn how to become one because the cougar was the guardian spirit that had come into this life with him. Jim recalled the special ceremony his mother's people had had for him when he was five years old. Since she was Chiricahua, they'd traveled back to that reservation and her people had honored him. The old, crippled medicine man had given him a leather thong with a small beaded pouch attached to it. Inside the pouch was his "medicine."

To this day, Jim wore that medicine bag around his neck. The beading had long ago fallen off and he'd had to change the leather thong yearly. Whether it was crazy or not, Jim had worn that medicine bag from the day it had been placed on him during that ceremony. The medicine man had told him that the fur of a cougar was in the bag, that it was his protector, teacher and guardian. Sighing, Jim looked down at the rapidly melting midday snow. Maybe that was why that mountain lion never charged him when he came upon him that fateful day so long ago. The cat had simply looked at him through wise, yellow eyes and waited. It was as if he knew Jim had to kill him, so he stood there, magnificent and proud, awaiting his fate.

Suddenly Jim felt as if the claw he wore next to his small medicine bag was burning in his chest. Without thinking, Jim rubbed that area of his chest. He wondered if this jaguar sensed his cougar medicine. He knew that the great cats were related to one another. Was that why she chose not to charge him? His Anglo side said that was foolish, but his Apache blood said that he was correct in this assumption. The jaguar saw him as one of them. She would not kill one of her own kind. And then a crazy smile tugged at a corner of Jim's mouth. Rachel must have jaguar medicine, for it was this cat that had saved her from a fiery death at the accident that occurred less than a mile down the road. It was this cat that had leaped into the middle of the highway to stop her.

With a shake of his head, he knew life was more mystical than practical at times. He recalled the dream Rachel had had of the jaguar turning into a warrior woman. Gazing up at the animal, he smiled. There was no question he was being given a second chance. This time he wasn't going to kill. He was going to trap her and have her taken to an area where no Anglo's rifle could rip into her beautiful gold-and-black fur.

Remembering Rachel, he glanced at his watch. To his surprise, fifteen minutes had already flown by! Jim wished he could slow down time and remain here, just watching the jaguar, who had finished her meal and was licking one paw with her long, pink tongue.

Rachel had just reached the snow-covered meadow when to her horror she saw two cowboys emerge from the other end of it. Halting her horse, she realized it was Bo and Chet Cunningham and they had spotted her. Hands tightening on the reins, Rachel was torn by indecision. Should she try and outrun them? Her horse danced nervously beneath her, which wasn't like the animal at all. When she saw the rifles they carried on their saddles and the grim looks on their unshaven faces, she felt leery and decided to stand her ground. When the two men saw her, they spurred their mounts forward, the horses slipping and sliding as they thundered across the small meadow.

"Who the hell are you?" Bo demanded, jerking hard on the reins when he reached her. His horse grunted, opened its mouth to escape the pain of the bit and slid down on its hindquarters momentarily.

Rachel's horse leaped sideways. Steadying the animal, she glared at Bo. The larger of the two brothers, he looked formidable in his black Stetson, sheepskin coat and red bandanna. Danger prickled at Rachel and she put a hand on her horse's neck to keep her calm.

"I'm Rachel Donovan. Your brother—"

"A Donovan!" Chet snarled, pulling up on the other side of her horse.

Suddenly Rachel and her lightweight Arabian were trapped by two beefy thirteen-hundred-pound quarter horses. Bo's eyes turned merciless. "What the hell you doin' on our property, bitch?" he growled. His hand shot out.

Giving a small cry of surprise, Rachel felt his fingers tangle in her long, thick hair. Her scalp radiated with pain as he gave her a yank, nearly unseating her from the saddle. She pulled back on the reins so her mare wouldn't leap forward.

"Oww!" she cried, "Let me go!"

Breathing savagely, Bo wrapped his fingers a little tighter in her hair. "You bossy bitch. What the hell you doin' on Cunningham property? You're not welcomed over here."

She could smell whiskey on his breath as he leaned over, his face inches from hers. Hanging at an angle, with only her legs keeping her aboard her nervous horse, Rachel tried to think. As the pain in her scalp intensified, the feral quality in Bo's eyes sent a sheet of fear through her.

"Let's get 'er down," Chet snapped. "Let's teach her a lesson she won't forget, Bo. A little rape oughta keep her in line, wouldn't ya say?"

Rachel cried out in terror. Without thinking, she raised her hand to slap Bo's away. Knocking her arm away, Bo cursed and balled his right hand into a fist. Before she could protect herself, she saw his fist swing forward. Suddenly the side of her head exploded in stars, light and pain.

She was falling. Semiconscious, she felt the horse bolt from beneath her. Landing on her back, she hit the ground hard, and her breath was torn from her. She saw Chet leap from his horse, his face twisted into a savage grin of confidence as he approached her. She struggled to sit up but he straddled her with his long, powerful legs, slamming her back down into the red mud and snow. She felt his hands like vises on her wrists, pulling them above her head. Screaming and kicking out, she tried to buck him off her body, but he had her securely pinned. Grinning triumphantly at her, he placed his hand on the open throat of her shirt and gave a savage yank. The material ripped with a sickening sound.

"No!" Rachel shrieked. "Get off me!" She managed to get one hand free and she struck at Chet. She heard Bo laugh as the blow landed on the side of Chet's head.

"Ride 'er strong, brother. Hold on, I'll dismount and come and help you."

Panic turned to overwhelming terror. Sobbing, Rachel fought on, pummeling Chet's face repeatedly until he lifted his arms to protect himself.

At the same time, she heard Bo give a warning scream.

"Look out! A cougar! There's that cougar comin'!"

As Chet slammed Rachel down to the ground again, her head snapped back. Blood flowed from her nose and as she tried to move, she felt darkness claiming her. Chet dragged himself off her and ran for his horse, which danced nervously next to where she lay in the snow.

Bo cursed and jerked his horse around as the large cat hurtled toward them.

"Son of a bitch!" he yelled to Chet, and he made a grab for his rifle. His horse shied sideways once it caught sight of the charging cat coming directly at him.

Chet gave a cry as he remounted, his horse bucking

violently beneath him as he clung to the saddle horn. The animal was wild with fear and trying to run.

Rachel rolled onto her stomach, dazed. The jaguar was charging directly down upon them. For a moment, she thought she was seeing things, but there was no way she could deny the reality of the huge cat's remarkable agility and speed, the massive power in her thick, short body as she made ground-covering strides right at them.

Snow and mud flew in sheets around the cat as she ran. Then suddenly the jaguar growled, and Rachel cried out as the sound reverberated through her entire being.

"Kill it!" Chet screeched, trying to stop his horse. He yanked savagely on one rein, causing his horse to begin to circle. *"Kill it!"* he howled again.

Bo pulled his horse to a standstill and made a grab for his rifle. But before he could clear the weapon from the scabbard, the jaguar leaped directly at him.

Rachel saw the cat's thick back legs flex as she leaped, saw the primal intent in her gold eyes rimmed in black. Everything seemed to move in slow motion. Rachel heard herself gasp and she raised her arms to protect herself from Bo's horse, which was dancing sideways next to her in order to escape the charge. Mud and snow flew everywhere, pelting Rachel as she watched the cat arch gracefully through the air directly at Bo, her huge claws bared like knives pulled from sheaths.

Bo gave a cry of surprise as the jaguar landed on the side of his horse. His mount reared and went over backward, carrying rider and cat with him. As Rachel rolled out of the way and jumped to her feet, she heard another shout. It was Jim's voice!

Staggering dazedly, Rachel looked toward where Jim was flying down the snow-covered slope at a hard gallop, his face stony with anger. The snarl of the jaguar behind her snagged Rachel's failing attention. Her knees weakened as she turned. To her horror, she saw the jaguar take one vicious swipe at the downed horse and rider. Bo cried out and the horse screamed, its legs flailing wildly as it tried to avoid another attack by the infuriated jaguar.

Within seconds, the jaguar leaped away, taking off toward the timberline at a dead run. Though Bo was on the ground his horse had managed to get to its feet and run away, back toward the ranch. Chet had gotten his horse under control finally, but his hands were shaking so badly he couldn't get his rifle out of its sheath.

Bo leaped to his feet with a curse. He glared as Jim slid his horse to a stop and dismounted. "Get that damn cougar before he gets away!" Bo shouted, pointing toward the forest where the cat had disappeared once again.

Ignoring his brother, Jim ran up to Rachel. When he saw the blood flowing down across her lips and chin, the bruise marks along her throat, her shirt torn and hanging open, rage tunneled up through him. He reached out to steady her and she sagged into his arms with a small, helpless cry. Gripping her hard, he eased her to the ground. Breathing raggedly he glanced up at Bo, who was looking down at his left leg, where one of his leather chaps had been ripped away. The meadow looked like a battlefield. Blood was all over the place.

"Are you all right, Rachel?" Jim asked urgently, touching her head and examining her.

"Y-yes...." Rachel whispered faintly.

"What happened? Did the jaguar—"

"No," she rattled, her voice cracking. "Bo hit me. They saw me, trapped me between their horses. Your brother jerked me by my hair. When he went for my throat to haul me off my horse, I tried to shove his arm away. That's when Bo hit me." Blinking, Rachel held Jim's darkening gaze. "Chet tried to rape me. Bo was coming to help him until the jaguar charged...." Gripping his hand, she rasped, "Jim, that jaguar came out of nowhere. She protected me. I—I...they were going to rape me.... They thought I was alone. They didn't give me a chance to explain why I was on their property. Bo and Chet just attacked."

"Don't move," Jim rasped.

Rachel watched dazedly as Jim leaped to his feet. The attack of the jaguar had left her shaking. Terror still pounded through her and she didn't want Jim to leave. In four strides, he approached Bo, grabbing him by the collar of his sheepskin coat.

"What the hell do you think you were doing?" Jim snarled, yanking Bo so hard that his neck snapped back. He saw his brother's face go stormy.

"Get your hands off me!"

"Not a chance," Jim breathed savagely. Then he doubled his fist and hit Bo with every ounce of strength he had. Fury pumped through him as he felt Bo's nose crack beneath the power of his assault. His brother crumpled like a rag doll.

Chet yelled at him to stop, but kept his fractious horse at a distance. "You can't hit him!" he shrieked.

Jim hunkered over Bo, who sat up, holding his badly

bleeding nose. "You stay down or next time it'll be your jaw," he warned thickly. Bo remained on the ground.

Straightening up, Jim glared at Chet. "Get the hell out of here," he ordered.

"But—"

"Now!" Jim thundered, his voice echoing around the small meadow. Jabbing his finger at Chet, he snarled, "You tell Father that this cat is under federal protection. The fish and game department is going to come in and trap it and take it to another area. If either of you think you're going to kill that jaguar, I'll make sure it doesn't happen. You got that?"

Chet glared at him, trying to hold his dancing horse in place. "Jaguar? You're crazy! That was a cougar. We saw it with our own eyes!"

Blinking in confusion, Jim looked over at Rachel. When he saw her sitting in the snow, packing some of it against the right side of her swollen face and bleeding nose, he wanted to kill Bo for hurting her. Leaning down, he grabbed his brother by his black hair. "You sick son of a bitch," he snarled in his face. "You had no *right* to do that to Rachel—to any woman!" He saw Bo's face tighten in pain as he gripped his hair hard. "How does it feel?" Jim rasped. "Hurts, doesn't it? You ever think about that before you beat up on someone, Bo?"

"Let go of me!"

"You bastard." Jim shoved him back into the snow. "Now you lay there and don't you move!" He turned and strode back to Rachel. Leaning down, his hands on her shoulders, he met her tear-filled eyes.

"Hang on," he whispered unsteadily, "I'm calling for help."

"Just get Bob Granby. I didn't make the call yet, Jim…."

Nodding, he went over to his horse and opened one of his saddlebags. His gaze nailed Bo, who was sitting up, nursing his bloody nose and sulking. Pulling out a small first-aid kit, he went back to Rachel.

"Get my homeopathic first-aid kit," she begged. "I can stop the bleeding and the swelling with it."

He went to her horse and got the small plastic kit. Kneeling beside her, his hand still shaking with rage, he opened the kit for her. "I'm sorry," he rasped, meaning it. As she opened one of the vials and poured several white pellets into her hand, he felt a desire to kill Bo and Chet for what they'd done to her. Rachel's cheek was swollen and he knew she'd have a black eye soon. Worse, her nose looked puffy, too, and he wondered if it was broken. Setting the kit down, he waited until she put the pellets in her mouth.

"Let me see if your nose is broken," he urged as he placed one hand behind her head. It was so easy, so natural between them. The tension he'd seen in her, the wariness in her eyes fled the moment he touched her. A fierce love for her swept through him. As gently as possible, he examined her fine, thin nose.

"Good," he whispered huskily, trying to smile down at her. "I don't think it's broken."

Rachel shut her eyes. With Jim close, she felt safe. "Did you see what happened?" she quavered.

"Yeah, I saw all of it," he told her grimly. Placing a dressing against her nose, he showed her how to hold it in place. "Stay here. I want to make that call to Bob and a second one to the sheriff."

Eyes widening, Rachel looked up at the grim set of his face. "The sheriff?"

"Damn straight. Bo's going up on assault charges. He's not going to hit you and get away with it," he growled as he rose to his feet.

Rachel closed her eyes once again. Her head, cheek and nose were throbbing. Within minutes, the homeopathic remedy stopped the bleeding and took away most of the pain in her cheekbone area. As she sat there in the wet snow, she began to shiver and realized shock was setting in. Lying down, she closed her eyes and tried to concentrate on taking slow, deep breaths to ward it off. The snort and stomp of nervous horses snagged her consciousness. She heard Jim's low, taut voice on the walkie-talkie, Chet's high, nervous voice as he talked to Bo in the background.

What had happened? Chet said a cougar had charged them. Yet Rachel had seen the female jaguar. And how had Jim known she was in trouble? He'd come off that mountain at a dangerous rate of speed. It was all so crazy and confusing, she thought, feeling blackness rim her vision. She hoped the homeopathic remedy would pull her out of the shock soon. It should. All she had to do was lie quietly for a few minutes and let it help her body heal itself from the trauma.

More than anything, Rachel wanted to be home. The violence in Bo's eyes had scared her as nothing else ever had. She knew that if the jaguar had not charged him, if Jim hadn't arrived when he did, they would have raped her—simply because she was a Donovan. The thought sickened her. Jim was right—the sheriff must be called. She had no problem laying charges against Bo and Chet.

If she had her way, it would be the last time Bo ever cocked his fist at a woman. The last time. Judging from the murderous look in Jim's eyes, he was ready to beat his older brother to a pulp. Rachel had seen the savagery in Jim's face, but she knew he wasn't like his two older brothers. He'd hit Bo just enough to disable him so he couldn't hurt either of them in the meantime. Unlike his brothers, Jim had shown remarkable restraint.

A fierce love welled up through Rachel as she lay there in the cooling snow. Though she felt very cold and emotionally fragile at the moment, the heat of the sun upon her felt good. No one had ever hurt her like this in her life. The shock had gone deep within her psyche. The last thing Rachel expected was to be physically attacked. Now all she wanted to do was get Bob Granby up here with the humane trap. And then she wanted to go home—and heal. More than anything, Rachel needed Jim right now, his arms around her, making a safe place for her in a world gone suddenly mad.

Chapter 10

Rachel's head ached as she sat on the edge of the gurney in the emergency room at the Flagstaff Hospital. If it weren't for Jim's presence and soothing stability through a host of X rays and numerous examinations by doctors and nurses who came into her cubical from time to time, her frayed nerves would be completely shot. Luckily, Jim knew everyone in the ER, making it easier for her to tolerate the busy, hectic place.

Rachel closed her eyes and held the ice pack against her badly swollen cheek. She'd found out moments earlier that her cheekbone had sustained a hairline fracture. At least her nose wasn't broken, she thought with a slight smile. Jim's hand rarely left hers. She could tell he was trying to hide his anger and upset from her. Bob Granby from the fish and game department had come out and met them on the Cunningham land about the same time a deputy sheriff, Scott Maitland, had rolled up. Chet and Bo were taken into custody and transported to the Flagstaff jail, awaiting charges.

Rachel was about to speak when the green curtains surrounding her cubical parted. She felt Jim's hand tighten slightly around hers as Deputy Scott Maitland approached the gurney. She knew Maitland was going to ask for a statement. Her head ached so badly that all she wanted to do was crawl off alone to a quiet place and just rest.

Maitland tipped his gray Stetson in her direction. "Ms. Donovan?"

Rachel sat up a little and tried to smile, but wasn't successful. "Yes?"

Apologetically, Maitland looked over at Jim and reached out to shake his hand. "Sorry about this, Jim."

"Thanks, Scott." He looked worriedly at Rachel. "She's in a lot of pain right now and some shock. Can you take her statement later?"

Maitland shook his head. He held a clipboard in his large hands. "I'm afraid not. Your father already has his attorney, Stuart Applebaum, up at the jail demanding bail information for your brothers. We can't do anything until I take your statements."

Rachel removed the ice pack and tried to focus on the very tall, broad-shouldered deputy. The Maitlands owned the third largest cattle ranch in Arizona. The spread was run by two brothers and two sisters and Scott was the second oldest, about twenty-eight years old. The history of the Maitland dynasty was a long and honorable one that Rachel, who was a history buff, knew well. For her senior thesis, she'd written up the history of cattle ranching for Arizona. She knew from her research that Cathan Maitland had come from Ireland during the Potato Famine in the mid-1800s and claimed acreage up around Flagstaff. He'd then married a woman Comanche warrior, whose raiding parties used to keep the area up in arms, as did the Apache attacks.

As Rachel looked up into Scott's clear gray eyes, she saw some of that Comanche heritage in him, from his thick, short black hair to his high cheekbones and golden skin. He had a kind face, not a stern one, so she relaxed a little, grateful for his gentle demeanor as he walked over and stood in front of her. His mouth was pulled into an apologetic line.

"Looks like you're going to be a raccoon pretty soon," he teased.

Rachel touched her right eye, which she knew was bruised and darkening. "You're right," she said huskily.

"I'll try and make this as painless and fast as possible," he told her. "I think the docs have pretty much wrapped you up and are ready to sign you out of here so you can go home and rest." His eyes sparkled. "I'll see if I can beat their discharge time for you."

"Thanks," Rachel whispered, and placed the ice pack back on her cheek very gently.

"Just tell me in your own words what happened," Maitland urged, "and I'll fill out this report."

Rachel tried to be as clear and specific as possible as she told the story. When she said that she had seen the jaguar, Scott's eyes widened.

"A jaguar?"

"Yes," Rachel murmured. She looked at Jim, who

continued to hold her hand as she leaned against his strong, unyielding frame. "Jim saw it, too."

"I did, Scott. A big, beautiful female jaguar."

"I'll be damned," he said, writing it down.

"Why are you acting so surprised?" Jim inquired.

"Well, your brothers swear they were attacked by a cougar." Maitland studied Rachel. "And you're saying you saw a jaguar come running down that hill and attack Bo?"

"I'm positive it was a jaguar," Rachel said.

"Scott, let me break in here and tell you something Rachel doesn't know yet. When she left to head down to the meadow, that female jaguar just sat at the opening to her lair, cleaning off her paws after finishing her jackrabbit. And then suddenly she jumped up, leaped off that ledge and ran right by me." Jim scratched his head. "She stopped about a hundred feet away from me, growled, looked down the mountain and then back at me. As crazy as this sounds, I got the impression I had to hurry—that something was wrong." Grimly, his eyes flashing, he added, "I leaped into the saddle and rode hell-bent-for-leather down that mountain. That jaguar was right in front of me, never more than a hundred yards away. She was running full bore. So were we. When I came out of the woods, I saw my brothers had Rachel down on the ground. That was when the jaguar really sped up. She was like a blur of motion as she ran right for Bo."

"I saw the jaguar leap," Rachel told Scott in a low voice. "I heard her growl and saw her jump. I saw her slash out with her claws at Bo." She frowned. "You saw Bo's chaps, didn't you?"

"Yeah." Scott chuckled. "No way around that. That cat slashed the hell out of them and that's thick cowhide leather." He scratched his jaw in thought. "The only disagreement we've got here is that two witnesses say it was a cougar and you both say it was a jaguar."

"Does it really matter?" Rachel asked grimly.

"No, I guess it doesn't. The fact that Bo assaulted you and Chet threatened you with rape is the real point of this report."

Shivering, Rachel closed her eyes. She felt Jim place his arm around her and draw her against him more tightly. Right now she felt cold and tired, and all she wanted was rest and quiet, not this interrogation.

"Let's try and get this done as soon as possible," Jim urged his friend. "She's getting paler by the moment and I want to get her home so she can rest."

"Sure," Maitland murmured.

Rachel never thought that being home—her new home on her family ranch—would ever feel so good. But it did. Kate and Jessica had come over as soon as Jim had driven into the homestead. They'd fussed over her like two broody hens. Kate got the fire going in the fireplace out in the living room and Jessica made her some chamomile tea to soothe her jangled nerves. Jim had gotten her two high-potency homeopathic remedies, one for her fracture and the other for her swollen cheek and black eye. She drank the tea and took the remedies. Five minutes later, she was so tired due to the healing effects of the remedies that she dropped off asleep on her bed, covered by the colorful afghan knitted by her mother many years before.

Jim moved quietly down the carpeted hall to Rachel's bedroom. The door was open and Kate and Jessica had just left. He'd told them he was going to stay with Rachel for a while just to make sure she was all right. The truth was he didn't want to leave her at all. Torn between going home and facing his infuriated father and remaining with her, he stood poised at the door.

Rachel lay on her right side, her hands beneath the pillow where her dark hair lay like a halo around her head. The colorful afghan wasn't large enough to cover her fully and he was concerned about the coolness in the house. The only heat supply was from the fireplace, and it would take awhile to warm the small adobe home. Moving quietly, he went to the other side of the old brass bed, pulled up a dark pink, cotton goose down bedspread and gently eased it over her. Snugging it gently over her shoulders, he smiled down at Rachel as she slept.

Her golden skin looked washed out, almost pasty. Reaching down, he grazed her left cheek, which was soft and firm beneath his touch. Her lips were slightly parted. She looked so vulnerable. Rage flowed through him as he straightened. His right hand still throbbed and he was sure he'd probably fractured one of his fingers in the process of slugging Bo. Flexing his fingers, Jim felt satisfaction thrum through him. At least Bo was suffering just a little from hurting Rachel. If Jim had his way, his brother was going to suffer a lot more. This was one time that neither his father's lawyer nor his money would dissuade Rachel from putting both his brothers up on charges that would stick. With their past criminal record, they were looking at federal prison time.

Jim needed to get home and he knew it. Leaning over, he cupped her shoulder and placed a light kiss on her unmarred brow.

"Sleep, princess," he whispered. *I love you.* And he did. A lump formed in his throat as he left the bedroom and walked quietly down the hall. Shrugging into his sheepskin coat and settling the black Stetson on his head, he left her house. Outside, the sun was hanging low in the west, the day nearly spent. What a hell of a day it had been. As he drove his pickup down the muddy red road, Jim's thoughts revolved around his love for Rachel. He knew it was too soon to share it with her. Time was needed to cultivate a relationship with her. If he'd had any doubt about his feelings for her, he'd lost them all out there in that meadow.

Working his mouth, Jim drove down 89A toward Sedona. Just before town was the turnoff for the Bar C. His hands tightened on the steering wheel as he wound down Oak Creek Canyon. The world-famous beauty of the tall Douglas firs, the red-and-white cliffs rising thousands of feet on both sides of the slash of asphalt, did not move him today as they normally did.

Would Rachel allow him to remain in her life after what had happened? Would his Cunningham blood taint her so that she retreated from him, from the love he held for her? He sighed. There would be a trial. And Jim was going to testify with Rachel against his brothers. Everything was so tenuous. So unsure. He felt fear. Fear of losing Rachel before he'd ever had her, before she could know his love for her.

Jim tried to gather his strewn emotions, knowing all hell would break loose once he stepped into the main ranch house when he got home. His father, because he was wheelchair bound, relied on one of them to drive him wherever he wanted to go. Jim was sure Frank was seething with anger and worry over Bo and Chet. But his father ought to be concerned about Rachel, and what they had done to her—and what they would have done had it not been for that jaguar attacking.

Shaking his head as he drove slowly down the dirt road toward home, Jim wondered about the discrepancy in the police report. How could Bo and Chet have seen a cougar when it was a jaguar? What the hell was going on here? No matter, the fish and game expert would see the tracks, would capture the jaguar in a special cage, and that would be proof enough. His brothers were well known for their lies. This was just one more.

"What the hell is going on?" Frank roared as Jim stepped through the door into the living room. He angrily wheeled his chair forward, his face livid.

Quietly shutting the door, Jim took off his hat and coat and hung them on hooks beside it. "Bo and Chet are up on assault charges," he said quietly as he turned and faced his father.

"Applebaum tells me Rachel Donovan is pressing charges. Is that true?"

Allowing his hands to rest tensely on his hips, Jim nodded. "Yes, and she's not going to withdraw them, either. And even if she did," he said in a level tone, holding his father's dark gaze, "I would keep my charges against them, anyway."

"How could you? Dammit!" Frank snarled, balling up his fist and striking the chair arm. "How can you do this to your own family? Blood's thicker than water, Jim. You *know* that! When there's a storm, the family goes through it together. We're supposed to help and protect one another, not—"

"Dammit, Father," he breathed savagely, "Bo hit Rachel. She's got a fractured cheekbone. Not that you care." His nostrils flared and his voice lowered to a growl. "You don't care because she's a Donovan. And you couldn't care less what happens to anyone with that last name." Punching his finger toward his father, he continued, "I happen to love her. And I don't know if she loves me. This situation isn't going to help at all. But whatever happens, I'll tell you one thing—they aren't getting away with it this time. All your money, your influence peddling and the political strings you pull aren't going to make the charges against them go away. Chet and Bo were going to rape her. Did you know that? Is that something you condone?" He straightened, fury in his voice. "Knowing you, you'd condone it because her last name was Donovan."

Stunned, Frank looked up at him. "They said nothing about rape. Applebaum said Bo threw a punch her way because she lashed out at him."

"Yeah, well, it connected, Father. Big-time." Jim pushed his fingers angrily through his short hair and moved over to the fireplace. He felt his father's glare follow him. Jim's stomach was in knots. He was breathing hard. A burning sensation in the middle of his chest told him just how much he wanted to cry with pure rage over this whole fiasco.

Frank slowly turned his wheelchair around. Scowling at Jim. "What's this you said about loving this woman?"

"Her name is Rachel Donovan, Father. And yes, I love her."

"She love you?" he asked, his voice suddenly weary and old sounding.

Jim pushed his shoulders back to release the terrible tension in them. "I don't know. It's too soon. And too damn much has happened. I'll be lucky if she doesn't tar and feather me with the same brush as Bo and Chet."

"My own son…falling in love with a Donovan…. My God, how could you do this to me, Jim? How?"

Looking into his father's eyes, Jim saw tears in them. That shook him. He'd never seen his father cry—ever. "You know," Jim rasped, "I would hope the tears I see in your eyes are for what Rachel suffered at their hands and not the fact that I love her."

Frank's mouth tightened. "Get out of here. Get out and don't ever come back. You're a turncoat, Jim. I'm ashamed of you. My youngest boy, a boy I'd hoped would someday run the Bar C with his brothers…." He shook his head. His voice cracked with raw emotion. "Just when I need you the most, you turn traitor on me. And you're willing to sell your brothers out, too. How could you? Your own family!"

Fighting back tears, Jim held his father's accusing gaze as a lump formed in his throat. He wanted to scream at the unfairness of it all. Suddenly, he didn't care anymore. "I've spent nearly a year here, trying to straighten out things between you, me, and my brothers," he said thickly, "and it backfired on me. I got warned more times than not that I can't fix three people who'd like to stay the way they are." He headed slowly to his coat and hat. "You can't see anything because you're blinded by hate, Father. The word *Donovan* makes you like a rabid dog. Well," he said, jerking his coat off the hook, "I won't be part and parcel of what you, Bo or Chet want to do. I don't give a damn about this ranch, either, if it means others will suffer in order to claim it." He shrugged on his coat. "You're willing to do anything to get revenge for transgressions that died with Kelly."

His heart hurt in his chest and his voice wobbled dangerously as he jerked open the door. Settling his hat on his head, he rasped unevenly, "I'll be moving out. In the next week, I'll come over and pick up my stuff. I'll be seeing you in court."

"Rachel, you look so sad," Jessica said with a sigh. She touched her sister's shoulder as she headed for the stove in Rachel's kitchen. "The homeopathy sure helped get rid of that shiner you had and there's hardly any swelling left on your cheek. But nothing has cheered you up yet." She smiled brightly and poured some tea for both of them. Sunlight lanced through the curtains, flooding the cheery kitchen.

Thanking Jessica for the tea, Rachel squeezed a bit of fresh lemon into it. "I'm okay…really, I am."

Jessica sat down across from her and frowned. "It's been four days now since it happened. You just mope around. Something's wrong. I can feel it around you."

The tart, sweet tea tasted good to Rachel. Gently setting the china cup down on the saucer, she stared at it and said softly, "I wonder why Jim hasn't come by?"

"Ahh," Jessica said with a burgeoning smile, "that's

it, isn't it? Why, I didn't know you were sweet on him, Rachel."

Looking up at her youngest sister, Rachel whispered, "I guess what happened out there in the meadow did something to me—ripped something away so I could see or feel more…." Lamely, she opened her hands. "I know he probably thinks I think less of him because of what his two brothers did to me."

"Hmm," Jessica murmured, "I don't sense that." She laughed, pressing her hand to the front of her green plaid, flannel, long-sleeved shirt.

"Your intuition?" Rachel valued Jessica's clairvoyant abilities.

"Maybe Jim hasn't come around because he's busy. You know, with two brothers in jail, someone has to run the Bar C, and he's got a part-time job as an EMT with the Sedona Fire Department. I imagine between the two, it has kept him hopping."

"Always the idealist."

Chortling, Jessica asked, "Do you like the alternative?"

"No," Rachel admitted sadly, sipping her tea. "I think Jim's avoiding me."

"I don't."

There was a knock on the front door. Jessica grinned and quickly stood up, her long blond braids swinging. "Are you expecting anyone?"

"No," Rachel said.

"I'll get it. You stay here."

Rachel was about to protest that she wasn't an invalid—and that Kate and Jessica were doting too much over her—when she heard a man's low, husky voice.

Jim. Instantly, her heart began to beat hard in her chest and she nearly spilled the contents of her cup as she set it askew on the saucer.

"Look who's here!" Jessica announced breathlessly as she hurried back into the kitchen, her eyes shining with laughter.

Jim took off the baseball cap he wore when he was on EMT duty. He saw Rachel stand, her fingertips resting tentatively on the table, her cheeks flushed a dull red. Would she rebuff him? Tell him to leave? He was unsure as he held her widening eyes.

"Hi," he said with a broken smile. "I just thought I'd drop over and see how you were coming along."

Jessica patted his arm in a motherly fashion. "Believe me, you're just what the doctor ordered, Jim. Listen, I gotta go! Dan is helping me repot several of my orchid girls over in the greenhouse and he needs my guidance." She flashed them both a smile, raised her hand and was gone, like the little whirlwind she was.

When Jim heard the front door close, he met and held Rachel's assessing, forest green gaze. "I wasn't sure if I should drop over unannounced or not," he began, the cap in his right hand.

"I—I'm glad to see you," she said. "Would you like to have some tea? Jessica just made some a little while ago." The look on his face tore at her. She saw dark smudges beneath his bloodshot eyes and a strain around his mouth. He looked as if he hadn't slept well at all.

"Uh…tea sounds great," he replied, maneuvering around to a chair and pulling it out. He placed his dark blue cap on the table and said, "I can't stay long." He patted the pager on his belt. "I'm on duty."

Nervously, Rachel went over to the kitchen cabinet and pulled out another cup and saucer. Jim was here. Here! How could she tell him how much she missed his presence in her life? Compressing her lips, she poured him some tea and placed it in front of him.

"Kate brought over some fresh doughnuts that Sam picked up from the bakery this morning. You look a little pasty. Maybe some food might help?"

Jim looked up. "That sounds good," he said. "I'll take a couple if you have them handy." He studied the woman before him. Rachel's hair was combed and hung well below her shoulders, glinting with red-gold highlights. She wore a pale yellow, long-sleeved blouse, tan slacks and dark brown loafers. In his eyes, she'd never looked more beautiful. Her black eye was gone and he saw only the slightest swelling along her right cheekbone. She almost looked as if nothing had happened. But it had.

Thanking her for the chocolate-covered doughnuts, he watched as she sat down next to him after pouring herself more hot tea. He gauged the guarded look on her features.

"How are you surviving?" he asked, munching on a doughnut. For the first time in four days, he found himself hungry. Ravenous, in fact—but even more, he was starved for her company, her voice, her presence.

"Oh, fine…fine…." Rachel waved her hands in a nervous gesture. "But you don't look too good." She avoided his eyes. "I've been worried about you, Jim. About you having to go over to your father's home and live there and take the heat from him about your brothers." She gestured toward his face. "You look like you haven't been sleeping well, either."

With a grimace, he wiped his mouth with a napkin. "A lot's changed since we last were together," he admitted slowly.

"Is your father okay?"

He heard the genuine worry in Rachel's voice. Her insight, her care of others was one of the many things he loved fiercely about her. Putting the cup aside, he laid his arms on the table and held her gaze.

"He had a stroke four days ago."

"Oh, no!" Rachel cried.

Scowling, Jim rasped, "Yeah…."

"And what's his prognosis?"

He shook his head and avoided her eyes. "The docs up in Flag say he's going to make it. His whole right side is paralyzed, though, and he can't talk anymore."

Squeezing her eyes shut, Rachel whispered, "Oh, Jim, I'm so sorry. This is awful." She opened her eyes. "Why didn't you call and tell me about it?"

Shrugging painfully, he put the doughnuts aside. "Honestly?"

"Always," she whispered, reaching out and slipping her fingers into his hand.

"I was afraid after what happened that you wouldn't want to be around me anymore…because of my brothers. You know, the Cunningham name and all…."

Rachel felt her heart break. Tears gathered in her eyes. "Oh, Jim, no! Never…not ever would I let how I feel toward you change just because of your last name." She reached out and took his other hand. "Is there anything we can do to help you? Or your father?" She knew Frank Cunningham would be an invalid now, confined to bed unless he went through therapy. And even then,

Frank would be bound to a wheelchair for the rest of his life. She saw tears glimmer in Jim's eyes and then he forced them away. His hands felt strong and good on hers.

Without a word, she released his hands, stood up and came around the table. Moving behind him, she slid her arms around him and pressed her uninjured cheek against his and just held him. She felt so much tension in him, and as she squeezed him gently, he released a ragged sigh. His hands slid across her lower arms, and she closed her eyes.

"I feel so awful for all of you," she whispered brokenly. "I'm sorry all this happened."

The firmness of her flesh made him need her even more. Without a word, Jim eased out of her arms and stood up. Putting the chair aside, he faced Rachel. Tears ran down her cheeks. She was crying for his father, for him and for the whole, ugly situation. Her generosity, her compassion, shook him as nothing else ever could.

"What I need," he said unsteadily as he held out his hand toward Rachel, "is you...just you...."

Chapter 11

As Rachel pressed herself to Jim, his arms went around her like steel bands. The air rushed out of her lungs, and she felt his shaven cheek against her own. A shudder went through him as he buried his face in her thick, dark hair. Clinging to her like a man who was dying and could be saved only by her. Her heart opened and she sniffled, the tears coming more and more quickly.

"I'm sorry, so sorry," she sobbed. "I didn't mean to cause this kind of trouble…and your father—"

"Hush," Jim whispered thickly, framing her face with his hands. He was mindful of her fractured right cheekbone, and he barely touched that area of her face. He looked deeply into her dark, pain-filled eyes. Tears beaded on her dark lashes. Her mouth was a tortured line. "This isn't your fault. None of it, princess."

He winced inwardly as he realized he'd allowed his endearment for her to slip out. Rachel blinked once, as if assimilating the word. She gulped, her hands caressing the back of his neck and shoulders.

"There's been so much misery between our families," she whispered unsteadily. "I was hoping…oh, how I was hoping things would settle down now that Kelly was gone."

Caressing her uninjured cheek, Jim wiped the tears away with his fingers. "We aren't going to pay the price that those two decided to pay one another, Rachel. We aren't. You and I—" he looked deeply into her eyes, his voice low and fervent "—can have a better life. A happier one if we want it. We can make better decisions than they ever have. We should learn from them, not duplicate their actions."

Closing her eyes, she felt a fine quiver go through her. "Not like Chet and Bo," she admitted painfully.

He nodded grimly. "We're nothing like those two. They have to find their own way now. Father is mute. He'll never speak again. He'll never be able to wield the power or call in the chips like he did before his stroke." Caressing her hair, Jim added wearily, "Chet and Bo will go to prison for at least a couple of years. I've talked to the district attorney for Coconino County, and he said that, based upon the evidence and our testimony and their past jail records, the judge won't be lenient. He shouldn't be."

Numbly, Rachel rested her brow against his chin. She felt the caress of his fingers through her hair and relaxed as he gently massaged her tense neck and shoulders.

"It's all so stupid," she said. "They could have done so many other things with their lives—good things."

"They made their bed," Jim told her harshly, flattening his hands against her supple back, "now let them lie in it."

Surrendering to his strength, Rachel flowed against him. She heard Jim groan in utter pleasure. Breathing in his masculine scent, she reveled in his warm, tender embrace. As the moments flowed by, she closed her eyes and simply absorbed his gentle and protective nature.

Pressing a kiss to her hair, Jim finally eased Rachel away just enough to look into her languid eyes. There was a sweet, spicy fragrance to her hair and he inhaled it deeply. Rachel was life. *His* life. He saw the gold flecks in the forest green depths of her eyes, and he fought the urge to lean down and take her delicious, parted lips. Instead, he asked wryly, "We never got to finish our conversation up on the Rim, do you realize that?"

Heat burned in Rachel's cheeks as she stood in his arms, her hands on his hard biceps. "You're right...we didn't."

"What do you think? Am I worth the risk? I know you are."

Shyly, Rachel searched his serious features. "Yesterday," she whispered, "I thought a lot about you...how long I've known you, and how I hadn't realized you had a crush on me back then."

"My crush on you," Jim told her, moving a strand of hair away from her flushed cheek, "never ended."

Swallowing hard, Rachel nodded. "I began to understand that."

"I'm scared. Are you?"

"Very," Rachel admitted in a strained voice, her fingers digging a little more firmly into his arms. "When Bo dragged me off the horse, I thought I was going to die, Jim. I could see the hatred in both your brothers' eyes and I knew..." She swallowed painfully. Her eyes misted and her voice softened. "I knew I loved you and I didn't have the courage to tell you I did. And I was sorry because I thought I'd never see you again." A sob stuck in her throat, and she felt hot tears spilling down her cheeks again.

Jim held her hard against him and gently rocked her back and forth. "It's okay, princess. I know you love me." He laughed a little shakily. "What a crazy time this is." He kissed her hair and then carefully cupped her face. "I love you, Rachel Donovan. And ten thousand stampeding horses aren't going to stop me from seeing you whenever I can."

His mouth was warm and strong as it settled against her tear-bathed lips. Rachel moaned, but it was a moan of surrender, of need of him. She tasted the sweet tartness of the lemon and sugar on his lips, the scent of juniper around him as he deepened his exploration of her. Her breath became ragged and her heart pounded. The power of his mouth, the searching heat of him surrounded her, drugged her, and she bent like a willow in his arms.

Just then, his beeper went off.

"Damn," he growled, tearing his mouth from hers. Apologetically, he eased Rachel into the nearest chair. "I'm sorry," he said, looking down at the pager. "Larry and I are on duty. It's probably an EMT call."

"The phone's in the living room," Rachel whispered,

dizzy from his unexpected, tender kiss. Touching her tingling lower lip, she felt euphoria sweep through her. Just the sound of his steady, low voice as he talked on the phone, was comforting to her. He loved her. The admission was sweet, filled with promise. And filled with terror. But as she sat there remembering the taste and touch of Jim, Rachel realized her terror hadn't won. It was still there, but not as overwhelming as before. Maybe the fact that she had almost died made her realize how good life was with Jim in it.

Jim walked back into the kitchen, his brow knitted. "I've got to go. There's been a multiple accident about a mile down 89A from here."

Rachel nodded and stood up. Her knees felt weak. Before she could speak, he slid his arm around her, drew her against him and captured her parted lips with his mouth. It was a hot, searching, almost desperate kiss. Before she could respond, he released her and rasped, "I get off tomorrow at noon. I'll bring lunch."

Then he was gone. Rachel swayed. Touching her lips gently, she felt a stab of fear—only this time she was worried over Jim and the accident scene. She remembered his promise of lunch tomorrow and the thought blanketed her, filling her with warmth. Never had she felt this way before. Her heart throbbed with a joy she'd never known. Love. She was in love with Jim Cunningham.

A little in shock over the realization, Rachel sat down before she fell down. She heard a knock at the front door, and then Kate's voice rang through the house.

"Rachel?"

"In here," she called. "Come on in."

Kate took off her cowboy hat and ran her fingers through her dark, tangled hair. She grinned as she came into the kitchen.

"I just saw Jim leaving in a hurry. He on call?"

"Yes. There's been a bad accident a mile down from our ranch on 89A. Are Dan and Sam here?"

"Yep," she said with a sigh, going over to the kitchen counter and pouring herself a cup of tea. "It's really nice," she murmured, "that you're home now. I like having an excuse to escape from vetting horses and cattle and to come over here and see you."

Smiling up at her older sister, Rachel patted the chair next to her own. "Isn't it great? Come, sit down. You're working too hard, Kate." Rachel knew her sister was up well before daybreak every day, and rarely did she and Sam hit the sack until around midnight. She didn't know how Kate did it. Perhaps she had Kelly's drive and passion for the ranch more than any of the sisters.

Flopping down on the chair, Kate sipped her tea. "Mmm, this hits the spot on a cold day." She crossed her legs. Her cowboy boots were scuffed and dusty. "Did you hear the latest? Sam and I just came in from Sedona."

"No." Rachel rolled her eyes. "I hate town gossip. You know that."

"Mmm, you'll be interested in this," Kate said. She took another gulp of the steaming tea and sat up. Tapping the table with her finger, she said, "We heard from Deputy Scott Maitland that Bo and Chet are probably going away to do federal prison time."

Rachel nodded. "Yes, Jim just told me the same thing."

"They deserve it," she growled. "If I'd been there, I'd probably have blown their heads off with my rifle, and then I'd never live outside of prison bars again."

Rachel grimaced. "Thank goodness you weren't there, then. You've seen enough of that place."

Kate made a face. "No kidding."

"Did you hear that Jim's father had a stroke? He's up at the Flag hospital recovering."

Shocked, Kate sat up. "No. What happened?"

"I'm not sure. Maybe it was the shock of Bo and Chet being in jail."

"Or you pressing charges," Kate muttered angrily. "I'm surprised that Old Man Cunningham didn't keel over of a stroke a decade ago. He's always blowing his top over some little thing."

"Two of your sons going to prison isn't little," Rachel said softly. "The ranch, from what Jim said, is in his brothers' names."

"Is Old Man Cunningham paralyzed?"

"Yes. He's pretty bad," Rachel murmured worriedly.

"Well," Kate said, pushing several strands of hair away from her flushed cheek, "that means Jim is going to have to assume the running of the Bar C."

Surprised, Rachel bolted upright. She stared at Kate. "What?"

"Sure," she said, leaning back in the chair and sipping her tea, "someone's got to run it now that the old man can't. Chet and Bo are probably looking at five years in the pen. Maybe they'll get off in two and a half for good behavior. If Jim doesn't quit his job as an EMT and return to the ranch, it will fall apart. Who will be there to pay the bills? Give the wranglers their checks?

Or manage the place?" With a shake of her head, Kate said, "Boy, what goes around comes around, doesn't it? Cunningham was trying to put us out of business and look what's happened to him." She brightened a little. "Come to think of it, that trumped-up lawsuit he's got against us will die on the vine, too." Smiling grimly, she got up and poured herself another cup of tea. "This disaster might be a blessing in disguise. If we can get his lawyer off our backs, we won't have to spend money filing—money we don't have."

Rachel nodded and watched her sister sit back down. She wondered about everything Kate had told her. Would Jim really settle down to ranching life on his father's spread? For the first time, she saw hope for a future with Jim.

The noontime sun streamed into Rachel's small but cozy kitchen as Jim sat sharing the lunch he'd promised with her. He'd stopped at a deli in town and gotten tuna sandwiches, sweet pickles and two thick slices of chocolate cake. Ever since he'd arrived, he'd been longing to take her in his arms again, to finish what they'd only started yesterday. But he could still see a slight swelling along her right cheekbone where it had been fractured. As badly as he wanted to make love to her, he would wait until she was healed. The way she carefully ate told him that moving her jaw caused her pain. Instead, he decided to tell her his news. "I quit my job at the fire department."

"To run the ranch?" Rachel asked, carefully chewing her sandwich and studying the man before her. Jim wore his dark blue uniform, leaving his baseball cap on the side of the table as he ate. He looked exhausted, and Rachel knew it was due to worrying over his father's condition. She was glad he'd come by, though—how she had looked forward to seeing him again!

"Yes," he said, sipping the hot coffee. "I talked to the hospital and they're beginning recovery therapy for my father. He's got all kinds of medical insurance, so it won't be a problem that way, thank God."

Rachel raised her brows. "It's a good thing he has insurance. We have none. Can't afford it."

"Like about one-third of all Americans," Jim agreed somberly.

"When will you bring him home?"

"In about a week, from the looks of it."

"How do you feel about running the Bar C?" she asked tentatively.

"Odd, I guess." He exchanged a warm look with her. "When I left after high school, I figured I'd never be back. When I did come home, Father told me Bo and Chet would take over the ranch after he died."

"How did you feel about that?"

"I didn't care."

"And now?"

He grinned a little. "I still don't." Reaching out, he captured her hand briefly. "I've got my priorities straight. I want a life with the woman who stole my heart when I was a teenager."

She smiled softly at the tenderness that burned in his eyes. "I still can't believe you loved me all those years, Jim. You never said a thing."

"I was a shy kid," he said with a laugh. "And I had

the curse of my father's Donovan-hating on top of it. That was the best reason not to approach you."

Rachel nodded and reluctantly released his hand. "I know," she whispered sadly. Holding his gaze, she asked, "Have you ever wondered what our lives might have been like if our fathers hadn't been carrying on that stupid feud?"

"Yeah," he said fondly, finishing off his second sandwich. Being around Rachel made him famished. "We'd probably have married at eighteen, had a brood of kids and been happy as hell."

Rachel couldn't deny the possible scenario. "And now? What do you want out of life, Jim?"

Somberly, he picked up her hand as she laid her own half-eaten sandwich aside. "You. Just you, princess."

Coloring, she smiled. "That's a beautiful endearment."

"Good, because as an awkward, shy teenager, I used to fantasize that you were a princess from a foreign country—so beautiful and yet untouchable."

Her voice grew strained with tears. "What a positive way to look at it, at the situation." Rachel gently pressed the back of his hand to her left cheek. The coals of desire burned in his eyes and she ached to love Jim. He'd made it clear earlier that, because her cheekbone was fractured, they should wait, and she'd agreed. To even try and kiss him was painful. Waiting was tough, but not impossible for Rachel. She understood on a deeper level that they needed the time to reacquaint themselves with one another, without all the family fireworks and dramatics going on around them.

He eased his hand from hers. "I brought something

with me that I've been saving for a long, long time." He grinned sheepishly and dug into the left pocket of his dark blue shirt. "Now," he cautioned her lightly, "you have to keep this in perspective, okay?"

Rachel smiled with him. Jim suddenly was boyish, looking years younger. His eyes sparkled mischievously as he pulled something wrapped in a tissue from his pocket. "Well, sure. What is it, Jim?"

Chuckling, he laid the lump of tissue on the table between them. "I had such a crush on you that I saved my money and I went to Mr. Foglesong's jewelry store and bought you this. I kept dreaming that someday you'd look at me, or give me a smile, and we would meet, and at the right moment, I could give you this." He gestured toward it. "Go ahead, it's yours. A few years late, but it's yours, anyway."

Jim saw Rachel's cheeks flush with pleasure as she carefully unwrapped the tissue on the table. He heard her audible gasp and saw her dark green eyes widen beautifully.

"Now, it's nothing expensive," he warned as she picked up a ring encrusted with colorful gems on a silver band. "It's base metal covered with electroplated silver. The stones are nothing more than cut glass."

Touched beyond words, Rachel gently held the ring encircled with sparkling, colorful "diamonds."

"Back then, every girl wore her boyfriend's ring around her neck on a chain."

He laughed. "Yeah, going steady."

"And you were going to give this to me?" She held it up in a slash of sunlight that crossed the table where they sat. The ring sparkled like a rainbow.

"I wanted to," Jim told her ruefully. "I saved my money and bought it the first year I saw you in junior high."

The realization that Jim had kept this ring through six years of school and never once had she even said hello to him or smiled at him broke her heart. No, he was a Cunningham, and Rachel, like her sisters, had avoided anyone with that name like the plague. She felt deep sadness move through her as she slipped the ring on the fourth finger of her right hand. It fit perfectly. Tears burned in her eyes as she held out her hand for him to inspect.

"How does it look?" she quavered.

Words choked in Jim's throat as he slid his hands around hers. "Nice. But what I'm looking at is beautiful."

Sniffing, Rachel wiped the tears from her eyes with trembling fingers. "This is so sad, Jim. You carried this ring for six years in school hoping I'd say hello to you, or at least look you in the eye. Every time I saw a Cunningham coming, I'd turn the other way and leave. I'm so sorry! I didn't know.... I really didn't know...."

"Hush, princess, it doesn't matter. You came home and so did I, and look what happened." His mouth curved into a gentle smile as he held her tear-filled eyes. "We have a chance to start over, Rachel. That's how I see it." Gripping her hand more firmly, he continued, "Life isn't exactly going to be a lot of fun this next six weeks, but after that, things should settle out a little."

"I know," she agreed. Six weeks. The trial would be coming up in a month and then Chet and Bo would get from the judge what they deserved. It would take six

weeks for her fractured cheekbone to heal. And then…
Her heart took off at a gallop. Then she could make love
to Jim. The thought was hot, melting and full of promise. She ached to have him, love him and join with him
in that beautiful oneness.

"I'm sure my brothers will be going to prison," Jim
said in a low voice. "And my father is going to take up
a lot of my time. I'll have to get used to running the
ranch. I was thinking of asking Sam for some help and
guidance. He was the manager of the Bar C for a while,
and he knows the inner workings of it. He can kind of
shadow me until I get into the full swing of things."

Rachel nodded. "I know Sam would do anything to
help out. We all will, Jim."

"Do you know how good that is to hear?" he rasped.
"No more fighting between the Donovans and the Cunninghams. Now we'll have peace. Isn't that something?"

It was. Rachel sat there in awe over the realization.
"I never thought of it in those terms before, but you're
right." She gave a little laugh. "Just think, the next time
your cattle stray onto our land or vice versa, no nasty
phone calls. Just a call saying, 'hey, your cows are stray-
ing again.'" She laughed. "Do you know how *good* that
will be?"

"The range war between us is over," he said, patting her hand and admiring the ring on her finger once
again. It was a child's innocent love that had bought that
present for her, but Jim felt his heart swell with pride
that Rachel had put it on, nevertheless.

"There's something I want to tell you," he said.
"When I left here the other day after Bo and Chet assaulted you, I went home and had it out with my father."

He frowned. "It probably contributed to him having a stroke, but I can't be sorry for what I told him." He held Rachel's soft green eyes. "I told him I was in love with you."

"Oh, dear, Jim."

"He needed to hear it from me," he rasped. "He didn't like it, but that's life."

"And he accused you of being a traitor?"

"Yes," Jim replied, amazed by her insight. But then, he shouldn't be surprised. She had always been a deep and caring person. "He said I was being a traitor to the family."

"What else? I can see it in your eyes."

Ordinarily, Jim would feel uncomfortable revealing so much of himself, but with Rachel, he felt not only safe in showing those depths within him, but he wanted to. "My father disowned me—for the second time."

"No...." Rachel pressed her hand against her heart as she felt and heard the pain in his voice, saw it clearly in his face and eyes. "And then he had that stroke?"

"He had one of the wranglers drive him up to the Flag jail. From what I hear from Scott Maitland, who was there when my father entered into the jail facility, he got into a hell of a fight with the sheriff of Coconino Country, Slade Cameron. That's when he had the stroke. They called 911 and he was taken right over to the hospital from there. Scott told me at the hospital, after I arrived, that my father was demanding that Cameron let my brothers go on bail. The judge had refused them bail, too, and Cameron was backing the judge's decision to the hilt."

Inwardly, Rachel shivered. She knew why the judge had not given them bail. The Cunningham brothers had a notorious history of taking revenge on people who pressed charges against them. That was why they had gotten away without punishment until now—they'd threatened their victims until they dropped the charges. But not this time. Rachel would have kept pressing charges even if they had gotten bail.

"So his anger blew a blood vessel in his brain," Jim told her quietly. "I'm surprised it hadn't happened before this, to tell you the truth."

She nodded and got up. Leaning against the counter, she studied him in the gathering warmth and silence. "How are you feeling about all this?"

Shrugging, Jim eased out of the chair and came to her side. He slid his arm around her shoulders and guided her into the living room. "Guilty. I can't help but feel that way, but I wasn't going to live a lie with my father, either. He had to know I loved you and that I was going to testify in your defense at Chet and Bo's trial."

She moved with him to the purple-pink-and-cream-colored couch near the fireplace. Sitting down, she leaned against him, contented as never before. "And even though he's disowned you a second time, you're going to stay and run the ranch?"

Jim absorbed the feel of her slender form. How natural, how good it felt to have Rachel in his arms. Outside the picture window, he saw snowflakes twirling down again. The fire crackled pleasantly, and he'd never felt happier—or sadder. "Yes. This disowning thing is a game with my father. I know he meant it, but now it doesn't matter."

Rachel rested her head against his strong, capable shoulder. "And you really want to run the Bar C?"

"Sure." He grinned down at her. "Once a cowboy, always a cowboy."

"An EMT cowboy. And a firefighter."

"All those things," Jim agreed.

"And when Bo and Chet get out of prison, what will you do? Hand the ranch over to them to run?"

Sobering, Jim nodded. He moved his fingers languidly down her shoulder and upper arm. "Yes," he said grimly, "I will."

"He'll never be able to run it," Rachel said worriedly.

"Bo and Chet are the owners, technically. I know they aren't going to want me around when they get out."

"And your father? What will you do? Continue to live there?"

Gently, he turned Rachel around so that she faced him. "When the time's right, I'm going to propose to you. And if you say yes, you'll live over on the Bar C with me. We have several other homes. I'll put my father in one of them and we'll live at the main ranch house. Even though he disowned me, he's going to need me now. And I'm hoping we can mend fences, at least for the sake of his health. When Bo and Chet get out, you and I will leave."

Rachel thrilled to the idea of being Jim's wife. His partner for life. All her previous fears were gone and she knew that was because she was certain of her love for Jim. Heat burned in her cheeks and she held his hopeful gaze. "Kate wants us to live here. In this house, Jim. She already told me we were welcome here in case we got 'serious' about one another."

Grinning, he caressed her hair and followed the sweep of it down her shoulder. "Kate saw us getting together?"

"Kate's not a dumb post."

Chuckling, Jim nodded. "No, I'd never accuse her of being that, ever."

Sliding her hand up his cheek, Rachel felt the sandpaper quality of his skin beneath her palm. She saw Jim's eyes go dark with longing—for her. It was such a delicious feeling to be wanted by him. "Then you wouldn't mind living here and working on the Donovan Ranch instead when the time came?"

"No," he whispered, leaning over and placing a very light kiss on the tip of her nose, "why should I? I'll have you. That's all I'll ever need, princess. Where I live with you doesn't matter at all. It never did."

Sliding into his waiting arms, Rachel closed her eyes and rested her head against Jim's shoulder. A broken sigh escaped her. The next six weeks were going to be a special hell for all of them on many levels. The trial would tear them all apart, she knew. And Jim would be away from her more than with her because he would have to be at the Bar C learning how to manage the huge ranch. And she, well, she had just rented an office in Sedona and there was a lot of pressure on her to get patients and start making money and contributing to paying off that huge debt against the ranch.

"I can hardly wait," Rachel quavered, "for these next six weeks to be done and gone."

Holding her tightly, Jim ran his hand along the line of her graceful back. Pressing a kiss to her hair, he murmured fervently, "I know, princess. Believe me, I know…"

Chapter 12

The mid-February sunlight was strong and bright as Rachel sat on her horse, her leg occasionally touching Jim's as the gelding moved to nibble the green grass shoots that surrounded them. The patches of snow here and there on the red clay soil of the Cunningham pasture was strong evidence of the fact that the steady snowfall would break some of the drought conditions that had held everyone captive.

"The cattle are going to eat well," Jim commented as he moved his hat up on his brow and gazed at Rachel. She looked beautiful in Levi's, a long-sleeved white blouse, leather vest and black Stetson cowboy hat. Her hair was caught up in a single braid that lay down the middle of her back.

Nodding, she leaned down and stroked the neck of her black Arabian mare. "For once."

They sat on their horses on a hill that overlooked both Donovan and Cunningham ranch land, a barbed wire fence marking the division line. Down below, on the Donovan side, Kate and Sam were working to repair fence so that their cattle wouldn't wander over onto Cunningham property. At least, Jim thought, this time there was going to be teamwork between the two families, and not angry words followed by violence.

"How's your father?" Rachel asked. Jim's face took on a pained expression. Frank Cunningham had never recovered after the stroke as the doctors had hoped. He was now bedridden, with twenty-four-hour nursing care at the ranch house. Jim divided his duties between managing the huge ranch and trying to help his father, who had given up on living. She knew it was just a matter of time. Frank hadn't been doing well since he'd found out that his two sons were going to prison. Bo got a year and Chet two years.

"Father's a little better today," he said, wiping the sweat off his brow. "That's why I came out with the line crew."

"It does you good to get out of that office you've been living in."

Grinning a little, he held Rachel's dancing, lively gaze. "I was going stir-crazy in there, if you want the truth." Jim knew that ever since the trial, which had taken place two weeks earlier, Rachel had been upset and strained. For the first time, he was seeing her more relaxed. Now she had a thriving office filled with patients who wanted natural medicine, like homeopathy, instead of drugs. To say she was a little busy was an understatement. Income from her growing business was helping to pay off some bills on the Donovan Ranch.

"What's the chances of you coming over for dinner tonight?" Rachel asked, her heart beating a little harder. The ache to be with Jim, to share more time with him, never left her. The last six weeks had been a hell for them. They needed a break. She needed him. The stolen kisses, the hot, lingering touches, weren't enough for her anymore.

Frowning, Jim said, "How about a picnic tomorrow? I wanted to go back up on the Rim and explore where they captured that jaguar and took her away." Reaching over, he closed his hand over hers. "Want to come along?"

"I'll provide the lunch?" Rachel asked, thrilling at his strong, steady grip on her hand. The burning hunger in his eyes matched her own feelings. How she hungered to have a few moments alone with Jim! The demands in their lives had kept them apart and she wanted to change that.

"You bet," he murmured with a smile.

"Have you heard from Bob Granby in the fish and game department about how the jaguar is getting along in her new haunt?"

Jim shifted in the saddle, the leather creaking pleasantly beneath him. "Matter of fact, I did. She's been taken over to the White Mountain area and is getting along fine there. He said two more jaguars have been spotted in the mountains north of Tucson, so they are migrating north for sure."

"I love how things in nature, if they are disturbed, will come back into harmony over time."

Reluctantly releasing Rachel's hand, Jim nodded. "I like the harmony we're establishing right now between the two ranches."

"It will last only a year," she commented sadly.

He studied her. "Not if you agree to marry me, Rachel."

Her heart thudded. She stared at Jim. "What?"

He grinned a little. "Well? Will you?"

She saw that boyish grin on his face, his eyes tender with love—for her. Lips parting, she tried to find the words to go along with her feelings.

"Is your stunned look a no or a yes?" he teased, his grin widening. Over the last six weeks, they had grown incredibly close. Nothing had ever felt so right or so good to Jim. He prayed silently that Rachel wanted marriage as much as he did.

Touching her flaming cheeks, Rachel said, "Let me think about it? I'll give you an answer tomorrow at lunch, okay?"

Nodding, he picked up the reins from the neck of the quarter horse he rode. A part of him felt terror that she'd say no. Another part whispered that Rachel truly needed the time. But that was something he could give her. Leaning over, he curved his hand behind her neck and drew her to him.

"What we have," he told her, his face inches from hers, "is good and beautiful, princess. I'll wait as long as you want me to." He smiled a little, recalling that she had made the other man in her life wait five years and even then she couldn't marry him. Things were different this time around and Jim knew it. Over the last six weeks, he'd watched Rachel's fear dissolve more and more. The fact that he'd loved her since he was a teenager, he was sure, had something to do with it. Leaning over a little more, he crushed her lips to his and tasted sunlight, the clean, fresh air on them. It was so easy to kiss Rachel. And how wonderful it would be to love her fully. Her cheek was healed now, and he didn't have to worry about possibly hurting her when he kissed her hard and swiftly. And he knew she wanted him, too, noting her hot response to his mouth skimming hers.

Easing away, Jim reluctantly released her. There was a delicious cloudiness in Rachel's eyes, and he read it as longing—for him. "I'll meet you at the north pasture at ten tomorrow morning?" he asked huskily.

Rachel felt dizzy with heat, with an aching longing for Jim. Every time he stole a kiss unexpectedly from her, she wanted him just that much more. Touching her lips, she nodded. He look so handsome and confident, sitting astride his bay gelding with that dangerous look glittering in his eyes, one corner of his mouth pulled into a slight, confident smile.

"Yes—tomorrow...."

Rachel found Kate out in the barn, feeding the broodmares for the evening. She helped her older sister finish off the feeding by giving the pregnant Arabian mares a ration of oats. When they were done, Rachel sat down on a bale of hay at one end of the barn. Kate walked up, took off her hat and, wiping her brow with the back of her hand, joined her.

"Thanks for the help."

Rachel nodded. "I need to share something with you, Kate, and I wanted you to hear it from me and not secondhand."

She saw Kate's face go on guard. Rachel smiled a little. "It's good news, Kate."

"Whew. Okay, what is it?" she asked, running her fingers through her hair. "I could use good news."

Wasn't that the truth? Rachel smiled tentatively. "Jim asked me to marry him today." She watched Kate's expression carefully. "I've already told Jessica and Dan. Now I want to tell you and Sam. I'd like to know how you feel about the possibility." Her gut clenched a little as she waited for Kate to speak.

"Jim's a good man," Kate said finally, in a low voice. She picked at some of the alfalfa hay between her legs where she'd straddled the bale. Her brows knitted as she chose her words. "I didn't like him before. But that's because his last name is Cunningham." Looking up, she smiled apologetically. "I'm the last one who should be holding a grudge. The more I saw of Jim in different circumstances, the more I realized that he was genuine. He's not like the others in his family. And he's trying to straighten things out between the two families."

"If I tell him yes," Rachel whispered, a catch in her voice, "that means I'll be living over there for a while, at least until Bo and Chet come back to claim the ranch."

"And then," Kate said, straightening and moving her shoulders a little, "you can come home and have your house back if you want."

"Then you don't mind if I tell Jim yes?"

Kate gave her a silly grin. Leaning over, she hugged Rachel tightly for a moment. "You love each other! Why should I stand in the way? Jim's a good person. He means to do right by others. He can't help it if he's got rattlesnakes for brothers."

Grinning, Rachel gripped Kate's long, callused hand. "Thanks, Kate. Your blessing means everything to me. I—I didn't want to come back here and not be welcomed."

Tears formed in Kate's eyes and she wiped them away self-consciously. "Listen, I've committed enough mistakes for the whole family. You've both forgiven me. Why can't I do the same for you and Jim? So, when's the big day?"

"I don't know—yet. Jim and I are going to ride up on the Rim tomorrow morning where we found the jaguar's den. I'm packing a lunch."

Rising, Kate said, "Great! I'm sure you'll know a lot more when you come down." Holding her hand out to Rachel, she sighed. "Isn't it wonderful? We've all come home from various parts of the world and we're getting our ranch back on its feet. Together."

Rachel released Kate's hand and walked slowly down the aisle with her. She slipped her arm around her sister's slender waist. "Dreams do come true," she agreed. "I hated leaving here when I did. I cried so much that first year I was gone. I was so homesick for Mama, for this wonderful land…."

Sighing, Kate wrapped her arm around Rachel's waist. The gloom of the barn cast long shadows down the aisle as they slowly walked together. "All three of us were. At least we had the guts to come back and work to save our ranch."

"And we're finally coming out from under the bank's

thumb!" Rachel laughed, feeling almost giddy about their good fortune. Kate and Sam had sold off half the Herefords for a good price. With the bank loan paid off, they now had a clear shot at keeping the ranch once and for all.

Kate looked down at her, smiling. "Want another piece of good news?"

"Sure? Gosh, two in a row, Katie. I don't know if I can handle it or not!"

She laughed huskily. Patting her abdomen, she said, "I'm pregnant."

Stunned, Rachel released her and turned, her mouth dropping open. "What?"

Coloring prettily, Kate kept her hand across her abdomen. "I just found out this afternoon. Doc Kaldenbaugh said I was two and a half months along. Isn't that wonderful?"

"And Sam? Does he know about it?" Rachel asked, feeling thrilled. She saw the shyness in Kate's face and the joy in it, too.

"Sure, he was with me."

"Oh!" Rachel cried, throwing her arms around Kate and hugging her. "This is so wonderful! I'm gonna be an aunt!"

Kate laughed self-consciously. "Hey, I'm going to need all the help I can get. This mothering role isn't one I know a whole lot about."

Tears trickled down Rachel's cheeks. "Don't worry," she whispered, choking up, "Jessica and I will love being aunts and helping you out. I think among the three of us, we can do the job, don't you?"

Kate grinned mischievously. "You mean Jessica hasn't told you yet?"

"Told me what?"

"She's expecting, too."

Stunned, Rachel stared. "What? When did this all happen? Where was I?"

Chuckling, Kate said, "We both went to Doc Kaldenbaugh today. Seems Jessica is expecting twins. They run in Dan Black's family, you know."

Rachel pressed her hands to her cheeks, dumbfounded. She saw Kate's eyes sparkle with laughter over her reaction.

"So, little sis, you and Jim had better get busy, eh? I'm assuming you want children?"

"More than anything," Rachel said, her voice soft and in awe. "You're *both* pregnant!"

"Yes." Kate gave her a satisfied smile. She turned and shut the barn doors for the night with Rachel's help. "Sam is going to hire a couple more wranglers now that we have some money. Then I can ease off on some of the work I've been doing. He wants me to take it easy." She laughed as she brought the latch down on the door. "I can't exactly see me knitting and crocheting in the house all day, can you?"

Rachel shook her head. "No, but Sam's right—you do need to ease off on some of that hard, physical labor you do on the ranch. I'm sure Jessica could use some help in her flower essence business. You like the greenhouse."

"I was thinking I would help her," Kate said. Patting Rachel on the shoulder, she said, "I'll let Jessica know I told you the big news. When you see Jim tomorrow, and say yes, tell him from me that I'm glad he's going to be a part of our family."

Rachel nodded and gripped her sister's hand for a moment. Kate's blessing made things right. "I will," she whispered. "And thanks for understanding."

"Around here," Kate said, looking up at the bright coverlet of stars in the black night above them, "everything is heart centered, Rachel. I like living out of my heart again. This ranch is our heart, our soul. I'm looking forward to having kids running around again. I'm really looking forward to seeing life and discoveries through their eyes. You know?"

Rachel did know. She lifted her hand. "Good night, Kate. That baby you're carrying will be one of the most loved children on the face of this earth." And it would be. As Rachel made her way through the darkness, broken by patches of light from the sulfur lamps placed here and there around the ranch, she smiled softly. They had suffered so much—each of them, and now life was giving them gifts in return for their courage. Her heart expanded and she longed to see Jim. Rachel could hardly wait for morning to arrive.

"Isn't that wonderful news?" Rachel asked as she sat on the red-and-white checkered blanket. Jim had spread the picnic blanket out at the mouth to the canyon, beneath an alligator juniper that was probably well over two hundred years old. Above them was the empty lair where the jaguar had once lived.

He munched thoughtfully on an apple. Lying on his side, his cowboy hat hung on a low tree limb, he nodded. "Twins. Wow. Jessica and Dan are going to be busy."

Chuckling, Rachel put the last of the chocolate cake and the half-empty bottle of sparkling grape juice back into the saddlebags. "No kidding."

"You like the idea of being an aunt?" Jim asked, slowly easing into a sitting position. He watched as Rachel put the items away. No matter what she did, there was always grace about her movements. Today she wore her hair loose and free, with dark strands cascading across her pale pink cowboy shirt.

"I love the idea."

He caught her hand. "What do you think about having children?"

His hand was warm and dry as she met and held his tender gaze. "I've always wanted them. And you?"

"They're a natural part of life—and love," he said slowly as he pulled a small box from his pocket. Placing the gray velvet box in the palm of her hand, he whispered, "Open it, Rachel…."

Heart pounding, she smiled tremulously. Rachel knew it was a wedding ring. She loved the idea of him asking to marry her here, in this special canyon the jaguar had come home to. In many ways, the Donovan women were like that jaguar—chased away by a man. And they, too, had finally returned home.

Her fingers trembled as she opened the tiny brass latch. Inside was a gold band. Instead of a diamond, however, there were eight channel-cut stones the same height as the surface of the ring so they wouldn't snag or catch on anything. Each stone was a different color, and as Rachel removed the ring, they sparkled wildly in the sunlight.

"This is so beautiful, Jim," she whispered. Tears

stung her eyes as she held it up to him. "It's like this ring." She held up her hand, showing him the "going steady" ring he'd bought so long ago and that she'd faithfully worn since he'd gotten up the courage to give it to her.

Touched, Jim nodded. "Do you like it?"

"Like it?" Rachel stroked the new ring. "I love it...."

"I had it made by a jeweler in Sedona. He's well known for one-of-a-kind pieces. I drew him a picture of the other ring and he said he could do it. Instead of cut glass, though, each of those are gemstones. There's a small emerald, topaz, pink tourmaline, ruby, white moonstone and opal set in it."

Amazed at the simple beauty of the wedding ring, Rachel sighed. "Oh, Jim, this is beyond anything I could imagine."

Wryly, he said, "Can you imagine being my wife?"

Lifting her chin, Rachel met and held his very serious gaze. "Yes, I can."

Satisfaction soared through him. "Let's see if it fits." He took the ring and slid it onto her finger. The fit was perfect. Holding her hand, he added huskily, "You name the date, okay?"

Sniffing, she wiped the tears from her cheeks with her fingers. "My mother's birthday was March 21. I'd love to get married on that day and honor her spirit, honor what she's given the three of us. Is that too soon?"

Grinning, Jim brought her into the circle of his arms. "Too soon?" He pressed a kiss to her hair as she settled against his tall, hard frame. "I was thinking, like, tomorrow?"

Rachel laughed giddily. "Jim! You don't mean that, do you?"

He leaned down and held Rachel in his arms, taking her mouth gently. She was soft and warm and giving. As her hand slid around his neck, a hot, trembling need poured through him. He skimmed her lips with his and felt her quiver in response. She tasted of sweet cherries and chocolate from the cake she'd just eaten. Running his hands through her thick, unbound hair, he was reminded of the strength that Rachel possessed.

Drawing her onto the blanket, he met her eyes, dazed with joy and need. "I want to love you," he rasped, threading his fingers through her hair as it fell against the blanket like a dark halo. Sunlight filtering through the juniper above them dappled the ground with gold. The breeze was warm and pine scented. Everything was perfect with Rachel beside him. Nothing had ever felt so right to Jim as this moment.

"Yes…" Rachel whispered as she moved her hands to his light blue chambray shirt. She began to unsnap the pearl buttons one at a time until the shirt fell away, exposing his darkly haired chest. Closing her eyes, Rachel spread her hands out across his torso, the thick, wiry hair beneath her palms sending tingles up her limbs. There was such strength to Jim, she realized, as she continued to languidly explore his deep, well-formed body. At the same time, she felt his fingers undoing the buttons on her blouse. Each touch was featherlight, evocative and teasing. Her nipples hardened in anticipation as he moved the material aside, easing it off her shoulders. The sunlight felt warm against her exposed skin as her bra was shed.

The first, skimming touch of his work-roughened fingers along her collarbone made her inhale sharply. Opening her eyes, she drowned in his stormy ones. They had always called him Cougar and she could see and feel his desire stalking her now. As he spread his hand outward to follow the curve of her breast, her lashes fluttered closed. Hot, wild tingling sped through her and she moaned as his fingers cupped her flesh.

Moments later, she felt his lips capture one hardened nipple and a cry of pleasure escaped her lips. Instinctively, she arched against him. His naked chest met hers. A galvanizing fire sizzled through her as he suckled her. The heat burned down her to her lower abdomen, an ache building so fiercely between her thighs that she moaned as his hand moved to release the snap on her Levi's. Never had Rachel felt so wanted and desired as now. As he lifted his head, he smiled down at her. His gaze burned through her, straight to her heart, to her soul. This was the man she wanted forever, she realized dazedly.

As he slipped out of his Levi's, after pulling hers from her legs, Rachel felt shaky with need. Her mind wasn't functioning; she was solely captive to her emotions, to the love she felt for Jim as he eased her back down on the blanket. As his strong, sun-darkened body met and flowed against hers, she released a ragged little sigh. Automatically, she pressed herself wantonly against him. His hand ranged down across her hip to her thigh. As she met his mouth, and he plundered her depths hotly, she slid her hand up and over his chest. Their breathing was hot and shallow. Their hearts pounded in fury and need.

The moment his hand slid between her thighs, silently asking her to open to him, she felt his tongue move into her mouth. Where did rapture begin and end? Rachel wasn't sure as his tongue stroked hers at the same time his fingers sought and found the moist opening to her womanhood. Sharp jolts of heat moved up through her. The cry in her throat turned to a moan of utter need. In moments, she felt him move across her, felt his knee guide her thighs open to receive all of him, and she clung to his capturing, cajoling mouth.

She throbbed with desire. She couldn't wait any longer. Thrusting her hips upward, she met him fearlessly, with equal passion. The moment he plunged into her, she gave a startled cry, but it was one of utter pleasure, not pain. His other hand settled beneath her hips and he moved rhythmically with her. The ache dissolved into hot honey within her. This warmth of the sunlight on her flesh, his mouth seeking and molding, their breaths wild and chaotic, all blended into an incredible collage of movement, sound, taste and pleasure. A white-hot explosion occurred deep within her, and Rachel threw back her head with a cry and arched hard against him. Through the haze of sensations she heard him growl like the cougar he really was. His hands were hard on her shoulders as he thrust repeatedly into her, heightening her pleasure as the volcanic release flowed wildly through her. In those moments, the world spun around them. There was only Jim, his powerful embrace, his heart thundering against hers as they clung to one another in that beautiful moment of creation between them.

Languidly, Rachel relaxed in his arms in the aftermath. Barely opening her eyes, she smiled tremulously up at him. His face glistened with perspiration; his eyes were banked with desire and love for her alone. Stretching fully, Rachel lay against his muscular length, his arms around her, holding her close to him.

"I love you," Jim rasped as he kissed her hair, her temple and her flushed cheek. "I always have, sweet woman of mine." And she was his. In every way. Never had Jim felt more powerful, more sure of himself as a man, as now. She was like sweet, hot honey in his arms, her body lithe, warm and trembling. How alive Rachel was! Not only was there such compassion in her, he was lucky to be able to share her passion as well. Moving several damp strands of hair from her brow, he drowned in her forest green eyes, which danced with gold flecks. Her lips were parted, glistening and well kissed. She had a mouth he wanted to kiss forever.

His words fell softly against her ears. Rachel sighed and closed her eyes, resting her brow against his jaw. Somewhere in the background, she heard the call of a raven far above the canyon where they lay. She felt the dappled sunlight dancing across her sated form. The breeze was like invisible hands drying and softly caressing her. More than anything, she absorbed Jim's love, the protectiveness he naturally accorded her as she lay in his arms. This was a man whose heart, whose morals and values were worth everything to her—and then some. It didn't matter that his last name was Cunningham. By them loving one another, Rachel thought dazedly, still lost in the memory of their lovemaking, a hundred-year-old feud no longer existed between their families.

Moving her hand in a weak motion across his damp

chest, she smiled softly. "I love you so much, darling." She looked up into his eyes. "I'm looking forward to spending the rest of my life showing you just how much."

Tenderly, he caught and held her lips beneath his. It was a soft kiss meant to seal her words between them. He felt as if his heart would explode with happiness. Did anyone deserve to feel this happy? He thought not as he wrapped her tightly against him. Chuckling a little, he told her, "Well, maybe as of today, we'll start a new family dynasty. A blend of Cunningham and Donovan blood."

The thought of having Jim's baby made her feel fulfilled as never before. Rachel laughed a little. "You can't have a feud this way, can you?"

"No," he answered, sighing. So much worry and strain sloughed off him in that moment as he moved his large hand across her rounded abdomen. Rachel had wide hips and he knew she'd carry a baby easily within her. Their children. The thought brought him a sense of serenity he'd never known before this moment.

As Jim looked down at Rachel, he cupped her cheek and whispered, "I'll love you forever, princess. You and as many children as we bring into the world because of the love we hold for one another."

* * * * *

Melissa Senate has written many novels for Harlequin and other publishers, including her debut, *See Jane Date*, which was made into a TV movie. She also wrote seven books for Harlequin Special Edition under the pen name Meg Maxwell. Her novels have been published in over twenty-five countries. Melissa lives on the coast of Maine with her teenage son; their rescue shepherd mix, Flash; and a lap cat named Cleo. For more information, please visit her website, melissasenate.com.

Books by Melissa Senate

Harlequin Special Edition

Dawson Family Ranch

For the Twins' Sake
Wyoming Special Delivery
A Family for a Week
The Long-Awaited Christmas Wish
Wyoming Cinderella
Wyoming Matchmaker
His Baby No Matter What
Heir to the Ranch

The Wyoming Multiples

The Baby Switch!
Detective Barelli's Legendary Triplets
Wyoming Christmas Surprise
To Keep Her Baby
A Promise for the Twins
A Wyoming Christmas to Remember

Visit the Author Profile page
at Harlequin.com for more titles.

THE MOST ELIGIBLE COWBOY

Melissa Senate

Chapter 1

All Brandon Taylor wanted was to finish his small plate of delicious shrimp pot stickers, grab a bottle of champagne and sneak out of his brother's wedding reception for a little while. Half hour tops.

He stood in the parklike backyard of the Taylor family ranch on this warm, breezy early September evening, behind a pillar wrapped in twinkling white lights and festooned with tiny red roses, eyeing the best route to escape. The wedding had started at six and though it was now only seven thirty, it felt like two in the morning. The ceremony had been *a lot*. Or maybe just a lot for him. The look on his brother's face when his bride had started down the aisle had slammed Brandon in his chest. Had he ever seen Jordan look like that? Not just happy, not just proud, but as if he finally understood the meaning of life.

Then there were the vows. Goose bumps had unexpectedly trailed up Brandon's arms when Jordan repeated his vows and then said some of his own, the reverence in his brother's voice holding Brandon completely still.

"Dang," their brother Dirk had whispered from where they'd stood to the side of their oldest brother. "Double dang," Dirk's twin, Dustin, had agreed, wonder in his voice. Their sister, Daphne, was on the other side, in the bridesmaid lineup, tears misting her eyes, but Daphne had always been a softie. Plus, she had an engagement ring on her finger and would be next to get married so, of course, she was a little emotional at a wedding. What Brandon's excuse was for choking up, he had no idea.

Likely he was just happy for his big brother, a guy who'd always been a hero to Brandon. That was all.

Given the Taylor track record at marriage, Brandon hadn't thought any of his four siblings would make lifetime commitments. But there had stood Jordan, vowing to love, honor and cherish Camilla Sanchez till death did them part. There had stood Daphne, whose problems with their thrice-married, controlling father were legendary in Bronco, also believing in *forever* with that diamond ring twinkling on her finger.

Brandon *was* truly happy for both siblings, but he knew one thing about love: it didn't last. It just didn't have a chance.

So, add all that to the hundredth time a wedding guest had said, "I bet you're next, Brandon," and he was ready for a breather. A cousin had even added, "Good golly, Brandon, aren't you thirty-four? And still single? It's high time you settled down."

Brandon had politely smiled through it all until he just couldn't take it and had snapped at another cousin, a know-it-all lawyer from Butte with a gold wedding band on his hand, "Statistics speak for themselves. No thanks."

He'd gotten the stink eye from the cousin and a shaking tsk-tsk of the head from an aunt, and he'd been about to apologize for being the cynical smart-ass he could sometimes be when someone clanked a spoon against a champagne glass and everyone started chanting, "Kiss, kiss, kiss!" Jordan and Camilla stood in the center of the dance area, and his brother laid one on his new bride that even had Brandon kind of blushing. Cheers, wolf whistles and clapping followed.

Brandon glanced toward a stand of Rocky Mountain maple trees, his favorite grouping in the yard, the leaves already shimmering their yellow in the white lights hung around the perimeter of the reception area. Surely no one would miss him for a half hour. He'd already dutifully made small talk with at least a hundred of the countless guests. He'd complimented his dad's wife— number three—on the great job she'd done turning the yard of their family ranch into an outdoor ballroom, complete with all the strung lights and huge pink-and-red flower displays, penguin-suited waitstaff mingling with trays of appetizers and cocktails. He *had* managed to get into an argument with his father about his sister— something he'd promised himself to avoid—but anytime

Cornelius Taylor, who had a king complex, complained about Daphne, Brandon was going to defend her.

Their dad, whose beef cattle operation made him one of the wealthiest men in Bronco Heights, Montana, had a "my way or the highway" mentality, and when Daphne had chosen the highway, Cornelius had blown his stack. She'd moved out to start her own ranch, and a very different one, at that.

Daphne, a vegetarian of all things in a family of cattle ranchers, owned the Happy Hearts Animal Sanctuary, and Cornelius was always muttering that all the place was missing was shuffleboard for the old bulls and recuperating horses, plus the many dogs, cats and small furry creatures available for adoption. Between Daphne getting engaged and Jordan marrying Camilla tonight, poor Cornelius was out two of his five offspring to boss around, and that was his favorite pastime. Brandon loved his dad, but the man was a control freak.

And Brandon Taylor would never let anyone tell him what to do, when, or how. He was his own man and always had been.

He glanced around. Lots of smooching. Dancing cheek to cheek. Brandon had arrived solo at the wedding, but he'd been paired with a very attractive single bridesmaid in the wedding party. When she'd asked how many kids he wanted someday and he said he hadn't even thought ahead to whether he wanted beef or chicken for his dinner, she'd rolled her eyes at him and walked off. Now, as he spied a determined-looking middle-aged woman coming toward him with what looked like a calling card in her hand, he gave a fast smile and hightailed it from his hiding spot. He had at least twenty-five cards and slips of papers with the cell phone numbers and social media handles of single daughters, nieces, granddaughters, neighbors he'd be "a sure match with."

Doubtful. Love and Brandon had never mixed. Love and Taylors had never mixed, either, not that Brandon didn't wish his two siblings well. Daphne seemed to have found the real thing with Evan Cruise, and his brother Jordan looked so sickeningly happy right now, staring into his new wife's eyes while slow dancing to Frank Sinatra, that Brandon really did have to hand it to him. The guy formerly known as He Who Would Not Be Tamed among the single women of Bronco had found his Ms. Right.

Brandon had spent the last few years making crystal clear to the women he dated that he would not commit. With his family history and not a single relationship working out for himself, Brandon put zero stock in romance and happily-ever-after, even when it was all around him—like at this wedding, a celebration of all things love and forever. Life had a way of not working out.

Cynical, sure. But true.

He popped the final pot sticker in his mouth, reminding himself to compliment his new sister-in-law on the catering her restaurant did for the wedding, then set the empty plate on a table. About to make off for the trees, he almost collided with a tiny elderly lady in her nineties.

Uh-oh.

There was no getting away from Winona Cobbs. No fast-talk, no evading. She had him pinned with her sharp gaze. Rumored to be mystic, Winona had a psychic shop at her great-grandson Evan's ghost tour business in town. Now that Evan was engaged to Brandon's sister, Winona was pretty much family. A psychic in the family sounded kind of scary. Not that he put much stock in mysticism, either, but with her long white hair, pale skin and mark-my-words look in her eyes, Winona Cobbs wasn't to be dismissed too easily. Plus, she deserved his respect. The lady had quite a family history of her own and had been through it all and then some.

"Brandon Taylor, you clean up well," Winona said, nodding as she looked him up and down through the rhinestone-dotted veil of her small purple cowboy hat. "Like a groom yourself in that spiffy tuxedo." She smiled wide and gave one end of her silver boa a toss over her shoulder.

He smiled back, shook his head and held up a palm. "No, ma'am. Not me. I'm more a lone wolf type."

"Oh please!" she scoffed. "I'll tell you what your problem is."

She sounded like his dad, he thought, his bow tie feeling tighter around his neck.

She leaned close. "Brandon Taylor, you don't know how to love. But I'll tell you something else. The universe has something in store for you. Oh yes sirree, it does."

Luckily for him, at the exact moment when he'd be expected to say something in response, two teenage girls approached Winona and asked if she'd do a reading for one of them. Apparently, the redhead had a crush on a boy who hadn't looked her way once during the entire reception.

"Oh, there are my twin brothers," Brandon said fast, eyeing Dirk and Dustin by the bar. "Nice to see you again, Miss Winona."

She narrowed her eyes at him, but turned her attention to the girls, and he fled for the stand of maples, grabbing an unopened bottle of champagne from a passing waiter's tray. He loosened his bow tie and slipped through the trees, the strains of Ella Fitzgerald's "At Last"—the band's version—following him. He glanced beyond at the side yard. Empty. Two trees to the left and one up ahead, he'd be hidden from view and could then take the short path to the stables. Horses always had a calming effect on him. A twenty-minute breather and he'd head back to the wedding.

Brandon entered the stables and walked down to the far end, where he knew he'd find an overstuffed chair with a little table beside it and a view of one of his favorite Appaloosas, Starlight, with her brown-and-white spotted back and flanks. But as he approached, he was surprised to see two long shapely legs crossed at the ankles, the feet bare, a pair of sexy silver high heels beside the chair. Who the gorgeous legs belonged to was a mystery, since the rest of the woman was hidden by a post.

Whoever she was, she clearly heard him coming because he heard a female voice mutter, "Not a moment to myself. Figures, right, pretty horsie?" and the legs pulled out of view.

Oh.

He knew that voice. Cassidy Ware.

She hated his guts. Had for over fifteen years. And *he* avoided her at all costs, which meant never going into

Bronco Java and Juice, the shop she owned in town. A shame since everyone said she had both the best coffee in Bronco and the best strawberry-banana smoothies, a favorite of his. In all these years of avoiding the shop, he still hadn't gotten better at making a decent mug of coffee or getting the ratios right for his smoothies. Made him add to his list of grievances against Cassidy.

As he approached in the dim lighting, he passed Starlight's stall and there Cassidy was, sitting straight, arms crossed, staring daggers at him.

"Oh, it's you," she practically spat.

"Ditto," he said, narrowing his eyes at her.

Damn, she was pretty. Long, swirly blond hair past her shoulders, huge hazel eyes and delicate features. He'd always thought she looked like an angel. But she had a mind and mouth like the devil.

"Look, Taylor, I know your family owns the place, but I came out here to be alone, so…"

"*I* came out here to be alone," he countered. "And like you said, my family owns the place, so…"

She scowled. "You're as insufferable as ever. God, even on my birthday I can't catch a break."

He tilted his head. "It's your birthday?" He must have known that at one point, but it had been a long time since he knew anything about Cassidy Ware.

She let a sigh pass over her glossy pink-red lips. "Happy thirtieth birthday to me," she sang.

"Happy birthday, dear Cassidy," he sang-added in his terrible baritone. "Happy birthday to you."

She laughed. "Well, thanks. But you can go now." She eyed the champagne. "Leave that, though, will you?"

Interesting. She'd also escaped the wedding to come out here, hiding from who knew what. He'd spotted her earlier in the kitchen, placing bite-size confections on a giant tray. His brother had mentioned that Camilla had hired Bronco Java and Juice to cater the nonalcoholic refreshments and desserts, including the wedding cake. Cassidy had probably been paid a small fortune. But she certainly didn't look happy. Then again, did she ever? Of course, it was possible that he associated her with a grimace because every time he ran into Cassidy around town, she crossed the street to avoid him. For all he knew, she could be the happiest woman on earth.

Except for her expression and slumped shoulders. Some birthday.

Oh, hell. He noticed a folding chair in the corner, grabbed it and then set it up beside her. "Tell you what. Because it's your birthday, you can have a slug. The rest is mine."

"You always were so thoughtful," she muttered, holding out her hand for the bottle.

He couldn't help but notice the lack of rings on her long, slender fingers. Not a surprise—first of all, Bronco was a very small town and he would have heard if she'd gotten married.

And second of all, she's completely *intolerable*, he thought, popping the champagne and handing her the bottle.

Some breather this would be.

Cassidy glanced over at Brandon, all six-feet-three of him stretched out in a well-fitting tux, bow tie askew, in a folding chair. His close-cropped dark hair made every angle of his gorgeous face visible, his strong nose and jaw, the intense dark eyes. Back when she'd had a mad crush on him as a freshman and had actually dated him for a few months, he'd been the cutest guy at Bronco High, and now he was so hot she could barely drag her eyes off him. His effortless hold over her had always been so unfair.

She took the bottle and lifted it in a silent *cheers*, then took a long sip. Then another. Ah, that was good.

Could her thirtieth birthday get any harder? The day had started out well enough. She'd been excited about tonight, taking part in the catering of such a fancy wedding at the Taylor Ranch. She'd been sure she wouldn't run into Brandon, nemesis for life, since the property was so big and there were three hundred and seventy-six guests. Everything had gone off without a hitch; she'd gotten so many compliments on her miniature pastries and tiny cookies and juice concoctions, which were available at the bar. But then word of her birthday had spread at the reception and the thirty-and-single nonsense had started.

Engaged and married former classmates had said, "Cassidy, be sure to line up for the bouquet toss so you can be next." Fake smile, giggle. Mariel Jones, a married accountant with two adorable twin toddlers, had said, "Oh, how sweet that you're catering the desserts. A big wedding like this probably pays months of your bills over at that little shop of yours."

Why were people so rude? And, dagnabbit, yes, this gig would help cover the slide into the cooler fall months and winter when business tended to slow down. April through early November, everyone wanted their mango-berry smoothies and ice mocha lattes and, of course, one of her decadent treats to go with them. Now, with the still beautiful early September weather, she had brisk business. But come December, folks wouldn't be venturing out as much in single-digit Montana temperatures. The fee for catering the Sanchez-Taylor wedding would be a nice boost, but she'd need more where that had come from.

And despite the great gig, she couldn't help but look around at all the accomplished, wealthy guests and wonder why she hadn't been able to make her goals come to fruition. Yes, she had her own business, and it was popular in Bronco Heights. But back when she'd been twenty-five, full of grit and determination, she'd made a business plan that had impressed Bronco Bank and Trust enough for the small loan she'd taken out to open the shop. She'd intended to have a chain of Java and Juices across Montana to start, including in city hotels like down in Billings. But, nope, five years later, at age thirty, everything was exactly the same. Cassidy was grateful for what she did have, but she'd really thought she'd be able to expand by now.

"Remember the bets we made?" Brandon asked, taking the bottle of champagne for a long slug and then handing it back to her.

She gaped at him, shocked *he* actually remembered. They'd been boyfriend-girlfriend for a few months when she'd been a freshman and he a big-man-on-campus senior. Between her mom giving her a hard time about dating a boy "who is too old for you and very likely used to getting *anything* he wants, given his family name" and the girls throwing themselves at him, she and Brandon hadn't really had a chance back then. She was constantly jealous of the older girls flirting with him and his friendliness back.

Once, toward the end, she'd accused him of standing her up for a date and catching him with another girl in the library, and then realized she'd made the mistake—the wrong day and the girl was Brandon's lab partner and already engaged to her own high school sweetheart. It had all just been bad timing back then and she'd been too young for Brandon Taylor in every way. She'd been in over her head and had broken up with him. But then he'd told everyone he'd broken up with her and, for some immature reason, that had rankled. She'd made a fuss, he'd shrugged, and they'd been antagonistic toward each other since, throwing little barbs that didn't really sting.

She'd tried to avoid him since, impossible in a town like Bronco, so the times they did run into each other, they'd just pretend they didn't see each other.

She thought back to that final day of their romance, the back-and-forth arguing in a back stairwell at Bronco High, Cassidy saying there was no way they'd make it as a couple to the end of the day, let alone the week. Brandon had agreed. That was when they'd flung their insult bets at each other.

"You'd bet that I'd be on my sixth child at age thirty," she said. "Well, I'm not even on number *one*. Hell, I don't even have a man in my life."

He stared at her and seemed about to say something, but didn't, just accepted the champagne bottle back from her and took another swig before handing it back. "And you'd bet that I'd be on my third marriage." He laughed, but his big grin soon faded.

"Instead, we're both single, no kids, hiding out in the stables during your brother's wedding. Whodathunk?" she asked.

"Gimme back that bottle," he said with a smile.

But she could see he was lost in thought and she wondered about what. An ex-girlfriend who'd gotten away? His own unfulfilled goals?

What *were* his goals, though? He was from the richest family in town, worked at Taylor Ranch in some cowboy-meets-executive capacity, and had everything he'd ever wanted. If Brandon Taylor wanted to be married, he would be.

"Why *are* you here?" she asked, surprised that she really wanted to know what had driven him from the wedding.

"The usual in-your-face questions from relatives I haven't seen in months or years," he said, his dark eyes on her. Then he looked toward the pretty horse in the stall across from them. "And my dad, as usual. One conversation with him and I need to decompress."

"Yeah?" she asked, her own father coming to mind. He'd left her mother—and her—when she was just shy of her first birthday. *I'm really sorry, but I'm just not cut out for marriage or fatherhood*, the cowboy had written in a note. He'd sent her mom money and a birthday card every year for Cassidy until she was eight, when he'd either completely forgotten she existed or had been just done with all that. Right or wrong, Cassidy had kept her distance from good-looking cowboys.

Brandon Taylor might not have to get his hands dirty, but he was a cowboy through and through. Mega rich made it worse. The entitlement and arrogance.

"He makes life on the ranch almost unbearable," he said, staring down at the floor. "You'd think trying to boss his three brothers—all equal partners in Taylor Beef—would keep him satisfied. But no, he has to try to control his five adult children." He shook his head and took another drink of the champagne, then passed it back. "Lately I've been thinking about what I really want out of life."

She stared at him, surprised he'd opened up. She didn't have experience with a controlling dad, of course. Her late mom had always been so busy trying to make ends meet that she'd given Cassidy a lot of responsibility to make the right choices. Cassidy always had. "Yeah, me, too. I mean, I know what I want. I just can't seem to make it happen."

"Those six kids?" he asked. "A husband?"

She narrowed her gaze. "I was referring to my goals for Bronco Java and Juice. I thought I'd have expanded by now. But it's just the one small place." She shrugged, taking another drink of champagne, then handing it over to him. She truly wasn't caught up in being thirty and single. Marriage wasn't on her mind. Maybe because she'd never found the right guy. She'd had relationships, but one of them always left. Sometimes she thought her heart just wasn't in the idea of marriage. She'd been too young to witness her mother's heartache at being abandoned by her child's father, but she'd grown up with her mom's dictums. *Never depend on a man... Make your own way... Be independent... Don't expect anyone to rescue you. If you get in trouble, rescue yourself.*

So here Cassidy was, Miss Independence. With not as much to show for it as she'd planned.

"I really did like you back in high school," he said suddenly, sliding his gaze to hers. "Sorry I acted like an idiot. You did dump me and I wanted to save face."

Cassidy smiled. She wasn't about to tell him how much she'd liked him then, that he was her first love and that she'd never really gotten over him. Yes, Brandon Taylor had been a golden boy. But a smart one who'd worked hard for good grades, who'd tutored classmates for free in math, his best subject, who'd been friendly to everyone instead of a stuck-up jerk like a few of his teammates on the football and baseball teams. He'd defended the picked-on from bullies. And the way he'd talk about horses, his admiration of them and knowledge and intention to make them his life's work at the Taylor Ranch, had held her rapt. She used to ask him about his family and it had taken her a while to realize he only talked about his three brothers and sister, never his parents, who were clearly a source of agita. Those times she'd seen Brandon in town over the years? The words *unfinished business* always echoed in her head along with the red alert to avoid him.

"Well," she said, feeling a little Brandon-size crack in her heart widen, "an apology fifteen years in the making. I'll take it."

He laughed and passed her the bottle, which she raised to him and then drank from before passing it back. There wasn't much left.

"So about our bets," she said. "You're supposed to be on wife number three. Did you just never meet the right woman?"

He leaned back in his chair, his eyes moving to the Appaloosa, then back to Cassidy. "Don't much believe in it, I guess. Marriage hasn't exactly worked out too well for my parents—my dad's the one who's been married three times, though he and Jessica do seem happy. For now. And my mom? Haven't seen her since she left when I was five."

She almost gasped. She hadn't known any of that. Brandon rarely talked about his parents back when they were dating. "I never knew my dad. And my mom never got married, which had once been a dream of hers. She fell in love with a ranch hand who sweet-talked her, and he left before I turned a year old. She kept asking where her ring was, and he kept saying he was saving up to afford a diamond worthy of her, with the next purse he won. He left instead. So, to be honest, I'm not much interested in marriage myself. Maybe I don't believe in it, either. I don't know anymore."

"Well, aren't we a pair," he said, tilting the bottle back. He handed it to her. "I saved you the last few sips."

She smiled. "Huh. I'd sarcastically called you thoughtful earlier, but you do seem to be just that."

"Not the bad guy you thought I was the last fifteen years."

"No," she said, finding herself leaning toward him just a bit, her gaze on his mouth. She'd kissed those lips many times ages ago. She remembered exactly how every nerve ending in her body had lit up when he'd held her close. That was Brandon the teenager. Brandon the man? Whew. She let her eyes travel down his long, muscular body in that black tux. Maybe *too* much man for her. Too much cowboy. He might be a good guy in general, but she'd seen him with a lot of different women over the years, one prettier than the next. Just last week she'd spied him through the window in Bronco Brick Oven Pizza with a gorgeous redhead. "When it comes to women, I'm sure you haven't changed a bit, Brandon Taylor."

He smiled that dazzling smile of this, the one that had always made her forget where she was—and all rational thought. "All I know for sure about you is that you're as beautiful as ever, Cassidy Ware."

Maybe she'd needed a compliment tonight on her thirtieth birthday. Because she was suddenly warming to Brandon. A little too much. She couldn't stop staring at his lips.

"What did we bet?" he asked. "I mean, what was the winner and loser supposed to get? That I actually can't remember."

She grinned. After they'd made their bets, she'd realized they were really just proclamations without anything to win or lose, and she'd demanded he eat his words if what he said about her didn't come true. "You said, and I quote, 'Fifteen years from now, whoever wins their bet gets bragging rights. Whoever loses has to wallow in being wrong. And if we both end up wrong, we'll have to kiss and make up and then go our separate ways forever.'"

"Well, we were both wrong," he said, holding her gaze, which dropped to her lips, then back up to her eyes. For a moment, she caught him slide a glance along her silky pale pink cocktail dress.

Kiss and make up. Kiss and make up...

Before she could even blink, the bottle was on the floor, empty, and they were kissing, Brandon's hands in her hair, her hands splayed against his chest, moving up to his neck and to his chiseled face.

He pulled back slightly. "Tell me to go back to the wedding. Or we might do something you'll probably regret. I *haven't* changed a bit. And we've had way too much to drink, Cass."

She liked how he used to sometimes call her Cass.

"We have," she agreed, the intoxicating scent of his cologne enveloping her. "But I don't think I'll regret anything."

Yes, she was tipsy. But it was her birthday and she'd been feeling sorry for herself not an hour ago. A secret birthday rendezvous with the man she'd never forgotten? The one who'd gotten away? *Finished* business after all these years?

"Me, either," he whispered. "But that might be the moment talking for both of us. You sure about this?"

He looked at her, his dark eyes probing and sincere instead of flirtatious and glib, and she knew he was giving her another moment to come to her senses.

She grabbed the lapels of his tux and kissed him hot and heavy on the lips. She would not regret this. After all, tomorrow, all kissed and made up, they'd go their separate ways—forever.

But tonight? She *needed* this.

Chapter 2

Oh, yeah! Cassidy thought, eyes closed, back arched, lips ready for more. *Happy birthday to me!*

She opened her eyes when she realized she was wasting precious seconds of not looking up close and very personal at Brandon. She'd already unbuttoned his fancy white shirt when they'd moved into an empty, clean stall, and he'd flung the garment into a heap by the door.

Her gaze roamed over his gorgeous face, down the strong cords of his neck to his magnificent rock-hard chest and farther down to where a line of soft dark hair disappeared into the waistband of his tuxedo pants.

Brandon kissed her lips, her forehead, her neck as both of his hands reached behind her to unzip her dress, and she shimmied out of it. The straw under her was both soft and rough, which was fine with her.

She hadn't been expecting anyone to see her in her sexy pale pink lacy bra and matching undies tonight, but she was darn glad she'd worn them.

"Oh, Cassidy," he breathed, looking her up and down, down and up. "You are still so damned beautiful."

"You, too," she whispered, taking his face in her hands and kissing him, softly, passionately, and then with all the desire coursing through her body.

He let out a groan and his fingers were suddenly inside her bra, which was then quickly removed, his mouth on her breasts, her hands in his hair. She was kissing his neck when she felt her undies being inched down her hips. They could not come off fast enough.

As he kissed his way down her stomach, she almost screamed with pleasure before she remembered, barely, where she was. She practically had to bite down on her fist.

She reached for the button on his pants and the zipper, which elicited another groan from Brandon. In moments they were naked on the hay, this man she'd never been able to forget lying on top of her. She heard him grab his pants and take something out, followed by the unmistakable tear of a condom wrapper.

And then he looked at her, his dark eyes intense, before he kissed her with so much passion she had to have him inside her, one with her, immediately.

"Cassidy," he whispered. "You're everything."

I'm everything, she thought tipsily and happily. *I'm everything to someone...* And not just someone. Brandon Taylor, still special to her after all these years, no matter what she'd said or thought.

But suddenly she couldn't form another thought. Because for the first time ever, Brandon Taylor was making love to her. And the reality was even hotter than her traitorous fantasies since her school days.

"You have a piece of hay in your hair," Brandon said on a smile, reaching to pluck it out.

Cassidy grinned. "You, too." She grabbed it from near his ear and tossed it on the floor.

Being with Brandon, even though they were tipsy, was like nothing she'd ever experienced.

It wasn't just the insane levels of passion. But the unexpected tenderness. The way he'd stop for a second and just looked into her eyes, gently holding her face. Like that old song said, it was in his kiss. It was in everything Brandon had done to her. And she'd given it back with everything she'd had.

Now they lay on the floor, the scratchy hay not exactly Egyptian cotton sheets, but she couldn't be any more comfortable or relaxed. She could lie there forever. They both were looking up at the ceiling, at the wood beams of the barn with the dangling electric lanterns, and as if he felt exactly the same way she did, he clasped her hand.

He'd said he hadn't changed, but he sure had. She could tell just in the way he held her hand, a silent acknowledgment of *something*. Though, of course, they hadn't had sex back in high school for her to make any comparisons, but there hadn't been much in the way of poetic gestures back then.

"Well," he said, turning his head to face her before letting go of her hand and suddenly sitting up. "I guess we'd better get back to the wedding or someone might send a search party for us." He reached for his white shirt and slipped it on, then found his bow tie half buried in the hay.

Dismissed. Could the splash of water over her head feel any icier?

She forced a fake chuckle and reached for her dress, suddenly feeling very exposed. She turned and put on her bra and undies, then slid the dress over her head and popped up, dusting herself off.

"Do I look like I was rolling around the floor of a barn?" she asked, trying to make light.

He studied her for a second. "No. You look absolutely beautiful, as always. No one would ever guess what went on here."

I barely would, she thought, turning away so he wouldn't see whatever strange expression was on her face. Disappointment. Embarrassment—for wanting more from him right now.

A half hour ago, she'd liked how earnest he could suddenly be, the sincerity in his voice moving. Now, a chill ran up the nape of her neck. This was Brandon Taylor. He could make you feel like the only woman in the world and then, a second later, remind you who he really was when it came to relationships.

A man who wanted to get the hell away from said woman and back to the wedding he hadn't been able to escape from fast enough.

That she really was slightly singed over this made her feel even worse. Stupider. What had she expected or wanted? Brandon to magically announce he was madly in love with her and carry her back to the wedding, where they'd dance every dance?

No, of course not. But something more than *wham-bam-thank-you-ma'am*, which was exactly what this felt like.

Oh, stop it, Cassidy, she told herself. *You're not Cinderella. He's no prince.* She spied her shoes—one wasn't lost on the castle steps, she hadn't gone from her pretty dress to tattered rags—and slid her feet into them. *This is exactly what you both set it up to be and he even made double sure you were in.*

So rescue yourself, she heard her mother say.

She was feeling a little bruised, so she'd simply go get happy and enjoy her thirtieth birthday. Go back to the wedding, listen to people compliment her on the gorgeous wedding cake that she knew would be scrumptious and bring in tons more business with future wedding cake orders. Have her prime rib dinner, dance a few dances with friends, and then go home.

And forget about Brandon.

Nothing to see here, nothing to be mad about.

"Well, well," she said as lightly as she could. "We made good on the bets. We kissed. We made up. Now we go our separate ways."

"Forever," he added.

She turned her head so suddenly to stare at him that she almost gave herself whiplash. *Forever.* Well, she knew where she stood with him.

He was dressed, too, now, but his bow tie was crooked, so she straightened it, aware that his eyes were on her. "Cassidy, I—"

She waited. "You what?" she asked when nothing else seemed to be coming.

"That was really something," he said, holding her gaze for a moment.

She felt a pang in her chest. What the hell was wrong with her? Why did she seem to be expecting something else from Brandon Taylor? Come on, Cassidy!

"Yeah, it was," she said, running a hand through her hair for more hay pieces.

"Shall we?" he asked, gesturing toward the high wooden gate of the stall.

There is no we, she wanted to scream. Instead, she calmly opened the door and walked out, then back along the long aisle of the stables and into the refreshing night air.

The last thing she needed was for anyone to notice her slipping into the yard with Brandon. She needed to keep this their little secret. "Well, I'll just scurry up ahead. Bronco is a small town and we don't want to be the big gossip of the wedding. Everyone knows we're supposed to hate each other."

"Actually, Cassidy, if people think we're a thing, maybe they'll stop telling me all about their single daughters, nieces and third cousins once removed and handing me phone numbers and cards."

"Yeah, that's gotta be rough," she said with a roll of her eyes. This was exactly what she needed. More of the Brandon Taylor she expected, the guy she always figured he was.

He nodded earnestly, adding to her ire. Perfect.

"Well, bye," she said and slipped off her heels again, grabbing them in one hand and dashing for the stand of majestic trees that would lead into the backyard where the reception was being held. Pressing a hand against the bark of a maple for support, she put her shoes on, lifted her chin, and came through the trees.

The good news was that the yard was the size of a football field, the reception area half of that, a vast space crowded with guests standing and chatting and enjoying refreshments. No one seemed to notice her as she slipped into the scene. The band was playing an old Bee Gees song. Cassidy headed to the buffet table, where she piled a plate with enough hors d'oeuvres to combat the effects of the champagne. She ate a smoked salmon crostini just as Brandon came through the trees.

Goose bumps trailed up the nape of her neck. Damn it. They'd just been as intimate as two people could be and now they were back to acquaintances. She didn't like how that felt one bit. She hadn't been intimate with a man in almost a year until now, but instead of feeling all energized and *yeah-I-needed-that*, she felt...alone. Cassidy and casual sex had never mixed.

At least she and Brandon had a truce, the old cold war settled. So now what? They'd politely smile if they ran into each other in the grocery store? Did Brandon Taylor even buy his own groceries? Probably not.

But he could finally come into Bronco Java and Juice, a place she'd long suspected he'd avoided because of her. Good. She could use his business. God knew the Taylor Beef boys didn't worry about the price of triple espresso lattes. Then again, she had a feeling Brandon would keep avoiding her, just for a very different reason this time.

She had no doubt there were many women in Bronco he took pains not to run into.

Cassidy ate a miniature mushroom empanada and watched as woman after woman chatted up Brandon as he moved through the crowd. Lots of cheek kisses. Lots of manicured hands running up his arms for no good reason. And there was Brandon Taylor's dazzling smile, loving it, no matter what he said about the rough life of having phone numbers thrown at him all night.

Now Sofia Sanchez, the bride's very attractive sister, whom Brandon had once dated, walked over to him and kissed his cheek, and they were both laughing at something.

Cassidy narrowed her eyes at them.

She knew what this awful feeling was. Jealousy. And she didn't like *that*, either.

She turned away and popped another tiny appetizer into her mouth. Dinner would be served at eight, her cake at nine. Once the cake was served, she could probably sneak out and head home—and hide under the covers till the morning light and a new day that would make this all feel like a dream.

Go our separate ways forever...

"May I have this dance?" said a familiar deep voice.

She whirled around to find Brandon holding out his hand. This was the opposite of avoiding her. Interesting.

Cassidy was so surprised that she reacted before she could think it through. She put her empty plate down and took his hand. He led her to the edge of the dance floor and they slow danced to the band's version of a Kacey Musgraves song that Cassidy loved. Brandon held her close and, with her eyes closed for a few moments, she was transported back to the stables, back to when they were one. All too soon, the song was over and Brandon was being called away for "extended family photos" with the bride and groom.

Completely off-kilter, Cassidy watched him head off with the group, taking a path that led to the front of the luxe log mansion. She could still smell that delicious cologne of his.

"Oooh, I thought you two hated each other," whispered a female voice from behind her.

Cassidy turned to find her friend Callie Sheldrick holding a small plate with a few hors d'oeuvres, her brown eyes wide with curiosity.

Cassidy bit her lip. "We ran into each other is all. A dance for old times."

"I thought old times were bad, though," Callie said with a gleam lighting her face. "You haven't had a good thing to say about Brandon since I've known you."

"He's a good dancer," Cassidy said.

Callie narrowed her eyes and grinned. "Something in the air between you two?"

Cassidy sighed. "Probably not. He's Brandon Taylor. Ultimate ladies' man."

"Eh, they're only ladies' men until they fall in love." Callie wriggled her eyebrows and popped a bite-size bruschetta in her mouth.

Cassidy took in that golden nugget. She supposed that could be true. Not that Callie had much experience with players, lucky for her. Her friend had fallen hard for Tyler Abernathy—anything but a ladies' man—a widowed rancher with an adorable baby daughter, and now they were a committed couple.

The band started playing a Frank Sinatra song and Callie was pulled away by her boyfriend, Tyler, for a dance. The song was almost over when Brandon reappeared and, once again, Cassidy was in his arms.

After the song, she would tell him to turn his attention elsewhere.

"Look, Cassidy," he said. "You probably expect the worst from me and I don't want to live up to that, so I'm going to be very honest."

She pulled back a bit to look up at him. "Okay," she said, bracing herself. She wanted honesty. She needed the second splash of cold water on her head.

"We had a pretty serious conversation earlier about how we both feel about marriage…" he began. "Neither of us is interested in all that, right? I just don't believe in commitment. That way, I don't hurt anyone, either."

"And you're telling me this because…?"

"Because for the twenty minutes I was away from you, I wanted to be back with you," he said. "I have a thing for you, Cassidy Ware."

She laughed despite herself. He wanted her to a point. Was that what he was saying? Unbelievable.

"And so I'd like to propose a possible arrangement," he added, "if you're interested."

She could feel the smile slide off her face. Oh, Brandon. She sighed inwardly, exhausted, and it wasn't even eight o'clock at night.

"Let's see each other," he said. "Date. With no strings. Just two people enjoying themselves and each other. Like earlier in the stables."

Yup, this was exactly what she'd expected of Brandon Taylor. "I don't think so. But thanks for your interest."

"I *am* interested, Cassidy. And, really, why not? We both want the same thing—no ties. And we're clearly good together. So let's have all the good parts of a relationship without the stuff that invariably mucks it up."

She'd said that, that she didn't believe much in marriage. But was that really true? She wasn't sure. She might not think much of relationships working out, given her family's past and her own track record, but that didn't mean the idea of a no-strings relationship held much appeal. There was just something…empty about it.

"Well, think about it," he said.

She wouldn't. But, for a moment, she pictured the two of them in her bed. Why was her body such a traitor? She stood there, looking at him, and yes, she wanted to be kissing him. *Could* they have a no-expectations fling until it ran its course? They'd get each other out of their systems. Maybe that was what this was about. The unexpected opening up in the stables. The rendezvous in the stall. The dances. A few weeks of dating and they'd fizzle, and then they truly could go their separate ways. Forever. With no one getting hurt.

It wasn't like she'd fall in love with Brandon Taylor. Not with what she knew about his romantic history. She had big plans and ideas for her future, all involving Bronco Java and Juice. That was her focus right now. Meeting her goals—which didn't include a serious relationship.

"What's your cell number?" he asked, taking out

his phone. "I'll text you a 'hi' right now so you'll have my number. Call or text anytime. Really. Any. Time."

She recited her number and, in moments, her phone pinged. "I'll sleep on it," she told him, but she wouldn't give it a moment's serious thought. Flings could be fun if everything lined up. But there was too much history between her and Brandon, too much...*there*. Cassidy couldn't quite explain what that *there* was, exactly, but he wasn't just some random hot guy. Or a guy she didn't have feelings for. Her unexpected disappointment at the way she'd felt dismissed at the stables came flooding back. The sex over, there had been no conversation, just one clasp of the hands that she'd foolishly read way too much into. And then, *Well, I guess we'd better get back to the wedding or someone might send a search party for us.*

That was what being involved with Brandon would be like. Cassidy just wasn't cut out for that. Maybe if she didn't care—again, about *what* exactly she didn't know. But she did care.

He was pulled away yet again—more family pictures. Then it was time for dinner, so everyone took their seats. Brandon was at the family table.

Cassidy had been invited to the wedding by the bride herself, who'd been so kind to offer her the job of catering dessert. She checked her table number. Fourteen. She was far, far away from the family table, which was a good thing. She needed a break from Brandon Taylor. And she also needed that prime rib to sober her up even more. But as she headed for her table, which seemed to be filled with singles, she felt eyes on her and, when she glanced around, she saw the very elderly Winona

Cobbs, with her purple cowboy hat and snazzy silver boa around her neck, staring at her with a strange smile.

Cassidy felt a chill go through her. Winona was psychic. Everyone knew that. She had her own little shop, Wisdom by Winona. Maybe Cassidy would stop in sometime and get herself a reading. Right about now, she could use a look into her future.

A few days later, Brandon sat at his desk in his home office on the first floor of the family ranch, trying to focus on the spreadsheet of numbers and accompanying graphs. Brandon was an executive vice president at Taylor Beef, which had its own office building, but he'd stayed close to home since the wedding. Since Cassidy. Right now he was supposed to be analyzing projected third-quarter sales figures, but all he could think about was her.

Thing was, his mind wasn't on what it was usually on when he thought about a woman he was very attracted to. Usually, he'd go over every delectable detail of their time together in anticipation of the next time. That would have him calling and texting. Instead, he was thinking about Cassidy herself. The girl he remembered—smart and opinionated and full of ideas and plans for herself. The woman she was now—a surprise. He hadn't expected to feel so…connected, as if they were on the same plane, same page. He'd thought they'd be like oil and water and instead they were like milk and cookies.

He could count on one hand the number of times he'd felt like that about a woman he was dating. Three times, to be exact.

Marley O'Kane's beautiful face appeared like a scary mask in his mind's eye. The former Miss Mid-Region Montana who "couldn't afford to pay for her gravely ill, beloved granny's cancer treatment" turned out to be a grifting liar. "Granny" was really a boyfriend in perfect health with a gambling addiction and a loan shark after him. Marley was a decent actress who'd actually studied up on Brandon to win him over because he was a Taylor and she'd thought her model-like looks would earn her some blank checks. He'd been twenty-two and about to write that first check to Marley until his sister had sat him down and reported seeing Marley and another man all over each other at an Italian restaurant. A look into her background had revealed everything.

It had taken two years to get past his stupidity and gullibility and to let himself feel something again for a woman he was dating. Didi Philbin might not have been a duplicitous cheat like Marley, but after six months, she'd broken up with him for someone else, and he'd been blindsided and more damned hurt than he'd admitted to anyone.

He'd let a good few years pass before he'd fallen for another woman, but he'd apparently had so many walls up that she'd told him being in a relationship with him was like being involved with a brick wall and that she'd had enough of trying to break through. His first reaction was that he'd work on it, he'd *try*, but not one brick dislodged and the lady had moved on.

So Brandon had stuck to flings and short-term romances where his lack of interest in commitment was stated up front. No one had gotten under his skin in a few years now, and Brandon found he liked it that way. There was something peaceful about it.

Except now he couldn't get Cassidy Ware out of his head. And that wasn't a good thing. Between his track record and his family history, he'd never commit and he'd never marry. His father had plenty of offspring to carry on the Taylor name. Jordan and Camilla would likely be giving Cornelius a new generation of heirs in no time. The way Brandon saw it, people either walked out on you or disappointed you or operated conditionally. And he was certainly no different or better than most. Ask any of the women he'd dated the past few years, many whom had deserved better than they'd gotten from him.

So in the few days since their night together, he hadn't gotten in touch with Cassidy. Not a word. That didn't sit right, but every time he grabbed his phone with the intention of sending a lighthearted text, he put it back in his pocket. And he felt all unsettled. Their last conversation had been about casual sex. A no-strings affair. Cassidy had agreed to "sleep on it," though he'd known full well she'd tell him to jump in a lake. Of course, she hadn't called or texted, either, to give her answer. So there was Brandon's "no." That was a good thing.

We kissed and made up and went our separate ways. Forever.

The idea of that—the word *forever*—left him weirdly unsettled, too.

He should just continue on, focus on work, and in a week or two, he'd barely remember the night in the stables. The Cassidy question settled somewhat, he picked up the printout of graphs on the quarter's numbers.

Before he could even attempt to concentrate, Brandon heard heavy footsteps approaching, which could only be his father. Cornelius Taylor was an imposing man, tall, like his sons, at six feet three with a shock of silver hair usually covered by a Stetson.

"Ah, just the son I wanted to see," his dad said, his large frame filling the doorway. "I have a surprise for you. Just turn around and take a look out the window and tell me what you think."

Probably a new horse, Brandon thought as he raised an eyebrow at his dad. Brandon's true passion on the ranch was the horses, but with a foreman, stable manager and many cowboys and cowgirls, the horses were covered. Brandon was a numbers guy, and Taylor Beef was about cattle, so his area of expertise had focused on that.

Brandon wheeled his chair around and looked out past the wide front porch to the vast property, the gorgeous view of land and trees and sky. He noticed a woman, a twentysomething brunette in a tight white dress and high heels, holding some kind of tablet and looking around. He had no idea who she was.

"She's single," his dad said. "Comes from a great family. Know the Farringtons? Relatively new to Bronco Heights. Bought the Double G."

Brandon turned to his father. "And you're telling me this because…?"

Cornelius Taylor walked over to the window. "Because two birds, my son. Two birds."

Birds? What?

"Leila's an award-winning architect," Cornelius added. "I've hired her to scope out a good section of our land for a prime location for the house she'll design—for you and your future family. Who knows? Maybe you two will fall madly in love like some Christmas TV movie." He chuckled. "You get your wife and your house in one."

Brandon was *not* chuckling. In fact, he was frowning so hard his face was beginning to ache. "There's a lot to cover in what you just said, Dad. But let's start with the house that I'm not interested in."

"Oh please," Cornelius said dismissively in a booming voice, waving his hand at Brandon. "Of course you need a grand house of your own. You're thirty-four. And when you find yourself a wife, you'll have your dream home waiting for you. Win-win. Let's go chat with Leila, shall we? Did I mention she was on the team of architects who designed BH247, that exclusive apartment complex right in town?"

Cornelius turned and headed for the door. Brandon stayed right where he was.

His dad stopped in the doorway. "Well, come on. You can talk about what style you're looking for. Log mansion? Luxe farmhouse? Of course we'll make sure the home is situated near this house so you and the family can easily come over for Sunday dinners."

It was that last part that had Brandon changing his tone. His dad was a control freak, but at heart, the man just wanted his family around the big table for pot roast. Brandon's sister had told him that, when she got really mad at their dad, she'd think of their mother, Cornelius's first wife, walking out on him, on her family, leaving him with confused young kids. Cornelius had been a workaholic, but he'd been there for his children in important ways back then. Daphne had said she knew it wasn't an excuse for their dad's controlling behavior, but it helped her understand him a bit better and be less hard on herself for not hating him for how he'd treated her since she'd moved out to start Happy Hearts.

Brandon got it. He really did. But he thought his father had gone too far with Daphne. And Cornelius was going too far now. Overstepping was the man's middle name.

"Dad, I know you mean well, but you're going to have to send Ms. Farrington on her way. I'm not in the market for a house. Or a wife. End of conversation."

Cornelius scowled. "I'll tell you what your problem is, Brandon."

Second time in a week that someone had said that to him.

"You're being offered a mansion on the property and you're turning it down," his father said. "You're your own worst enemy."

"I like my life the way it is," Brandon said. His father's only reason for building him a home on the ranch was to keep him on the ranch. That wasn't in doubt.

His father shook his head and raised his pointer finger to make another accusatory pronouncement, but he rolled his eyes and left, shaking his head.

Brandon turned toward the window and watched his father walk up to the architect and throw up his hands. Then he heard his dad calling out, "Hey, Dirk," and saw his brother getting out of his pickup. The twins—sons from his second marriage—hadn't grown up on the ranch and didn't live here now, but Cornelius had always told them they were welcome anytime. Both liked to ride and often made use of the stables.

Run, Dirk, run, Brandon said to himself, shaking his own head. But his younger brother was trapped, and now the three of them were getting into the brunette's Range Rover and off to scout house locations. Poor Dirk probably didn't know what had hit him. Brandon had no doubt Dirk would warn Dustin to make himself scarce in the days ahead.

Brandon spun himself back around and put his feet up on the desk, next to the work he was supposed to be doing. At least he wasn't in a hot fury.

A few months ago, this kind of controlling stunt from his dad would have had Brandon all pissed off, especially because of the way Cornelius was keeping up his pointless cold war with Daphne, who'd had the gall to want her own life. His conversation with his dad would have ended quickly in raised voices and a slammed door. Now, thanks to his sister's empathy, Brandon had been focusing on trying to understand his father more, even if he didn't like it. Cornelius Taylor didn't want to lose any of his children, plain and simple. He wanted them right there in the main house, which was why he'd built addition after addition, usually with each of his marriages, to make the wings bigger and bigger. He still referred to the wing where Brandon's suite was located as the "kids' wing." Brandon could go weeks in the kids' wing without hearing another suite door open. That was how huge it was.

Brandon fully believed that his father was happy about Jordan's marriage, but he also had no doubt Cornelius was hatching plans to build Jordan and Camilla a villa on the property. Luckily, the two were on their honeymoon for a couple of weeks and didn't have to deal with Cornelius. But with Daphne having left the nest, Cornelius Taylor was digging his hooks into his second born—Brandon—who'd always been something of a wild card that couldn't be labeled or boxed. His father had a problem with that.

Cassidy Ware's lovely face and big hazel eyes floated into his mind, and what a lovely distraction it was. Perhaps he'd head over to Bronco Java and Juice for a strawberry-banana smoothie just to see Cassidy, to say hello. He could say something to let her know he hadn't just disappeared on her, that he knew she'd never take him up on his casual sex offer and he wanted to give them both some time to put the past to rest—again.

But just as he grabbed his jacket, he started thinking. And thinking. And thinking some more. He'd see Cassidy and want to kiss her. He'd ask her out on a proper date and maybe she'd say yes. Then suddenly they'd be dating. Seeing each other. She'd want more than he could give, and they'd be at each other's throats.

A montage of the romances that had almost undone him went barreling through his head. He had a thing for Cassidy and, if he gave in to it, he'd no doubt be adding her to his record of relationships that had come to a bruising end for whatever reason. Stick to the usual, he told himself. Flings and the short-term.

He threw his jacket on the love seat, sat back down and picked up the sheet of sales projections, but every time he tried to focus on the graphs, all he saw was Cassidy's beautiful face.

Chapter 3

Two weeks later

At two thirty, closing time for a café that opened at 7:00 a.m., Cassidy turned over the Open sign on the front door of Bronco Java and Juice and very slowly walked back behind the counter, her eyes on her purse. The red-leather bag with its long beaded strap was on its usual hook beside the bookcase containing her binders of recipes and special mugs and beautiful glasses she'd collected over the years. She stared at the purse, which contained something so scary she was afraid to step too close.

A pregnancy test.

It had barely been three weeks since the wedding where she and Brandon Taylor had made love in a hay-strewed stall in the stables. She tried to think of the exact date of her last period, but her head was a jumble. She only knew she should have gotten it by now. If she *was* pregnant, she'd conceived the night of the wedding.

Come on. She wasn't pregnant. First of all, she and Brandon had used a condom.

But her formerly very regular period *always* announced itself with the usual symptoms. When she'd had those for days without the actual period, she'd stopped in her tracks in the middle of the sidewalk, wondering if her strange cravings lately for a loaded baked potato with sour cream and bacon crumbles was another sign.

For peace of mind, so she could focus on her constant special orders for birthday cakes and wedding cakes— thank you Sanchez-Taylor wedding—she'd stopped into the drugstore on her break. She'd bought a test when the aisles were clear and no one was behind the counter but the kind pharmacist, who'd long been a keeper of secrets in town. What that man knew could fill a very juicy tell-all about the citizens of Bronco Heights.

Could she actually be pregnant? Barely a few weeks along? With Brandon Taylor's baby? She'd never gotten back to him on his proposal for a no-strings affair. And he hadn't followed up, which told her he hadn't been all that serious about even the most casual of relationships. A moment had presented itself in the stables and they'd both been in. Now they were both out. Fine.

Except it wasn't fine and hadn't been way before she'd even thought she might be pregnant. During the past few weeks, she'd tried to force away her traitorous feelings every time one conked her over the head or grabbed at her heart. Her feelings for Brandon Taylor had come rushing back the night of the wedding. She'd worked hard to put those feelings in their place. *You can't always get what you want and you have to deal with it.*

She thought a slightly bruised heart was all she had to contend with.

Cassidy slowly walked to her purse and dug inside for the box, then went into the employee restroom. Heart thumping, she read the instructions enclosed with the test. *"'Wait two full minutes. If an orange check mark appears in the small window, you are pregnant...'"*

She was sure there would be no orange check mark as she carefully followed the instructions and noted the exact time, to the second, that she placed the stick onto the sink counter. She bit her lip and paced the small bathroom without darting a single glance at the test.

You're not pregnant, she told herself. *You're just taking the test to rule it out. After this, you'll wash your hands of Brandon Taylor and how he almost scared you half to death.*

Imagine if she were pregnant with his baby? She shook her head. The man couldn't even commit to his own proposal for a no-strings fling! She let out a snort but then immediately wanted to cry.

She stared hard at the second hand of her watch. Ten, nine, eight, seven, six, five, four, three, two...one.

Cassidy swallowed. She squeezed her eyes shut and then opened them and grabbed the stick.

Bright orange check mark.

She gasped and staggered backward, grabbing the edge of the sink to steady herself.

What?

She stood staring at the check mark, one hand going instinctively to her belly.

Pregnant.

But they'd used a condom. Could it have broken?

She closed her eyes, her heart thumping, her head feeling like it was stuffed with hay.

Maybe because she was in shock, she grabbed her phone and found the "hi" text Brandon had sent her at the wedding. At least she had his number and didn't have to track him down at the ranch. She texted him.

I'm at Java and Juice. Can you come here now? Very important.

He texted back within five seconds, which she found sort of comforting.

Sure thing. Be right there.

Well, at least he responded fast—not only to her text, but to the word *important*. He'd get here soon, she'd tell him, and they could be in shock together.

She stood in front of the mirror, looking for differences. She had to look different if she were pregnant. Something telling in the eyes. But she looked just the same as she had this morning.

Cassidy paced with the stick of the pregnancy test, eyeing the orange check mark. Pregnant, pregnant, pregnant.

Maybe she should have *first* called a trusted friend, like Callie. Talked it out and come to some kind of understanding about the different possible scenarios. But there was only one scenario she could think of right now. Having this baby on her own because Brandon Taylor was going to move to Alaska when he found out.

Cassidy Ware, a single mother. Like her mother before her.

Whatever you do, Cassidy, don't get yourself pregnant by some guy, her late mother had said quite a few times over the years. *Yeah, a baby is a beautiful and precious thing, but the reality of raising a child alone— emotionally, physically, financially and spiritually—is harder than most people can imagine. Be smart with yourself, girl.*

Tears stung Cassidy's eyes and she blinked them away. What she would give to have her mother back right now. Her mother's mother had been gone when Cassidy wasn't even two years old, and there had been very little in the way of a support system for her mom.

"Hello?" a deep male voice called out from the front of the shop. "Cass?"

He was as good as his word. Not ten minutes had elapsed since they'd texted.

"Cass?" he called again.

The sound of his voice sent a surge of protectiveness through her and she put her right hand on her belly.

No matter what, she said to her stomach. *I will do right by you. That's a promise.*

She wasn't sure she meant to, but she came out of the bathroom with the stick in her hand. Brandon was standing in front of the counter, concern on his face.

She stared at him, then looked at the stick.

He gaze went right to it, his dark eyes widening.

"What's that?" he asked, staring from it to her and back to the stick. He stepped closer, staring harder.

"According to this, I'm pregnant."

His head leaned slightly forward and now his expression held confusion and shock. "Pregnant?"

"Pregnant," she repeated.

He didn't say anything for a few moments. "And how do you feel about this?"

The question surprised her. She'd expected him to ask why she was telling him this. Then demand a paternity test. Then head for Alaska.

How do I feel about this? she asked herself. *I don't know. I don't know. I don't know.* She hadn't had time to even think about it. "I don't know yet. I'm processing. I'm still in shock, which is probably why I called you instead of a close girlfriend to help me get my head around it."

The one thing she did know? She was going to have a baby. A sudden elation whirled through her, but in seconds it was gone, replaced by fear.

She needed a little time to get her bearings here. "Coffee?" she asked, her throat dry. "Smoothie?" She pointed at the colorful chalkboard listing the offerings. "We can sit down and talk. But for a few minutes, our most pressing issue can be what we're in the mood for. I think I'll have the Berry Explosion smoothie."

He looked at her, head slightly tilted, expression unreadable. "Actually, I would love a strawberry-banana smoothie. I've kind of been avoiding this place ever since you opened it despite my love of juices. And coffee. And pastries."

She smiled. "Coming right up. And since the blender

is so loud, we can be spared having to make small talk." She grabbed her big knife and headed for the baskets of fruit and the chopping board.

He looked relieved and dropped into a chair at a table for two, then immediately sprang up. "Can I help? Should you be up and about?"

She stared at him, not expecting that, either. Her guard was way up with Brandon Taylor, but every now and then, he'd make it dip a bit. She had to be on guard against that. "Pregnant women can lift bananas. No worries."

He nodded a few times, then sat back down. Every time she looked over at him, he was looking at her.

I am pregnant with your child. The words kept echoing in her head. How was this her reality? A literal roll in the hay, a half hour after fifteen years of avoidance, and she was pregnant. With Brandon's baby.

She gave her head a little shake, snapped lids on their cups and brought over a berry smoothie for herself and his strawberry banana. She sat across from him. He pulled out his wallet, and she covered his hand with hers. "On the house."

"Thanks," he said, putting his wallet away. He very slowly unwrapped his straw and then slid it into the lid, finally taking a long sip. "Delicious. And fortifying. I actually don't feel like I might fall over anymore."

"Is that how *you* feel about it?" she asked.

He took another sip of his drink. "The news is a shock, I won't lie. But everything's going to be fine. We'll get married."

She froze. "Married?"

"Married. We're having a baby, Cassidy. So, yes, let's get married."

"Just like that, you're proposing marriage?" She reached up and put the back of her hand to his forehead. Not hot at all. "Brandon, you didn't even follow through on proposing a no-strings affair."

"Because you deserve more than that, Cassidy."

"You mean because you don't want to deal with me demanding more from you," she countered. She had this guy's number. Please.

"Maybe both. But all that is moot now. We're having a baby. So let's get married for the baby's sake."

Part of her wanted to cry. The other part was drawn to the practicality of it. But her answer was no.

"Never in a million years would I marry without love being the driving force," she said.

"Marriage can be about partnership. It can be about us as a team, taking care of our child."

"Ah, so how would that work? You would have 'married hours' where you would dote on your child and make dinner for the family and then in your free time you'd sleep with other women as if you weren't married?"

"Of course not!" he said. Loudly. "Sorry. If we marry, we're married. I'm not going to date, Cassidy. Jeez."

"So you'd be all-in for a partnership to raise our baby. Interesting. I have to say, you've surprised me. I didn't think you'd take the news well at all, and here you are, preparing to forsake all others. But the wedding vows include loving your spouse. You can't pick and choose the parts of the vows you'll honor."

"We can do whatever we want, Cassidy."

She shook her head. "Some things are nonnegotiable to me. I won't marry a man who doesn't love me. You don't believe in love, so you don't seem to need it. I get it. But my answer is no."

He reached for her hand. "Well, I'm here for you, Cassidy. One hundred percent. Anything you need, say the word. I'm going to be someone's father—and I'm going to take that very seriously."

Tears stung her eyes and she looked down at her berry smoothie. Her father hadn't felt that way. But her baby's father did. Her hand went to her belly and she wanted to whisper, *Hear that, boo?*

"I'm going to be someone's father," he repeated, shaking his head. "Wow."

She smiled for the first time since seeing the orange check mark. "I'm going to be someone's mother."

He leaned over and pulled her into a hug, and she went willingly into his arms, all her fear and worry disappearing as he tightened his hold on her. The moment he let go, all the scary emotions were back.

That made her even more unsettled. She seemed to *need* Brandon. His steady strength in the face of shocking news, his declaration to be there for both her and their baby, the comfort of his arms around her.

And because he was being so damned wonderful, she'd start relying on him.

A knock sounded at the door and a group of teens appeared, pointing at the Closed sign. "Sorry, we're closed," she called out and the group left.

"I forgot to lock up," she said.

"Why don't we go somewhere more private to talk?" he suggested. "Where do you live, anyway?"

"There are two apartments upstairs. I'm on the top floor. We can talk there. I just need to clean up."

"I'll help," he said, standing and rolling up his sleeves as he headed behind the counter.

Who are you and what have you done with the real Brandon Taylor? she wanted to say. *The arrogant rich boy who grew up with a silver spoon and gets whatever he wants because of his looks and family name.* But she realized she didn't really know Brandon at all and hadn't in fifteen years.

She was beginning to like this Brandon a little too much.

"Well, you'll have to move," Brandon said as he surveyed the tiny space that Cassidy called home. "This place is too small for one person, forget adding a baby."

He'd estimate the apartment was seven hundred square feet, if that. There was a galley kitchen that two people couldn't pass each other in, a small living room, a bedroom, a small spare room without a closet and a bathroom with a very old and tired tiled floor. The place was functional, but that was about it. No charm, no character—and not enough room for a child.

Cassidy lifted her chin. "I happen to like my apartment. It's plenty big enough for me, and a baby barely takes up any room. I'll just move my desk from the spare room to my bedroom or the living room and set up the baby's things to make a nursery."

He poked his head into the minuscule spare room,

which currently held a narrow desk and chair. "How is a crib going to fit in here?"

She came up behind him and peered in. For a second, he was distracted by the scent of her perfume, something light and flowery. "I only need a bassinet to start. They're pretty small—like the baby that will sleep inside."

What else did babies need? He wasn't sure. Did he even know anyone with a baby? He tried to picture a furnished nursery.

He closed his eyes for a moment, trying to remember being very young and his dad telling him, Jordan and Daphne that he was on the way back to the hospital to bring home their stepmother, Tania, and their new twin baby brothers, Dirk and Dustin. When they'd arrived, Brandon, Jordan and Daphne had followed their dad and Tania into the enormous nursery that had two of everything. Brandon tried to picture what had been in that room.

He'd never forget the cribs—sleigh-style polished wood stenciled with the twins' names, each with a Taylor Beef cattle logo beside it. There were a few huge stuffed animals, including a giraffe whose head was practically at the ceiling. Two plush blue-and-white rocking chairs.

"Ah—you'll need a rocking chair," he said. "No way will a rocking chair fit in here."

"I'm not sure I need a rocking chair at all," she countered. "The sofa will suffice. Or I can just rock the baby as I stand."

He looked from the room to Cassidy. "You'll need a

dresser. A dresser won't fit in here. And what about a bookshelf to hold the baby's books?"

"Brandon, I'm not even one month along. The baby's not reading yet."

"I like to be prepared."

"Spoken like a man who's never had to make do." She crossed her arms over her chest, chin lifted again.

He tilted his head. "Cassidy, you don't *have* to make do. You can move right into one of the furnished guesthouses on the Taylor Ranch. I'll have everything you need for you and the baby delivered immediately."

She stepped back and shoved her hands in the pockets of her white jeans. "Brandon, that's very generous of you and all, but I'm fine right here."

"Are you?" he asked, eyeing the place. The wood floors were scuffed and the apartment looked tired and old. Cassidy had done what she could—there was a plush sofa and an area rug and some framed vintage posters. But still. "I mean, when you're nine months along and can't turn around in that narrow kitchen…"

"I've been living here for five years," she said, crossing her arms over her chest again. "This is home. Sorry it's not good enough for a Taylor." She turned away, and he immediately felt like a heel.

"Cass, I'm sorry. I don't mean to pick apart your home. But right now, I'm looking at it from a different perspective—the home of the mother of my baby. I just want you to have everything. I want our baby to have everything."

She turned back to him, her expression softening— for just a moment. "Well, I do appreciate that. I mean, it's very nice that you feel that way. But our baby doesn't need *everything*."

"Were you always so stubborn?" he asked.

"Were you always so controlling?" she countered.

Knife to the heart. He could feel his frown deepening. Call him what you want, but never call him controlling, like his father. That was going too far.

"I see I hit a nerve," she said.

Yeah, you did, he wanted to say. But he was too stung and proud for that. Controlling. Him? How was wanting the best for her and their baby being controlling? Brandon was nothing like Cornelius Taylor.

He moved into the living room, shaking off the unsettling comparison. "I think we should make a list of what we'll need for the baby. If you insist on staying here, we'll need two of everything since he or she will have two homes."

Now she was frowning. "Wait a minute. Two homes?"

"You said no to marrying me, so yes, two homes. Yours and mine. I figure we'll split the week. Anyway, I'm getting ahead of myself. We won't need anything for quite a while."

"Way ahead of yourself," she agreed with a nod.

"Don't mind me, Cassidy. I think I'm just trying to wrap my mind around this as we go. Maybe it just hasn't been enough time for me to process it, so I'm throwing everything out there, trying to understand what needs to be done."

"Maybe when it does sink in, the reality of it, you won't even want to be involved," she said.

He stared at her—hard. "Not going to happen. I told you, I take this responsibility very seriously."

She stared back harder, but now there was something he couldn't quite name in her expression, in her eyes. She seemed to be trying to figure him out.

"Look, I found out I was pregnant an hour ago and four seconds later, I called you. We both need to process." She let out a yawn. "I definitely need a nap. Could be a side effect of pregnancy, but I was up till the wee hours doing a couple of test recipes for birthday cakes. Thanks to your brother's wedding, my side business is picking up serious steam."

"Side business?"

"Specialty cakes," she said. "Birthday parties, weddings. I did a seven-year-old's birthday cake for a prominent Bronco Height's family. They wanted seven layers, one for each year, each layer with a different filling— and the cake in the shape of a race car. When they said they needed it in two days and I had to turn it down, which killed me, they offered me *three hundred dollars* to do it. Three hundred dollars! Can you believe that?"

"Actually, yes. My father does stuff like that all time. 'I want it now and I'll pay for it.' That's Cornelius Taylor's motto."

"Is it yours?" she asked.

"No! Of course not. Well, I mean, if there's something important I must have, of course I'm willing to pay to make it happen."

She smiled. "I see."

He did not like the direction this conversation was going. He was nothing like his father.

"Tell me more about your side business," he suggested as she dropped down on the sofa, curling her legs up to her side.

He remembered coming into the stables the night of Jordan's wedding and seeing those legs. The legs that had started it all.

"Well, I'm trying to think of a way to put the two together," she explained. "The cake business with expanding Bronco Java and Juice. Or maybe it's two separate entities. I'm not sure yet."

"Or you could move into a bigger shop with a baker's kitchen. You already sell baked goods, so that would be a natural expansion. You've already built a great reputation and a name for yourself in both areas."

She smiled, but then it faded. "A bigger location will mean a lot more seven-layer birthday cakes. I do have two wedding cake orders that'll help that dream along."

"And I can help," he said. "We can start scouting bigger locations in the morning."

The legs unfurled and she straightened, one eyebrow raised. "Because I'm having your baby?"

"Well, yes. I'm here to help."

The legs curled back underneath her. "Brandon, I appreciate that you're generous. But I've been on my own a long time and I can take care of myself. I can make my own dreams come true."

Ah, he'd offended her at her core, but he hadn't meant to. He sat beside her, took her hands and held them. "I admire you, Cassidy. I might think you're crazy and stubborn, but I admire your independence. You're your own woman."

"I am," she said, then yawned again. She leaned back a bit so he had to let go of her hand, and she pulled the fleece throw over her and laid her head on the armrest. "I'm so sleepy."

"I'll let you get some rest." He smoothed the top of the throw and reached over to kiss her cheek.

"You're different than I thought," she whispered.

"What do you mean?" he asked, not sure he wanted her to answer that.

But she was already asleep.

Chapter 4

After leaving Cassidy's apartment—reluctantly, since he'd just wanted to sit there as she napped and let the news permeate his very thick skull—Brandon found himself driving aimlessly around town. Now that he was alone, stone-cold fear skittered up his spine and goose bumps broke out on his arms. He was going to be a dad? Someone's father? Him? Brandon was a serious enough guy, was responsible for millions of dollars at Taylor Beef, but the concept of being a helpless, dependent little being's father was scarier than it had first seemed when he was still with Cassidy. Maybe because he wasn't physically alone in the parenthood; Cassidy was the other half of that equation. But now, alone in his silver truck, he'd never felt so unsure of himself.

I need info, he thought. Information and facts. He

didn't feel like going back to the ranch and using his computer because if he ran into his father, Brandon might spontaneously combust. The words *I am not like Dad* echoed through his head. Not that Cornelius didn't have his good points. But he was a know-it-all about everything, including his children's lives, and he added conflict by just being himself. Brandon did not want to be that kind of father.

But that was the question. Could a man be what his child needed instead of the fully formed person he already was? Could Brandon put his child's heart, mind and soul first? He had no idea how that worked. He'd always lived by the adages "trust your instincts" and "go with your gut." But what if his instincts were way off when it came to child-rearing? What if he'd be a terrible father? He didn't know anything about babies or children. He was about to pull over and type *How to be a Good Dad* into his phone's search engine, but who could read that tiny type?

Ah—he knew where he needed to go. A destination that would give him a good half hour to drive with purpose and end up exactly where he needed to be—in a bookstore.

He didn't bother blasting music on the way to Lewistown; he let himself sit with the startling revelation that he, Brandon Taylor, was going to be a father in eight months. That he shared this enormous responsibility with Cassidy Ware, a woman he'd had very little contact with since high school. *You'll study up, you'll be on surer footing*, he told himself as he arrived in Lewistown, a much bigger town than Bronco.

He found a bookstore and headed in, relieved that parenthood had its own section and he didn't have to ask for help. *Um, hi, do you have a book about babies for the very clueless?* He plucked out titles that sounded helpful, then put most back after flipping through them. Some had so much information jammed into the pages, including sidebar lists and illustrations that Brandon's head had started to spin. Others seemed to be written in a baby jargon he couldn't decipher. Then he found exactly what he looking for: *Baby 101 for the First-Time Father: Navigating the Unknown of a Pregnant Partner and Baby's First Year.*

He'd breathed a sigh of relief, bought two copies in case he accidentally left one somewhere, and sat in his truck in the parking space, reading. *"'You've got nine months till the baby is a living, breathing, crying, pooping part of your life. But your pregnant partner is the one carrying the baby. Check out the chart on pages 21–22 for a fetus's week-by-week development and you'll have a better understanding of just what's going on in that growing belly. Pregnancy is exhausting and exhilarating. Be there for your partner...'"*

Yes, that was it. He couldn't do anything for the baby yet; he or she wouldn't be here for months. But he could be there for Cassidy, as he'd told her he would be. He pulled out his phone and texted her.

Have any cravings? I'm in Lewistown and parked right in front of a gourmet takeout. Want some pickles? Their menu board lists some great-sounding soups.

She texted back immediately.

I was asleep till the phone chime from your text woke me.

She added an emoji of a smiley face yawning.

He winced. A being-there-for-her fail. Do not wake up the exhausted pregnant woman!

He waited a beat for her to text what food she wanted since she was now awake, but five minutes later, he was still waiting. "Guess she fell back to sleep," he said to his phone.

He let the window down, the perfect midsixties breeziness and bright September sunshine a balm. He glanced at the book he'd set on the passenger seat. Suddenly *he* was exhausted.

What he needed was to talk to someone, someone he could trust, share this with and get some guidance from a person who actually knew him.

His sister.

Thirty minutes later he was back in Bronco, pulling into the Happy Hearts Animal Sanctuary. Happy Hearts was a registered charity animal rescue that helped farm and companion animals through rescue, adoption and education. Potbellied pigs, sheep, dogs and cats, and lots of farm animals called the place home. He texted Daphne to see if she was free to talk for a minute. She texted back that she was in the cat barn, that it was feeding time and he was just in time to help.

That was how he found himself setting down bowls of wet cat food and kibble on little mats against the walls of the adoption barn. One slinky black cat was more interested in sniffing his shoe than the food. He knelt to give the cat a scratch on her back. She eyed him and then padded over to a bowl.

His sister, in her usual jeans and Happy Hearts long-sleeved T-shirt, her long strawberry-blond hair in a po-nytail, tossed him a smile and then surveyed the room. She jotted down notes about who wasn't eating and which cats still needed their special diet, then looked at him. "Can we talk and work at the same time?" she asked. "I can hand out the bland diets while you collect kitty blankies for a load of laundry."

"Absolutely," he said, grabbing a basket in the cor-ner, surprised when a striped gray cat jumped out and gave him a dirty look before curling up on a hay bale.

Daphne laughed. "You never know where you'll find a furry creature around here."

He started collecting the small blankets and stuff-ing them in the basket. Daphne sure worked hard. She had volunteers to help, but the cat barn alone was a ton of work. Then there was the dog section, and the farm animals, and who knew what else was living out its best life at Happy Hearts Animal Sanctuary, in peace and harmony. He was pretty sure there was even a very old reindeer.

"I have news," he said. "But I have to swear you to secrecy, Daphne. I need your solemn oath. Not a word to anyone."

Her mouth dropped open. "Jessica's pregnant?"

He tilted his head. Jessica? His father's third wife was not pregnant. At least, Brandon didn't think so. Then again, she was considerably younger than their dad, so anything was possible.

"Not Jessica. Cassidy Ware."

"Cassidy from Java and Juice?" Daphne asked, checking off cat names on her tablet. "What does that have to do with y—" Before she could even finish the word *you*, his sister's eyes widened. "Oh my gosh. Brandon, are you saying that you're going to make Dad a grandfather before any of us? Are you kidding me?"

"I just found out a little while ago. I'm going to be a father."

Daphne was very slowly shaking her head. "Wow. Wow!"

"I know. I don't think it's sunk in yet. Because I'm not freaking out. I mean I am, but not to the extent you'd expect."

"Interesting," she said, and he was aware that she was studying him. "And I didn't even know you and Cassidy were a couple. How long have you been together?"

When you shared one thing you might as well let it all out, he reasoned. He explained about Jordan's wedding. The stables. The champagne. Yada yada yada. Cassidy was pregnant.

Daphne was slowly shaking her head again, her blue eyes gleaming. "Wow. Wow!"

"I know," he said.

"So…since you're not even *dating*, what's the plan?"

"I immediately suggested we get married. She said no. She doesn't want to marry solely for the baby's sake. She said the man she marries has to love her."

"I'm with her," Daphne said. "No offense."

"Offense taken," he said, staring at his sibling. "What about a smooth-running partnership based on respect, shared parenthood, friendship and responsibility? That's a marriage that'll last, Daph."

She glanced at her twinkling engagement ring, then at him. "Marriages start with love. Everyone goes into it expecting the best."

"How can you be so optimistic given who our parents are?" he asked.

"I'm not saying love isn't kind of scary. Just that it's worth it. I can't wait to marry Evan next month. We're going to grow old and gray together—I have no doubt about it."

Scary? Brandon wasn't *scared* of love. He'd tried, hadn't he? Three serious relationships that had all ended miserably. If anything, thousand-year-old Winona Cobbs had been right to say he didn't know *how* to love. Anymore, that was. But he fully intended to stay rusty in that department.

Except when it came to his baby. Surely that would come naturally. Right? He needed to read more of that book. There was probably a chapter or five all about that.

He felt his shoulders slump. "Doesn't our family history make you...uneasy about it all?"

She surveyed the cats eating and checked off more boxes on her tablet, then turned it off and looked at him. "I'm not Mom. Or Dad. I make my own choices, blaze my own path."

As another black cat wound between his legs, he nodded. "That you do, Daphne Taylor." He knelt down, setting the basket on the floor, and gave the cat a scratch on the head. He was done talking about this. Yes, he'd brought it up. He'd made a special trip over here. But he didn't feel any more in control of his own life. Control. There was that word again. Ha—he could hardly be *controlling* if he didn't even feel in control. Right?

A change of subject was definitely in order. "How do you not keep all these majestic creatures?" he asked, admiring the sleek cat.

Daphne smiled. "They have fun here. And I know they'll all find loving homes soon. They always do. Even the prickly ones who hide when a potential adopter comes in."

He gave the cat another scratch and stood. "I have this overwhelming urge to take care of Cassidy," he said out of the clear blue.

"Well, given your role in the big news, I'm glad to hear that, Brandon."

His role was father. Father. Daddy. He accepted the responsibility—absolutely. But the word itself still felt so strange applied to him. When would it feel more real? When would he be more comfortable?

"I just want to make everything easy for her," he said, his gaze on an orange tabby playing with a piece of hay. "She's pushing back. Isn't that nuts? I can give her anything she wants or needs. She can have all the creature comforts and yet she insists on staying in her tiny apartment above the shop."

Daphne smiled. "She's independent. She's been on her own since her mom died, has her own business." She scooped up the basket. She studied him for a moment and then nodded, which meant she was about to lay some of her wisdom on him. He sorely needed it. "If you want a way in, find out what she really needs,

Brandon. That's how you make yourself indispensable to someone used to handling things herself."

"What she needs? But she doesn't seem to need *any-thing.*"

"We all need something. Even you. Find out what that is for Cassidy. Maybe you can't provide it."

"With my bank accounts? Of course I can."

Daphne shook her head. "No, Brandon. I'm talking about the intangible."

He threw up his hands, and Daphne grinned.

"Get to know her," she added. "Start there. How about that?"

Get to know her. Yes, of course. He really didn't know Cassidy very well, what made her tick, what she hated and loved.

What she *needed.*

It hit him like a lightning bolt. Suddenly he understood. What Cassidy needed had nothing to do with money or diapers or cribs. He had no idea what it was, but he could find out. Then he could really be there for her.

"What would I do without you, Daph?" Brandon asked, bending to give his sister a kiss on the cheek. He took the laundry basket from her. "I'll pop this in on my way out. I have to learn how to do laundry sometime if I'm going to be someone's father."

Daphne gaped at him. "I think you're gonna be just fine, Brandon."

Maybe. Maybe not. Because the more he was getting used to thinking of himself as a dad, responsible for an innocent, precious child that he helped bring about, the more he wasn't all that sure.

* * *

Ever since Brandon's text had woken her from her nap on the sofa, Cassidy had been sitting with her laptop, feet up on the coffee table, a cup of herbal tea beside her knees, researching everything baby and motherhood. Including single motherhood. There were articles and blogs and book recommendations on the subject and everything she read had one thing in common: as a single mother, she would need a support system.

At first, she hadn't put herself in the single mother camp. Yes, she was single and she'd be a mother. But her baby's father was from the richest family in town, and whether she liked it or not, her baby would have everything he or she needed and then some. Cassidy might be independent and practical, but she wasn't stupid or stubborn to the point that she'd turn down the basics she couldn't afford on her own. She also had to consider that there were two parents here. She had her way and style and Brandon had his, and she needed to remember that she wasn't the queen; they were equal partners as parents.

And Brandon had said, more than once, that he was fully committed to being the baby's father. She wasn't on her own. But some of the articles she read had interviews with single mothers who talked about the loneliness of it all, not having the emotional support of someone who loved you. Someone to truly lean on.

Cassidy had always filled her time with work and her friends, and volunteering and dreaming of growing her business. But sometimes, when she'd come home after a particularly hard day, she'd wish there was someone special waiting for her. Someone to massage her aching shoulders and to tell her she'd make her dreams come true, that she had what it took. She'd been that for herself for years, sometimes feeling empowered and sometimes feeling so alone she'd tear up. Maybe she'd been rationalizing the freedom and focus that being single gave her.

All night she'd thought about Brandon's text, asking if she'd like anything from the gourmet place, if she had a craving for something, and she'd been so surprised and touched that she'd had a runaway fantasy for a good twenty minutes—of imagining them together. Really together. Like married. With a baby.

She could have that, if she wanted. The man had proposed. She could have the ring, and the husband, and a nice house and everything her baby could possibly want, including a large extended family. Hadn't she very recently told Brandon she wasn't interested in marriage? That she didn't believe in it? She didn't know what she really felt and what she'd been rationalizing. What she did know was that with her mother and grandparents gone, and a couple of aunts and uncles scattered across the west, Cassidy was grateful that her baby would have all that family in the Taylors.

But she'd never been about pretending. She'd always been firmly rooted in reality. That was how her mother had raised her, and Cassidy appreciated it. Brandon might be kinder and more generous than she'd expected, but his proposal was…cold. What would be the point of marrying if there was no love? Love *was* the point.

Her phone pinged. A text from Brandon.

I got you some takeout from that place in Lewistown. Hungry?

Cassidy smiled and glanced at the clock. It was just after seven, and she was starving. I actually am, she texted back.

Be right there.

Fifteen minutes later, she buzzed him in and listened to his boots on the stairs up to the top floor. She stood in the doorway, ostensibly anticipating her deli feast but just as equally anticipating him.

She was just a little off-kilter emotionally speaking, so of course she wanted company. Company that was in the same position she was in: suddenly going to be a parent. She'd have to be careful not to get wrapped up in Brandon Taylor's grand gestures.

There he was, holding two big plastic bags from Grammy's Gourmet, one in each hand. For a moment, she couldn't take her eyes off him, all of him. The broad shoulders, that gorgeous face with the dark twinkling eyes. He wore a green Henley shirt and faded low-slung jeans that were so sexy she swallowed. And his cowboy boots. She found them sexy, too.

"I didn't know what your favorites were, so I got you a little of everything," he said. "Grammy said everything would keep in the fridge for four days."

"Did you actually ask her that?"

"Yes," he said.

She grinned. "You keep surprising me, Brandon."

"Oh, I'm full of surprises." He gave the bags a heft.

He came inside and headed to the kitchen, where he set the bags on the small round table. He took out so much food, she gasped. "Everything's labeled. I got you four quarts of soup—potato leek, Hungarian mushroom, butternut squash and roasted vegetable. I also got a lasagna, a shepherd's pie, a chicken potpie and two kinds of quiche. Also a cheesecake sampler. Oh, and a pound of ginger snaps. I remember when we dated a million years ago that ginger snaps were your favorite."

Cassidy felt tears well in her eyes. A half hour ago, she'd been uncomfortably aware that she wanted this kind of TLC in her life, and here was Brandon—the last person she'd expect it from—providing it. "Thank you, Brandon. Beyond thoughtful." She wanted to say more, but she was so touched, overwhelmed at his kindness, that she was a little speechless at the moment.

"So what are you in the mood for?" he asked.

She surveyed the crowded table. "Ever since you said chicken potpie, I've been craving it. I can taste the potatoes and carrots already."

"Coming right up," he said. "You go relax. Grammy gave me heating instructions for everything."

She stared at him. Was he for real or working some angle? What, though?

Stop being so cynical and expecting the worst, she told herself. *If a gorgeous, sexy man wants to take care of you for a change and heat up your chicken potpie, let him.*

She sat back on the sofa, charmed by the sounds of lids opening and utensils clanking on a plate. Twenty minutes later, he came into the living room with a tray and set it on the coffee table. He'd even included the salt and pepper shakers and a glass of ice water.

"Bon appétit," he said, sitting in the club chair adjacent to the sofa. "I snagged one of the ginger snaps for myself."

She was surprised to see he hadn't fixed himself a plate of something. "Not hungry?" she asked, the aroma of the chicken potpie making her mouth water.

He shook his head. "I ended up having a late lunch at my sister's farm. Do you know Happy Hearts?"

"Of course. Daphne's one of my best customers. Tries all my interesting vegetarian combos."

"Speaking of vegetarian," he said, "she insisted I try something called a seitan barbecue po'boy since she'd made one for herself earlier and had leftovers. It was so good, I had two of them, and I'm still stuffed. *Seitan barbecue*. We're talking wheat meat, Cassidy. It shouldn't be delicious, but it was."

Cassidy laughed. "Well, if you liked that, I make some amazing smoothies with silken tofu. You should try one sometime. Now that you don't have to avoid Java and Juice." She dug her fork into the potpie and blew on the steaming mouthful, then ate. Scrumptious. "This is so good. Thanks, Brandon. I owe you."

"So…does that mean you'll consider my proposal?" he asked.

She gaped at him. "I meant a smoothie on the house or something. Not marriage."

"I'll wear you down," he said, taking a bite of the cookie.

She froze, her fork midair. "Why do you want to? I

mean, why do you want to get married? You don't believe in the institution."

"Because we have a different situation. We're not two people in lust who think we're going to last for the next sixty, seventy years. As I said, we'd be entering into a partnership based on shared commitment and responsibility to our baby. I believe in *that*."

She poked her fork into a chunk of potato. Romantic. Real romantic. Then again, that was what he was going for—the opposite of romance. "So, let me get this straight. For the baby's sake, for our partnership in raising our child, you'll give up the possibility of meeting someone and falling in love and wanting to marry that person for all the right reasons?"

"My reasons for wanting to marry you *are* right," he said. "But yes, I have no trouble kicking all that nonsense to the curb. Love doesn't last. People change. Love fades or dies."

Tears stung her eyes and she blinked them away fast. She wasn't even sure why she'd gotten so triggered by what he'd said, but she thought it was because of how completely down on love he was. He *really* didn't believe in it. And that was sad.

"Did you tell your sister that I'm pregnant?" she asked, taking another bite of the potpie even though her appetite was waning.

"I did. I hope you don't mind. I know it's your business, too, and I probably should have checked with you first. I did swear her to secrecy and Daphne can be trusted."

She nodded. "It's really early in the pregnancy, but if you want to tell your family, that's fine."

"How many people have you told?" he asked.

"None. Who would I tell?"

He stared at her. "What do you mean?"

"The first person I'd tell would be my mom, but I lost her five years ago. No dad to tell, and his family was never in my life. I do have a couple of aunts and cousins on my mom's side, but they live far away and we've never been close."

"Want some of my relatives?" he asked, his expression so soft on her that she had the urge to catapult herself into his arms for a hug. Just one hug to fortify her and she'd be okay again. "You can have my dad."

She laughed. "I once heard Cornelius Taylor give someone holy hell in the middle of downtown Bronco Heights. A man in a Range Rover wanted to make a right turn on red while an elderly woman was in the crosswalk and going too slow for the jerk. Boy, did your father let loose on him and his lack of respect. Cornelius took that lady's arm and helped her across the street, shooting daggers at the Range Rover dude."

"Really? Huh. My dad can *occasionally* surprise me. I wouldn't think he'd notice, let alone help anyone cross a street. No one would call him champion of the underdog. Particularly if the underdog is his own daughter. Do you know he's still mad at her for daring to leave home to start an animal sanctuary? 'How dare she mock the family business!' he bellows at least once a day. It's been *six* years. Get the hell over it, Dad."

"She's his only daughter," Cassidy said. "Surely he's supportive of her no matter what."

"Nope. He won't even acknowledge her. Turns and walks away anytime he sees her in town."

Cassidy gasped. "That's awful."

"That's family," he said. "The good, the bad and the really ugly. No one can count on anything in this world. I mean, we both know that. We learned at very early ages that even your own parent can walk out on you. My mom. Your dad." He shook his head.

Cassidy put her fork down. She nodded; the long-running on-and-off ache in her chest fully in On mode. "I don't know which is worse. A dad walking away from his young child and never looking back? Or a dad who's been there the whole time but then turns his back because he doesn't like your choices—choices that not only hurt no one, particularly him, but help so many."

"Both bad," he said. He turned slightly, staring out the window where a big oak was just visible in the moonlight.

She studied him, and he seemed lost in thought. She wanted to ask what he was thinking about, to get him talking about the sore spots their conversation seemed to rub raw, but from his expression, she knew that would be a mistake.

"Well," he said, standing, "I'd better get going."

No, don't leave, she wanted to say. She longed to jump up and hug him.

"You okay, Brandon?" He was all tied up in knots over his family history—past and present. She understood, but if even Daphne, who'd experienced both a mother walking out *and* her father turning his back, could open herself up to love and believe in it, surely Brandon could.

Then again, she'd known siblings who were night-and-day different, so much so, she wouldn't have believed they'd been raised in the same home by the same parents.

"Okay as ever," he finally said, but she didn't understand what that meant.

You don't really know him anymore, she reminded herself. *Be careful. Protect your heart. This is not a man who's going to give you what you need most.*

He gave her hand a squeeze and then was gone, her apartment suddenly feeling so empty.

Their conversation had chased him out, but she wanted nothing more than to just be there with him, not talking. Just sitting, sharing the ginger snaps. Sharing understanding.

Yes, she was headed for big trouble where Brandon Taylor was concerned.

Chapter 5

Brandon switched on the lamp in his office, the only illumination in the room. He'd left Cassidy's almost an hour ago, and he was still too wound up to do anything relaxing, like watch the game he'd recorded or a movie. He could work; that might distract him from the thoughts jumping around in his head.

He stared at his computer screen. Yeah, right. He had way too much on his mind right now.

He thought he could commit to being a father, but how the hell did he know if he could? He was his mother's son. He was his father's son. And both Marge Taylor and Cornelius Taylor had let down their own children in the worst ways.

When Brandon was five, his father had basically bought off Margaret, who'd won custody of Jordan,

Brandon and Daphne in the divorce. Back then, Brandon had thought that his mother seeking custody meant she'd loved them, cared about them—she'd fought to keep them. But she'd really been waiting for the payoff, for her mega-wealthy ex-husband to make her an offer that would justify her leaving her children. Millions. Not that Cornelius had paid her to leave them, exactly; the man had simply understood that money was more important to her than her own kids, and that had made her a poison in their lives. It was the poison Cornelius had found an antidote for. Brandon had had a love-hate relationship with his family's wealth ever since he'd learned the whole sordid story when he was a young teenager.

It was all so ugly that Brandon tried never to think about it. The screwed-up blood that ran through his veins scared him, though. Because it meant he couldn't entirely trust himself. He could say all he wanted that he'd be Father of the Year. But with his family's past, who the hell knew? And talking about it with Cassidy had gotten him so turned around that he'd had to get away before the walls closed in on him. He'd felt so claustrophobic in that moment. Not because her place was tiny but because of how uncomfortably personal their conversation had turned.

Cassidy Ware always got him talking. How did she do it? He'd had two missions in mind for going over to her place. One was to bring her the food, but the other was to answer the question Daphne had raised: what did Cassidy need?

Instead of finding out so that he could offer her what she needed and more easily convince her to marry him, they'd gotten off track. He did believe they should marry, for all the reasons he'd already stated. But also because he felt he could be a better father, a more present, everyday father, if the two of them were a couple, living in the same home, making decisions together. Given how easy it was for a Taylor to mess up when it came to relationships and family, Brandon wanted the setup to produce the best possible results. That meant marriage. Not him living at the Taylor Ranch and being a father half the week or checking in. He didn't want to be a part-time father. But unless Cassidy accepted his proposal, he'd have little choice.

Damn it.

He took a deep breath and tried to clear his mind by turning around in his chair and looking out the big windows onto the yard. But all he saw was Cassidy's face. Cassidy's swirly blond hair. Her hazel eyes. Her sexy body in her skinny jeans.

Her belly. That would soon swell with pregnancy. With his child.

His chest started to squeeze, and Brandon knew he had stop thinking, had to get his head back in his everyday world and not the life-changing bombshell that had been dropped on him.

He grabbed his phone and checked his schedule; his day had gone off the rails with the news and the trip to Lewistown and then the hour he'd spent at his sister's farm. Scanning his to-do list, he saw he needed to get in touch with Geoff Burris, Bronco's most famous son, to sign on to promote Taylor Beef in a major advertising campaign. One of the most talented ropers Brandon had ever seen, Geoff was a huge celebrity on the

Montana circuit. He'd just unseated the reigning champ over the Fourth of July weekend, and he was on his way to becoming a national hero. Scoring him ahead of the Mistletoe Rodeo in November would have Taylor Beef numbers skyrocketing.

Because Brandon had gone to high school with Geoff, though Geoff was a few years younger, Cornelius had given Brandon the job of wooing the guy into promoting Taylor Beef. Abernathy Meats, a major competitor, was after Geoff, too, and that made the negotiations harder than Brandon expected. The champ had already made clear through his management team that he'd listen to both family's pitches, but that he wasn't ready to make a decision. Brandon had some great ideas—from traditional to out of the box—but Geoff's team wasn't committing. Brandon needed to get the guy signed before the Abernathys did, or that family, with whom the Taylors had had a mostly friendly rivalry for generations, would rub it in their faces. Taylor Beef was number one, Abernathy Meats a close second. His dad and uncles wanted to keep it that way—or actually, widen the gap. Securing a star like Geoff Burris would do that.

He could try Geoff's cell phone right now. He'd had the number from years back when they'd been on the same sports team at Bronco High, Brandon as the captain and Geoff as a rising star. But calling after business hours to talk business could also piss the guy off, and that was the last thing Brandon wanted to do. He'd call in the morning. For now, he'd do some old-fashioned brainstorming with pen and paper to drum up a few new ideas for the potential advertising campaign. But ten minutes later, all he'd done was write Geoff Burris and Taylor Beef across a legal pad and tap the pen against all the blank space. Tap. Tap. Tap.

As if he could concentrate.

The fact that he could suddenly hear music playing wasn't helping. Was that a Blake Shelton song? Brandon got up and went to investigate, but stopped in his tracks the second he left his office. He could see his father and stepmother slow-dancing in the living room to the strains of a country ballad, Jessica's head on Cornelius's shoulder. Then she lifted her head and they were gazing into each other's eyes before Cornelius kissed her.

Brandon quickly backtracked into his office and shut the door. Whoa. *That* was unexpected. Had he ever seen his father and Jessica like that? He didn't think so. Honestly, he'd never paid much attention.

The two did seem happy. But was it a *for now* thing? Two marriages hadn't lasted. Why would the third be the charm?

Brandon switched off the lamp and left his office, heading for the grand stairs in the opposite direction of the living room. The music had stopped, and when Brandon started up the steps, he could see into the living room where his father and Jessica were in each other's arms.

Why the hell is life so confusing? he wondered as he went into his suite.

He pulled out his phone, the urge to call Cassidy so strong. He needed to fight that urge, tamp it down. It was one thing to want to make the mother of his child comfortable, to make sure she had what she wanted. It was another to *need* to hear her voice. He put his phone away, grumbling as he flopped onto his bed. He couldn't let himself get all twisted around. He was committing to *fatherhood*. He needed to focus on ensuring he'd be a great parent. That had to be his only personal mission.

He reached for the book he'd bought and flipped it open to his bookmark. He hadn't gotten far. But he'd read long into the night, needing to fortify himself with how to be the dad he *wanted* to be.

At 7:00 a.m., when Java and Juice opened for the day, a group of customers waited for Cassidy to unlock and flip the sign from Closed to Open. The waiting group always made her heart happy. And no surprise—they were all parents or caregivers with babies.

Cassidy loved having the kiddo crowd in the early mornings. She'd figured her early-morning hours would attract tired parents who'd be happy for somewhere to go before the rest of Bronco Heights opened, and she'd been right. So Cassidy had added a baby and toddler area with a playpen and foam mats and soft toys. Parents always told her how much they appreciated being able to set down their toddler at the little choo choo train table while they sipped an iced drink and had a brownie on the plush tan sofa along the wall beside it, or on the overstuffed chairs she'd picked up from thrift stores.

When the babies and toddlers went home for their naps, the en-route-to-work folks stopped in for espressos and bagels, then she had coffee-breakers and snack-needers who poured in and out till noon when the lunch crowd started arriving. The menu, offering everything from sandwiches and soups to crepes and pastries, brought in a varied customer base from the 7:00 a.m. to 2:30 p.m. hours.

A baby squealed as Cassidy was headed back behind the counter, and she turned to smile at the babies on laps and in the playpen, a toddler picking up one of the little colorful trains.

I'm going to be a mother, she thought, her smile turning into a grin. *Maybe not the way I'd always imagined, but that's okay. More than okay.*

She'd spent a lot of time thinking about Brandon last night, about what a surprise he'd turned out to be, including hidden depths, and she'd had to issue another warning to protect herself. She had a lot going on. Running a business required her full attention, and now she had to split that attention with everything being pregnant required—from getting used to the idea itself, to doing some research and making lists.

As Hank and Helen, a wonderful married couple in their late sixties who'd started working for Java and Juice after their retirement, were in the kitchen making the popular breakfast sandwiches and slathering various kinds of cream cheese on bagels, Cassidy took orders and made drinks. There was a good number of people waiting in line, babies and strollers inching up, and she felt her heart ping with pride. *I might not have achieved everything I intended, but this is my shop and it's paying the bills. I can take care of my baby just fine. And I don't have to do that from a luxe guest cabin at the Taylor Ranch.*

As the morning wore on, Cassidy made smoothies and juices and coffee drinks, selected pastries from the display, handed over turkey BLTs, soups, and banana-chocolate crepes, and swiped many a credit card. She grinned when she saw her next two customers. Her friend Callie Sheldrick holding ten-month-old Maeve Abernathy. Maeve was the daughter of Tyler Abernathy, Callie's widowed boyfriend. Callie explained she had the day off from her job as an admin at Bronco's Ghost Tours so she was caring for the little one today.

"A little on-the-job training for someday," her friend whispered down to the baby in a stroller beside her. Callie's brown eyes shone with pure happiness. Cassidy could tell she adored the baby.

Speaking of… Maybe she'd share her big news with Callie. Aside from Brandon's family, Cassidy didn't want everyone to know, not this early in the pregnancy, but she'd sure like to talk over motherhood with a good friend. She glanced up at the big round clock on the wall. Ten minutes till her break.

Cassidy handed Callie her chocolate-almond smoothie, then hurried around the counter to say hi to the sweet baby when a little fist reached out and grabbed the end of her long ponytail. She swallowed her yelp. Maeve let out a huge laugh that couldn't possibly come from such a small body.

Cassidy grinned at her friend. "That's some grip!"

Callie gave the baby a tickle and she immediately let go. "Tricks of the trade. She once had my hair in a death grip and I finally learned that blowing a raspberry on her shoulder made her release and give out that great belly laugh."

Cassidy wished she were writing all this down. These were the small details she'd need to know. "I go on break in a few. I'll join you. I have news," she whispered.

"Oooh, I will be all ears," Callie said and then settled at a table near the baby section.

Cassidy made many more drinks, had to restock her cinnamon crumb cake, a big hit today, and the coconut-chocolate-chip scones, and then finally it was break time. She fixed herself a berry smoothie and headed over.

The baby was in her stroller beside Callie's seat, her blue eyes drooping. Cassidy pulled over a chair, unable to take her eyes off Maeve, her soft blond-brown wispy curls, beautiful face and pink bow lips, the tiny nose, the rise and fall of her chest as she dozed off. Cassidy was suddenly overcome with a wave of butterflies flying around her stomach. At the responsibility of raising a child. Unlike Brandon, Cassidy had no doubt of her capacity to be a good parent, but that didn't mean she wouldn't make mistakes. And the sight of baby Maeve, such a marvel of a tiny human being, made her long to be perfect, a TV mom who had all the answers.

She bit her lip, suddenly overwhelmed and unable to get any words out.

Callie peered at her. "What? What's wrong, Cass?"

"I'm pregnant," she whispered, glancing around to make sure no one was listening to their conversation.

Her friend's eyes widened. "Tell me everything."

Cassidy did. Starting with the stables, then describing the business-like marriage proposal and ending with how incredibly kind and thoughtful Brandon had been. She even told her friend about him bringing her four kinds of soup and heating up her chicken potpie.

"Wow," Callie said. "Sure sounds like he's going to be a great dad if he's that caring."

Cassidy took a sip of her smoothie to try to stop herself from what she was about to say. It didn't work. "And a man a little too easy to fall in love with."

There it was. Maybe what really had her so anxious.

"Ah, gotcha," Callie said. "I see the problem. But eight months is a long time, Cass. And perhaps just the right amount of time for a self-confirmed bachelor like Brandon to come to a few realizations."

Cassidy felt herself brighten. That was true. Maybe Brandon did just need some time with all these new developments. Becoming a dad and dealing with the hold his family's past had on him. Realizing that a marriage without love was cold and empty. She certainly didn't expect him to want to marry her because he loved her; they barely knew each other at this point. But she *would* like him to propose they begin a real relationship—a good start.

"I'm just starting to get to know Brandon," Cassidy said. "And, to my big surprise, I like him. A lot. But that might be just the situation talking, the newness, the shock, and the reaction to how insanely sweet Brandon is being. Aside from the business deal of a marriage proposal."

"Well, even that was sweet," Callie said, taking a sip of her smoothie. "He's giving up everyone else for you and the baby. That says something."

"It really just says he doesn't care about love. That's what he's giving up."

Callie shook her head. "Hardly, my friend. Bronco's Most Eligible Bachelor is giving up *other* women, Cass. No dating. No sex. If he's proposing a marriage without love or romance, obviously he knows he's saying 'see ya' to sex, too."

Now it was Cassidy's eyes that widened. "I didn't think about it. I mean, I really didn't have a chance to consider what his idea of partnership-marriage would mean…how we'd operate, you know?"

"If he's giving up sex with all the hot singles in Bronco, then he either intends to have a sexual relationship with his wife or he's truly suggesting a partnership and he cares more about you and the baby than he does about his sex life."

"Huh. We already nixed a no-strings romance," Cassidy explained.

"Um, Cassidy? I'd say a legal document like a marriage license is strings aplenty."

Cassidy tilted her head. "Callie, you're blowing my mind. I can't take this all in! Don't say anything else."

Callie chuckled. "You have a lot to think about. But I suggest having a conversation with Mr. Taylor about exactly how he envisions this marriage to go. Not that you'd say yes, but you should have all the information."

It *was* a lot to think about. Cassidy sat back and sipped her berry smoothie. Jeez. Now she understood a little of how Brandon had felt last night, why he'd up and bolted. Cassidy felt like doing that right now— running out the back door to just stop and breathe for a few minutes, digest what her friend was saying. It was all too much.

Woof! Woof, woof!

Cassidy bolted up. "That might be Maggie! The dog you said went missing from a Happy Hearts adoption event."

Before Cassidy had known about the missing Maggie—she'd sort of named the adorable stray who'd been coming around the back door at Java and Juice Scooter. At first she thought Scooter must belong to someone nearby and was allowed to roam around the back alleys. She'd put out treats and spend a little too much time talking to Scooter, sharing her hopes and dreams. Animals sure were easy to talk to.

Cassidy was hopeful that the dog would still be there when she opened the back door, but the sweet pooch was gone.

"Hopefully she'll come back," Callie said as Cassidy returned to the table. "If she does and you can leash her, call Daphne and she can come by to check to see if it's Maggie."

"I definitely will," Cassidy said.

The front door opened and a bunch of customers came in, including Tyler Abernathy, Callie's boyfriend. The tall, lean rancher took off his cowboy hat, nodded at Cassidy and then smiled at Callie. "I was missing my two sweethearts so I figured I'd come in for a coffee and get to see you both even for just a few minutes."

Tyler leaned down to give Callie a kiss, then gazed at her and his napping daughter with such love that Cassidy's heart skipped a beat.

Love. Pure love. *It might be really hard to come by, but it exists and I'm holding out for it*, Cassidy thought.

"So your mom is all set with babysitting tonight, right?" Callie asked him. She turned to Cassidy. "An old friend of mine is in a community theater production of *Romeo and Juliet*. I'm so excited about a night on the town."

Ping!

Tyler pulled out his phone. "Uh-oh," he said. "Guess who just texted me she can't babysit tonight because Dad just came down with a cold."

Cassidy looked at Maeve. *She* could watch the baby. And learn something in the process. "I'd be happy to babysit this little pumpkin."

"I really appreciate that," Tyler said, "but we need an *overnight* sitter. The play starts late and ends late and then there's a dinner and party after."

Oooh, Cassidy thought, *an overnight with a baby. Now that would provide some serious on-the-job training.* "No worries. I'll babysit at my place. Just drop off her bassinet, and whatever she might need for the night. Then just pick her up in the morning from here."

Callie slid her a happy glance that told Cassidy her friend understood why she was so eager to babysit— and overnight, at that.

Tyler looked so relieved. "You sure you don't mind? She's an easy baby, but she might wake up once during the night. She's pretty good at soothing herself back to sleep, though."

Cassidy grinned. "I'd *love* to watch Maeve. Really, it's my pleasure."

Callie smiled and squeezed her hand. "We'll drop her off on the way. Seven?"

"Sounds good," Cassidy said, so excited about her evening's adventure.

As the trio left, Cassidy wondered if she should invite Brandon over to help. So that he could get a sneak peek at what taking care of a baby was all about. He seemed truly committed to his role as a father, and she doubted he was all talk; his actions truly said otherwise. But a preview of what caring for a baby entailed, particularly in the wee hours of the morning, might have him changing his tune. And if it did, she needed to know that now. That would easily call a screeching halt to her blossoming feelings for Brandon.

As if he knew she was thinking about him, her phone pinged with a text from him.

How are you feeling today? Need anything?

The warm fuzzies enveloped her. He probably had no idea how such a simple question, maybe just a nicety for him, meant to her. If her mother were still alive, she'd be calling Cassidy every hour on the hour to check in. She'd bring tons of comfort food, all safe for pregnancy. She'd bring her wool socks and a new cozy throw. She'd care the way mothers cared.

And here was Brandon, a man who professed that he wasn't interested in love, being very loving.

I feel great—thanks for asking. I told Callie the big news. And I'm babysitting little Maeve Abernathy tonight at my place if you want a sneak preview of what to expect. Anytime after 7:00.

She waited, wondering if this would be it, when he would show his true colors, make an excuse about why he couldn't. As if he'd want to babysit with her. As if he'd want to take care of a baby any earlier than he absolutely had to. Come on, Cassidy.

I'll be there, he texted back.

She let out a wistful sigh. Of course, he would. Because that seemed to be who Brandon was. A man she could count on. Though a man she could count on to be exactly what he'd said he'd be: a committed father to their baby, a committed platonic partner to Cassidy. Nothing more.

Just remember where you stand and you'll be fine, she told herself.

Chapter 6

"You're doing *what*?" Cornelius asked, confusion-tinged anger exploding on his face.

"I'm babysitting," Brandon repeated, never so grateful to have an excuse for getting out of the fundraiser his dad was trying to get him to go to in his stead tonight. Brandon had lost count of the number of high-ticket fundraisers he'd gone to this year. Between the monkey suit and the small talk, he couldn't take another.

The two stood in the grand foyer of the ranch house, Brandon slipping on his jacket.

"Not that part!" his father bellowed. "Though why you would be babysitting is beyond me, but I'll tell you, Brandon, you're not always easy to understand."

Brandon stared at his dad. "Then what part?"

"You're helping an *Abernathy*? Consorting with the enemy!"

Oh brother. "I don't think fifteen-pound Maeve Abernathy is any threat to us, Dad."

"Those Abernathys are living for the day they catch up to Taylor Beef in revenue," Cornelius said, waving his index finger around. "This has to be a setup. Tyler is probably going to pick your brain for how you're planning to secure Geoff Burris in our new ad campaign, then steal all the ideas and Burris himself!"

Good Lord. "There's not going to be any discussion of business. In fact, I doubt Tyler even knows I'll be helping out tonight."

Cornelius perked up at that. "Oh. Helping out who?"

"Cassidy Ware. She's the actual babysitter."

"Cassidy? That nice gal who owns Java and Juice?"

He knew the place? That was a surprise. "Yes. You've been there?" Despite his fortune, his dad wasn't one to "throw good money away" on what he could "have for free at home." Like coffee. And lunch. And would Cornelius Taylor ever drink a concoction made from silken tofu and kale? No. *Vegan nonsense*, he called smoothies, even the ones made with milk.

"Jessica likes that place, so we stop in there on occasion," Cornelius said. "Last time, she had many questions about the juice blends and wasn't sure which she wanted to order, and Cassidy offered to make her as many samples as she wanted to try. Now that's good business sense. Jessica liked so many of the samples, she ordered a bunch of quart containers to bring home. Cassidy said we were the first to order by the quart. We must have dropped a hundred bucks in there that day."

Brandon almost pumped a fist in the air. *Go, Cassidy.*

"And I thought you two hated each other," his dad added. "Something about a bad romance in high school?"

"We've become…friends," Brandon said. He made a show of pulling out his phone and checking the time. "I'd better get going."

"Fine," Cornelius grumbled. "But if you see that Abernathy, you tell him nothing! Not a word to him about Taylor Beef or Burris. Nothing! Tyler will probably come out with the baby in his arms to seem all harmless and fatherly, then go in for the kill about your pitch to Burris's team."

Brandon shook his head with a smile. "Don't worry, Dad."

"Oh, I will. That's my job."

Brandon clapped his dad on the shoulder. "See you later."

Once in his truck, Brandon let out a deep breath. Talking about Cassidy with his father had felt so strange, given the big news Brandon was withholding. *Yes, Cassidy from Java and Juice—generous with samples and the mother of your soon-to-be grandchild.*

He was far from ready to share that last part.

Brandon made a brief stop in town to pick up a few things, and when he finally pulled into a spot near Cassidy's place, he saw Tyler and Callie getting into their car and driving off. *See, Dad, I told you. No worries. No point of contact made.*

He pressed the intercom for Cassidy's apartment and she buzzed him in. He took the steps two at a time, his anticipation at seeing her making him a little uncomfortable. She was waiting in her doorway when he reached the top floor. Her blond hair was in a bun, exposing the neck he'd kissed every inch of not too long ago. She wore a long-sleeved, green-and-white Bronco Java and Juice T-shirt and soft, faded jeans. He thought she was sexy in a slinky cocktail dress? Whoa.

She held the baby in her arms. The little girl had a small purple rattle in her hand. "Look who it is, Maeve! It's Brandon!"

He grinned. "Hi there, Maeve. I'm going to help babysit tonight."

Maeve stared at him and shook the rattle. "Abda!"

"Nice to meet you, too," he said. "I'm just learning how to speak Baby, so go slow, okay?"

Cassidy smiled. "I love her babbles. She's just the cutest," she added, giving the baby a snuggle.

He followed Cassidy inside and lifted his gift bags. "So, I brought over a couple of things."

Her hazel eyes sparkled. "Do you ever just show up?"

"No. How could I not get a little something for the baby?"

She laughed, shaking her head. "I wish you'd stop being thoughtful, Brandon. You make it hard for me to put you in a certain box."

"Right. Because labels are ever accurate. People are never just one thing."

"Touché," she said with a nod. "He's got me there," she added to Maeve, then sat in the living room, the baby on her lap, Brandon beside her.

"So, for you, Miss Big Cheeks, I have this." He pulled out the soft, floppy, stuffed bunny with bright orange ears and a yellow body. Maeve dropped the rattle on the floor, grabbed the bunny and started shaking it. Its hands rattled and were chewable, which the teething baby apparently discovered because a hand went right in her mouth.

Cassidy grinned. "It's a hit."

"I did get help picking it out from the salesclerk at the gift shop. I had no idea what to get a baby, but she asked me the age and came back with a few suggestions." He picked up the other bag and handed it to her. "Just a little something for you."

"Brandon! You didn't have to get me anything." She peered inside and pulled out the small hardcover book. *Comforting Quotes, Wisdom, and Lullabies for the New Mother.* She touched her hand to her heart. "Darn you, there you go again. I love books like this. Thank you." She flipped through it, stopping on a page near the beginning. "'Nap when the baby naps,'" she read. "'Ignore the laundry, the dust bunnies, your to-do list, turn off your phone, and rest.' Sounds like excellent advice to me."

He nodded. "I saw it by the counter and thought you might like it."

"I do. Very much. Thank you."

"So what's on the agenda?" he asked, eyes on the baby. "Does she have a schedule? According to my fatherhood book, schedules are everything." He was only on chapter four, but he'd learned quite a bit and was looking forward to putting what he knew in practice tonight.

"You have a book on fatherhood?" she asked.

"Yup. Bought it the day I found out I was going to be a dad. I have to read every sentence very slowly since all the lingo is new. Did you know there are different kinds of cries? Pick me up *now* cry. Hungry cry. Tired cry. Bored cry. My belly hurts cry."

Cassidy laughed. "I've also been doing research and reading. Baby world is definitely its own universe. And yes, Maeve has a schedule. Tyler gave me a cheat sheet of everything to know about Maeve. When to feed her, when to put her down for the night, what to do if she cries in the middle of the night, when to expect her to wake up in the morning, how much to feed her. Everything."

Whoa. He hadn't gotten that far in the book. The subject of "sleep" alone had three chapters. "That sounds like a lot to keep track of. What is she up to now?"

"Just chillin'," Cassidy said. "She'll be ready for her bottle soon and then we'll have more playtime and then we'll put her in her crib for the night. Tyler said she tends to sleep through. Well, till five, five thirty."

"Hey, I work at a ranch. We get up with the roosters. Five is nothing to me."

"I hadn't considered that. You'll be fine with the early mornings, then. Me, too, since the shop opens at seven, and I bake fresh beforehand."

He immediately pictured himself beside her in bed, Cassidy naked and sleeping, her blond hair splayed on the pillow. He'd hear their baby cry in the middle of the night and go take care of him or her, letting Cassidy sleep. He'd follow the schedule and, when the baby was ready for a nap, he'd get back under the covers with Cassidy. No problem. He'd heard that taking care of a baby was tough stuff, but between his fatherhood book and some practice like tonight, he'd pick it up in no time. He'd have a *schedule*. Just like he had for his workdays. And didn't babies nap all day in their cribs or strollers? Most times he noticed a baby in a stroller in town, the little one was snoozing away peacefully, not making a peep.

He liked everything about his middle-of-the-night scenario and baby-rearing with Cassidy, except getting out of their bed. Of course, there wasn't going to be a "their bed." She'd turned down the no-strings romance. She'd turned down the platonic marriage proposal. Maybe he'd broach the subject of marriage again tonight. Taking care of a baby while talking about providing a united Team Parents might sway Cassidy.

"Would you like to hold her?" she asked.

He almost jumped. Did he want to hold her? *No*, he thought. Maeve seemed pretty fragile. Droppable. Breakable. Had he ever held a baby? He couldn't remember ever doing so. Damn. A minute ago he was all "there's nothing to taking care of a baby." Now he was afraid to hold one. No one ever said he didn't talk a good game; he was kind of famous for it. But usually he came through. Now he just wanted to inch away. "Do you need a break?"

She tilted her head. "Not necessarily. I just thought you'd want to. You don't have to. But unless you've had lots of interactions with babies, you might like to see what's it all about."

"I've had zero interaction with babies," he admitted. He wasn't sure why that was so hard to say. He didn't like coming up short. But this was one area where Brandon Taylor, Executive VP, had absolutely no experience.

"See how I'm holding her?" Cassidy asked. "Supporting her against my chest with an arm around her back and one under her bottom? That's what you do. It'll be instinctive once you take her," she added. "How tightly to hold her, all that."

"Okay," he said, holding out his hands.

He didn't have his arms in the correct position, so Cassidy adjusted them and suddenly Maeve Abernathy was against his chest, holding on to her bunny and chewing away on its toe. He stared down at the top of her head in complete wonder. He had a baby in his arms!

"She barely weighs anything and yet feels so substantial." He sniffed the top of her head. "Baby shampoo. I remember when my twin brothers were babies and smelled like that." He looked down at Maeve, then over at Cassidy.

"I love that smell," she said. "I think everyone does. And you're doing great, by the way," she added with a nod. "You look like a natural."

He raised an eyebrow. "You're lying through your teeth."

"Nope," she said, shaking her head. "You really do."

Huh. That gave him a bit more confidence. Could he move and hold Maeve at the same time? He stood and walked over to the windows. That shouldn't have felt like such an accomplishment, but it absolutely did. "Look, Maeve, that's a tree. And there's a man walking a little dog. I think it's a Boston terrier." She turned her huge eyes to him and shook her bunny. "Yeah, the doggie is very cute. I agree."

"Bah!" Maeve said, waving her bunny before dropping it.

He eyed the stuffed animal on the wood floor.

"Hmm, do I have the super powers of kneeling down while holding a baby and picking that up?" he asked Cassidy.

She grinned. "Slowly."

He knelt as slowly as he could, keeping a tight hold on Maeve, and reached out an arm and grabbed the stuffed animal, which Maeve batted right out his hand and back onto the floor. She then exploded into baby laughter. He picked it up again, and again she knocked it to the floor, giggling away.

"Oh, it's like that, is it?" he asked, giving her a little tickle on her belly. More baby laughter. He had no idea babies could laugh that loud.

He looked over at Cassidy, who wasn't laughing. Or smiling. "Everything okay?" he asked.

"Yeah," she said. "Everything's fine." She turned away and sat on the sofa, straightening the little pile of white burp cloths that were already perfectly stacked on the coffee table.

Hmm. Something was not fine. He walked to the couch and stood beside it, Maeve now batting his chin with the stuffed animal. He gave her another tickle and she dropped the bunny with a giggle.

"So this is how babies play games," he said. "I thought they just sat around or napped. I'm getting a first-rate education here, thanks to you," he added, giving Maeve's impossibly soft cheek a gentle caress. He sat beside Cassidy, the baby now nibbling on her fingers. "You have a lot of experience with babies? Kids of your friends? Relatives?"

"Neither," she said. "But I have done a lot of babysitting. It's how I put myself through school and got my associate's degree. Well, that and waitressing."

"Are all babies like Maeve? I like her. She has spunk."

Cassidy laughed and he was so glad to hear that sound. She'd seemed a bit down a minute ago. "There's a huge range. You've got your colicky screamers." She shivered. "Then you've got never-nappers. Then there are the easy-peasies, like Maeve seems to be."

As if on cue to take issue with that, the baby let out a cry, not a cry-cry, more like a fussy whine.

"Ah, let me check the schedule," Cassidy said. "I think it's time for her dinner and bottle." She scanned the typed, stapled pages and stopped midpage with her fingertip. "Seven thirty, dinner. One container of mac and cheese, two peach slices and four ounces of formula in her bottle."

"Wow, she eats mac and cheese?" he asked. "I figured she'd eat jarred baby food. Sweet potato purée. Apple sauce."

"She's a few months past solids, so she can eat tiny bites of just about anything," Cassidy said. "Tyler dropped off a small container for her. He told me he makes a batch of her meals for the week and freezes them and sometimes she eats whatever he and Callie are having, just little pieces."

Brandon smiled. "Tyler sounds like a great dad. I should talk to him. Not that I'm *allowed* to talk to him." He groaned and rolled his eyes.

"Not allowed?" she asked with a raised eyebrow as she stood and headed into the kitchen.

Brandon followed. "My father thinks Tyler set up this

entire babysitting scenario so that he can corner me for information about Geoff Burris. Taylor Beef and Abernathy Meats are major competitors and both want Geoff to sign on to promote the company in an ad campaign."

"Ah," she said. "Your dad doesn't really believe Tyler set this up, does he?" She slid Maeve into the baby seat rigged to the table, then went to the refrigerator and took out a small container and a baby bottle.

"Oh, he probably does. Two plus two always equals a lot more than four with my dad. He has all sorts of equations to make facts add up the way he wants. All he needed to hear was that I was going over to your place to help babysit an Abernathy."

Cassidy smiled. "Maeve is totally innocent!"

"He figures Tyler will jump out of the woodwork at some point to get me to talk about my secret plan to sign Burris."

"Landing the biggest rodeo star in Montana would be major," she said. "*Do* you have a secret plan?"

"Well, I've tried every business tactic I've learned over the years and that didn't get me past his 'team,' so yes, I now do have a secret plan that I will put into effect tomorrow."

"Can I hear it?" she asked, pouring the contents of the container into a small pot and turning on the burner.

"Sure. It's called 'I knew you in high school.'"

Cassidy laughed. "Will that work with him? If it were me in his shoes, I would sign with Abernathy Meats just to spite you."

He grinned. "Yes, you would have. Before you re-knew me. Admit it, now you'd sign with Taylor Beef."

"Well, I am going to have a little Taylor, so yes," she said.

His gaze went right to her belly, still completely flat. But in there was a tiny, growing mix of the two of them. He swallowed and suddenly had to sit.

He pulled out a chair and sank down on it, right next to Maeve, who was banging her bunny on the tray top of her seat. *I get you, Maeve*, he said silently to her. *You're a little frustrated, just like I am, so you're slamming your bunny. If it were okay for me to do that, I would.* She swiveled her big blue eyes to him. *Not that I don't like babies. I'm gonna have one in, what...eight months? Sometimes that sinks in and scares the bejesus out of me, Maeve. Again, no offense.*

"So we're okay?" he asked the baby.

"Ba la!" Maeve said and flung the bunny across the table.

She let out a giggle before her face crumpled and her eyes got teary. Boy, did her face go from its normal complexion to bright red.

"Just in time!" Cassidy said, bringing over a little plate of mac and cheese.

Maeve's expression changed in a snap at what was before her. Cassidy slid a baby spoon into one piece of macaroni and brought it up to the baby's lips. Maeve gobbled it up.

Looked easy enough. "I'll feed her," Brandon said. "You cooked, so I've got this."

Cassidy smiled and handed him the spoon. "I'll get her peaches cut up." She walked over to the refrigerator again, her back to him.

Again, he got the feeling that something was wrong, that *something* was bothering her. Ask? Don't ask?

"Everything okay?" came tumbling out of his mouth, even though he probably should have just let her be with whatever was going on inside her head. He didn't always want to answer that very question whenever it was asked of him. In fact, he never did. So he should extend the same courtesy to Cassidy.

She turned toward him with a tight smile. He could see something was warring within her. Her hazel eyes seemed half happy and half upset. "Of course," she said—too brightly—then got busy with a knife and the peach slices.

Brandon nodded and turned back to Maeve, feeding her another little cheesy macaroni, then another and another. She batted the next spoonful at his face, and the gooey pasta clung to his chin. "Oh, thanks, Maeve."

Cassidy laughed, so hard that he couldn't help but laugh, too. Then she stopped, kind of suddenly, and looked like she might burst into tears.

As he wiped the macaroni off his face, he thought about his sister telling him to find out what Cassidy *needed* and that once he did, he'd become indispensable and then she'd come around to marrying him. Whatever it was that she needed, she wasn't getting it right now. That was for sure.

Something was definitely bothering Cassidy. And he was going to find out what.

Yes, something was wrong, she thought as she watched Brandon settle onto the sofa with Maeve on his lap. After he fed the baby, Cassidy had changed

Maeve into her jammies, a soft cotton one-piece with blue moons and yellow stars. While she'd done that, Brandon had taken the storybook from Maeve's bag and flipped through it. Now, with Maeve reclining against him, her head in the crook of his elbow, he began reading aloud from *Doolie the Duck's Big Adventure*.

A few pages in, he noticed the baby's eyes drooping and his voice lowered, the sound almost lulling Cassidy to sleep, too. "Well, Maeve, I only got to read you four pages. Maybe next time I'll get to find out if Doolie and the beaver become buddies." He smiled, gently pushing back a baby curl from near Maeve's eye.

This. This was what was wrong.

The man was a revelation. She kept expecting him to revert to the Brandon Taylor she'd thought he was the past fifteen years. An arrogant hotshot leaving behind the ole trail of broken hearts, used to getting whatever he wanted because of his family name, looks and money, not caring about anyone but himself. But she certainly hadn't met that guy. Maybe for a few minutes in the stables, right after they'd made love, when she'd thought he'd been dismissing her. She'd come to realize he hadn't been. He'd truly had to get back to his brother's wedding; he was a groomsman and was supposed to be there, not cavorting in the barn with a guest-slash-the-help. She'd been the one to insist they arrive back separately. And then what had he done? Asked her to dance quite a few times.

He'd also asked her for a no-strings romance.

And a platonic marriage.

So here was a truly great guy, sweet to babies and to

the mother of his child, but who could not, would not, commit to a relationship.

So was he great or not great at all? The answer: not great for *her*. The more time she spent with Brandon, the more she liked him. No, she more than liked him. She was falling for him hard, despite all her warnings not to let that happen. But there was powerful stuff going on outside of her control.

He'd been her first love, even if it was just a few months of a high school romance and all they'd done was kiss. It made him special. Unforgettable. That he was so insanely good-looking and sexy, his dark eyes equally intense and playful, made him impossible to ignore. And that he was so thoughtful and made himself so available to her touched her deeply. She'd missed having "a person," someone who'd be there in a heartbeat for her, who'd drop everything if she needed them, as she'd do for them. Her "person" had always been her mom, and her loss had left a gaping hole inside Cassidy's heart that she hadn't even fully understood until Brandon Taylor came along and started filling it in.

"Someone's asleep," Brandon whispered, pointing a finger down at Maeve. He then brought that finger up to his lips in a *shh* gesture.

And somehow, that was all it took for a little voice inside her to say *I love you, damn it*.

Uneasy as that thought ping-ponged around her head, she bolted up. "I'll settle her in her bassinet." She reached out to take Maeve, but Brandon stood.

"I've got it," he said. "Transferring her to you and then to the bassinet might wake her. This way we skip a step." He looked at her for agreement, his dark eyes so warm it was hard to look away.

"Good point." She backed away, glad to have a moment to compose herself. *You don't love him, you just really like him. He's a surprise is all. And your baby's father. It's not love, it's not love, it's not love.*

Maybe she'd snap out of it by the end of the night like Olympia Dukakis's character thought her daughter should do in the movie *Moonstruck*.

Cassidy led the way into her bedroom, where she'd had Tyler put the bassinet. Brandon easily settled Maeve, her little bunny beside her. The baby stirred, but then let out a sigh, her eyes remaining closed, her chest slowly rising and falling with her sleeping breaths.

"That went better than I thought," he said. "I'm not half bad at this."

She smiled. "Not half bad at all. Were you worried? Did you think she might barf all over you or that she'd scream every time you tried to hold her?"

"Yes, actually. I did. I never would have considered myself baby friendly."

"Me, either," she said. "But you're consistently full of surprises."

"In a good way, I hope."

She felt her smile fade. Not in a good way for her well-being. Or for her heart.

Once again he was staring at her, his gaze soft. He reached out a hand to her hair and tucked a swath behind her ear. "I hope our baby gets your eyes. So pretty."

She swallowed. She couldn't say anything.

He moved closer, the hand moving to her cheek. "So beautiful," he murmured.

You, too. You, too. You, too, she thought, unable to take her eyes off his face. He was so close. And so irresistible.

In moments she was backed up against the wall, their mouths fused, his hands in her hair, hers on his rock-solid chest.

She could feel him pulsating against her. All she had to do was to keep kissing him, to keep touching him, to say *yes*, and they'd be in her bed.

Back away from the hot man, she told herself. *All getting naked with Brandon again will do is leave you wanting more from him. And he's told you he's not up for grabs.*

"You drive me wild, Cassidy," he whispered into her ear, and she closed her eyes, giving herself a few more seconds of such delicious pleasure.

But she couldn't exactly tell him they had to stop when she was so busy kissing him.

Chapter 7

Cassidy came to her senses in the nick of time, her T-shirt in a heap at her feet, his jeans unsnapped.

"Brandon," she said as his lips grazed her neck and his hands traveled across the lacy cups of her bra. "We can't do this. First of all, we're babysitting. What if Tyler and Callie stop by to pick up Maeve early and we're naked in bed? They asked me to babysit—not fool around while taking care of their daughter."

There. A very good reason to stop this craziness. They weren't in high school, making out on a couch while her little charge was fast asleep. They were adults and this was wrong on too many levels.

"Tomorrow night then?" he asked, reaching down to pick up her shirt for her.

She sighed and hurried into her T-shirt. "We'd better talk."

"My least favorite words," he said.

Her heart went south. This was the Brandon she'd been expecting all along. The one who wanted sex but not romance or love. The one who wasn't interested in the details, such as every messy step of what they'd gotten themselves into with the pregnancy. He was more big picture. She was pregnant, therefore he'd buy out pricey Baby Central in Lewistown and stash her in a luxe cabin on his property, wearing a wedding ring to a point, which would let him come and go as he pleased.

No sirree. Not with this woman.

She smoothed her hair and lifted her chin. He snapped his jeans.

She needed to make sure he understood that she was vulnerable to him—without saying it outright. She hated that he had the control here. He was the one who wasn't interested in a real relationship. Or love. She could either accept that or ignore it like an idiot, give in to her attraction for him, and end up potentially so hurt that it created a terrible rift between them. As parents, they couldn't afford that. They needed to be Team Baby.

So just stop it, Cassidy. You know how he feels. There's really nothing to talk about.

Except, as she watched him tiptoe over to the bassinet and check on Maeve, who was sleeping soundly, she was struck by the fact that this man had hidden depths he wasn't aware of. He could love; he simply chose not to. There was more to it than his family history. She'd experienced parental abandonment just as he had, but she knew her heart was open to love. Guarded, sure.

But open to it. With the right person. Brandon was completely closed.

She suddenly realized that he must have been very hurt by previous romantic relationships. All that meant was that he'd been willing once to let himself feel *everything*. Therefore, he could do it again.

"Wow," he said, standing at the bassinet in the dimly lit room and looking down at the sleeping baby. "Look at that. Everything awaiting her, the entire world, all the possibilities."

Oh, Brandon. If it takes me every single day until my due date, I'm going to get that heart of yours back and running.

He turned just as she put her hands on her belly. Her expression must have been a mixture of a million things because he said, "A thousand pennies for your thoughts."

"Inflation or the Taylor riches?" she asked, shaking her head with a smile.

"Li'l of both."

"Just what you said. Our baby will have the whole world waiting for him or her. I want to do everything right by this little one." Suddenly, tears poked at the backs of her eyes. "I don't want to make mistakes and I know mistakes are easily made." She turned away, overcome by a burst of fear.

"Hey," he said, coming over and slinging an arm around her shoulder. "We're all human. No one's perfect, so yes, we're going to make mistakes. But mistakes can be healthy and teach us how to be better."

She nodded, the tears drying up. The man needed to take his own wisdom to heart.

"You're going to be a great mom, Cassidy."

A warmth spread inside her and she truly felt better. One minute he could make her feel there was no hope for them, and a second later, remind her that he just needed time to turn his heart around.

"Thank you. That means a lot to me. And you're going to be a great dad. I can see that in everything you do, Brandon."

"Am I blushing?" he asked, touching his cheeks with a twinkly-eyed smile.

He could be jokey all he wanted, but she knew she'd touched him as deeply as he'd touched her.

She did want to talk—though where the conversation would lead she had no idea—and doing so over dinner might help. "I have a ton of food, as you know." She headed to the doorway of her kitchen. "Want to try the lasagna?"

"I never turn down lasagna," he said with a bright smile. Trying to make nice, to make light. Diffuse the tension.

In the kitchen she poured herself a glass of her new decaf iced tea, took a gulp and instantly felt better. She poured another for Brandon and handed it to him.

He parked himself in a chair at the table, his gaze on her. "I guess we do have a lot to talk about," he said then took a long sip of the tea.

She let out a breath. "Yeah, we do."

He set the glass down on the table. "What do you *need*?"

"Need?" she repeated, glancing at him before reaching into the refrigerator for the container of lasagna.

"I just want to make sure I'm there for you. Here for

you. I've been accused of being dense when it comes to women and what they want. Or need. Maybe what you need is for me not to kiss you. Maybe you need a really solid friend. Whatever it is, I want to be there for you."

She really didn't know what to make of that. *Not kiss her. Solid friend.* She wanted him to fall for her the way she was falling for him, damn it. But clearly, he wasn't. "You've been very kind, Brandon. So—"

"Thanks, but what do you need from me?"

"That's hard to answer." It really was. If he proposed a real relationship, the two of them really trying to make this work because they were about to share a child, she would be all-in.

"I'm not sure what I need from you," she said. "You're here, you're committed to the baby." She bit her lip. She wanted a hell of a lot more than that.

"And that's what you *need*?" he asked. "Me to be there for both of you?"

"It's a little more complicated than that," she said, feeling a frown form. There was a whole universe in that question of his.

He looked at her, sort of biting his lip, his expression somewhat confused. What was he trying to get at?

"What I need is kind of a big question, Brandon. I mean…what do *you* need?"

He leaned back in his chair, hooking his thumbs into his jeans' pockets. "I guess it *is* harder to answer than it seems. Maybe you could just give me a list of tangibles. What you'd like to start getting for our baby. A bassinet like Maeve's, a crib, pj's, stuffed animals. Whatever you want."

Was that what he was talking about? *Stuff?*

"Need and want are different," she said, turning and sliding the lasagna into the oven.

"Are they really, though?" he asked when she spun around, his eyes steady on her.

"Yes. Very. There's a lot I want but don't need."

"Like what?" he asked.

She held back a sigh. She'd started this conversation and she just wanted to end it. They weren't on the same page. Or in the same realm.

"Come on," he said, taking a sip of his drink. "Like what?"

Fine. Though it annoyed her to explain something so basic that anyone who wasn't filthy rich would understand. "Like…the gorgeous, long red wool coat I saw in a shop window. That coat stops my heart every time I pass that shop. But it's *way* out of my budget. I have a perfectly nice wool coat already. And a down jacket. I don't need that red coat. I just want it. See?"

"But want can become need," he said. "I think if you want something bad enough, you begin to need it. You must have it."

She stared at him for a second. Yes, exactly. That was how she was beginning to think about him. But she had no idea what *he* was talking about. How it related to *them*. Unless she was giving him too much credit and he was thinking about a Range Rover or a trip to Tahiti. She got out two plates and utensils, her appetite diminishing by the second.

"Have you thought more about getting married?" he asked.

She whirled to face him. Was this the route he was

on? How did want and need get him to this question? He didn't want or need to get married, not in the real sense.

You want to know what I need? To understand you. Just when I think I do, you throw me for a major loop.

"No. There's nothing to think about, Brandon." She sucked in a breath, remembering her conversation with Callie at Java and Juice about what a marriage would actually entail. "But tell me. Let's say we did get married. How exactly do you envision it? I mean, we wouldn't be a normal husband and wife. So we'd live together like roommates? Friends but sharing in the responsibility of raising our child?"

"Well, I guess I didn't think too far down the line. But it's a good question."

Aha. Didn't think it through. Once he did, he'd take back the proposal in a snap.

"What do you mean by roommates, exactly?" he asked—warily.

"Well, it would be a platonic marriage, right? So we'd be roommates. Housemates, I should say. We'd have separate bedrooms."

"But we'd be married," he said. Earnestly. "So, we'd share the master suite."

"Oh, the master suite," she sing-songed. "Brandon. Platonic couples, an oxymoron in itself, don't share bedrooms. Because they're not sleeping together. There's no sex."

He stared at her. "There could be."

Of course he expected sex. Brandon Taylor giving up all the hot singles of Bronco for a truly platonic marriage? No way. "So you see us married, having a sexual relationship, as married couples do, just without the emotional angle? It wouldn't be a love match. Is that it?"

She'd known from the get-go that love wouldn't be part of it. But she hadn't known he'd been counting on the shared bed.

"We already know how good we are together, Cass. Sexually."

"Didn't we have this exact conversation at the wedding? A no-strings romance? I said no thanks."

"Right," he said. "Except now we're expecting a baby. So it's a different conversation."

She laughed—but not happily. "I see. Now that we're having a baby, the conversation has morphed to *marriage* instead of just a *relationship*. Legally binding. Do you really believe any of this complete and utter crap you're saying?"

He frowned. "It makes sense to me, Cassidy."

No kidding. "It doesn't work for me. It's not what I *need*."

Fury whirred in her stomach. The smell of the lasagna was suddenly too much. She ran into the bathroom, thinking she had to throw up, but she didn't. She just needed to catch her breath. Splash some cool water on her face.

When she came out, Brandon was standing by the oven with her big yellow oven mitts. She'd heard the timer go off when she'd been in the bathroom, but hadn't had it in her to rush out. He took out the container of lasagna and began cutting and plating.

Ever helpful. Grr. *Be just one thing!* she wanted to scream like a crazy person. Of course, no one was or should be. But he needed to stop getting A pluses for kindness and generosity and thoughtfulness and Fs for relationships.

He brought the plates to the table and set them down. "I'm sorry, Cassidy. But I am who I am. I don't see myself changing. It took a lot to make me this way, and I'm fine with who I turned out to be."

She forced herself to sit. "Fine with not having a real relationship? How can you be so sure you'll love our baby if you can't love your wife?"

He stared at her, something shifting in his expression that told her she'd pushed a button he didn't want pushed.

She was about to apologize, to say that she knew full well there was a difference, but his phone pinged.

He pulled it out. "Oh, damn it. Text from my dad. There's a problem with Starlight. My favorite horse at the ranch. She's the one who eavesdropped on us talking the night of the wedding." He scanned the text. "My dad wants my help."

"Go," she said. "I think we could both use a break from our conversation anyway."

He nodded. "I'll take a rain check on the lasagna."

The moment the door closed behind him, she felt his absence so acutely that she had to sit and give herself a moment.

And she knew she'd already crossed her own line. There was no turning back from her feelings for Brandon. So she'd just put her energy to better use: turning *him* back from a life without love.

That somewhat settled, she dug into the lasagna. She was eating for two now, so she added his to her own plate.

* * *

"Let's go take the chocolate-coconut scones from the oven," Cassidy told Maeve, scooping the baby from the playpen in the kiddie section of Bronco Java and Juice. "You can take your bunny with you."

"La ba!" Maeve said, waving her new lovey.

It was six forty in the morning; the sky a beautiful dark pink and gray as the sun began to rise. Cassidy had been awake since just before five o'clock, when Maeve had let out a little shriek to let her sitter know she was ready to begin her day. Despite not having had a great night's sleep, thanks to some tossing and turning over her conversation with Brandon, Cassidy had excitedly rushed over to get Maeve, elated at caring for a baby and grateful for the practice.

She loved everything about the experience of caring for Maeve, from holding the sweet baby against her, feeding, changing, bathing, dressing, even getting spit up on. At one point, Cassidy realized she was talking to Maeve nonstop, detailing her every move, thinking out loud, and it occurred to her what good company a baby was, even if silent company.

One thing that had kept Cassidy awake last night was her quiet phone. She'd kept expecting it to ping with a text from Brandon, checking in, quipping about something, anything. But he hadn't texted at all. Maybe Starlight was very ill. Or maybe their conversation had been too much for him, as well. Granted, he would have left to help out at the ranch no matter what the two of them had been doing. Brandon wasn't a responsibility shirker. But he'd left very quickly and she'd been able to tell that he was relieved for the excuse to get out of there.

How can you be so sure you'll love our baby if you can't love your wife?

She'd hit below the belt on that one. First of all, there was no wife and wouldn't be unless she agreed to his plan of *being* an unloved wife. She'd apologize when she saw him next, and she had no doubt she'd see him today. If she wanted to help Brandon be able to love again, she had to be smart about it, not fling shaming accusations at him.

"Today's a new day, Maeve," she told the baby. "I'll start fresh with Brandon. What's my grand plan, you ask? To just be myself. To not talk so much about what's to come and what will be, and how this and how that, but just to *be*. Two people figuring things out as they go because they were thrown together into something huge. A you, Maeve. A baby." She scooped her up and twirled around, a rookie move when she knew better because a tiny fist grabbed the end of her ponytail and yanked.

"Oh yeah?" Cassidy said, giving the baby a tickle. Maeve giggled, her beautiful eyes twinkling. "And I have a much more fun activity for you instead of hair yanking. Let's go into the kitchen and take out the scones. Maybe we'll each swipe a piece. Yum!"

As she turned to put the baby in her stroller to wheel her into the kitchen, Cassidy had that funny feeling that someone was watching her. Not Maeve, who only had eyes for her bunny, which she was alternately shaking and chewing. Some *early* early birds outside awaiting their smoothies and lattes? Or maybe Tyler was a bit early to pick up his daughter? She expected him just before seven. Or perhaps Helen and Hank had arrived for their shift? Cassidy glanced at the glass front door, but there was no sign of anyone.

She was about to wheel Maeve behind the counter and into the kitchen when she had the feeling again. This time, she looked to the glass back door, which could be accessed from the kitchen and the shop.

Cassidy jumped. Winona Cobbs stood at the door, her razor-sharp gaze right on Cassidy. Ninety-four years old, Winona was a relative newcomer to Bronco. Cassidy had heard from Callie, who worked for Winona's great-grandson, that Winona was originally from a tiny town called Rust Creek Falls. She'd gotten pregnant as a teenager and had been told the baby had died and had then been separated from her beau, a man named Josiah Abernathy. But the baby girl had been alive the whole time. Thanks to sleuthing, caring folks, that baby had been located, and Winona had been reunited with her long-lost daughter, Daisy, with whom she now lived in Bronco.

Cassidy hurried through the kitchen and opened the door. "Morning, Miss Winona. We're not quite open yet, not till seven, but if you're wanting a quick cup of coffee or tea, I'd be happy to get you something."

"I've had my morning tea, thank you," Winona said. Her long white hair was in a ponytail down one shoulder of her purple tracksuit. "I was taking my morning stroll through the back nooks and crannies of the shops, and noticed you."

"Oh, well thanks for saying hi. Sure I can't get you a pastry? I have six kinds of muffins and three kinds of scones. Maybe a bagel? You can have your pick before the morning crowd shows up to devour them any minute now."

"I had sourdough toast and jam with my tea, so I'm just fine," Winona said. "But I'll tell you something, Cassidy Ware. You'll be glad you did it. Yes, you will."

Cassidy stared at the elderly woman. *Glad I did what?* she wondered.

Everyone said Winona was psychic and she did have her own business, Wisdom by Winona. Callie ran into Winona often since she worked for Winona's great-grandson at Bronco's Ghost Tours, where Winona had her shop in an office. Callie had told Cassidy that she'd come around to believing that Winona had a gift.

"What do you mean by that?" Cassidy asked Winona. "Glad I did what exactly?"

"You'll see. Oh yes, you will. You have a nice day now." Winona turned on her heel and walked away.

Cassidy tried not to frown. "You, too," she called. *You'll be glad you did it.* Did what?

She wanted to chase after Winona and demand she answer the question. But she couldn't leave Maeve alone and she had to tend to the scones.

Did *what*? Was it something she'd already done? Or something she was going to do?

Hmm. Maybe Cassidy would make an appointment with Winona at her shop. Get an answer *and* have a formal sit-down reading of her fortunes, her future. Not that she necessarily believed in psychics. But she didn't *not* believe, either.

As Cassidy was coming to realize, anything was possible.

Chapter 8

At seven in the morning, Brandon was finally ready for bed. The veterinarian had instructed him and the stable manager to watch the horse all night; she was having stomach issues, but neither Brandon nor the manager could figure out what the Appaloosa could have possibly eaten that could have resulted in this kind of colic. With Starlight more comfortable after getting some medicine, Brandon had settled in for the night in her stall, knowing full well he'd be unable to sleep a wink anyway. Not with that conversation with Cassidy knocking through his head. And not with all the reminders of where his present and future had begun. Right here.

He got up, pulled hay from his neck and hair, and rolled up the sleeping bag, talking gently to Starlight, who was much perkier this morning. He was about to text his dad that the horse was on the mend when he heard footsteps. One of the cowboys, Paul Fielding, came into view, holding the hand of a young boy, seven or eight at most. The boy was crying, his head hung. The cowboy looked grim. What was this about?

Paul nodded in greeting at Brandon then looked at the boy. "My son Kyle has something to say."

The boy's face crumpled and tears slipped down his freckled cheeks.

"Go ahead, Kyle," his dad said firmly.

The boy slashed two hands under his damp eyes, his shoulders shaking. "I didn't mean to make Starlight sick. I swear it!"

Ah. Mystery solved of how a horse with a restricted diet managed to eat something that made her so ill.

A teary-eyed, nervous Kyle looked down. "After school yesterday, I came to see her and Firecracker, my other favorite horse. And I had leftovers in my lunch-box so I gave them to Starlight. I'm really sorry," he added, the boy's remorse evident in his face and voice.

"Do you remember what you gave her?" Brandon asked.

Kyle nodded. "Apple slices. And the rest of my turkey and cheese sandwich. There was half left."

"Well, that doesn't sound too bad," Brandon said. "Definitely didn't agree with her, though."

Kyle hung his head again and scuffed the floor with one of his blue sneakers.

"Tell Mr. Taylor what else," his father said. "It's important he knows so that Starlight can get the best care."

Yeah, apple slices and a turkey sandwich, even the

whole thing, wouldn't have gotten Starlight as sick as she'd been.

Kyle looked up, biting his lip. "There were a few Pop Rocks left in the pack, so I shook them out on my palm and held them out to her and she ate them. She seemed to like them. They were the cherry ones. I didn't know she'd get sick. I'm sorry." He burst into a fresh round of tears, the narrow shoulders trembling before he threw his arms around his dad's waist and buried his face in his hip.

"Kyle, you've got to face Mr. Taylor and your mistake," Paul said, his voice gentle but firm.

The boy slowly looked up at Brandon. "I'm really sorry. I'm sorry, Starlight," he called out to the horse.

Brandon knelt in front of Kyle. "The thing about horses is that, unlike people, they can't throw up or burp. So food that doesn't agree with them just stays in their bellies, making trouble."

Kyle wiped under his eyes again. "I didn't know that. Did you know that, Daddy?" he asked, turning to the cowboy.

Paul nodded. "I did, son. Animals and people have very different kinds of bodies. So you have to know what an animal can and can't eat before you offer it anything. If you want to work on a ranch someday, that's important to know."

"That's right," Brandon said, standing. "You want to be a cowboy like your dad, Kyle?"

Kyle nodded. "And I want to be a champion roper like Geoff Burris. He's my favorite. But my dad said I can't go to the holiday rodeo in November like we were gonna because of what I did to Starlight."

Brandon glanced at Paul, who looked pretty miserable himself. "Well, Kyle, you didn't know you would make Starlight ill and now you do. I'll bet anything you'll never feed the horses again without getting permission. Starlight was probably very happy to get those apple slices, but she can't have stuff like Pop Rocks."

Kyle nodded. "She did seem to like the apples best of all. My dad also said I'm not allowed to come in the stables anymore and I promise I won't."

Brandon slid a compassionate glance over to Paul, then looked at the boy. "Tell you what, Kyle. You obviously love horses, since you were just trying to share your lunch leftovers with Starlight. She happens to be my favorite, too. If it's okay with your dad, it's okay with me for you come see her and any of the horses anytime you want. Just don't feed them without permission from a grown-up. Okay?"

Paul's shoulders visibly sagged with relief, and Brandon realized the guy was probably worried for his job.

Kyle's face broke into a smile. "Wow, thank you. I'm really sorry for what I did."

"I know you are," Brandon said. "Starlight's going to be fine. And I'm just glad she ate everything so that you couldn't give any Pop Rocks to Firecracker or we'd have had two horses with serious bellyaches."

Kyle's eyes widened. "Oh yeah. I'm glad, too."

"And," Brandon added, "if your dad thinks it's okay to take you to the rodeo to see Geoff Burris win again, like I know he will, I also think that's okay. Geoff's a Bronco hero."

"He's the best!" Kyle exclaimed. He looked at his dad. "Does that mean we can still go?"

"We'll talk about that on the way to school," Paul said, smoothing the boy's rumpled brown hair. "If Mr. Taylor's good with it, then maybe we can, after all. I know how much seeing your hero in person means to you."

"All right!" Kyle said and ran over to Brandon, throwing his skinny arms around Brandon's hips for a hug.

Brandon grinned and gave the boy a squeeze.

After more apologies and a handshake from Paul, father and son headed down the long aisle, and Brandon heard Kyle say, "Daddy, Geoff Burris is my hero, but so are you."

Not much could bring a tear to Brandon's eyes, but that did. Funny, Cassidy was the one with all the new hormones coursing through her, and here he was, impending fatherhood making him all emotional.

He gave Starlight a pat on the nose and let her know he'd be back in an hour, then texted his father that the Appaloosa had come through fine and that the vet would be back around nine to check on her. He headed out of the stables, watching Paul and Kyle walk away holding hands, the boy's backpack dangling from one of Paul's shoulders.

That'll be me someday. Dealing with all the scrapes kids got themselves into. He thought Paul had handled the whole thing very well, and he'd be sure to seek him out later this morning to let him know. He tried to imagine himself with a child that age, helping out with homework, giving advice, going fishing, riding, hiking, and teaching them all about the ranch. Dragging the crying kid to apologize for this or that. He saw himself teaching his young daughter how to get up on a horse, her hair blond like Cassidy's, eyes dark like his. He saw himself helping his young son, his hair dark like Brandon's, eyes big and hazel like Cassidy's, with his math homework, then the three of them having dinner, walking the dog they'd adopt, talking about their days, sharing, laughing.

Fantasy? Or possible reality? He certainly hadn't experienced days like that with his own parents. He didn't remember his parents being married at all, though of course they had been. Maybe he was romanticizing a family scene because one didn't exist in his head. Therefore, the Norman Rockwell version was easy to make up. For all Brandon knew, he'd be a mediocre dad and say, *Sorry, I can't teach you to ride today, I have to work. Sorry, I can't help with long division, I need to make a business call.*

Nah. Brandon wouldn't be an "I'm too busy" dad. He'd be there 100 percent, putting his child first. He'd felt that deeply from the get-go.

How can you be so sure you'll love our baby if you can't love your wife?

Cassidy's words from last night, right before his dad's text, slammed into his head. *Was* he romanticizing? Maybe Cassidy was right. If he couldn't stand the thought of commitment, didn't believe in a real marriage, what made him think he believed in the bonds of a parent and child?

Brandon stared out at the fence line, barely seeing ranch staff coming and going. He shivered as a chill snaked up his spine, though it was a perfect sixty-four-degree morning.

There was only one thing to do when Brandon's head got all turned around like this. Work.

Kyle Fielding had lit a fire under Brandon to call Geoff Burris and, for that alone, the kid deserved to go to the holiday rodeo. He headed into the main house, glad no one was around, and wound his way to his office. He'd focus on his job and his schedule and the word *love* would disappear from his head. He picked up his cell phone and scrolled his contacts until he reached Geoff Burris.

Time to get this done.

He pressed Send and waited.

"Okay," said a familiar deep voice, "my phone screen just told me Captain T was calling. I'm thinking the last time I had a captain named T was back in my sophomore year of high school, on the baseball team. Brandon Taylor?"

Brandon laughed. "I guess it's been a while since we've talked. Fifteen years. Though I've followed your career every step of the way. I'm a major fan, Geoff."

"Well, thanks. I'm doing what I love. What about you? I know from the rare times I get back to Bronco that you and your brothers all work for Taylor Beef at the family ranch. Is that where you saw yourself back in the day?"

Had he? Working for the family corporation had forever been expected, and despite Brandon always forging his own path, he'd simply assumed he'd take his place at Taylor Beef. Obligation? Real interest? Family ties? He wasn't even sure he'd really ever thought about it, which was surprising in itself. Maybe it meant that the notion of family meant more to him than he'd been willing to consider. "I just saw myself working with horses, and I do spend a lot of time in our stables. Otherwise, I'm an executive VP for Taylor Beef. I like being part of the family business. Somehow I'm pretty good with number crunching."

"My team has been alerting me to your calls. Sorry I haven't personally called back. I'm pulled in a million directions every day and my schedule is nuts."

Brandon had no doubt. "Yeah, I bet. In fact, the man you've become, the champion you are, and your ties to Bronco are the reasons it would mean so much to Taylor Beef to have you promote our company in our new ad campaign, especially during the November rodeo. I hear you might be doing some promo shots for the rodeo and local TV and radio spots soon, so I'm hoping when you're in town, we can get together."

"You saying you don't have a date lined up for every night of the week, Taylor?" Geoff asked on a laugh. "You can't tell me *the* Brandon Taylor has changed."

"I want to say I haven't. But things are complicated right now."

"Oh? Complicated is interesting. But maybe not for a guy who's used to playing the field. Someone's got you all turned around, huh?"

"I don't know, to be honest. But something is happening." He pictured Cassidy, hands on her belly... *Change the subject, Taylor*, he told himself. He had no idea what he thought or felt when it came to Cassidy Ware. "Your social life must be pretty amazing."

"I rarely have an evening to myself. Rodeos, promos, fundraisers, this event, that event. Everything seems to require a date, and yeah, there are plenty of very attractive women. Sometimes I love the life and sometimes I don't."

"I hear you," Brandon said. "All I know is that life is full of wild surprises."

Geoff let out a whistle. "Tell me about it."

"How about if I tell you more about why you should sign with Taylor Beef?"

Geoff chuckled. "You're good, I'll give you that. I've got five more minutes before I have to be at a press conference. Convince me right now to sign with you, and I'll let you know if you did by end of the week."

It was the only in he needed.

Brandon talked for a bit about what having a great man, hometown hero, and the roping champion of Montana as the Taylor Beef spokesman would mean to Brandon's father and uncles. He rattled off Taylor Beef numbers, family history, name recognition, product excellence, and talked about how Taylor Beef and the Taylor Ranch helped out in the community with fundraisers that benefited underserved ranching families in Bronco. How the ranch worked with the young cowboys and cowgirls associations of the county. Then he spoke of what Geoff meant to the company, to the town, to adults and children alike, and he told him the story of Kyle Fielding and Starlight. He even mentioned the boy managing to choke Brandon up with that hero comment.

When he finally stopped talking, he was 99 percent sure he'd done all the convincing he'd needed. Geoff even asked for the Fieldings' address to send them complimentary tickets and a T-shirt for both father and son. They ended the call, Geoff promising that his management team would be in touch by week's end with a decision.

I've got this in the bag, Brandon thought. But that was always his problem. Overconfidence. Arrogance.

Nothing was guaranteed. Not signing Geoff Burris. Not getting Cassidy to agree to marry him. Not being a good father.

I'll tell you what your problem is. Brandon Taylor, you don't know how to love.

Elderly Winona Cobbs, with her snow-white long hair and purple cowboy hat, came to mind. He recalled her pronouncement before he'd snuck out of his brother's wedding.

Fine, he didn't know how to love. But you didn't have to learn to love a baby. That was automatic. He was— there was his overconfidence again—99 percent sure. Your child had your heart the moment you met him or her. That was how life worked.

Not for his mother. Not for Cassidy's father. But for most parents. Right?

Suddenly he wasn't so confident. He had *evidence* that he was wrong. In his own immediate family. Cassidy's, too.

He leaned back in his chair and put his feet up on his desk with a sigh.

Maybe he'd make an appointment at Wisdom by Winona. Ask a few questions. Talk through some of these burning issues. See what Winona said. If he *couldn't* love, then maybe he had no business being anyone's father.

Kind of late for that, he silently chided.

He was giving himself a headache. He thought he'd

known himself so well until the bombshell of all bomb-shells had dropped on his head. Yes, a sit-down with Winona Cobbs, local psychic, might be just what he needed.

At twelve thirty that afternoon, Brandon peered at the turquoise wooden shed in the yard of Bronco's Ghost Tours. Stars and crescent moons were painted on the rough planks. A sign hung on the purple door: Wisdom by Winona. Below it was another sign: Moved Inside Bronco's Ghost Tours 'Til Summer.

Brandon glanced up at the bigger building and headed inside. He saw Callie Sheldrick at the front desk, but she was on the phone explaining about the various tours customers could sign up for. Bronco had a leg-endary history, and Evan Cruise, his sister's fiancé, had started a successful business that people flocked to. He held up a hand in greeting to Callie and she smiled. He peered at the doors down the hall. One was painted purple with crescent moons and stars. He warily walked over and knocked.

Winona Cobbs opened the door. Standing between two heavy purple drapes tied on each side, the elderly woman reminded him of an old-time rodeo queen. She wore a purple shirt with all sorts of colorful jewels on it, purple jeans, purple cowboy boots, and a purple tur-ban on her head with a huge gold brooch in the shape of a crescent moon.

"Well, come on in," she said.

He peered in past her. Wasn't there a light in there? He stepped in and followed her through the drapes into a small room. Some illumination came from antique-looking lamps. The smell of incense infused the air.

"You may sit there," she added, pointing at a faded pink wing chair across from a purple one, which she sat on. A small table was between them.

"So how does this work?" he asked. "Do you use a crystal ball?"

She didn't respond. She was just staring at him. Not hard. No expression. Just staring. "Oh, Brandon. Brandon, Brandon, Brandon."

He raised an eyebrow.

She reached into a purple tote bag and pulled out a piece of purple paper and a pen, then jotted something down. "Here."

She slid the paper over to him. A scent wafted up to his nose. Lilac, maybe.

"'Lewistown Community Center,'" he read. "'Gwen and Paul Woodsley. This Thursday and Friday—9:00 a.m. to 12:00 p.m. Two hundred and fifty dollars per couple.'"

He looked up at Winona. "Uh, what's this?"

"It's a class for first-time parents," she said, holding his gaze. "It covers pregnancy up to age two. Just right for you and Miss Ware."

He could feel his mouth drop open. He studied Winona for a moment. She had to be the real deal. How else would she *know*?

"I suggest you head over to Bronco Java and Juice right now and tell Miss Ware that you think the two of you should attend the parenting class. There's a lovely inn called the Blossom Bed and Breakfast where you can book a room for Thursday night. Tell the proprietor Winona sent you. She'll take care of you two real nice."

He tried to find words but his head was spinning. There was just too much to unpack here. "Let me ask you this, Miss Winona. You told me at my brother's wedding that my problem is that I don't know how to love. That may be true. So what's the point of any of this? I'm going to mess things up with Cassidy and I'll probably bomb at being a father, despite my intentions."

"I *also* said that the universe has something in store for you."

He hadn't forgotten; he just hadn't focused on that since it had sounded kind of silly. "I assumed the 'something' was the pregnancy. That I'm going to be a father."

"That's one of the somethings, yes."

One of them? "What else?" he asked.

"Brandon, I'd like to tell you that everything is going to work out just fine for you. But when it comes to some people, they have to do the work first. You're one of those people."

"The work?" he repeated.

"The *work*. You've got to invest the time in yourself. If you want it, make it happen."

He tried not to sigh. "I thought this was supposed to be a psychic reading. I'm really just interested in knowing the end result."

A long wrinkled finger came pointing at him. "You're a fine man, Brandon Taylor."

He waited. Surely that was the start of the sentence and more was coming. But Winona didn't say anything.

"You're a fine man," she finally repeated, frustrating the hell out of him. "And your sister is a lovely person. Happy to have her join the family. She makes my dear great-grandson Evan very happy." Winona stood.

He did, too. He'd go talk to Cassidy about the parenting class. Taking it certainly couldn't hurt. He'd likely come out of it feeling more prepared for what was to come than just reading about fatherhood could do for him. He could ask his questions, get real answers, unlike the kind Winona gave, and learn something. And he and Cassidy would do it together; they needed to come at this more united than they were at the moment. There was tension between them and he didn't like that.

He also liked the idea of staying overnight in Lewistown. Even in separate rooms, which he had no doubt she'd insist on. They could both use a couple of days away—for a lot of reasons.

He glanced at Winona, who was staring at him again, but this time, she wasn't expressionless or scowling at him.

"By George, I think he's got it," she said on a chuckle.

He gave her wrinkled hand a gentle pat of thanks and got out of there fast.

Chapter 9

Cassidy had never been a clock-watcher. But today, closing time couldn't come fast enough. Since noon alone, it had been one little problem after another.

Two customers had gotten into a huge political argument and she'd had to ask them to take their ranting outside. She'd been met with applause from those who'd been listening to the raised voices. Then a toddler took his mother's cream-cheese-slathered bagel half and slapped it, facedown, on a velvet love seat. Once Cassidy had gotten that all cleaned up, a man dropped his red berry smoothie on the floor, missing one of the rugs by a few inches. A little while later, Cassidy had heard barking and had beelined for the back door, where she'd earlier set down a plate of kibble for the stray who might be Maggie, the lost dog from Happy Hearts, in the hope of attracting her. But by the time she'd gotten there, the dog was gone. As was the kibble. Darn.

For the past fifteen minutes, at least, nothing was going wrong. Two women dressed to the nines came in and ordered pricey green juices, full of compliments for how fresh the offerings were. Now this was more like it. Bring on the compliments.

As Cassidy stepped back to chop and slice and drop the veggies in the blender, she heard one of the women say Brandon's name. Naturally her ears perked right up. She moved around the side of the little island so she could eavesdrop better, knowing full well that she'd probably not like what she heard and should stand closer to the whirring blender.

"I still can't believe Brandon ghosted me last summer," the blonde said with a pout of her glossy lips. "We went out three times and he never called again. And *trust* me, I gave him reason to call." She ran a hand down the length of her excellent body.

Ugh, why did Cassidy think she wanted to hear this slop? Knowing Brandon had dated half the town's singles was bad enough. Listening to details of his sexcapades? No thanks. She moved closer to the blender.

And still heard every word.

Her brunette friend gave her a commiserating smile. "Men are such dogs. Did I tell you I dated Brandon, too?" she asked, a faux sheepish expression on her pretty face.

"What? After I did?"

"Well, you said it was over so… I ran into him at a fundraiser my PR firm was working. He is so damned hot I couldn't help myself."

Double ugh. Take your juices and go!

"How many times did you go out?" the blonde asked as Cassidy came over with their orders, wishing she could plug her ears. Could this day get any worse?

"Twice. On our second date he took me to Coeur de l'Ouest, that excellent French restaurant just outside town, and he got all holier-than-thou because I told our waitress that the service was slow and that would be reflected in her tip. He had the nerve to say, 'Oh, are you planning to pay for this dinner?' We got into a huge argument and I huffed out."

"He probably asked *her* out right after you left," the blonde said, handing over her credit card.

Her friend nodded. "Right?"

Thank the heavens they took their juices to go. Cassidy had heard enough. Who hadn't Brandon dated in Bronco? Who hadn't he ghosted or dumped or pissed off in a fancy restaurant, even deservedly?

At least Brandon hadn't been going to undertip the waitress. That did not seem like his style, slow service or not, which was rarely if ever the waitstaff's fault.

Because he probably *had* wanted to ask her out, she thought with a scowl.

She wondered if she should even try chipping away at the bricks around his heart. The man was thirty-four and very likely set in his ways, used to living on his terms only, not having to account for anyone else. But now he did have someone else to account for: their child.

Chip away, she would. She owed it to herself and their baby to try. There was so much potential for them, if only he'd let her in. Maybe they'd be terrible together.

Maybe they wouldn't work and they'd become a statistic like the ones he liked to throw around. But maybe they'd be great together. She just wanted a chance.

Cassidy looked at the clock on the wall. One forty-five. She couldn't wait to go upstairs, take a long, soothing shower, put on a face mask, and binge-watch the hot new regency romance series everyone was talking about. She was all caught up on her private baking orders, had started a nest egg and new business plan for her future expansion plans, and could just put her feet up and relax for the rest of the day. Ah. Just the thought of it made her feel better—and helped put Brandon Taylor, his trail of women and his antilove mindset out of her head.

"Hi, Cassidy!"

She turned to find her friend Susanna Henry smiling as she stepped up to the counter. Susanna was several years younger than Cassidy and an office manager for Abernathy Meats. Cassidy knew that Susanna had once dreamed of becoming an actress, and though she did volunteer at the community theater, Cassidy wondered if Susanna was happy. There was just something in her friend's expression sometimes—Cassidy couldn't quite put her finger on it

"I definitely need my caffeine fix," Susanna said, pushing her layered brown hair from her face and adjusting her long, filmy scarf. Susanna had great style. "I'd love a caramel macchiato."

Cassidy smiled. "Coming right up. How about a treat to go with it? There's only one chocolate-fudge cupcake left. So good."

"Oooh, I'll take it. I need chocolate to get me through

the afternoon. I've been trying to get in touch with Geoff Burris all day and his team isn't returning my calls."

Cassidy held up a hand as she set Susanna's cupcake in a small box on the counter. "I'd better stop you there. I'm...friends with Brandon Taylor and he was talking recently about trying to get in touch with Geoff for Taylor Beef, so neither of us should say anything else. Conflict of interest or whatever."

"Definitely," Susanna said with a smile. "May the best company win—which will be Abernathy Meats, of course."

Cassidy grinned. Susanna had been working for the company since high school, so she clearly had pride in her employer. Cassidy had always thought her friend had a little crush on Dean Abernathy, one of the five heirs to the Abernathy Meats company and the family cattle ranch. Dean was eight years older than twenty-five-year-old Susanna and, according to Susanna, he'd always treated her like the kid sister he'd never had.

A few more customers came in, so Susanna waved goodbye and left. Finally, it was two thirty and closing time, and Cassidy headed to the front door to turn the sign around. Ah, a little me time was definitely in order. This had been some day. On top of some night.

Just as she turned the sign, Brandon Taylor appeared in front of Java and Juice, holding up a hand in greeting. Surprised to see him, she opened the door, wondering what had made him stop by. Maybe just to check on her to see how she was feeling.

He looked too good in dark jeans, a white T-shirt, black leather jacket and cowboy boots.

"Have I got a story for you," he said, his dark eyes sparkling. "Firsthand, or I wouldn't believe it myself."

Cassidy tilted her head in curiosity, then walked back behind the counter to start cleaning up. "A story?"

He closed the door behind him and followed her, stopping at the counter. "I made an appointment at Wisdom by Winona. Do you want to know what my fortune is?"

She gaped at him. He'd had a reading? Brandon Taylor? He didn't strike her as the psychic-reading type. "Yes, I really do."

"A parenting class in Lewistown. It's for both of us."

Okay, now she was really confused. "What? A parenting class?"

He launched into the story, from knocking on the purple moon-and-stars-painted door of Wisdom by Winona to the startling result of the reading: the class. "I was expecting having my palm read. A crystal ball. Tea leaves. And a real reading of my future. I mean, Winona sure looks the part."

Cassidy gasped. "Brandon, I just realized something. There's only one way Winona could have known I'm pregnant and that you're the father. If she's truly psychic. Only two people know in town—your sister and Callie. And I doubt either told a soul."

"Yeah, I thought about that, too. I'm sure they didn't tell anyone, so it's not like Winona could have heard about the pregnancy from gossip. So maybe there's more to this parenting class? Maybe the teacher is a wizard or something."

Cassidy laughed. A magic wand on Brandon would speed things along for sure. "Or maybe Winona is wise enough to know we could use a little help in all areas going forward—the class, some time away from Bronco and everyday life."

"Yeah, she also seemed to know what I was thinking at the end of our session, when I was sitting there trying to figure it all out." He chuckled. "So what do you think? Getting out of Dodge might be just what we need. I know I can use a parenting class, and being away will give us a chance to talk on neutral ground."

She nodded. "I'll need my own room at the B and B."

"I figured you'd say that. I'll register us for the class and call the inn the minute I leave here."

"Okay," she said. "Pick me up at seven forty-five on Thursday morning? That should give us time to get there and find the place."

"Will do." He held her gaze. "I have a good feeling about this, Cassidy."

She was too surprised to have a good feeling—yet. But she could use a parenting class, too. And some time away from Bronco. And the opportunity to work on Brandon Taylor in a neutral setting.

Yes. The more she thought about it, the more comfortable she became.

Excited, almost. If she would allow herself to go there.

And when she got back from the trip, she'd make an appointment with Winona herself. Who knew where she'd send her and Brandon next?

Last night, Brandon's father had a tirade when he'd heard that his executive VP was taking two days off—today and tomorrow—for personal reasons. Cornelius had demanded to know what those personal reasons were, but Brandon had been tightlipped, which had infuriated his father even more. "That's *my* business," Brandon had said.

"Your business *is* my business," Cornelius had bellowed, but Brandon had reiterated that it actually was not, resulting in the stink eye, a finger jabbed at him, steam coming out of Cornelius's ears, and a tantrum about Brandon taking valuable time off to "gallivant around Lewistown."

Two words finally had made Cornelius not only calm down but change his tune completely.

Geoff Burris.

Brandon had assured his father that he expected positive news from Geoff about agreeing to sign with Taylor Beef for the ad campaign by tomorrow at the latest. Suddenly the man had been smiling and clapping Brandon on back saying, "You go enjoy yourself, son. You deserve some time off."

Now, as Brandon drove through the gates of the Taylor Ranch at seven thirty, he let out a relaxed sigh. He hadn't realized just how much he needed a break from his father's controlling ways and booming voice. Not that this trip would be a vacation, but Brandon sure was looking forward to it. To the class. The B and B. And spending two full days—and one long night—with Cassidy.

She was waiting in front of Java and Juice with a cardboard tray of coffees in her hand and a small suitcase beside her feet as he pulled up. She looked so pretty in black skinny jeans, ankle boots and a thick, long, off-white cardigan that belted around her waist. Her blond hair was in a loose bun, soft tendrils around her face. He wished he could kiss her hello. Maybe he could—on the cheek, anyway. But what he really wanted was a long, hot kiss, not a friendly kiss, and she'd already made it clear that friends was all they could be.

He parked and hopped out to open her door for her.

"Thanks," she said, sliding into her seat. "I made you a mocha latte and a mixed berry scone." She held up another bag. "I snagged a molasses cookie for myself—I had the strangest cravings for it this morning."

"Appreciated. I could use the caffeine boost," he said, taking a long sip before he set it into the console cup holder and pulled out of the spot. "What else do you find yourself craving?"

"All sorts of things. From soups—like the ones you brought me—to twice-baked potatoes with a ton of sour cream. And lemon zinger tea. I'm having that now." She took a sip, then set it in the other console holder and glanced out her window. "Wow, I can't believe I'm actually taking two days off. My trusty employee Helen will take over the front counter, and my part-timer, a hardworking community college student, will help Hank in the kitchen, so the place is all set. They're great staff."

"I'm glad you won't have to worry about your business. You can just focus on yourself, the class, doing some shopping in Lewistown, if you want, relaxing. Whatever you're up for."

She smiled. "Sounds pretty dreamy, actually. I owe Winona one."

"Have you seen her for a reading?" he asked as he turned onto the freeway.

"Not yet, but I've wanted to for a while. Part of me

doesn't want to know what's to be. I mean, I'm not supposed to know till I get there, right? But part of me wants assurances. Then again, psychics don't give assurances—they give you truth."

"My truth is a parenting class?" he asked on a chuckle before taking a sip of his coffee, then another. It hit the spot. Between being on the road, having Cassidy in his car, and the caffeine, everything was A-OK right now.

"She must mean *something* by it. That's all she gave you? The date and time of a parenting class?"

"Well, at my brother's wedding, she told me my problem was that I didn't know how to love. So she got that out of the way already." He hadn't meant to say that. But it did sort of validate what he'd said the night they'd babysat, right before he'd had to leave. It was important to him that Cassidy knew he wasn't just making stuff up about his abilities—or lack, rather—on the subject of romance and relationships.

Her words echoed in his head.

So you see us married, having a sexual relationship, as married couples do, just without the emotional angle? It wouldn't be a love match. Is that it?

Yes, that was exactly it. And now a psychic had explained why. He didn't know how to love. He'd known how once, clearly. But he'd given all that up and so, at this point, he'd not only forgotten how to love, he planned to remain blissfully ignorant. For the rest of time.

And as he'd told Cassidy the night they'd looked after Maeve Abernathy, he was strictly talking romantic relationships. Not the parental one he'd have with his child. He believed there was a difference. But man, had that gotten Cassidy up in arms.

He felt her eyes on him. "Does Winona think the parenting class is an answer for that?"

"How could it be?" he asked. "What's the connection? It's just a how-to class for first-timers."

She seemed to be thinking that over. He glanced at her and could see her hazel eyes working furiously, pondering what he'd told her.

"A couple days ago," she said, "I found Winona staring at me through the back door at Java and Juice. She told me, 'You'll be glad you did it.' I asked her what she meant, but she wouldn't say. I mean, I do a lot of things all day long. What, specifically, will I be glad I did?"

"She's a cryptic one, that Winona Cobbs," Brandon said. "Frankly, she scares me a little. Maybe more than a little."

Cassidy smiled but instead of responding she took a long sip of her herbal tea, wrapping both hands around the cup. He sensed she needed some time to just sit and think, so he stayed silent. And so did she.

When they arrived in Lewistown at eight forty-five, the bigger town was bustling, people walking, jogging, window-shopping. Brandon used his maps app to find the community center. He parked in the back lot, and then he and Cassidy walked up the brick path to the double doors. He checked his registration receipt on his phone. Room 225. Inside, they took the elevator to the second floor and found the class.

A tall blond couple in their thirties stood at the front of the medium-size room. The woman was pregnant, but Brandon had no idea how far along. Three rows of chairs formed a semicircle in front of a table they stood behind. There were all kinds of props on the table, from a weird-looking plastic contraption that Brandon didn't recognize to a few stuffed animals and bottles of laundry detergent. There was a basket with a sign reading *Class Syllabus. Take One!* Cassidy took two and handed him one.

He followed Cassidy to the second row, where she chose seats near the aisle. There were at least forty people of varied ages in the class; from a few who looked too young to be parents to a few in their fifties and sixties. Perhaps grandparents with responsibility for childcare needing a refresher. In any case, Brandon appreciated being one of many instead of a smaller, more intimate group where the teachers might make him talk. He was about to scan the syllabus, but one of the teachers started speaking.

"Welcome!" the blonde woman said. "I'm Gwen Woodsley and this is my husband, Paul Woodsley." She touched her belly. "As you can see, I'm expecting. I'm six months along and due right around Christmas. We also have a fourteen-month-old, an adorable girl who just started to walk, so whether you're expecting or have a baby, we've got you covered."

So far, so good, Brandon thought. The teachers were right there in the trenches.

Gwen nodded. "Now, if you look around the room, you'll see a varied mix. Single parents-to-be. Divorced. Partners who are not married. And married couples. No matter the type of family you'll form, first-time parenting can be challenging."

Paul then went on to describe those challenges, some

of which Brandon had never thought about. Such as: if you're divorced or not married but sharing custody, who gets the child on Christmas? Who gets the child on his birthday? Making those kinds of choices couldn't be easy, Brandon figured. He made a mental note to tell Cassidy that it was exactly one of the reasons they should get married. Neither would be away from their child on holidays. Neither would miss their kid's birthday.

"Okay," Gwen said with a clap of her hands. She went on to describe needing a support system in every sense of the word.

There were murmurings of agreement.

Brandon made a running list of who he could call in an emergency. His dad and Jessica in a heartbeat. And they'd come running. Interesting and unexpected, he thought. But the truth. And his siblings. Each and every one. He had some good friends he could count on, too. He sat a little straighter, already feeling more in control now that he had that vital aspect covered.

He felt Cassidy's eyes on him and turned to her, but she shifted her gaze straight ahead toward the teachers. Her expression seemed a little…stony.

"I want you all to take out your syllabus," Gwen said, "and a pen. And I want you to underline the heading of paragraph one—Support System."

He watched Cassidy underline *Support System*. He wondered what hers was.

"Okay, next, this is for all of you who are expecting," Paul said. "Three-quarters of you." He went on to describe the importance of reading and research, knowing what foods were toxic to pregnant women, seeing your OB for prenatal checkups and taking prenatal vitamins. "Your syllabus has a list of no-no's and super yeses—but your homework is to read up on those lists and the reasons behind it."

Brandon was writing furiously, taking more notes in the past twenty minutes than he had in all of high school combined.

Cassidy turned to face him. "I like that you're taking the class seriously."

He held up two fingers. "Scouts honor that I will give up Caesar dressing—a no-no for pregnant women—on my salad in solidarity."

She laughed. "You don't have to do that."

"Yes, I do."

For the next hour and a half, the Woodsleys talked about how to know it was time to call your doctor and go to the hospital, how to time contractions, that there was something called false contractions. They talked breastfeeding and formula, how to care for the umbilical stump, when to introduce solids, teething, self-soothing, sleep schedules. Brandon's head was beginning to spin. Finally, the Woodsleys called for a fifteen-minute break, noting that light refreshments were on the buffet table at the back of the room.

"I seriously need coffee," Brandon said. "My third cup of the morning."

"I wish I could have caffeine. But I'll settle for decaf. It'll trick my brain."

They made their way to the back of the room, waiting in line for the refreshments table.

"So, how are you finding all the info?" Cassidy asked. "It's a lot."

"I feel like my head must have expanded by five sizes—that's how much new information is stuffed inside. And we're only halfway through the first day." He slapped a palm to his forehead. "But seriously, I'm getting a lot out of the class. I didn't know three-quarters of this stuff."

She nodded. "A lot is new to me, too. I don't have a ton of experience with newborns. And, um, the, *umbilical stump*? What?"

"Right?" he said with a conspiratorial smile. "You can be in charge of that."

"Well, you'll have to be when the baby is with you."

"Not if we get married," he whispered.

"Brandon. We covered that."

They reached the coffee urns and made their drinks, Brandon adding an extra pack of sugar for the rush or he might not survive the second half.

Based on everything he'd heard so far, convincing Cassidy to marry him was now number one on his to-do list. Who *was* her support system? She didn't have family.

And if they got married, they could trade off tasks. She would take care of the umbilical cord stump with the alcohol-soaked cotton balls, and he'd do the bathing, breathing in that baby-shampoo scent.

He had to convince her. And he had this entire little trip to do it.

Chapter 10

After class was dismissed for the day at noon, Cassidy suggested having lunch first and then heading to their bed-and-breakfast, since check-in time wasn't until two o'clock.

"If you still have a craving for that twice-baked potato," Brandon said, "I know a great bar and grill that has them. And a little bit of everything."

"Sounds perfect." After that information overload, Cassidy wanted comfort food and then a nap.

He held out the crook his arm and she was so touched by the gesture that she stopped walking for a moment. She looped her arm around his. How long had it been since she'd walked down the street like this with a man? Forever. Part of a pair. Coupled. And this time, with the father of her baby. She was already deeply drawn to Brandon, but their connection made it all the more powerful.

An hour and a half later they'd finished lunch, Cassidy with a happy belly full of a healthful green salad with pregnancy-cleared dressing and a scrumptious twice-baked potato with extra sour cream. She'd been unable to resist trying one of Brandon's onion rings, and she wasn't surprised that he was a sharer.

Close to two, they arrived at their bed-and-breakfast, a charming Victorian just a couple of blocks off the main street but tucked away in its own private circle of huge trees. Following her into the inn, Brandon had his duffel slung over his shoulder and Cassidy's small, wheeled suitcase.

She headed for the front desk and the smiling woman behind it, who introduced herself as the proprietor, Amy Peterman. Cassidy gave their names.

Amy typed at the tablet in front of her. "There's a reservation for one room for Brandon Taylor. I don't see a reservation for a Cassidy Ware, and I'm very sorry, but we're fully booked."

Cassidy narrowed her eyes at Brandon. Had he only booked one room when she'd made a point of saying she wanted her own?

He stepped up to the desk. "When I called two days ago to make the reservations, I asked for two rooms and was told I was all set."

The woman frowned. "By any chance, did the person you spoke to sound like a bored teenage girl?"

Brandon raised an eyebrow. "You know, now that you mention it, kind of."

"Sarah Peterman!" the woman called toward a room behind the desk. "Come out here."

A girl around sixteen came out. "Oh my God, what did I do now, Mom?"

Amy had her hands on her hips. "Two days ago, when I asked you to cover the phone for me for a half hour, did you take a reservation for *two* people, Brandon Taylor and Cassidy Ware, and then only enter one reservation?"

The girl tilted her head. "I do remember the name Cassidy. The new girl at school is named Cassidy. I like it."

Her mother stared at her. "You entered only *one* reservation for *one* of them."

The girl grimaced. "Sorry. I waited to enter the reservations until after I disconnected because I hate having to hold the phone against my ear while I type, but then the phone rang again and I got distracted. I'm really sorry."

Amy sighed. "And *I'm* really sorry," she said, turning back to Cassidy and Brandon. "We do only have the one room. The good news is that it's one of our largest and has a king-size bed."

Now it was Cassidy's turn to sigh. To Brandon, she said, "Ever see that old movie with Clark Gable and Carol Lombard when they hang a sheet between their sides of the bed? That'll be us."

"You take the room," he said. "I'll find a room somewhere else. You go relax, and I'll be back in a jiff."

The proprietor shook her head. "Oh, you won't find a room in Lewistown this week. Three conventions in town. Everyone's thrilled to be booked solid."

"It's okay, Brandon," Cassidy said, maybe a little glad that they were forced to share a room. Maybe some intimacy—of the close proximity kind—would work a little magic on him.

Amy showed them to their room, insisting that her daughter, Sarah, be the porter. The girl scowled but complied, carrying their bags ahead of them up the short flight of steps to the second floor.

The room was lovely. Big and airy, with a sliding-glass door that led to a balcony holding a small café table and two chairs. Soothing pale blue walls with watercolors of the mountains and a couple of Montana landmarks. A huge, white-wood four-poster with a soft down comforter and a ton of pillows. A side table holding a welcome basket and bottles of water.

When the proprietor and her daughter left, Cassidy kicked off her boots and tried the bed, the pillows so cuddly.

"Ah, heaven," she said. She was about ready for that nap.

"Mind if I try?" he asked.

"Go right ahead."

She was never so aware of anything as when Brandon lay beside her, both of them looking up at the beamed ceiling.

"Very comfortable," he said, turning his head toward her. He was so tall and strong and…sexy.

Do not look at him or you will want to kiss him, she ordered herself.

"So, what's on the agenda for the rest of the day and night?" he asked.

"Definitely a short nap in this amazing bed," she

said. "Then maybe we could go exploring. I haven't spent much time in Lewistown."

"Sounds like a plan. You nap and I'll read the longest class syllabus I've ever seen. I want to be prepared for tomorrow so I'm not scared out of my mind."

She laughed. "Were you overwhelmed today?"

"Maybe just a little. Or a lot."

"I was, too," she admitted. "But now that I'm here, on this insane bed with this amazing down comforter, all the info is gelling and clicking instead of stacking."

"Maybe that'll happen for me if I close my eyes." He did, and she smiled. "Nope, just stacks upon stacks of information about bottle nipples and diaper sizing."

He turned onto his side, propped himself up on his elbow and faced her, tucking a strand of her hair behind her ear.

She froze, almost afraid of his touch, of wanting him so bad she might grab him and pull him to her.

"I'm glad we're here," she whispered.

He reached for her hand and found it and held it, the warmth so comforting that she relaxed and felt herself drifting off.

When her eyes opened, the room was dimly lit, and Brandon was sitting in the club chair at the desk, reading the class syllabus. She glanced at the alarm clock on the bedside table. She'd been sleeping for almost an hour. Had he been reading this whole time? She smiled at the thought.

"Give me ten minutes to make myself presentable, and we'll go explore," she said.

He turned with that smile that always went straight

to her heart. "I told you in the stables, Cassidy. You always look beautiful."

Aw, God. Stop making yourself so necessary to me, she wanted to say, But she was tongue-tied. She slipped out of bed and rummaged in her suitcase for jeans and a sweater and her toiletry bag, then headed into the bathroom, which was practically the size of her apartment's bedroom. Every amenity was on the counter or bolted into the wall. And two fluffy white spa robes hung on the back of the door. Oh yeah, she would definitely be wearing one of those later.

She washed her face with the delicious-smelling soap, patted her face dry with a soft, thick towel, then put on a little makeup, brushed her hair, and changed into the fresh clothes. Ah, she felt so good now.

When she came out, Brandon was sitting on the edge of the bed with a very large plastic shopping bag with BH Couture written across it. Only the most exclusive, expensive clothing boutique in Bronco Heights.

"Bought yourself a pair of jeans?" she teased. "No, socks. For a hundred bucks."

"Actually, this is for you," he said, standing and holding out the bag.

"For me?"

She took the bag over to the bed, set it down, and opened it up—and gasped. She pulled out The Coat. The long red wool coat that she'd fallen in love with in the window of BH Couture but would never in a million years be able to afford.

"Brandon." That was all she could manage to say.

"I happened to pass the boutique and notice this coat. It looked just like you described it the other day, so I went in and asked the saleswoman if she happened to notice anyone stopping to ogle this coat. She said that Cassidy Ware stops in front of the window almost every day and stares at it with a dreamy expression, but never comes in."

Um, a little embarrassing. "Who noticed me?"

"Sofia Sanchez," Brandon said. "My new sister-in-law's sister."

You mean your ex-girlfriend. She knew the two had dated, but she really didn't know if they'd been serious or not. Then again, did Brandon get serious about any woman?

"Brandon, you can't go around buying me expensive coats."

"Why not?"

She knew how much this coat cost. A lot of smoothies and lattes. Months' worth. "Because it's not a normal gift. And there's no gift required. It's not my birthday."

"I just wanted to do something nice for you, Cassidy. Besides, the weather's turned a bit. It's fifty-five degrees. Now you'll be warm enough."

She bit her lip and stared at the gorgeous coat, such a perfect shade of deep red, such fine wool. She loved it so much.

"At least try it on," he said.

She did. And once it was on, she was never, ever taking it off. She went to the ornate wrought-iron floor-length mirror attached to the wall and buttoned it, then tied the belt around her waist. "I love it to pieces."

He smiled, and she walked over to where he stood by the bed. She lifted her face to kiss him on the cheek but he turned at that exact moment and their lips met instead.

"Thank you," she whispered. "I feel a little bit like Cinderella right now. But I'll tell you, Brandon Taylor, I'm my own fairy godmother. You hear me? I don't need a prince. I love this coat and I'm sleeping it in, but no more gifts, okay?"

"Okay," he said, leaning forward and capturing her mouth in another kiss. Her knees went slightly weak and she was so intoxicated by him that she didn't pull away.

"None of that, either," she said, stepping back.

He didn't respond, just smiled, and she knew she was in big trouble here. She loved this room. She loved her coat. She loved *him*.

I love you, Brandon Taylor.

There it was. The truth. And once Cassidy admitted something to herself, she was stuck with it. There was no going back from this. That meant she had her work cut out for her.

After walking around Lewistown, window-shopping and going in and out of shops, Cassidy looking so beautiful in her red coat, they decided to bring takeout back to the inn and call it a day.

Brandon had heard raves about a Mexican restaurant named Manuel's, so they picked up burritos, chips and salsa, and walked back to the Blossom Bed and Breakfast, where teenage Sarah was behind the desk, typing away at her own phone instead of answering the ringing inn phone. Her mother came out from the back room, muttering her daughter's name.

Brandon chuckled as they took the stairs. "When our

daughter is a teenager, she'll answer the phone." He fit the old-fashioned key into their room door. "She'll be one of those perfect teenagers who's never sullen, always smiles, does her homework, doesn't date till she's twenty-one."

Cassidy laughed. "Honestly, I can't imagine the baby any older than six months. Past that is too scary. Teething? Walking? It's all too much!"

Once inside, Brandon took off his leather jacket and hung it up, but Cassidy wrapped her arms around herself.

"If I wasn't so nervous about black beans and salsa falling out of my burrito and onto my coat, I'd keep it on while we eat. But I can't risk it." She took it off. "Bye, my beauty."

He smiled as she hung up her coat beside his. He loved how happy the coat made her. "A bit too cold to eat on the balcony," he said, setting their food and their drinks on the small table by the window.

They sat and dug in, both agreeing that Manuel's was delicious. Even the tortilla chips were unusually good, light and crisp with a hint of lime.

Cassidy took another bite of her veggie burrito then a sip of her water. "So, after everything we learned today at class, I think we should talk about how we see things working when the baby comes. I mean, since we're not getting married."

"Or we could just get married," he said, swiping a chip through the excellent salsa.

She moved her burrito from in front of her face to stare at him, a slight frown on her beautiful forehead.

"We can't. I told you, I'm holding out for true love, Brandon."

His stomach churned. True love. *Come on*. Hadn't she been through enough herself? Maybe she hadn't. "Are you telling me that after your own failed romances, you still believe in love?"

Cassidy nodded. "I learned something from those failed romances. So, yes."

"Like what?"

She sipped her water, then set down the bottle. "Well, with my most serious relationship, I learned that I give it all I have until I know it's hopeless. That's both good and bad. I fell hard for a guy who really couldn't love. I didn't understand that at first, though. I thought he was just not demonstrative. I overlooked a lot because I thought he was a very busy ER doctor, dedicated to his work."

"So you understand, then. I mean I'm sorry you had to go through that, but you understand why I stay uninvolved from the start. That way, no one gets hurt."

"There's a big difference between Dr. Dead Inside and you, Brandon Taylor. He was a true cold fish. You're the opposite of that. You're warm and kind and thoughtful. He never would have brought me soup or remembered my mentioning a coat I loved in a shop window."

"I don't have to be dead inside to know relationships never work out." He took another bite of his burrito, thinking of how to change the subject without her noticing. "Did you know that by the end of the first month of pregnancy, babies are a quarter inch long? So tiny!"

Yeah, nothing obvious about that change of subject. She was staring at him, but didn't respond.

"I brought my fatherhood book with me and was reading while you were napping earlier," he explained. "I like knowing what's going on in there," he added, gesturing at her stomach. "I highlighted a few areas I wanted to ask the Woodsleys about tomorrow."

She put down her burrito and cleared her throat, then her gaze was back on him. Intensely. "The other day, you asked me what I needed, Brandon. Remember that?"

He sat back in his chair, slightly worried where this was going. "I remember."

"Do you want to know? Really want to know? Because I know the answer now."

Oh hell. What if what she wanted wasn't what he wanted? What if the one thing she wanted was the one thing he couldn't give her? Even with all his money.

But he couldn't deny that he did want to know. He wanted to know everything about Cassidy Ware, even the harder-to-deal-with stuff. "Yes, tell me. I don't want secrets between us. Everything should be out in the open."

"Good. It means a lot that you feel that way. So here it is—what I need. A *real* relationship with you. I want you to try. We're going to have a baby, so we're going to be in each other's lives forever. I have feelings for you and I know you have feelings for me. So let's see where we can take this. You want to get married without love for the sake of the baby? Let's try a real relationship for the sake of the baby. There, I said it." She let out a breath. "And trust me, that wasn't easy, given your stance."

Brandon shook his head and stood, his stomach really twisting now. "I'm not willing to destroy things between us, Cassidy. Our relationship—as our baby's parents—is too important. My own parents aside, I had some friends growing up with divorced parents who hated each other's guts and used their kids as pawns. I'm not going there, Cassidy."

"So you can't even imagine that we'll work out? That we'll be one of those elderly couples on a porch, sharing a glass of sweet tea and waiting for our great-grandkids to come over?"

"Statistics say we have a fifty-fifty shot," he reminded her. "Those are crap odds. You want to risk us hating each other when we have a child to raise? I don't want to make trouble for my kid. I don't want strife in my own house. There's enough of that in the world."

She looked so frustrated that he told himself to shut up and sit down.

"How do I fight this?" she asked, her voice cracking. "How do I get you to see that some risks are worth it when everything you're saying isn't wrong?" Tears shone in her eyes and she shook her head, turning away from him.

He knelt in front of her and took her hands. "Cassidy, are you kidding me? Being here with you is a risk. Seeing you every day is a risk. I've never cared about anyone the way I care about you."

She swiveled and looked at him.

"There, I said it," he added with a gentle smile. "And trust me, that wasn't easy, given my stance."

His stealing her line got a small smile out of her. She squeezed his hand back, a good sign.

"What if we *try*," she said, "and at the first sign

that we're not meant to be, we agree to our old high school bet—to go our separate ways forever, romantically speaking. I think we'll know pretty fast if we're not a real match, Brandon. Right now, we've got something really huge in common and it's running the show in terms of a relationship. So let's find out if we have the fundamentals in common. Let's find out if we can really talk to each other. Let's find out if we're good together."

Something inside his chest untwisted and twisted, untwisted and twisted. "Damn it, Cassidy. Stop making it impossible for me to tell you no."

"If you want to give me what I need, this is what I need. Your willingness to try us out."

He stood and reached out a hand, and she looked at him with so much hope in her eyes. She stood, too, and he pulled her against him, holding her close. "Okay," he finally said.

But now his chest was tightening in on itself. Squeezing. This was a mistake, he knew. They were headed for heartache and everything was going to fall apart. He was going to disappoint her and then his doomsday predictions for joint custody would come to fruition.

But how could he not try when she was asking? Because everything *she* was saying wasn't wrong.

She tightened her hold on him, resting her head against his chest. *Just go with it and maybe you'll be proved wrong*, he told himself. *For right now, put it out of your mind and just enjoy Cassidy in your arms.* He could stand like this for hours.

"When I'm a hundred and two and look back on my life, this moment will be one of the tops, Brandon."

He tilted up her chin with his hand. "Guess it's okay for me to kiss you now."

"Yup," she whispered. "And more."

"That does sweeten the pot," he said.

She unbuttoned her cardigan slowly, her gaze on his, and tossed it to the chair. She wore a tight, silky black cami with lace at the V-neck. He lifted that off her in seconds. As he kissed her neck and made quick work of her sexy black bra, she wriggled out of her jeans and then unsnapped and unzipped his.

"You might have waited to ask me to try *now*," he said. "I would have promised you anything for this."

"First of all, we wouldn't have gotten this far right now without your yes. And I'll always know I got it out of you without getting you all hot and bothered," she whispered, a hand slipping into his boxer briefs.

He back-walked her to the bed, kissing her sexy pink-red mouth and neck en route, and all thought was replaced by pure sensation. Then he was under the covers with a naked Cassidy, the ends of her silky hair tickling his chest as her hands and mouth moved down his body.

As she slid back up his body to kiss him, he was half-aware that this felt different, *was* different from the first time just weeks ago. Back then, he'd whispered that she was "everything," and he'd meant *in that moment*.

But now, Cassidy Ware was everything in every moment. Now. An hour from now. Tomorrow. Eight months in the future when they'd have a baby. Forever. He *did* care about her more than he was willing to dig into. She was going to be the mother of his child. She had his full attention, and not just because her tongue was roaming across his lower belly.

He wanted to stop thinking so he kissed her, hot and passionately as his hands explored every inch of her soft body. He nudged her over so he was on top, and when he looked at her, his beautiful Cassidy naked before him, he was hit by a rush of feeling so startling that he blinked against it. He clasped both her hands and brought them up past her head, trying not to think as he kissed her neck, then lingered on her breasts, then licked his way down her torso.

"Oh, Brandon," she murmured, writhing. Moaning. Arching her back.

It took every bit of control not to enter her. If he did, it would be over way too soon.

But if he waited, he'd be aware of how his heart was beating too fast, of the fullness in his chest—a good fullness. Because Cassidy was in there.

He could talk about statistics all he wanted, but the way he felt was a fact, too.

Scary as hell.

She wrapped her arms around him as she pulled him up her body, her nails slightly digging into his back, her lips on his neck, her tongue dangerously close to his ear.

And then he couldn't wait a moment longer. He had to be one with her.

"Brandon!" she whisper-screamed as he moved against her, slow at first, driving them both wild if their muffled moans were any indication. Then faster, faster, faster, building, building, building.

When he was one hundred and two and looked back on his life, he knew this moment would be tops for him, too. Not the sex, though he could barely control himself. But the okay, the yes, that he was going to try.

Chapter 11

Cassidy woke the next morning alone in the king-size bed. She sat up, listening for sounds of the shower running. But the room was silent. And dark. Brandon wasn't in the club chair, reading. He wasn't *there*.

Her heart plummeted and she lay down slowly, closing her eyes. *Fool, fool, fool*, she thought. *Of course he's gone before dawn.* He might have meant his *okay* yesterday—and she knew he meant it while they were having incredible sex—but he probably woke at 4:00 a.m., hyperventilating, and headed for the hills.

Fine, she thought, straightening, determined not to let him make her miserable and ruin her day. She would get herself up, showered and dressed, and go have breakfast downstairs. Inn breakfasts were the best. Then she'd go to part two of the class and somehow get herself back to Bronco. Surely, Brandon wouldn't have stranded her here, though. No, he'd never do that, no matter how freaked out he was about saying yes to a real relationship.

What was she doing? Why was she reading the worst into him being gone? If they were going to have a real chance, she needed to have more trust in him. She turned on the bedside lamp and there it was. The note it hadn't even occurred to her to look for.

Friday, 6:15ish

Went down to get coffee for us. We can have breakfast here or go to the diner we passed yesterday. If Sleeping Beauty wakes up in time before class.

—B

That sludgy feeling in her stomach dissolved. *You know him better than you think you do. Trust what you're doing to work and it will.*

She dashed into the shower, recalling every moment of last night. At first he'd been a little too gentle until she showed him he didn't have to be. They were a match in bed and out of bed. They could talk about anything. They found the same things funny and *not* funny. They were going to have a baby.

They were meant to be. She believed that. And now that they were a couple, he would come to see that in no time. She knew she would hit a roadblock or two when he'd feel overwhelmed, and she'd deal with it, get him through it. Hey, if he was so overcome with emotion for her that it tripped him up, wasn't it her job to help?

Cassidy smiled as she stepped onto the bath mat and toweled off, then put on that fluffy spa robe. Heavenly. When she came out of the bathroom combing her hair, Brandon was back, sitting at the desk with two foam cups of coffee in front of him.

"You should have waited," he said. "Now you're just going to get all dirty again."

For a second she had no idea what he meant, until he walked over to her and untied her robe, his hands roaming as he kept his dark eyes on hers. She had to close hers, she was so lost in desire for him. Before she could even process it, his clothes were off and they were back in bed.

An hour later, she had her second shower of the morning, but this time not alone.

"So far, I'm okay with having a real relationship with you," he said as he put on his own fluffy robe.

She fake socked him in the arm. "I admit I'm having a grand old time myself."

He hugged her to him. "Now I'm ravenous for food."

She grinned. "Me, too."

At just past eight they were downstairs in the dining room. Four tables were occupied by other guests, so Cassidy chose the small round one by the side window. Amy was running between the tables, serving plates, refilling orange juice glasses. Her daughter, Sarah, appeared with her backpack and a muttered, "Bye," as she headed for the door.

"Sarah Peterman, you come here this instant," Amy called out.

Sarah groaned. "Oh my God, Mom, what did I do now?" That was definitely her favorite refrain.

"Let me give you a kiss goodbye," Amy said, hugging the girl to her. "I've barely seen you all morning. Have a great day, honey."

Sarah brightened and grabbed a scone from the basket on the buffet table. "Bye, Mom."

Cassidy grinned at Brandon. "I think those two are a lot closer than they let on."

"Were you close with your mom?" he asked.

She waited to answer until Amy had poured their coffee and taken their orders for the special—French toast with cinnamon sugar.

"We were, but my mom was busy, like Amy," she whispered. "I was on my own a lot. I think it made me more independent. My mother was very supportive of my goal to have my own business. For some reason, opening a shop in Bronco Heights seemed like the height of making it when I was in high school. To her, too."

"Because you lived in Bronco Valley then?" he asked.

She nodded. "I was surprised that you deigned to date a Valley girl. The two sides of town didn't really mix much back then."

"I liked you, and that's all I needed to know," he said.

She reached for his hand and gave it a squeeze. She loved so much about him. She loved *him.*

"I was only at your house a couple of times since your mom didn't exactly approve of me, but I do remember wondering how you two fit in that tiny place. There was only one bedroom."

"My mom insisted I take it. I was so blind back then, I didn't realize how much she was sacrificing. She should have had the private room and instead she slept on a pullout in the living room." She shook her head. "I always dreamed that one day I'd be able to buy her a pretty house in Bronco Heights. She thought moving to the Heights meant she'd made it." She felt tears prick her eyes and she blinked them away.

"You still own that house in Bronco Valley?" he asked as Amy set down their French toast.

Cassidy shook her head. "When my mom was very sick, she told me to get rid of it once she was gone and use the sale money to start my business. The house sold for peanuts and I had to take out a small loan to get Bronco Java and Juice started, but I knew I was making her proud in heaven. To the very end, my mother was my biggest champion and support system. God, I miss her."

"Your mom sounds like an incredible person."

"She was. And though I do know she'd be proud of me, I also feel like I let her down. It's been five years since I opened the shop, and I really thought I'd have expanded—a sidebar in a fancy hotel in one of the cities or a second location."

"What's keeping you from expanding?" he asked, swiping a bite of cinnamon-sugar-dotted French toast in syrup.

"Well, I'd been hoping to expand into an adjacent shop, but neither has been available and won't be for years. I think I'll be able to open a second location in a couple of years, especially now that I have the specialty-cake side business going strong. I just have to be patient."

"I have no doubt you'll achieve your goals and dreams, Cassidy. You've been focused and driven since I met you fifteen years ago. You'll make it happen."

Warmth spread through her. As a bigwig for the most successful company in town, let alone the county, Brandon's praise meant a lot to her.

His phone pinged and he took it from his pocket and glanced at it. "I didn't think today could get any better, but it actually has. The one and only Geoff Burris, rodeo champion, just texted that he's a yes to promote Taylor Beef. My dad's going to be ecstatic."

"Great news!" she said. "Congratulations." She raised her glass of orange juice to him, and he clinked it with his own. She thought of her friend Susanna trying to get through to Geoff Burris's team. It would a disappointment for Abernathy Meats, for sure.

He took her hand and held it, then took a bite of his French toast with the other. She recalled that he'd do this when they were in high school. They'd go to a pizza place and he'd hold her hand and eat a slice of pizza with the other. She used to think it was the most romantic thing. Kind of still was.

Three and a half hours later, when they'd returned from the second day of their parenting class and were checking out of the inn, Cassidy could hardly believe what a magical experience this had been.

And she had Winona Cobbs to thank. While Brandon was settling up at the desk, Cassidy stepped outside and looked up the telephone number for Wisdom by Winona. She pressed in the numbers and waited, hoping Winona would answer.

"Hello, Miss Ware."

"Goodness, you are psychic! Though I have proof of that already."

"Well, I also have caller ID," Winona deadpanned.

Cassidy felt her cheeks burn. "Ah, right. Well, I'm calling because Brandon Taylor and I are just leaving Lewistown now—we attended the parenting class on your advice and stayed at the lovely Blossom B and B, and the trip was just wonderful on every level."

"No surprise there," Winona said.

Cassidy grinned. "It was for me. I'd like to make an appointment with you for a reading."

"Delightful. You can pay me in a fancy coffee drink and two kinds of Danish, one for the road. I'll be at Bronco Java and Juice on Monday morning at six thirty. We'll chat there."

"Oh! Well, that sounds fine. I'll see you then."

"Yes, you will," Winona said before disconnecting.

"Checking in at the shop?" Brandon asked as he stepped out into the breezy sunshine with their bags.

"Actually, I just made an appointment with Winona Cobbs. She gave you this trip and it turned out to be everything we needed. Who knows what she'll tell me?"

He smiled. "She sure doesn't say much, but then much *happens*. And you know, I just realized she didn't charge me a cent. I usually get the Taylor name upcharge for everything."

"She's charging *me* a fancy coffee drink and two Danishes, one for the road."

"She could charge folks big bucks. Turns out my reading was priceless."

Cassidy leaned up and kissed him on the lips. "Agreed."

Barely an hour later, Brandon reluctantly pulled into a spot in front of Java and Juice, not ready to say goodbye to Cassidy, even for a few hours this afternoon. He zipped around to the passenger side and opened her door for her.

"I may never get used to that," she said.

"Sorry, you'll have to. It's the Taylor way. The pregnancy makes me doubly chivalrous." He got her suitcase from the cargo area and they headed upstairs.

Cassidy unlocked the door and they stepped inside. She slipped her arms around his neck. "Thank you for an incredible couple of days. Who knew taking a parenting class could be so life-changing? Plus, I can now properly swaddle an infant. Well, a doll."

He grinned and kissed her on the lips. "Winona Cobbs knew."

"I'm so excited for my reading on Monday morning. I'll let you know what she says."

He kissed her again. "Oh, you think you won't see me before Monday? I can't wait that long."

"Good. Want to come over tonight? We can cook or order in, watch a movie or bad reality TV."

"I'll see you at seven thirty," he said.

One more kiss—a long, hot one—and he was out the door. So far, being in a real relationship wasn't the straitjacket he'd thought it would be. He had no idea why, but he was grateful. He could give Cassidy what she needed and not feel the walls closing in on him. Win-win. He wasn't going to think about it; he'd just go with it.

He might have stayed a bit longer at Cassidy's, but he was itching to tell his dad the good news about Geoff Burris.

He found his father in his office, scanning and signing invoices.

"Dad, I told you I was confident that Geoff Burris would agree to star in our ad campaign, particularly ahead of the Mistletoe Rodeo in November," Brandon said, stopping in the doorway. "Mission accomplished."

He'd never seen his father get out of a chair so fast.

"Yes! Excellent." Cornelius pumped his fist in the air—three times. "Jessica," he called at the top of his lungs. "Jessica!"

Brandon's stepmother came rushing in. "What on earth is all this yelling?"

"Brandon got Geoff Burris!" Cornelius exclaimed. "Taylor Beef will continue its reign over Abernathy Meats!" He actually did a little dance where he turned in a circle then grabbed Jessica into a dip.

"Great work, Brandon," his stepmother said with a grin. "Cornelius should be in a grand mood for a least three days." She chuckled, kissed her husband and then left the room.

"We'll have a small party to celebrate," Cornelius said. "Next Saturday night. Then we'll have our ad people get the word out to build excitement and we'll throw a big shindig at The Association."

"Sounds good, Dad." Brandon had no doubt his father would be in a good mood for weeks, not days.

"And the party will be just family," Cornelius added. "Your uncles, your siblings. Text them, will you?"

"Daphne is one of my siblings," Brandon said, staring at his father. Hard.

"Well, I did say siblings, didn't I? So yes, of course Daphne is invited."

Would wonders never cease. This good mood of Cornelius's might last a *month*. Maybe even forever.

"Daphne is family even if I don't like how she's living her life," Cornelius said. He moved over to the bar against the wall and took down two glasses. "She can invite her fiancé, too."

Brandon extended his hand. "I'm proud of you, Dad. But it's about damned time."

His father scowled and waved his hand dismissively, but he was too happy for the frown to last. He reached for the Scotch, top label. "I didn't say I'd actually *talk* to Daphne, just that she was welcome to attend. Vegetarian lifestyle. Animal sanctuary. Who in their right mind ever heard of such a thing from an heir of a cattle ranching empire? I figure a family party celebrating a Taylor Beef score will make her see that family comes first, not personal nonsense."

Now that was more like Cornelius Taylor. Brandon shook his head, wishing he could actually get through to his father, but years of dealing with him had told him he wouldn't. The man was completely self-absorbed.

Brandon was about to rescind the *I'm proud of you*, but his father grabbed him into a bear hug.

"*I'm* so damned proud of *you*," Cornelius said. "Did the personal days you took have anything to do with winning over Burris?"

"Actually, no. I attended a two-day class with someone special. And in fact, since this will be a family party, you can add one more to the guest list."

"You get married or something?" Cornelius asked, eyes narrowed on him. He looked like he was bracing himself for terrible news.

"No. But I'm going to be a father. Cassidy Ware is pregnant."

Cornelius's eyes practically popped out. "Am I supposed to congratulate you? I can't tell."

He felt like he'd just taken a left hook to the jaw. His father had to ask?

"Yes, Dad. Congratulations are in order. Cassidy and I are a couple and we're expecting."

Cornelius picked up the Scotches and handed him one. "A new generation of Taylor Beef heirs! Brandon, that's wonderful. Today just keeps getting better."

Hadn't Brandon just thought that earlier about his own day?

"You're happy about having a grandchild or happy that you're getting a baby heir?" Brandon asked.

"They're one and the same, son. I couldn't be more thrilled."

So Cornelius Taylor. "I expect you to babysit, Dad," Brandon said with a smile.

"With Jessica's help, sure. Where's my cell phone?" he asked, looking at his desk and the credenza and the bar. "Who can ever find that thing? I have some gloating calls to make around town. A new generation of heirs! That is something else. Well done, Brandon. Well done, indeed."

Good Lord. He really hadn't known how his father

would take the news. Part of him had expected Cornelius to erupt with rage over losing another son to a personal life—and this time a baby. His dad might be 100 percent focused on the word *heir*, but maybe deep down where he barely knew his father, the man was actually happy about being a granddad.

"Hold off on making any calls, Dad. Cassidy's very newly pregnant. I'll let you know when you can call everyone you know."

"Fine, fine," Cornelius said. "You get in touch with your sister about the party. We'll have it here at the ranch. Oh, and I'll call that nice architect back and set up a meeting for you. She can design you a grand house right here on the ranch with a nursery."

Cornelius took that moment to raise his glass in a toast.

Brandon kept his glass down. "I'm not sure of my plans, Dad. Or what Cassidy wants." Now that they were a couple, getting married was definitely off the table. He had to ease into being in a real relationship. A platonic marriage—no problem. A real marriage? A shiver ran up Brandon's spine.

Cornelius scowled, but again, he was too happy about his heir-to-be that it didn't last long. The mirth was back in his eyes. "Well, you bring Cassidy to the party."

Brandon clinked to that.

Chapter 12

A potbellied pig named Tiny Tim was sniffing his cowboy boot. Brandon had wanted to stop by Happy Hearts, his sister's animal sanctuary, this afternoon before he got bogged down in a few hours of work. Daphne, in overalls and muck boots, was feeding the pig and a surly-looking goat in their pens. Tiny Tim's snout was more interested in Brandon's boot than in his breakfast.

"Aw, he likes you," Daphne said, pushing her long strawberry-blond ponytail behind her shoulder. "So you said you had some very interesting news for me. I'm all ears."

He explained about Geoff Burris. And their father's invitation.

"So he envisions my attendance as an opportunity

to reprogram me, is that it?" She rolled her eyes good-naturedly and shook her head. "Dad will never change, will he?"

"Nope," Brandon said. "Think you'll come?"

"To spend time with the whole family, yes, I absolutely will. Having Evan by my side, even figuratively, will give me strength to deal with Dad. To be completely ignored by Dad, I should say."

Brandon grinned. "I'm glad you'll be there.

"So how are things with you and Cassidy?" she asked, adding what looked like kale and spinach to Tiny Tim's huge food bowl.

"I found out what she needed," Brandon said. "And came through."

Daphne's blue eyes lit up. "Yeah? Can I ask? I'm dying to know."

"She needs us to be a couple, a real couple. She needs me to try to give it my all. So that's what I'm doing."

"Brandon, that's great. Good for both of you."

"Not necessarily good for the baby," he said on a sulky note.

"What? How could it not be? The baby's parents are in a committed relationship."

"And if it doesn't work out? If Cassidy and I just piss each other off after this honeymoon phase and suddenly we're fighting and break up? Then we're both all bitter and arguing over who gets the baby what days."

Daphne turned to look at him. "Why get so ahead of yourself—and to a place that you very likely won't go?"

"How can you know, though? Not one relationship of mine has worked out. Why would this one?"

"Because of how you feel about Cassidy," Daphne

said. "Plain and simple. And I'll tell you, Brandon. I don't even think how you feel about her is connected to her being pregnant. I mean, it's powerful stuff—she's going to be the mother of your child. But your feelings for Cassidy are because of *her*."

"How could you possibly know that?" he asked, reaching down to touch Tiny Tim's soft ear. He got a snort of thanks before the pig went back to eating.

"I could tell from the way you were talking about her the day you told me she was pregnant. You feel about Cassidy the way I feel about Evan. When someone is that right for you, it's obvious. It's also out of your control."

He frowned. "I like to be in control of myself."

Daphne chuckled. "Love is big stuff. Just let it do its thing. Stop trying to mess with it."

"I never said anything about love. Cassidy and I are in a relationship, a romantic relationship. Stop putting words in my mouth."

Daphne laughed again. "Poor Brandon. Madly in love and fighting like hell against it."

"Those are more words, Daphne."

Luckily, her phone rang and she had to get over to the adoptable animals barn. He couldn't take much more of his sister right now.

Madly in love. He and Cassidy were testing things out. No one said anything about love.

He and Cassidy were about *need*. She needed real romance out of him. He needed—

Brandon froze, realizing that what he needed was at odds with what she'd gotten from him.

He needed a platonic marriage so that they could

raise their child in peace and harmony. But instead, she would be leading him to a real marriage—the natural progression from a real relationship.

For a smart guy, he sure was stupid sometimes. She'd all but spelled it out, that for their baby's sake, they should try the real thing. What the hell had he thought she'd meant? He shook his head.

Calm the hell down, he told himself. *Just go slow.*

"Later, Tiny Tim," he told the potbellied pig and stalked toward his truck.

He got in, his shoulders bunched, his head out of sorts. A drive would do him good.

Distracted, he ended up turning onto a road that would lead him right into Bronco Valley, the area of town where Cassidy had grown up. He remembered where she lived: 401 Elm Street.

He didn't spend much time in the Valley since his life was focused in the Heights. And now that he thought about it, he didn't have any friends in this part of Bronco, either. But he had no doubt that many employees of the Taylor Ranch lived in the Valley, and the Taylor family should be more involved in the community than it was. Fancy fundraisers were one thing. Real involvement, doing the work itself, was another. Taylor Beef was deeply involved in investing in ranching communities, but Bronco wasn't all ranches.

He found the house by memory, almost surprised it came back to him. The peeling, faded yellow one-story home was the same boxlike structure, with a chain-link fence on one side. He parked across the street and stared at the uninviting residence, having a hard time imagining Cassidy, as a young girl or a teenager, finding inspiration walking that uneven path and up the broken steps—the top one, raised on the left side, had a dangerous gash in the concrete—and going inside. Then again, she must have, given how driven she was. She'd wanted to have her own business since she was a preteen. She'd seen it as a way out, something that was hers.

A young couple with a toddler wearing a pink wool hat with bear ears came out of the house. The woman, her long dark hair in a ponytail, was singing a song about a meatball rolling off a table and out the door, and the toddler joined in when she knew a word, making the man with them laugh. They looked happy. Very happy.

You didn't need money to be happy, Brandon knew. He had too much money and he hadn't been happy for a long time—until Cassidy had come back into his life.

But then the man tripped on the uneven step and almost fell, and the little girl screamed, "Daddy!"

Brandon grimaced, got out of his car and held up a hand. "You okay?"

"I'm fine," the guy said. "Do it every day even though I know it's there." He shook his head on a chuckle.

The woman smiled. "You always forget to step over that part of the step where it's split. Amanda and I always remember, right, honey bunny?"

"Right!" the little girl said. She looked up at Brandon. "I'm two." She held up two fingers.

Brandon grinned at her. "I like your hat," he told her. He turned toward the couple. "I know the family that used to live here. Do you own this house now?"

"Yeah," the man said. "Bought it five years ago and meant to fix it up, but times are tough."

Brandon looked at the steps. Were they like that

when Cassidy lived there? He couldn't remember. The couple of times he'd dropped Cassidy off here, he did recall staring at the house and being confused that anyone could live in a tiny box like this. Rich privilege, he thought, shaking his head. And snotty and wrong. People did the best they could with what they had.

Brandon looked at the couple. "As I said, I know the family that lived here and, in their honor, I'd like to send out a mason to take care of these steps. No charge to you whatsoever."

They stared at each other then turned to Brandon.

"You're serious?" the man asked. "What's the catch?"

"No catch. Just in memory of the woman who owned the house. She was a single mother and raised one heck of a daughter. Now you're raising a daughter here. I'd just like to do something in her memory."

"That's really nice," the woman said. "No strings?"

"No strings."

"Thank you," the man said. "We'll definitely take you up on that. The people that lived here, we didn't meet them, but they must have been good folks if you care that much about them."

Brandon extended a hand and both shook it. "The steps will be repaired this week. Take care."

As he walked back to his truck, he wasn't sure if he'd mention this to Cassidy. It seemed like something that was between him and her mother, who he'd never gotten to meet because she'd been at work the couple of times he'd been over. Or maybe it was just between him and his conscience—for not doing more to build up Bronco Valley. He'd talk to his brother Jordan about forming a revitalization company; he had no doubt the entire family would get involved.

As he headed back to Bronco Heights, he thought about her mother's sacrifices, her dreams for her daughter, her support of Cassidy. And Cassidy's own dreams, her goals. An idea fixed in his head and the more he thought it over, the more right it felt. He wouldn't tell Cassidy about this, either. He'd let it be a surprise.

With that idea taking center stage in his brain, he was thankfully distracted from his conversation with his sister, which now seemed like yesterday. He made a call, then a stop in town, then drove to the Taylor Ranch, ready to get back to work. Because he'd spend most of it anticipating tonight with Cassidy.

Then again, maybe he should cancel. Given his frame of mind, he'd be on the quiet side and she'd know something was wrong. And something *was* wrong.

But he wanted to see her, *had* to see her, even if their very real relationship was causing his chest to tighten on him.

"Something smells amazing," Brandon said, sniffing the air as he stepped through the door of Cassidy's apartment.

She kissed him on the lips and then closed it behind him. "I'm making a stir-fry and it's almost done. Go make yourself comfortable. You can root through the TV for a movie or show. I love how domestic all this is," she called in a happy voice from the kitchen.

Domestic. He'd never really liked that word. He dropped down on the sofa, aiming the cable remote at the television on the wooden stand. He scrolled through the channel guide—movies, reality shows, documentaries, romantic comedies. Nothing caught his eye. He shifted on the sofa, crossing a foot over his knee. Uncrossing. Trying to get comfortable. The back of his neck itched. Now his shoulders felt tight. Bunched.

Weird. What the hell was wrong with him?

I love how domestic all this is...

He stood up, shutting off the TV. Something was bugging him.

Suddenly, the smell of the stir-fry seemed cloying more than anything. This whole setup seemed kind of... homey. Marriage-y. The kind of thing married people did. Domestic.

When they'd originally made these plans, he hadn't realized *how* domestic it all was. A home-cooked meal. Watching TV. Sharing popcorn on the couch and talking about their days. When was the last time he'd done that with a woman? Brandon and his dates always went out to fine restaurants. And if they went back to the woman's place, it wasn't to watch a romantic comedy while snuggling on the sofa.

He stared at her sofa and it suddenly seemed like the gateway to walking down the aisle in a tuxedo, his bow tie strangling him. He didn't want to get married. He didn't want this beautiful thing with Cassidy to turn bitter and ugly. He had to protect his relationship with his child.

Okay, calm down, buddy. You're having some kind of confirmed bachelor panic attack.

Cassidy used the words *try us out* and *give us a chance*, he reminded himself. She hadn't been talking about marriage.

But that's what she wants. That's where this is all leading.

He dropped back onto the sofa, half expecting ropes to come darting out of the cushions to trap him forever.

"Dinner's ready!" Cassidy called.

He slowly got up. No ropes pulled him back.

He had to be losing his mind. What the hell was going on with him? His head and heart and mind and body seemed to be at war, each yanking him in a different direction.

Poor Brandon, he heard his sister say in his head. *Madly in love and fighting like hell against it.*

No. Once again, he'd never said anything about love. This was a trial romance. Feeling each other out to see if they were good together. It wasn't going to last. He'd known that when he'd agreed to give it a shot. He'd tried and now he was quickly discovering that he wasn't cut out for a real relationship. No surprise there.

He also knew he'd have to get out before things got too out of hand. Maybe he should tell Cassidy tonight that he thought they should go back to the way things were before Lewistown. Platonic partners in pregnancy and child-rearing. He could make a stronger case for marriage now that they'd tried this real relationship thing and it wasn't working out. For *him*, anyway. Cassidy seemed fine with it.

She was happy.

Very happy.

And he was going destroy that? *Um, Cassidy, we have to break up because this isn't what I want and it's messing with me. Love doesn't last. Marriage doesn't last. Let's just get out of this now and save our friend-ship. For the baby's sake.*

He told himself to wait for a pause in their conversation and go from there.

He stepped into the kitchen, hoping his expression didn't match the turmoil inside his head. Cassidy was bringing two plates of steaming stir-fry to the table. A bouquet of flowers was in the center of that table, and he realized he hadn't brought them.

"I should have brought you flowers," he said. "I got caught up in conversation with my dad and then my sister, and my head exploded."

That was an in. Of sorts.

"Yikes, what was the gist?" she asked, sitting.

He sat, as well, and explained about the celebration party and how Cornelius had only invited Daphne to reprogram her into someone she wasn't and would never be.

"Why isn't it enough to be his daughter?" Brandon asked. "Why must she be a meat-eater? Why can't she protect animals? Why can't she just be who she is?"

"I agree," Cassidy said.

"People should be allowed to be who they are, not who others want them to be." Yes. That was true. He was who he was. Cassidy was trying to turn him into a TV husband and father.

No. *She's not trying to do anything but be who she is,* he corrected. *Leave her alone.*

Losing. His. Mind.

"You know what?" he said. "Let's change the subject to something that has nothing to do with my father."

He couldn't say a word about the rest of the conversation with Daphne. About them. Him. And how uneasy he'd felt in the Happy Hearts' barn, being accused of *loving* Cassidy.

She took a bite of her stir-fry, then popped up and grabbed a magazine off the counter. "How's this for a change of subject? A parenting quiz in *Baby* magazine."

He ate a bite of the chicken and vegetables and rice, which was delicious and did not turn to sludge in his stomach. The change of subject had helped already. "With all the reading I've done and the two-day class, I should ace this."

She smiled. "Me, too." She quickly ate another bite of stir-fry. "Okay, first question. 'Your newborn is crying inconsolably. You rock her, you feed her, you change her. Still crying her eyes out. You…(A) Call her pediatrician and ask for advice, even if it's midnight. Every doctor has an after-hours service. (B) Let her cry. She has to learn to self-soothe! (C) You're too busy crying yourself from frustration at how hard parenthood is to help your newborn.'"

"Um, the last one?" he said. "Kidding. Although I can see that happening. I'm going to say A. According to my fatherhood book and Paul Woodsley, newborns shouldn't be left to cry and self-soothe because they're too young for that."

Cassidy grinned. "Correct! Now you ask me the next one."

He slid the magazine over. "'Your baby is ten months old. You've never left him with a sitter because, to be honest, it makes you a little nervous. You now have two tickets—great seats!—to your dream event. You…(A) Get over yourself and ask the teenager next door if she can sit for you. (B) Give the tickets away. (C) Call a trusted sitter from the list you've been adding to since the baby was born, developed from friends and family and neighbors—'

"Wait," he said, looking at Cassidy. "People go ten months without leaving their homes?"

She laughed. "I'm sure some do. I can imagine being a very protective parent, not wanting to leave my baby with a stranger. If none of my friends are available and I desperately need a sitter, I'd probably cancel on the event. I sure wouldn't choose A, desperately asking sullen teen Sarah Peterman from the Blossom B and B!"

"I'd watch the baby for you," he said.

She reached across and squeezed his hand. "And I for you." She took a sip of her water. "But hopefully we'd be attending the events *together*. I'm gonna go with C. The one with the trusted list."

"Correct," he said. "Though think about all the events I'll be able to get *out of* once the baby is born. Dreaded fundraisers. I'm fine with writing the check. It's the small talk that kills me."

"I've always liked small talk. Nice and light conversation. I chat with people in line at the grocery store, while waiting to get my car inspected, with the mail carrier, you name it."

"Weirdo," he said with a smile. "A weirdo who makes great chicken stir-fry."

She laughed. "Did you find a movie for us to watch?"

Such a normal, easy question. Much easier than any of those in the parenting quiz. And yet it made his throat close up to the point he had to put his fork down.

The craziest thing was that he *wanted* to be sitting

there with Cassidy, having this home-cooked meal and taking parenting quizzes and then watching a romantic comedy or thriller. It was just the concept itself that made the walls of this tiny apartment feel like they were closing in. How did that make sense?

Hell, maybe Daphne was right. Maybe he was fighting against his feelings for Cassidy. He clearly was.

Why had he talked to his father earlier? Why had he gone to Daphne's? The key to him being okay with a real relationship with Cassidy was being completely out of his own life, away from memories—past and present—that reinforced how he felt. Love and marriage didn't last. People got hurt. One of his uncles always said, "Start as you mean to continue," and Brandon thought that was a great saying, important advice. If he didn't get emotionally involved, no one would get hurt. He and Cassidy could have a terrific platonic relationship, and their child would be raised happily. No yelling parents. No *You said. You promised. Why didn't you. I hate you.* None of that.

Watching a movie would just make things worse. He'd be too in his own head, overthinking, getting way ahead of himself. What he needed was to distract himself. To lose himself. He needed Lewistown in Cassidy's tiny apartment.

"I have a better idea," he said. "Let's make our own unfilmed love scene in your bedroom."

That brought a giggle out of her and a slight blush to her cheeks. "Sounds good to me. Best movie possible."

"Right?" he asked, reaching for her hand and kissing it. *I just don't want to hurt you. I'd hate myself forever.*

As they finished dinner, he felt better. He could sway things, as he'd just done, to make domesticity in a real relationship bearable. Maybe that would help. But for how long?

Once in the bedroom, Brandon forgot all about being claustrophobic and commitment-phobic. Cassidy was like a dream come true in bed, much better than his fantasies had ever been. They fit together so well, in perfect rhythm, in total sync.

When the alarm on the bedside table went off at 5:00 a.m. the next morning, his eyes were already open, the walls once again moving in. He just needed a little time to regroup, to think. He'd go riding, get his bearings, figure out what he was going to do. He had to tread very carefully.

As she stirred in bed and then sat up, he quickly dressed, turned down her kind offer to come down to the shop for coffee and breakfast, and for a moment, just admired how beautiful Cassidy looked all sleepy-eyed, her blond hair a little wild. He kissed her good-bye, his head a jumble.

As she walked him to the door, he realized he'd never mentioned that she was invited to the family party. "I completely forgot to mention this last night. That party my dad's throwing? He personally invited you because you're now family. He's the only one besides Daphne who knows about the pregnancy. We can tell my brothers and uncles at the party Saturday night."

She stared at him. "You completely forgot to mention this? How?"

"I had a lot on my mind last night. The talk with my dad was weird. Then I went to Daphne's and that got weird, too. Then the day went unexpected places and by the time I arrived here, I was tied in knots, I guess. And once we were in bed, I forgot *everything*."

He tried to smile, but it must have come out awkwardly. He sighed inwardly, hating what he was doing. Hating how unsettled and off balance he was. How damned uncomfortable. With the only woman he'd ever been completely himself with. Hell, maybe that was a lot of the problem here.

"You okay, Brandon?" she asked, studying him.

Not really. I don't know what I'm doing. I want to be with you. But it feels wrong, like we're on a kiddie roller coaster that's about turn wild and crash.

How did he explain all that?

"You did seem kind of distant last night," Cassidy said. "Same thing this morning. You can talk to me, you know."

"I know." He made a show of looking at his phone for the time. "I have to go. Early-morning video-conference call. Have a good day."

"You, too," she said…hesitantly.

The last thing he wanted was to make her feel insecure. He *was* being distant and he knew it.

But I don't want to talk about it until I work it out for myself. I want to give this a bit more time. I'm not ready to tell her it's not working for me.

If he did tell her he wanted to go back to the way things were before Lewistown, who knew what she'd do? Maybe she'd be brokenhearted and he'd feel like the pits of hell. Maybe she'd be furious and tell him she'd see him in court to discuss custody issues. A cold blast ran up his spine.

He really needed some wisdom from Winona Cobbs, but the elderly woman would just give him some cryptic two-liner and send him on his way.

He was going to have to figure this out for himself.

Chapter 13

Cassidy practically flew down the steps to Java and Juice at five thirty on Monday morning. She wanted to make sure the bulk of her baking was done by the time Winona Cobbs would arrive at six thirty for her reading.

And especially given the new direction of her relationship with Brandon—and the awkwardness between them Friday night and Saturday morning—Cassidy wanted to hear that all would be well. Plus, she was dying to know what Winona had meant the other day. *You'll be glad you did it.*

Glad she did *what*? Told Brandon what she needed? What else had she done lately?

As she let herself in the back door, she wondered if Brandon was already regretting agreeing to a committed relationship. She'd gotten to know him so well that when he'd come over on Friday night and was a little quieter than usual, she'd taken it as him distancing himself. Sure, maybe he had been preoccupied with whatever had gone on with his father, then Daphne, and the rest of the afternoon, which he'd mentioned had been heavy.

But forgetting to mention that she was invited to his family party until he was about to leave the next morning? That was telling. Did he not want her there? Did putting her and family in the same sentence make him uncomfortable? Was it too much too soon?

Something was bothering him. Maybe being home, back on his own turf, had him feeling uneasy about being in a real relationship, opening himself up to risk. The magic of getting away for two days was one thing, but being home, business as usual, might have gotten its grips on him. He hadn't suggested getting together Saturday night, and though she'd picked up her phone ten times to text him to come over and talk, she wanted to give him some breathing room.

He'd texted twice on Sunday, a meme that had made her laugh and a link to an article on what type of music babies in the womb should listen to—all kinds. His getting in touch had made her feel better, and she'd had a busy bunch of hours at Java and Juice, then had spent the rest of the afternoon working on an expansion plan for the business. She'd had a brainstorm of opening up another location in Lewistown, where she'd made so many happy memories. The bustling town would be perfect. She couldn't put the ole cart before the horse, though; she'd make an appointment with her bank and, if she got approved for a loan based on her business plan, she'd go scout out locations.

Incredible, she thought. Not too long ago, she was moping around a barn on her thirtieth birthday. Now she was in love. Going to be a mother. And possibly have her business dreams realized. She had to stop worrying about Brandon. If they weren't okay, he'd tell her. Brandon was honest and forthright. And anyway, Winona Cobbs would set her straight very soon.

The next hour went by too slowly, even though Cassidy was super busy, making muffins and scones and her special English muffins for the breakfast sandwiches that Hank and Helen would cook up. Finally, dozens of baked goods out of the oven and in the display case, a knock came at the back door.

Cassidy dashed over. Winona stood there, wearing a purple turban, a long purple sweater, and silver-colored leggings. She also wore purple cowboy boots. Cassidy loved the way Winona dressed. Ninety-four and full of style.

"Morning, Winona," she said. "I've got your Danishes waiting for you. What's your coffee order?" she asked, heading back to the counter.

"I'd like something fun instead of the boring old regular coffee I always have at home. Maybe something with caramel. You pick."

"I've got just the drink for you," Cassidy said. "A caramel macchiato. Vanilla syrup, steamed milk, espresso and a drizzle of caramel syrup. So comforting and delicious."

Winona winked. "I'll take it."

Cassidy made the drink and plated a Danish, bagging

up one more as promised in case it slipped her mind later. "Here you are."

"Let's talk in the kitchen," Winona said. "I know you have some cleanup to do."

"Right you are."

Winona eyed her. "I know."

Cassidy smiled and led the way into the kitchen. She started cleaning up bits of dough and powdered sugar and icing. "First, I'd like to ask you what you meant by 'You'll be glad you did it.'"

"You haven't done it yet," Winona said. "Let's just leave it at that."

Cassidy brightened. "Oh. Well, since I'll be glad, that's fine, then."

"Yes, it is." Winona sat in the chair Helen always used when she needed a break from standing. "Here's what I have to tell you, Miss Ware. You are not the captain of your own ship—not anymore."

Cassidy frowned. "But my mother loved that saying. She always told me that I *was* the captain of my own ship."

"You used to be. But not anymore. You have a co-captain now."

"Oh! Of course, you mean Brandon."

"Yes, I mean Brandon." Winona sipped her drink. "My, is this good. So rich and decadent. I just love it."

Cassidy smiled. "I'm glad."

Winona took a bite of her Danish. "Delicious. Absolutely delicious." She stood and put the rest of the Danish into the bag with the other one, then took another sip of her coffee. "Have a lovely day, dear."

Cassidy stared at her. "Wait. What about my reading?"

Winona tilted her head. "Weren't you listening?"

"I'm not the captain of my own ship, not anymore?" Cassidy asked, trying not to sound too disappointed. That was her *entire* reading?

Winona adjusted her turban. "Exactly."

With that, Winona took her bag of Danishes and left by the back door.

Humph.

Cassidy glanced at the clock. Six forty-five. That meant her appointment had lasted all of fifteen minutes. And half that time was spent making the caramel macchiato!

She couldn't think too much more about it because Helen and Hank arrived, and then a lot of customers, helping Cassidy's mood by ordering a lot of pricey drinks and smoothies.

"Hi, Cassidy!"

She turned to find Sofia Sanchez coming up to the counter. A beautiful young woman, Sofia's usually straight long red hair was styled in beachy waves past her shoulders, her dark brown eyes on the beautiful red coat hanging on a hook by the aprons. Sofia was a stylist at BH Couture, where Brandon had bought the coat.

"I love that coat so much," Sofia said with a grin. "It's one of my favorites at BH Couture."

Cassidy grinned back. "And I hear I have you to thank. I'm a little mortified to know you caught me staring all dreamily at the coat for weeks to confirm it for Brandon."

"Are you kidding? What do you think I do all day at

work? Stare at items totally out of my price range, even with my employee discount."

Cassidy laughed. "Well, thank you. I love it."

"I have to say, I never thought Brandon Taylor would settle down. We only went out a couple times before he told me he'd just like to be friends. But I got the sense immediately that he was the ultimate confirmed bachelor. That no woman would ever win his heart to get him down the aisle."

Had Cassidy won his heart? She really wasn't sure. Sometimes she thought so, based on how he looked at her, how he acted. Then sometimes, like Friday night and Saturday morning… "Sofia, what do you mean you never thought he would settle down?" Sofia must think he *had* settled down. Because of the coat?

"Oh, it's clear you're the one," Sofia said. "Just like my sister Camilla was the one for the *former* Most Eligible Bachelor in Bronco—he-who-supposedly-wouldn't-be-tamed Jordan Taylor. Seems like when Taylor men finally fall, they fall hard and that's that." She glanced at the coat. "Oh yes. He fell hard."

Cassidy glanced at the coat also. "Men have been buying women expensive gifts since the dawn of time. Hard to read anything into that."

"Yeah, but I saw the look in his eyes and heard the emotion in his voice when he was double-checking about the coat. Love knocks a man upside the head. For a while there, he's all disoriented. Then he comes to and fully wakes up. Brandon strikes me as someone who's been trying to control his single status for years. But no one can control how they feel deep down. Not Jordan Taylor and not Brandon."

"Thank you," Cassidy whispered. "I might have needed to hear that right now. Any coffee drink or smoothie on the house."

"Oooh, I'll take a berry explosion smoothie," Sofia said.

As Cassidy made the drink, she couldn't help but wonder what Sofia's love life was like. Given the personal conversation they'd just had about Cassidy, she could probably ask. But she didn't want to pry since Sofia hadn't brought it up herself.

A few minutes later, when Cassidy handed over her drink and then watched her walk away, she was amazed at how full of surprises life really was. At Jordan and Camilla's wedding, Cassidy had been a little jealous of Sofia, especially when she and Brandon had been talking so close. And now, Sofia was the one who'd lifted Cassidy's spirits.

Her phone pinged with a text, a much-needed interruption from her thoughts. Except the text was from Brandon.

How'd the reading go?

Cassidy bit her lip and texted her reply.

Not sure. She told me I wasn't the captain of my own ship anymore, that I had a co-captain.

Am I the co-captain or is the baby?

Cassidy hadn't even considered the baby in that equation.

You are—I confirmed. Winona left after fifteen minutes.

Yeah, she shooed me out after fifteen minutes, too.

Winona wasn't much of a talker. But what she did say ran deep. It was up to Cassidy to figure out what Winona had meant. If she could.

I was hoping for something a little more substantial.

I'd give it time. Winona's wisdom works in mysterious ways.

Cassidy smiled. She sent a smiley cowboy emoticon and Brandon texted back a thumbs-up.

But after Friday night and Saturday morning, she was just slightly worried about what was going on with Brandon. Maybe she didn't want to know anything else.

Woof! Woof, woof!

Maggie? Cassidy rushed to the back door, and there she was. The brown-and-white Australian shepherd. This could very well be Maggie, escapee from Happy Hearts. She couldn't let the dog in the shop, so she went outside to pet her while she called Daphne Taylor.

"Oh my gosh! I'm on my way!" Daphne said.

Cassidy texted her part-time employee to cover the counter while she dashed in to get the leash hanging from the hook, leaving the door slightly open so she could soothingly talk to the dog. "You can't run away this time. Don't you want your forever home? If you're not Maggie, I'll bet Daphne will take you in and find you a home. Don't you want to go where you truly belong?"

Woof! the dog responded.

"You are such a good dog." Cassidy carefully slipped the leash around Maggie's neck, trying to attach the clasp to the corded part, but Maggie gave a woof and slipped out of the makeshift collar. She took off, leaving Cassidy with an empty leash.

Noooo!

"Pup, come back!"

Cassidy went racing down the little alley, looking in every direction for the dog, but she didn't see her. She caught her breath then called Daphne again.

"I'm so sorry," Cassidy said. "The dog got away while I was trying to attach the leash I bought."

"Oh darn." Daphne sighed. "We'll get her eventually. Thanks for trying, Cassidy. Oh, and I'll see you Saturday where I can properly congratulate you."

Cassidy beamed. "I'm excited about meeting the Taylors. And by the way, what's the dress code? Should I dress up?"

"Family party at the ranch? Let's see…my father will be in his crispest jeans, a Western shirt and one of his hundreds of Stetsons. Jessica, my stepmother, will be in a shift dress with a tiny cardigan over her shoulders and high heels. I'll be in a Happy Hearts T-shirt."

Cassidy almost gasped. Based on what Brandon had told her, their father would go nuts. "Really?"

Daphne laughed. "No way. Totally joking. I'll wear a casual dress."

"A casual dress—perfect. I appreciate the help. I'm really sorry about Maggie."

"We'll find her. See you soon."

The chat with Daphne made her feel a little more connected to the Taylor family. The last time she'd gone to a Taylor function was Jordan's wedding, and she'd been part of the catering team. Now she was going to be a guest at a family party. Her baby *was* a Taylor.

Suddenly she did want to know her future, what was going to be. Were she and Brandon going to work out just fine, get married, live happily-ever-after?

If she had a Magic 8-Ball, she was pretty sure it would tell her to ask again later.

Chapter 14

On Tuesday morning, Cassidy was surprised to look up from the cash register in Java and Juice to find Brandon next in line. He was in business casual, which meant he was working from home at the cattle ranch instead of the Taylor Beef offices in town. Dark jeans, long-sleeved button-down shirt, and cowboy boots. Could he be any sexier?

"Hey, beautiful."

She most definitely did not look beautiful. She was tired, had powdered sugar in her hair, and her apron was covered with icing from a doughnut a toddler pressed against her "to see if it would stick." Her face *had* to register the crazy morning, and the shop had only been open for a little over an hour. "Hi, yourself." Her face also had to register how good it was to see him.

"I mentioned to my stepmother that I was headed into town and she asked me to pick up four quarts of juice. She said the same as her last order."

Ah, Jessica Taylor and her quarts of juice. Cassidy loved that. It was like having twenty customers in one. "Ah, I can easily call it up." Cassidy typed "Taylor" into her tablet and Jessica's last order appeared. Half were green juices and half were fruit.

"I wish I could see you tonight," he said, "but I've got late meetings with our ad agency to go over concepts for the Burris ad campaign." He wasn't quite looking at her since he was reaching for his wallet. Brandon was different since Lewistown. Or the same as he'd been *before*.

Her heart went south. "Oh…well, another night then." She tried to keep the disappointment out of her voice. She knew Brandon was going through a "thing" and she had to let him work it out. He'd gone from "I will never be in a committed romantic relationship with strings again" to being in exactly that. She couldn't expect that he'd always find it comfortable. Still, she had an important appointment today that could result in good news and she'd been hoping they could celebrate if there was cause.

"Definitely," he said. But he didn't suggest a night.

"Brandon, I'm a straight shooter. Are we okay?" Nothing wrong with asking, she told herself. You didn't ask, you didn't find out. She'd kept it light and simple.

He gave her hand a squeeze. "We're okay. I've just got a lot on my plate. I will definitely see you Saturday night."

Saturday night? It was *Tuesday*.

They definitely were not okay.

"Text me if you need anything," he said and then left with his shopping bag of pricey juices for his step-mother.

At least he came in. If he were truly trying to avoid her, he would have made an excuse not to do Jessica the favor.

The shop got busy and didn't let up. As usual, Cassidy was grateful for the distraction. And then, finally, at two thirty, she took off her apron, speed-cleaned and was grateful her service was coming in for the weekly deep clean. Cassidy had to get ready for her appointment. The appointment of all appointments!

Butterflies let loose in her stomach. Today she was meeting with a loan officer at Bronco Bank and Trust about her goal to open a second location in Lewistown. She was confident she'd be approved. But not *too* confident. The bank could easily say no. That she was doing fine with one location but not fine enough to justify them giving her money for a second. Her business plan was sound, though. She'd added the revenue her side business had brought in and what she expected going forward. She had her papers in order. She even had testimonials from Bronco residents.

If she got the loan, she'd let Brandon know a celebration was in order, and they could have a magical night in Lewistown sometime this week, scouting locations for her second shop. When she'd opened the shop in Bronco Heights, she'd been alone, her mother freshly gone. Now she'd have Brandon by her side, sharing in her joy, her success.

If he didn't let his head start controlling his heart again.

Cassidy headed upstairs, showered and changed into a black pantsuit and her pumps, packing her business plan into a leather folder that her mother had bought her for her eighteenth birthday. *Dear Future Business-woman, you'll need this*, her mother had written on the card. She hugged it against her chest. "I'm gonna make you proud, Mom," she said heavenward.

At four o'clock, Cassidy sat across from David Harwood, loan officer. Despite her being prepared in every way, the man was intimidating because of his title. He held her future in his hands.

No, she corrected. *He doesn't. You do. You've got this*.

She took out her business plan and was about to begin her well-rehearsed speech when Harwood held up a hand.

"No need to convince me," he said. "You're approved for a half million dollars. I've drawn up the paperwork, so if you'll just sign here." He slid the paperwork across the desk.

"Wait, *what*?" she said. "Approved for five hundred thousand dollars? I didn't ask for even *half* that much in my online application."

"A benefactor has backed you, Miss Ware," he said. "Brandon Taylor. You're all set."

The air whooshed out of her and she sat back, stunned.

And angry.

What. The. Hell.

"I don't understand," she said. "When did he do this?" Brandon didn't know she was coming here today.

"Mr. Taylor called the owner of the bank personally this past Friday afternoon to discuss it, then came in just before closing to sign the necessary documents to transfer funds on an as-requested basis by you."

Good Lord. The day they'd gotten back from Lewistown. She remembered they'd talked about her hopes of expanding. She'd mentioned it was still a "someday" goal financially speaking.

She slid the paperwork back across the desk. "I filled out an online application. And I have a solid business plan typed up. I'd like you to consider me on my own merits."

The loan officer's mouth dropped open. "Are you saying you don't want the preapproved funding?"

"Yes, that is exactly what I'm saying. Mr. Harwood, please consider my application and read over my business plan. I've worked hard to build Bronco Java and Juice into a successful shop and I know a second location in a town with a much larger population will be even more successful."

He accepted her leather folder. "I'll be in touch," he said and shook her hand.

With that, she stood and walked away, fury mingling with embarrassment. Cassidy had never been one to care what anyone thought. But did the entire bank think her boyfriend was bankrolling her?

She stalked back to the shop and got in her car. She was about to tell Brandon Taylor what he could do with his half million dollars.

* * *

Cassidy had been to the Taylor Ranch twice before, once when Camilla Sanchez had first hired her to cater drinks and desserts for her wedding and had showed her where she'd set up, and then for the wedding itself. She drove up the winding road toward the main house, just able to catch a glimpse of the stables through the trees. How different would her life be at this moment if she hadn't escaped to see the horses that night? Or if she'd gone back to the wedding before Brandon had arrived at the stables?

One thing she knew was that she would have still gone to the bank with her business plan, full speed ahead on her goals and dreams. She parked and bit her lip, actually not so sure about that, after all. Had Brandon's belief in her spurred her on? Maybe. Being in a supportive, happy relationship had done wonders for her and had absolutely boosted her self-confidence. Regardless, Brandon should have known she wouldn't want his truckload of ready cash. He knew she was independent and believed in working hard for what she had and what she got. His grand gesture was about *him*, she realized. Not her. He was able to throw his money around and had.

As she opened her car door, Cornelius Taylor was coming out of the grand house, a tablet in his hand. Tall and imposing, he wore a leather vest over a Western shirt and dark jeans and boots.

He didn't even glance over to see who'd arrived. She rolled her eyes. The MO of someone who didn't have to care who'd arrived. He had people to care.

She got out and walked up to him. "Mr. Taylor, nice to see you again."

He finally looked up. "Miss Ware!" He clasped both her hands. "As mother of my future grandheir, I'm thrilled to welcome you to the Taylor Ranch. Congratulations, by the way. Jessica and I are thrilled. This will be her first stepgrandbaby."

Cassidy smiled. Huh. She wasn't expecting him to be this effusive. He seemed a lot less scary. "I'm thrilled, too. Due in the springtime."

"Fabulous. I can envision an outdoor nursery in the backyard. I'll have our architect look into that. That little one will want for nothing. Now, as someone who doesn't have any people, you don't have to worry. Did you know you can special order a handcrafted marble crib with an inset of diamonds in the shape of cows? Jessica found that on a baby website. We can use the Taylor Beef logo itself. You and Jessica can discuss all that on Saturday."

"People?" she repeated, stuck on that and grateful since she'd heard the words *cow-shaped diamonds* and couldn't process *that*.

"Family. You're all alone. But not anymore. You're a Taylor now because of my grandheir. You make a list of what you need now and for when the baby comes, give it to Brandon and we'll get going on it. Jessica suggested a separate playroom in the house you build. We're thinking a wading pool, ball pit, climbing equipment, a children's library and art area. We'll have the playroom staffed with qualified childcare associates, of course." His phone rang and he glanced at it, giving her a moment to breathe.

Whoa. A little overbearing there, Mr. Taylor.

"Is Brandon here?" she asked as he typed something onto the tablet with two fingers. "I need to discuss something with him."

"In his home office," he said, still typing. "Make a left at the entry, second door on the right."

"Thanks," she called as she headed for the steps.

The house never failed to take her breath. Like a luxe log mansion, it stretched on forever, the mountains in the distance, the rustic landscape surrounding it so gorgeous and peaceful. She went inside, stopping and slowly turning, taking in the grand scale of the foyer alone, all polished wood and beams that managed to look rustic. The house reminded her of photos she'd seen of luxury guest ranches—the massive stone fireplace and the natural furnishings that made you feel as though you were in the wilds of Montana and a luxe spa at the same time.

She went down the long hall and came to the second door on the right.

Her anger came rushing back. It wasn't only that he'd assumed she needed him to achieve her goals. It was also the insane amount. Five hundred thousand dollars. As if that were nothing to him! *Oh, here's half a mil, Cassidy. Have fun with it, honey.* She shook her head. The arrogance!

Indoor wading pool. Qualified childcare associates in her baby's playroom! It was all too much for her to even digest.

Cassidy sucked in a breath, lifted her chin and knocked—hard.

"Come on in," Brandon called.

Cassidy opened the door and he looked up from where he sat at his desk, surprise lighting his handsome face.

She walked in, stopping halfway between the door and his huge desk. "I went to my bank today with my business plan to discuss my loan application for a new location in Lewistown," she said. "To my surprise, the loan officer told me I didn't need the paltry amount I asked for because I had a cool half million ready to be transferred into my account. All I had to do was sign."

He stood and came around the desk, half sitting against it. He was studying her, and could clearly see that she wasn't grateful. "I did want to surprise you. I figured when you were ready to open the second location, whenever that would be, it meant you believed in yourself and your business plan, and I wanted the money to be at your disposal whether that was now or another five years from now. *I* believe in you, Cassidy. Always have, always will."

Damn it. Why did he have to explain it that way, which tempered her anger. He was still in the wrong, but he'd acted from a place of kindness, not arrogance.

"Brandon, I don't want your funding. If I meet my goal to expand, it'll be on my own merit, with my own money—or borrowed money from my bank because *they* trust in my company and my business plan. So thank you, but no thank you."

He stared at her—and almost looked a bit hurt. "I admire you for that. But Cassidy, you're forgetting one thing. You're going to be the mother of my child. My money is your money."

No, you're forgetting one thing, Brandon. "We're not

married, remember?" She closed her eyes, wishing she hadn't said that.

"Is that what you want?" he asked.

"Not with how things have been between us," she said, the emotion in her voice making her wince. "You're the one who wanted to get married—but your way. The loveless way. The cold, emotionless way. I can't and won't do that. But marriage isn't what I'm here about. I'm here about the money you arranged for me at my bank."

He glanced down for a moment, then back up at her. "I never want you to have financial issues, Cassidy. I never want money to come between you and your dreams. I *have* gobs of money. I want to share it with you. It's that simple." He turned and looked out the window.

She closed her eyes, shaking her head. He just didn't understand.

Or maybe she wasn't understanding him, not that she had to in this situation. But she had the feeling he was thinking about his mother. Looking for a huge payday and leaving her own children once she had it. But he quite obviously knew that Cassidy wasn't in any of this for the money.

"Brandon, I just want you to understand how important it is to me to make my own way. It's not that I don't appreciate what a generous person you are."

Cassidy heard footsteps and then Cornelius Taylor appeared in the doorway.

"Trust me, Miss Ware, *you* need the money," Cornelius said. "Take it as a safety net. Who the hell knows what will happen with you two? One day, you and Brandon likely won't be speaking to each other, and he'll have to pay you off anyway to keep our heir."

Cassidy gasped.

Brandon bolted up from where he'd been leaning against the desk, his expression angrier than Cassidy had ever seen. "Now you listen to me, Dad," he began, steam coming out of his ears.

"I most certainly will not," Cornelius said and huffed away.

"I'll deal with my father later," Brandon said to her, his dark eyes glinting. "Mark my words. Right now, I want to finish our conversation."

"I said what I came to say." She waited, hoping *he'd* say something that would make everything okay again.

But he didn't say anything. She could see, plain as day on his face, that he wanted to. But he remained silent.

Cassidy turned and left, wishing he'd come after her, but she got to her car and he didn't appear in the doorway. *Fine. Whatever. I said my piece.*

She had no idea what was going to happen between them, where they'd go from here.

She only knew her heart was breaking.

When Cassidy left, Brandon thought about going after her, but he was still too furious at his father to think straight. He needed to clear his head before he could figure out how to make things right with her when everything was so wrong in so many ways. So he headed to the stables and got Starlight ready to go.

He passed the corrals and rode into the open land, his chest less tight, his head clearing the farther he went. The sun was setting, and the glare made it hard to see, but he was pretty sure a man who looked a lot like his brother Jordan was standing in front of a big, weirdly shaped rock by the creek. He rode over and, the closer he got, he was shocked to see it *was* Jordan, a mare grazing nearby. What the hell was he doing all the way out here?

Jordan turned at the approach, his gold wedding band glinting in the setting sun. Jordan and Camilla had recently returned from their honeymoon, both tanned and looking very happy whenever Brandon ran into them. His brother held a chamois cloth in one hand and a plastic container of something in the other. "Got in a fight with Dad?"

Brandon gave a bitter chuckle. "You know it." He peered closer at the big rock that Jordan had been facing. Wait a minute. He hopped off Starlight and moved closer to the rock. It was a heart. What? The rock, made from granite, was around two feet in circumference. It had to have been huge before someone had gone at it with a circular saw. "What's this?"

"Just something I've been doing when I get into it with Dad," Jordan said, rubbing it down with the cloth. "When Camilla and I were…trying to make it work, we came riding out here once, and we had a moment right at this spot, sitting on this rock, that turned my head around. So I wanted to immortalize it for Camilla. It's finished and I'll show it to her this weekend. I was just giving it a final polish."

"Damn. That's romantic."

"And practical," Jordan said. "Every time I ride out here and see my heart, I know where my priorities are."

Man, had Jordan changed. But Brandon was too caught up in the word *priorities* to focus on his brother. *Brandon's* priority was the baby. He had to remember that. His relationship with Cassidy was up there, yes. But a relationship that would enable him to be a good father. Not a bitter angry one arguing about who disappointed whom.

Except you want that relationship to include sex. That's the opposite of platonic.

He sighed inwardly. He was a spoiled rich guy who wanted it both ways. And Cassidy wasn't about to give in to that. That was another reason he admired her so much.

But that didn't change how he *felt*.

"This party on Saturday…" Brandon said. "It's where I was going to announce that I'm about to become a father. Cassidy Ware is pregnant. I'll be a dad next spring."

Jordan's mouth dropped open. "Holy hell, Brandon. Congratulations." He pulled Brandon into a bear hug.

"Things are a little…rough right now."

"Ah," Jordan said, "in that case, find or make your own priority rock, whatever that may be. It'll help."

Brandon stared at the rock. His mind was going in so many directions, he wasn't really homing in on what his brother was saying. "I need to keep riding."

Jordan nodded. "That helps, too."

Yeah, it always did. Except this time, Brandon would have to ride for hours and he wasn't sure he'd ever find his answers.

Chapter 15

Cassidy spent the rest of the week baking, working at Java and Juice, reading the book on motherhood she'd bought and keeping to herself. She'd avoided the sweet little book—wisdom and quotes for the new mother—that Brandon had bought her. It reminded her too much of how thoughtful he could be. He'd texted on Tuesday night that he was sorry how they'd left things and that he needed to take some time to think, to let things settle.

Fine with her. And not. Things had been so up and down with Brandon after such a whirlwind of heaven that she couldn't have taken any more of it. She needed to know where they stood so that she could know what her future was: with Brandon at her side or as a single mother with joint custody.

Now, on Friday morning, a new text came from him.

My dad's been avoiding me, easier than it sounds given we live in the same house. I'll be going to the party to confront him—privately. I'd like you to be there so that we can announce our news to the rest of the family together.

How warm and fuzzy, she thought, shaking her head. What a lovely invitation. She felt so much more comfortable. Not!

This is a family matter and I'm not family. We also need to talk and I don't intend to do that in earshot of your father ever again.

His response was quick.

Touché. But please. It's important to me that you're there.

She almost typed back a *why*, because she honestly had no idea. But she couldn't do this right now, couldn't handle texting back and forth when everything they had to talk about was so important. Fridays were always super busy at Java and Juice. There was already a line of customers and she was also expecting to hear from the loan officer at the bank. *Focus on where you are*, she told herself. *Not your up-and-down romance.* Were they even a couple anymore? They were *something*—the baby on the way ensured that.

I'll be there. I'll drive myself so I can easily escape, if need be.

Touché, again, he texted back.

She'd made what seemed like a thousand complicated coffee drinks and plated pastry after pastry, ringing up snack and lunch orders when her phone pinged again.

This time it wasn't Brandon. She didn't recognize the cell phone number, but she did recognize the words.

You'll be glad you did it.

Oh, Winona, she thought, her heart all over the place. *Whatever it is I'm gonna do, I sure hope so.*

Because the family room at the Taylor Ranch was so huge, Brandon hadn't gotten near enough to his dad to demand an apology Cornelius would likely not give. As he'd told Cassidy yesterday via text, he'd do that privately. Jordan and Camilla were by the bar, Dirk and Dustin were chatting with all three of their uncles, and Cornelius and Jessica were deep in conversation. His father was throwing up his hands a lot. The two might be talking about the fact that Daphne was due to arrive any moment—or about the big blowup with Brandon and Cassidy, what Cornelius had said to her. That was, if his father even talked to Jessica about down-and-dirty stuff. Who knew what their relationship was really like. Maybe it was all superficial.

Jessica was much younger than Cornelius, but she truly seemed to like him. She was affectionate in a way that seemed natural and not forced. Brandon thought back to catching the couple dancing to a Blake Shelton tune. There was real romance in that dance; Brandon had seen it with his own eyes.

Part of him wanted to talk to his father about that, how Cornelius had found this third chance at love with Jessica when his first two marriages had collapsed. Heck, maybe he'd talk to Jessica about it. Even though they lived in the same house, albeit huge, they didn't see much of each other. Brandon should work on that. Spend more time with Jessica, especially now that she was going to be a grandmother to his child. He wondered if Jessica would open up about her marriage— not the details, but enough for Brandon to get a real sense about the depth of his stepmother's feelings for his blustery father—and his for her.

His father wasn't one to talk about marriage except to wave his hands around dramatically. Cornelius didn't talk much about Dirk and Dustin's mother, and he rarely talked about his first wife, Jordan, Brandon and Daphne's mother.

Speak of the devil. Daphne and Evan walked into the family room. He only thought of *Daphne* and *devil* in the same sentence because she'd gotten his head so turned around when he'd stopped by Happy Hearts to invite her to this party. Fighting against love. Please. He hadn't let himself get there in the first place. He didn't *love*. He *cared*. There was a difference.

He watched his father eye Daphne, the man's gaze moving to Evan. Cornelius whispered something to his wife then crossed the room to talk to his brothers. Brandon picked up his glass of wine and took a good long sip, then went to greet his sister.

He shook hands with Evan and hugged Daphne. "Party's a real blast," Brandon said. "I should tell you,

Dad and I are on the outs, so I don't know how festive this evening will be."

Daphne nodded. "Well, festive and Dad aren't really a thing, so it's business as usual."

As she and her fiancé crossed the room to the bar, Brandon's gaze was drawn to the open French doors and the beautiful woman who had just walked in.

Oh, Cassidy. Her blond hair was loose past her shoulders. She wore a floral black dress that swished around her knees and black cowboy boots. He'd missed her so much.

He walked over to her and wanted to envelop her in a hug, but her expression kept him from touching her. She was wary. With every reason.

"Ah! Everyone's here!" bellowed Cornelius Taylor's voice. "I'll make this short and sweet. Thanks to Brandon, Taylor Beef has scored rodeo champion Geoff Burris to star in the ad campaign, a particular boon ahead of the rodeo in November. Eat that, Abernathy Meats!"

Brandon's uncles clapped and laughed uproariously.

His father held up his glass of champagne. "To Brandon. To Taylor Beef! To Geoff Burris!"

Everyone turned toward Brandon and held up their glass then drank. Brandon downed his. Cassidy was sipping ginger ale.

Cornelius cleared his throat. "I'd also like to say that I'm glad Daphne is here with her fiancé, Evan Cruise. I may not always show it the best way, but you are family, Daphne. Sell that ridiculous Hoofy Hearts, have a steak, and you'll be welcomed back to the family with open arms." He raised his glass again, his eyes on his daughter.

If looks could maim, Cornelius Taylor would be flat on his back.

Daphne glared at him. "I will not drink to that. But I will toast to my brother's success in landing Geoff Burris. That's a major feat. Despite my leanings, I'm very much invested in the success of my siblings. Now, if you'll excuse me, Evan and I are out of here."

Cornelius scowled. Jessica had an *Oh dear* expression.

Jordan and Camilla were shaking their heads.

Dirk and Dustin were on their phones, probably also making plans to get away.

Cassidy was sort of nodding, as though this was expected. As if everything she'd been through with Cornelius made perfect sense.

"Now you listen to me, Cornelius Taylor," Cassidy suddenly said. Everyone stopped what they were doing and stared at her. "If you think I'm going to raise my child, your 'grandheir' as you refer to him or her, in this kind of intolerance for family, you have another think coming. I may not have money. I may not have people. But I have my values. Family should be everything. You have no idea how lucky you are, Mr. Taylor." With that, she turned and walked out.

The room erupted in claps and wolf whistles. Brandon heard his brother Dirk say to Dustin, "Wait, Cassidy is pregnant?"

Cornelius stood glowering, his arms across his chest. Jessica stared at her husband, her *Oh dear* expression morphed into something a little more hardcore. Maybe she'd try to talk some sense into her husband.

"Woman after my own heart," Camilla Sanchez Taylor whispered to Brandon. "I had a moment just like that with my father-in-law before Jordan and I got married. Not sure it got through. But it felt good. You tell Cassidy she's one hundred percent right."

Brandon squeezed Camilla's hand and took off through the French doors, hoping to catch Cassidy before she drove off.

He did. She stood with her hands at her sides then paced, as if trying to calm down before getting in her car.

"Cassidy," he called.

"Guess I'll never be invited back," she said, throwing up her hands. "Not that I want to be. But these are my baby's relatives. Your father is my baby's grandpa. I can't avoid that the way your father avoids your sister. Family *is* everything."

"I know," he said. "And I'm sorry you were put in that position. But I'm glad you spoke your mind. Camilla did that, too, before she married Jordan. She said to tell you you're a hundred percent right."

She stared at him. Hard. Studying him. She looked so beautiful in the moonlight, so equally strong and vulnerable, that he just wanted to gather her to him and hold her—and not let her go.

"Well, here's what I want to know, Brandon. Are *you* one hundred percent in? None of this 'one foot in, one foot out' bull. Are we together?"

He looked at the stars for a moment then back at Cassidy. "I…" He tried to find the words to explain how much she meant to him, but that the brick wall around his heart was impenetrable. He'd been through too much, seen too much. He wanted her in his life, but on his terms. And he wasn't even sure what those terms were.

"I love you, Brandon Taylor. Deeply. Can you say the same?"

Love. That word almost made him physically ill.

He could barely look at her. He tried to force himself, but he couldn't. *Don't love me*, he wanted to say. *I don't know how to love back. Even Winona said so, and she knows what she's talking about.*

"If we can have that platonic marriage, we can have it all," he said, knowing he sounded insane. "A united team for our child. Parents who care about each other, in the same house, with a shared goal of raising their kid together, putting the child first. Neither of us will miss anything. I know it's not exactly what you want, Cassidy, but it's a compromise, isn't it? Marriage is about a lasting partnership, making a relationship work. We can do that."

"You really don't see it, do you?" she asked.

"See what?" He didn't want to know, though.

"How like your father you really are. You believe in everything he said to me in your office the other day, Brandon. That one day we won't be speaking to each other. That you'll probably have to pay me off to keep your child. You actually *believe* that. It informs everything you do and controls you. It's *why* you can't love."

Red-hot anger swirled in his gut, but it was tamped by what felt like cold dirt being kicked up inside him. He didn't want to have this conversation. He couldn't.

"Goodbye, Brandon," Cassidy said, sounding so sad, but so firm. "We'll work out a schedule for the baby.

We'll keep things friendly for his or her sake. But good-bye." With that, she ran to her car.

No. No, no, no. "Cassidy," he called, but he couldn't even hear himself. His voice was clogged with emotion.

He heard her car start, saw the lights come on.

She drove off, fast, leaving him standing there feeling like absolute hell.

The cramping started the next morning, when Cassidy should have been getting out of bed for an early morning of baking. But the pains low in her belly were too intense. She turned onto her other side.

Oh God. What was this? She was barely a month along. She'd conceived the first week of September and now it was the last week. These couldn't be contractions.

A cold rush of fear gripped her. *Please, please, please, let everything be okay.* Please.

She grabbed her phone and called Brandon. Brandon—whom she'd said goodbye to last night.

"Cassidy?"

"My belly," she managed to blurt out between breaths. "It hurts so bad, Brandon."

"I'll be right there," he said, the desperation in his voice matching her own. "You stay on the phone with me." She could hear him moving, a door shutting, another door shutting, his truck starting. "I'm on my way. I'll be there in five minutes. Should I call an ambulance?"

Breathe, breathe, breathe, she told herself. "I don't think so. I just need to get to the hospital."

"I'm getting closer and closer," he said every minute

as he drove, till he reached her apartment. "I'm here. I'm coming up. Can you unlock the front door for me?"

"I'll try," she said, getting out bed, doubled over, one hand on her belly as she staggered to the intercom to buzz him in and then unlocked the door. She turned and dropped onto the overstuffed chair that had been her mother's favorite.

The pains were getting worse.

"I'm coming up the stairs now," he said and then burst into her apartment, putting his phone in his pocket.

She could see the worry and fear on his face. But she could only focus on the pain and trying to breathe through it.

Please let my baby be okay, she prayed with all her might.

Panicked, Brandon got Cassidy downstairs and to Bronco Valley Hospital as fast as he could without driving recklessly. When she was wheeled down the hall and out of sight, his heart split in two, half going with her.

He paced the waiting room, texting Daphne what was going on. Within fifteen minutes, his entire family was there, including his father and Jessica. He told the group what he knew, which was absolutely nothing. A nurse had told him the doctor would be out to talk to him when he finished his full examination of the patient.

Brandon paced some more then dropped into a chair, his forearms resting on his knees, his head down.

"Money poisoned my two marriages," Cornelius whispered when he sat beside Brandon. Or whispered as much as Cornelius Taylor's naturally booming voice *could* whisper. "I don't know a soul who'd turn down half a million dollars to make it on her own merit. That's a woman you should marry, Brandon. And not because it would make good business sense, though it does, but because that woman is one in a million."

Brandon looked at his dad, the clog in his chest clearing somewhat. He hadn't realized how much the strife with his father had bothered him until his father just undid it.

"Jessica made me go to a couples workshop not too long ago, and I learned about projection," Cornelius added. "I realized on the way over that I was doing just that to you and Cassidy. Projecting. Just because my first two marriages didn't work out doesn't mean yours won't."

Brandon straightened and turned toward his dad. "I appreciate that." He'd appreciate it more if he wasn't so worried about Cassidy. He'd also be more focused on the fact that his dad went to a couples workshop.

"You love that woman," Cornelius said. "Like I love Jessica, God help me." He turned to look at his wife, who sat across the room, talking to Dirk and Dustin.

The air whooshed out of Brandon. He'd known in the Lewistown B and B that his feelings for Cassidy had gone rogue and were beyond his control. His subconscious must have been working behind the scenes the past days to keep him held back just enough. Self-preservation.

But now? All he could think about was Cassidy. Cassidy and his baby. If he had to punch himself in the head to wake the hell up about what was important, he'd do it.

Actually, Cassidy walking away last night had done that. Knocked him upside the head.

"I do," Brandon said, realizing he'd lost the fight against love. He'd tried and failed spectacularly and for that he was grateful. It shouldn't have taken an emergency to conk him over the head and free his heart, but it had. And now he knew the truth. "I love her very much."

I love you, Cassidy Ware! He wanted to jump on his chair and scream it for everyone to hear. *I love you!*

"Told ya," Daphne whispered as she walked by, stopping to give his hand a squeeze. She nodded at Cornelius, her expression deservedly hard on the man, but still acknowledging their dad had done something right here.

Poor Brandon. Madly in love and fighting like hell against it.

What he needed right now was for Cassidy to be okay. For their baby to be okay. His baby was his priority rock, he knew, his brother's words coming back to him. *Find or make your own priority rock… It'll help.*

Actually, the baby alone wasn't his priority rock. Cassidy was, too. They both were. He loved them both. Cassidy because of the woman she was. The baby because he was Brandon's child. And when he met that child this spring, Brandon would love him for who he was, as well.

Understanding slammed into his head and his heart with such force that he almost tipped over.

He *did* love Cassidy. Madly. But he had a terrible feeling that he'd come to that realization too late.

Chapter 16

Cassidy knew Brandon had to be sick with worry. Over an hour had passed since she'd arrived at the hospital, waiting, filling out forms, getting poked and prodded. She was fine. *The baby was fine.*

The moment she'd heard those words from the doctor she'd known that nothing else would matter as much. She would be okay.

With or without Brandon Taylor.

Her heart was broken, but her baby was just fine. And for that, she would be forever grateful.

The doctor had just signed her discharge papers, and as soon as she could get out of this hospital gown and into her clothes, she could leave.

According to a nurse, the waiting area was full of Taylors, one in particular who'd been pacing and constantly asking about her and the baby's condition.

That Brandon cared wasn't at issue. Of course he cared. But caring and loving were two different things.

A knock came on the door, and Cassidy called out for the person to come in. Brandon appeared, his face ashen, his dark eyes worried.

Her heart squeezed in her chest. How she loved this man. How was she supposed to let him go?

"Please tell me everything's okay, Cass," he said, sitting on the bed and taking her hands. "No one would tell me anything."

"The baby and I are both fine. The doctor ran tests. All is well. He said it was just some natural cramping, but that it's good I came in to be checked out. I have my discharge papers so I'm good to go once I get dressed."

She could see the relief hit him—so hard that he dropped his head in her lap.

He sat up straight and looked at her. "Cassidy, I have so much to say. So much to tell you."

"Oh yeah?" she asked. More of the same, she was sure. *Sorry. Sorry. Sorry. I can't. I can't. I can't.* Tears stung the backs of her eyes.

He nodded. "Yeah."

"Not here. Not while I'm in this bed and in this dumb backless gown. I want to go home."

"I'll give you some privacy to get dressed," he said. "My family's outside. They may mob you. My dad included. I'll let them know you're okay and they should go to give you space."

"I appreciate that," she said. She wasn't a part of that family. Her baby would be.

But not her.

He left and she let out a haggard, heartbroken sigh,

then quickly got dressed. She waited a solid ten minutes before peeking outside. The Taylors were gone. Only Brandon remained.

He was quiet on the way to her apartment, quiet as he gently helped her up the stairs.

When the door closed behind him, she crossed her arms over her chest.

"Okay, I'm listening, Brandon."

Go ahead. Break my heart all over again.

Somehow, she was going to have to accept that he didn't love her, couldn't love, wouldn't love her.

She sat down on the sofa. He sat beside her and took both her hands, his eyes serious on hers.

"I'm so sorry about last night, Cassidy. You asked me if I loved you, and I didn't respond, like a total fool, but the truth is, I love you more than anything in the world. You mean everything to me. You and our baby. I love you so much. So, so much."

She stared at him. Everything she'd wanted him to say last night he was saying now. A few hours and a scare made that much difference?

She wasn't buying it. He *cared*. He'd been very afraid for her and the baby just an hour ago. But he didn't love her.

"That's the fear talking, I guess, Brandon. You were afraid you'd lose me or the baby and realized how much you care about both of us. That's a beautiful thing. But it's not love."

He gaped at her.

"Brandon, tonight, tomorrow, you'll realize what I'm saying is true."

"Now who doesn't want to believe the truth because

she's scared?" he said softly. "I deserve not to be believed, Cassidy. You're right to be wary. And yeah, you scared the hell out of me. But I knew in Lewistown while sitting next to you in that baby seminar that I loved you like crazy."

"Lewistown?" she repeated. She remembered how he'd said he'd try. How he'd made love to her at the B and B. Like a man in love. Like a man who'd never let her go. That night, she'd believed in him, in them. That they really had a chance.

"I love you, Cassidy. You. And I love our baby-to-be. I will spend the rest of my life showing you how much."

She gasped. She could see the sincerity in his eyes, in his expression. She felt it in his hands. "You do love me. You really do."

He moved the coffee table back a bit and then got down on one knee. "The ring is coming, Cassidy. But will you marry me? Will you make me the happiest man on this planet?"

Her eyes brimmed with tears. *Oh, Brandon.* "I will marry you. Yes, yes, yes!" she screamed.

He grinned and stood up and scooped her into his arms and kissed her. "I love you, Cassidy Ware."

"Guess we're not going our separate ways forever," she said with a smile.

"No, in fact, I want to marry you as soon as possible. Not because of the baby. Because of *you*. Oh, and my dad helped knock some sense into me. He said you were one in a million, and he's right."

"Speaking of millions… Well, a *tenth* of that, I got my loan. The bank officer left a message for me last night."

"Congratulations!" he said "I had nothing to do with that. I swear," he said, pressing a hand to his heart.

"I know," she said. "The loan officer assured me of that."

"I'm sorry I was so stubborn. That I fought against us. I'm so grateful to you for sticking by me, Cassidy."

She gasped again. "I'm glad I did it," she said slowly. "That's it! That's what Winona knew I'd be glad that I did. Not give up on you. I knew my goodbye last night wasn't permanent. It never could be. We have a baby between us. I believed at the very beginning that you'd come around, and you did."

"I love you with all my heart," Brandon said, then kissed her again.

"We kissed and made up and it turns out we're staying together forever. Take that, fifteen-year-old bet."

He smiled. "Can I call the Taylors with the good news? I'll start with my Dad and Jessica."

"Go right ahead. Put them on speaker."

A few minutes later, there was whooping and wolf whistles, Cornelius and Jessica talking over each other in their excitement, yelling for Dirk and Dustin to come hear the great news.

"We all bought out the hospital gift shop," Cornelius said. "Lots of flowers, balloons and stuffed animals await you two. Sorry, but a quarter of it won't fit in that tiny apartment of yours. Guess we'll be seeing you around the ranch?"

Cassidy laughed. She and Cornelius would find their way. And she couldn't wait to get to know Jessica better. All the Taylors.

Cassidy Taylor. She liked the sound of it.

Finally, it was just the two of them again.

"Selfie of this special moment," Brandon said, getting out his phone. "I'm going to send the photo to the family."

"You're going to be a great dad—and a great husband."

He hugged her, then held out the phone and snapped a photo, their smiles big like the love in their hearts.

Brandon grinned at the selfie. "You, me and our baby. Our family. Now I really know the meaning of the word *priceless*."

"Love you, Brandon Taylor."

"Love you times a million, Cassidy Ware Taylor to-be."

This time, she had no doubts of that.

Priceless, indeed.

* * * * *

Get 4 FREE REWARDS!

We'll send you 2 FREE Books plus 2 FREE Mystery Gifts.

FREE Value Over **$20**

Both the **Harlequin® Special Edition** and **Harlequin® Heartwarming™** series feature compelling novels filled with stories of love and strength where the bonds of friendship, family and community unite.

YES! Please send me 2 FREE novels from the Harlequin Special Edition or Harlequin Heartwarming series and my 2 FREE gifts (gifts are worth about $10 retail). After receiving them, if I don't wish to receive any more books, I can return the shipping statement marked "cancel." If I don't cancel, I will receive 6 brand-new Harlequin Special Edition books every month and be billed just $5.49 each in the U.S. or $6.24 each in Canada, a savings of at least 12% off the cover price, or 4 brand-new Harlequin Heartwarming Larger-Print books every month and be billed just $6.24 each in the U.S. or $6.74 each in Canada, a savings of at least 19% off the cover price. It's quite a bargain! Shipping and handling is just 50¢ per book in the U.S. and $1.25 per book in Canada.* I understand that accepting the 2 free books and gifts places me under no obligation to buy anything. I can always return a shipment and cancel at any time by calling the number below. The free books and gifts are mine to keep no matter what I decide.

Choose one: ☐ **Harlequin Special Edition**
(235/335 HDN GRJV)

☐ **Harlequin Heartwarming**
Larger-Print
(161/361 HDN GRJV)

Name (please print)

Address _____ Apt. #

City _____ State/Province _____ Zip/Postal Code

Email: Please check this box ☐ if you would like to receive newsletters and promotional emails from Harlequin Enterprises ULC and its affiliates. You can unsubscribe anytime.

Mail to the Harlequin Reader Service:
IN U.S.A.: P.O. Box 1341, Buffalo, NY 14240-8531
IN CANADA: P.O. Box 603, Fort Erie, Ontario L2A 5X3

Want to try 2 free books from another series! Call 1-800-873-8635 or visit www.ReaderService.com.

---

*Terms and prices subject to change without notice. Prices do not include sales taxes, which will be charged (if applicable) based on your state or country of residence. Canadian residents will be charged applicable taxes. Offer not valid in Quebec. This offer is limited to one order per household. Books received may not be as shown. Not valid for current subscribers to the Harlequin Special Edition or Harlequin Heartwarming series. All orders subject to approval. Credit or debit balances in a customer's account(s) may be offset by any other outstanding balance owed by or to the customer. Please allow 4 to 6 weeks for delivery. Offer available while quantities last.

Your Privacy—Your information is being collected by Harlequin Enterprises ULC, operating as Harlequin Reader Service. For a complete summary of the information we collect, how we use this information and to whom it is disclosed, please visit our privacy notice located at corporate.harlequin.com/privacy-notice. From time to time we may also exchange your personal information with reputable third parties. If you wish to opt out of this sharing of your personal information, please visit readerservice.com/consumerschoice or call 1-800-873-8635. **Notice to California Residents**—Under California law, you have specific rights to control and access your data. For more information on these rights and how to exercise them, visit corporate.harlequin.com/california-privacy.

HSEHW22R3

HARLEQUIN
PLUS

Try the best multimedia subscription service for romance readers like you!

Read, Watch and Play.

Experience the easiest way to get the romance content you crave.

Start your **FREE TRIAL** at
<u>www.harlequinplus.com/freetrial</u>.